PRAISE F

'A deadly debut, ambi
A very promising s
— Allan Guthrie

'This is a great debut book, introducing a detective with loads of appeal who deserves, and seems destined for, a series.'
— *Sunday Times*

'... this debut captures the desolate coastal essence with just a touch of the Wintons.'
— *Qantas The Australian Way*

'[The characters] all speak with that authentic voice which you only find in the best crime novels.'
— *Courier Mail*

'... an excellent read – let's hope we get to see more of Carter's hero, DSC Cato Kwong.'
— *West Australian*

'As with all good crime fiction there are many layers to this story, genuine "aha" moments and a very strong cast of main and supporting characters.' ★★★★
— *Australian Bookseller+Publisher*

'... riveting reading.'
— *The Examiner*

'There is a great cast of characters in this very entertaining book.'
— *NT News*

ALAN CARTER

PRIME CUT

Michael O'Mara Books Limited

ABOUT THE AUTHOR

Alan Carter was born in Sunderland, UK, in 1959. He holds a degree in Communication Studies from Sunderland Polytechnic and immigrated to Australia in 1991. Alan lives in Fremantle with his wife Kath and son Liam. He works as a television documentary director. In his spare time he follows a black line up and down the Fremantle pool. *Prime Cut* is Alan Carter's first novel. He wrote it while he was living in Hopetoun as a kept man.

To my beautiful wife Kath
for helping me chase the dream

PROLOGUE

Saturday, May 5th, 1973. Late afternoon.
Sunderland, England.

Something is changing, he can tell. There's a shift in power. The underdog is snarling. The meek are about to inherit the earth. Colours from the screen flicker in his eyes and he leans forward, fingers tightening into the arms of the chair. The hairs on the back of his arm stiffen and crackle like a crop before the approaching storm.

'... Hughes with the corner, the ball falls to Porterfield. It's in! Porterfield scores for Sunderland ...'

He leaps to his feet, splashing the colour telly with Double Diamond ale and turns to his wife Chrissy and little Stephen sitting on the settee.

'Did you see that pet? Eh son? Brilliant!'

He takes a long gulp from the can. Some escapes and runs down his chin and on to his red and white striped shirt. He does a little jig. On the telly the players hug and kiss. This wasn't the way the script was meant to go. He fires up an Embassy Regal and draws the smoke deep into his lungs. In slow motion the goal is replayed a third time, a fourth. He says it again.

'Did you see that? Magic.'

Chrissy's hand rests lightly on her pregnant bump. Little Stevie is leaning into his mum. No, Chrissy and Stevie didn't see the goal. By that time they've already been dead at least two hours. The black and tan Yorkshire terrier licks uncertainly at the blood on the cheap paisley-patterned carpet.

Maud Street: redbrick two-storey terraced houses, thirty either side of the road. Huddled together like ill-fitting dentures. A crowd was already forming around the tape at number 11. This house, like many others, had the red and white team colours in the windows and a 'Ha'way the Lads' poster from the *Sunderland Echo.* Detective Sergeant Stuart Miller walked across the threshold. His young offsider, Chris Lawton, followed.

In the front room a uniform was interviewing the neighbour. According to the call-out she'd dropped by to share the winning moment and found them. She was a small, thin, bottle-brunette with the yellowed fingers of a chain-smoker. With shaking hands she lit another off the end of the last, chucking the dead one in the fireplace. The uniform looked up, caught Miller's eye, and nodded her head back in the direction of the room next door.

'Not pretty, sir.'

Miller took a deep breath and walked in.

The telly in the corner was still on. Post-match interviews and celebrations: an ecstatic rolling sea of red and white engulfing a bemused Wembley Stadium. Nobody had turned it off yet, maybe in case fingerprints could be taken from it, maybe because they wanted to keep on watching, to hold on to that magic, and never let go. Second division Sunderland had beaten first division Leeds United. A single goal had delivered them the coveted FA Cup. The post-match pundits all agreed this was a day to remember. Miller had no argument with that.

Just inside the doorway a framed wedding photo hung slightly askew on the wall; the groom, mid-to-late twenties, looking like the guitarist from Slade but with a suit on like he was due in court. Big eyes, dark shoulder-length hair and a lopsided fringe with smile to match; maybe he'd stopped off for a couple of bevvies on the way to church. There was already an APB out on him, last seen by a neighbour walking up the street at half-time. He was the prime suspect. You couldn't argue with the statistics, Miller thought: murder and marriage go together like a horse and carriage.

The bride had a California look, long blonde flowing hair like those lasses in the 'I'd Like to Teach the World to Sing' Coke ad. She'd have gone down a storm on the grey, grimy streets of Sunderland. It was her big day, but the smile didn't seem to match the occasion: a bit uncertain, not sure what she was getting herself into. Next to that was another photo of a little boy, maybe five or six. He had his mother's blonde hair and his dad's big wide smile. And perhaps two years left to live.

It wasn't a big room and now seemed even less so with Miller's own bulky frame, the gangly DC Lawton, a photographer and a doctor all jostling for space. And there were the two bodies.

'Christ,' whispered DC Lawton, his hand over his open mouth.

They were on the settee; if you half-closed your eyes and forgot where you were for just a moment they looked like they could have fallen asleep in front of the telly. But it was a grisly illusion. A young woman, heavily pregnant; the same one in the photograph, Miller presumed, but he only had the hair to go on. Her head was a bloody mush. She'd been bludgeoned with something heavy, a hammer or a big spanner perhaps. There were brown scorch marks on both her earlobes. He could smell it now, in with the stale cigarettes in the overflowing ashtray down by the fireplace and the metallic sweet smell of blood and other crime-scene odours – a hint of something smoky or burnt.

The little boy was beside her, his hand resting on her knee and his head against her shoulder. He looked about the same age as Stuart's own son, seven or eight. His head was less of a mess than the woman's but still caked with blood from one big gash on the right side. His earlobes were also burnt. DC Chris Lawton stumbled out of the room and Miller heard him dry-retching in the backyard.

On the floor at their feet was some kind of transformer box. One end was plugged into the mains and at the other, car jump leads with alligator clips. The box looked like it could have come off a Scalextric racing-car set or something similar. The doctor plucked his dandruff-flecked jacket from a door hook, shrugged it over his narrow shoulders and snapped his case shut.

'Electrocution or bludgeoning, either would have been enough. So why both?'

Miller shook his head slowly. Why indeed? One was the cold application of science and gadgetry, the other was the heated application of brute force. What were they dealing with here?

The room was a dingy box, ten feet by twelve, dimly lit by a narrow window which looked out on to a postage stamp backyard patterned with curls of dog shit. It was the same kind of room Miller had grown up in. Same cheap carpet, same bitter fug of old cigarettes. If you're lucky, you grow up and better yourself and never take for granted where you came from. If you're not so lucky you spend the rest of your life drowned in piss and self-pity and lashing out at those you claim to love. Miller's hand wandered instinctively to the small scar at the corner of his eye where his father's wedding ring had caught him on his twelfth birthday.

Is that what happened here? A domestic gone too far? He looked at the bodies propped side by side on the settee. Cuddled together, hands on knees, posed in a cruel parody of happy families. No, this was something else. He had experienced blood and death and tragedy and stupidity and all the other daily horrors included in his job description. But he'd never encountered anything like this before. Miller's vision blurred, his throat tightened. The room was closing in on him, the low hum of the TV, the rolling ecstatic waves of red and white, the jubilant players lifting the trophy in constant replay.

'All fucking nonsense.' Miller switched it off.

He walked out into the street to get some air. A little Yorkshire terrier was hanging around the front door looking inquisitive and expectant. Miller crouched and patted it.

'Nothing for you here son, off you go.'

A gang of lads, decked out in red and white, were headed for the Royal Marine pub at the top of the street to continue the victory celebrations, chanting and clapping 'We are the champions!' The leader caught Stuart Miller's eye and grinned. 'Best fucken day of me life this, mate, best fucken day!'

1

Wednesday, October 8th, 2008. Late morning.
Katanning, Western Australia.

The way the body was lying, it was obvious she hadn't seen it coming. The limbs were splayed at a grotesque angle. A pool of blood beside the head had dried in the sun before it could make it the few centimetres to the side of the road. Blowflies hovered impatiently. The October sun was high and unseasonably nasty. Anybody with any sense was sitting under the shade of the only tree for miles. Or they were somewhere else.

The sergeant was crouched beside the rapidly ripening corpse, talking into a small digital recorder. Cato Kwong squinted at the sergeant and took a swig of lukewarm water from a bottle that felt like it was melting in his hands. On his iPod, La Bohème was reaching a screeching crescendo. He turned it off and removed the earphones. He checked his watch: still only midmorning.

Time seemed to move so slowly these days. The sergeant's name was Jim Buckley: he chattered to himself, loving every minute, every detail of the task at hand. For a big bloke his movements were graceful. Pavarotti in a butcher's apron.

'Bullet number one entered just behind the left ear and exited through the right cheek; bullet number two entered the left eye. No apparent signs of an exit wound so we presume bullet number two is still lodged inside. I now intend to conduct an on-the-spot autopsy to confirm. Recording suspended at ... 10.22 a.m. Detective Sergeant James Buckley.'

Buckley reached over and opened his toolbox. He pulled out a handsaw.

That's one big difference between Homicide Squad and Stock

Squad, Cato mused, you don't have to wait for the autopsy, just do it yourself. He was still getting used to the idea: Detective Senior Constable Philip Kwong–Stock Squad. Homicide Squad, Major Crime, even Gangs, they had a ring to them that made you puff out your chest and stand a bit taller. Stock Squad? They were there to deal with cattle duffers, sheep theft, stolen tractors. They were touted as industry experts, they knew the farmers, knew the lingo. In Cato's view they were washed-up has-beens recycled as detectives. Mutton dressed as lamb? The Laughing Stock Squad. So if you come across a suspicious cow will you take it back to the station and grill it? Or leave it to stew?

So far Cato felt like little more than a glorified agricultural inspector. Stock Squad. It kind of escaped from the corner of your mouth like a coward's curse. Coward's curse pretty well summed up his situation. He was here because he'd been hung out to dry by a bunch of cowards he'd once worshipped and he couldn't do anything about it because of the Code, the Brotherhood, the whatever other bullshit name that might conceal a multitude of sins.

The Stock Squad was on tour: hearts and minds. The other two members of the squad taking the high road to the north, Cato Kwong and Jim Buckley on the low road south. A week of 'intelligence gathering' was how Buckley saw it: pressing the flesh, nosing around, random checks and a healthy per-diem budget–it would keep them in piss until they got back to Perth. A week of chewing straw, swatting flies and nodding sagely at stuff he didn't give a rat's arse about was how Cato saw it.

Cato Kwong: Stock Squad. Cato, like Peter Sellers' Chinese butler and martial arts sparring partner in The Pink Panther. A nickname inflicted on him at police academy. Cato hadn't seen any of the movies so he'd rented the videos to see what they were getting at. Cato, the manic manservant? Cato, the loyal punch-bag? Or just simply Cato the Chinaman?

The beginning of day three and Cato felt like he'd been on the road for a month.

'Oi, Kwongie, you gonna give us a hand, mate?'

Jim Buckley was already red-faced with effort as the saw bit into the back of the cow's neck. Blood spurting, blowflies going berko, he was in hog heaven. Cato winced primly; he preferred his meat plastic-wrapped and barcoded.

'Jim. Sir. Sarge ...'

Cato still didn't know how to address Jim Buckley. It wasn't that he didn't have any respect for authority, it was just that he was still working on it in Jim Buckley's case.

'Look, do we really need to do all this stuff? It's pretty obvious. The cow was run over, finished off with a couple of bullets to the head. The back leg was chopped off with a chainsaw and taken home to the barbie. End of story.'

Cato took another swig of the mountain spring water. He didn't function well in excessive heat. Maybe he should join the Canadian Mounties, or the Tasmanian ones, somewhere nice and cool.

Jim Buckley frowned, a tad disappointed with the younger man's attitude. 'It's still a crime, Cato mate. And it's our job to find the bad guys.'

Cato knew he was banging his head against the proverbial. Buckley, after twenty-five years in the force, had finally found his niche. Stock Squad was Jim's domain and he was in no mood for negativity. He mopped a sodden brow with a wipe of his shirtsleeve and passed the blood-soaked implement to Cato.

'So, as your senior officer, I'd advise you to shut the fuck up and start sawing.'

2

Four hours earlier.
Wednesday, October 8th. Dawn.
Hopetoun, Western Australia.

Her lungs were bursting and her left hip was agony: two kilometres from home and four behind her. For the last twenty minutes she'd been feeling a bit old, worn out. Too many twinges these days and getting harder to keep them at bay. But then she rounded the corner, hit the top of the sand dune and there was the ocean. Beautiful, she thought, gorgeous. A slight breeze rippled the surface and the sun was just coming up, dispelling the shadows on the hills in the national park over to the west. The huge open sky was striped orange, pink, purple, and blue.

And would you believe it, dolphins, two of them, splashing in the shallows near the groyne. She semi-sprinted the last two hundred metres along the sand where it was packed hard at the water's edge, never taking her eyes off the dolphins. As she drew nearer something changed. The way those dolphins were moving, the shape of the fins, the frolicking and splashing; no, it wasn't splashing–it was more like thrashing. Sharks. And there was something in the water with them, something brown, floppy, lifeless. A seal maybe, from the colony on the rock a few hundred metres out from the groyne. She quickened her step. This would be something a bit special to share with her primary class in news today.

One of the sharks seemed to be shaking the seal in its jaws, like a puppy with an old sock. Finally it let go and the seal flew a few feet through the air, landing with a soft plop at the water's edge. From five metres away she could see they'd ripped the poor little bugger to shreds; just one flipper remained and the thing didn't seem to have a head. She was right on top of the carcass now. She stopped, caught her breath, shivered. It wasn't a seal; it was a human torso. It wasn't a flipper; it was an arm – a left arm, no hand. She'd been right about the head though – there wasn't one.

She bowed forward, hands on knees, and threw up. Behind her she could hear the sharks still splashing in the shallows like a couple of dolphins, playfully taking the piss.

Hot flush. Senior Sergeant Tess Maguire put down her coffee, opened her jacket and cracked a car window. The smell of rotting roadkill nearby forced her to shut it again, quickly. Tess swore and flicked on the air conditioning. Six-twenty on a sharp, spring south-coast morning and she was sweating like a pig. Suddenly cold again, she flicked the air conditioner back off. She felt completely out of sorts. How could she be getting hot flushes when she'd only just turned forty-two? Tess looked at herself in the rear-view. The short-cropped blonde hair was losing its fight against the wispy greys. She kept on threatening to let it grow out to all-over grey. It was natural. What's so bad about grey anyway? She tried to think of some attractive, well-known, grey-haired women. She couldn't get beyond Germaine Greer. Tess added hair dye to her mental shopping list and turned the radio on.

The interviewer sounded young enough to be her daughter. She'd countried her voice up a bit, talking with an authoritative twang to a primary commodities broker about the grain and wool prices. Apparently one was up and the other was down, in contrast to the stock market in general which was still in freefall. Tess couldn't get her head around how a handful of venal mortgage-brokers in America could trigger what seemed to be a global financial tsunami and the end of the world as we know it. Never mind, it was unlikely to hit them here in Hopetoun – the end of the world and proud of it. This was Tess's first posting since she came off sick leave. Nine months. Most of the first month in hospital and out-patients, the next three in physio, the rest in therapy. She wondered how Melissa would go: new to town, year nine in high school, sharing a classroom with a bunch of teenage hard-cases whose dads had come down to work at the new mine. She'd seen them hanging around the park–the kids, not the dads. Testosterone. The pushing and shoving, swearing and shouting: youthful high spirits, some called it. Only these days it sent her into cold sweats and panic attacks, fighting for breath, tears welling up. Even now, just at the thought of them.

A new life, a new start, new hope in Hopetoun, they'd promised her. The place hadn't warranted a permanent police post in the past. For decades it had been a laid-back holiday or retirement spot for wheatbelt farmers. There was nothing to police except maybe the occasional drunk driver or domestic. Now, with the nearby nickel mine, the population had steadily grown from a stable four hundred in the old days to a whopping two thousand–and rising. It would still be a while before it was Gotham City but with more houses, plenty of money being tossed around and the pub getting busier it meant more bad behaviour, temptation, vandalism, domestics and drugs. Hopetoun was a good place to put ageing or wounded or useless cops out to pasture. Tess ticked all three boxes. At first she'd turned it down. Senior Sergeant Tess Maguire–the bump up to 'Senior' was a reward for getting the shit kicked out of her–wanted to tough it out. But after a few weeks at a desk in Perth HQ with the concerned but embarrassed stares, the traffic, the noise and the crowds, Tess was sold on the sea change. Hopetoun. No crime to speak of, she reasoned, no stress, just sunshine and sea breezes to clear out the cobwebs.

First she heard him. Then she smelled him. Then she saw him: weaving down the road, screeching and roaring, the acrid stench of burning rubber from the smoking tyres. Tess checked the clock on her dashboard: he was right on time. She had parked the paddy wagon by the turn-off to the mine. The swirling black tyre marks at the junction were a testament to his earlier handiwork. They were the kind of marks you'd see on any road in any Australian suburb these days but the big nobs of the Shire wanted an end to it. It was rampant hoonism, it created a bad impression, it was a bloody disgrace. And it was Tess Maguire's job to nip it in the bud. Tess started up her motor, switched on the flashing lights and swung across the road blocking his path. He stopped. She tapped on his window until he opened it.

'Having fun, Kane?'

Kane Stevenson, Doughnut King: a drongo kid from a drongo family. There was a time Tess might have avoided pinning labels on to people. Give them a chance, that kind of thing. Not any more. Drongo is as drongo does. But what the Shire bigwigs might find hard to swallow was the fact that this particular drongo was a local boy, born and bred. They couldn't blame this on miners, outsiders or incomers; Kane was home-grown trouble. Now that he was working at the mine, he had money to burn along with those tyres.

He wound down his window, all innocent. 'Morning Tess, early start?'

'Sergeant, or Officer, to you. What do you think you're doing?

'Sorry mate, had to swerve. Roo on the road, I couldn't kill it, animal lover me.'

'Right.'

'No: straight up.'

Tess stepped back and made a show of admiring what she saw.

'Company ute, nice. Been promoted, Kane?'

He slapped the steering wheel proudly. 'Yeah, Team Leader; extra fifteen grand.'

'Congratulations. Thing is, Kane, under our lovely new hoon laws, I've got every right to impound this vehicle.' She snapped her fingers. 'Gone in sixty seconds. I don't think your employers are going to be too impressed.'

His employers being Western Minerals, one of the biggest

and richest companies in the world with mines in all corners of the globe. They paid their employees extremely well but were very unforgiving of transgressions. Their motto: Zero Tolerance. Everybody assumed they were talking about bad behaviour.

'Ah fuck, Tess, c'mon,' Kane pleaded, for the first time a flicker of recognition of consequences in his big brown eyes.

Tess's mobile trilled: caller ID, Greg, her offsider.

'Tess? You'd better get back to town. There's been a body.'

She squinted menacingly at the Doughnut King. 'First and last warning,' and took off in the paddy wagon, burning a bit of rubber on the way.

As the sky brightened, Tess passed a convoy of white utes heading in the opposite direction out to the mine, forty kilometres away. On the outskirts of town she climbed the low hill to the roundabout leading off to the light industrial on one side and the new sprawling off-the-peg Legoland housing estate on the other. Cresting the rise she relaxed a notch or two at the view down the main street to the bright blue Southern Ocean at the bottom of the hill. After three months she still hadn't got over how small, quiet and, yes, beautiful the place was. And she hoped she never would.

Tess pulled into the beachside gravel car park. Her colleague, Constable Greg Fisher, was on the beach talking to a middle-aged woman dressed in running gear, while the town GP crouched examining something on the sand; it was hidden from view by a makeshift canvas windbreak. Greg's initiative: he was in his first year out of police academy and eager to impress. Tess had long forgotten that feeling. A pair of pied oystercatchers pecked the sand irritably with scarlet stiletto beaks. A small handful of early-rising onlookers strained to get a glimpse of the body, careful not to overstep the invisible line established by Constable Fisher.

As she got closer, Tess recognised the woman as a teacher

from the primary school: she'd seen her around, hard not to in a town this small. The teacher was a bit green around the gills; her eyes were puffy, her lower lip trembled as she talked, Greg taking notes. Tess left them to it and walked, white sand squeaking beneath her feet, over to the doctor and the body. The torso glistened in the morning sun; green tendrils of seaweed sparkled on the mottled, lightly tanned flesh. There was no head, no legs, only part of one arm and a pale grey mush where the missing pieces should have been.

The doctor stood up, broad-shouldered, early fifties. Tess had met him once before, a few weeks back when she dropped in a young miner who'd been on a bender and tried to punch out the pub ATM when it argued with him about his PIN number.

'What's the word, Doctor Terhorst?'

'Well he's dead, that's for sure.' His lip curled slightly at his little joke, then he continued in his clipped Afrikaans accent. 'But at this stage I can't accurately say what age bracket or even, for sure, what race. From the torso length I'd estimate medium height, medium build. Don't ask me for a time of death, with something that's been in the water it's too hard without the proper tests. Ball park? Less than a week.'

'Shark attack?' Hopetoun. Southern Ocean. Not an unreasonable question.

'Well I've seen a few of these back in Cape Town and the injuries are consistent with sharks.'

Tess pointed to the mush at the base of the spine where the legs were meant to start. 'Looks like they bit clean through him.'

The doctor nodded grimly then scratched his chin. 'Possibly. I'd be more worried about the sever wound at the neck.'

'Why?'

'It's very neat compared to the punctures and tears everywhere else. The spinal column looks like it's been sheared with a clean straight edge. Either our shark had meticulous table manners ... or somebody cut this poor man's head off.'

3

Wednesday, October 8th. Midmorning.
Busselton, Western Australia.

The floorboard creaks under Stuart Miller's size tens. The passageway seems shorter than he remembers it and that bitter ashtray smell is back in his nostrils. The lights are out, another power cut, bloody miners on strike again. So why can he hear the telly on the other side of the door? A football match. He turns the handle and steps into the dim room lit only by the flickering TV screen: a sea of red and white rolling and roaring. Jenny and Graeme are on the settee, cuddled up, watching the game. On the floor, Graeme's Scalextric cars race around the track giving off sparks at each corner.

'Home, pet, what you got the lights out for?'

His hand goes to the light switch but nothing happens.

'Shite, the bulb must have gone. What's the score?' he nods at the TV.

'Nil all,' says little Graeme, finally acknowledging his dad's presence. Jenny must be in a huff about something: him working late again probably. She hasn't moved or said a word. Miller looks at the screen again, the Cup Final, Sunderland and Leeds. Billy Hughes steps up for the corner, the ball lands for Porterfield. He's seen this before: the goal, the setting. That's when the panic kicks in. He touches his wife's shoulder and head, and his fingers come away sticky with blood. Graeme is nestled into her, hand resting on her knee, a deep crimson gash above his ear.

Stuart Miller jerked awake gasping for breath. The bed was empty and Jenny was gone.

4

Wednesday, October 8th. Late morning.

Sergeant Jim Buckley was heaving, puffing and fit to have a coronary. His normally flushed drinker's face was nearly purple and his ginger-grey sideburns glistened with sweat. The cow's head was now separated from the body after a joint effort by himself, Cato and three hacksaw blades. Its neck was flat to the ground and the eyes were staring skywards to cow heaven. Buckley had a foot planted firmly on either side of the head, pinning the ears to the ground. With his left hand pushing down hard on the nose for extra leverage, he gave one last mighty tug with the right. His hand emerged triumphant from the cow's face, pliers gripping a small blood-soaked lump of metal.

'A .22, just as I thought.'

Cato finished pissing against a ghost gum and zipped back up. He had retired to the shade and was halfway through today's cryptic from the *West*. He'd managed to snaffle it from the neighbouring breakfast table at the Katanning Motel. It had been a close shave though, the guy had only gone to the toilet and when he came back for his paper Cato had to plead ignorance and suggest that the breakfast lady had cleared it away. Buckley had shaken his head in disgust.

'Why don't you ever buy your own, they're only a dollar, you tight-arsed bastard.'

'Dollar thirty. All I need is the crossword, I don't need to read all the other crap.'

His father had taught him how to crack the cryptic codes a couple of years ago and now he was hooked. There was something about the search for clear reasoning among the insane ramblings, and identifying the cold calculation behind the crafty wordplay. It came in useful in the interview room sometimes. Dad meanwhile had moved on to Sudokus to enrich his widowed dotage; he'd knock them off in ten minutes if his hands weren't shaking too much. He'd tried to get Cato onto it, reckoned the process of patient, logical elimination would be good for training his detective brain. Cato was sticking with the cryptics; intuition, flights of fancy, twisted logic and inspiration backed up later by the facts – that was more his style.

Merit Cup for perfect roast.

Cup, roast, something to do with coffee? The heat was curdling his brain. Cato stretched out his long legs and smiled encouragingly.

'Good work, Sarge. Any idea whose gun it came from?'

Jim Buckley's good mood had withered in the heat.

'Get fucked. Bag this evidence while I clean up.'

'What, the head as well?'

'In the esky; sooner it's on ice the better.'

'No worries,' Cato sighed. He wondered if he should resign now or after next payday. That was the intention after all: disgraced, demoted, demeaned, despised – until he had taken enough and went of his own accord. They wouldn't sack him; he knew too much. But they certainly had their ways.

Cato grabbed a Ziploc bag out of the Land Cruiser glove box, hauled the esky off the back seat, and kick-closed the car door, planting his heel dead centre of the bull's-head logo. He popped the bullet in the bag and crammed the head into the esky. A mobile buzzed in his trousers. It took Cato by surprise; he hadn't expected a signal out here.

'That you, Cato?'

'Detective Senior Constable Kwong speaking, who's this?'

'Hutchens.'

DI Mick Hutchens, his old boss from Fremantle Detectives. Now with Albany Detectives, enjoying a south-coast sea change in Bogan Town. He'd fared better in the fallout than Cato had.

'What can I do for you, sir?'

'Cut the crap, it's me, Mick. Where are you?'

Cato looked around at the parched, blistered landscape.

'Somewhere near Katanning.'

Hutchens chuckled. 'Enjoying life with the Sheep-Shagging Squad then?'

'Not sure the Commissioner would appreciate your cynical tone, sir.'

'Right. That fuckwit Buckley with you?'

'Want a word with him?'

'No. Listen up. Got some real work for you. A body, well, half a one anyway. Human though; would make a nice change for you.'

Cato's pulse quickened like it hadn't done for a long time.

'Where is it?'

'Down in Hopetoun; maybe three hours drive for you.'

Cato racked his brain – Hopetoun, south coast, fishing spot? Other than that, the place meant nothing to him.

'Why aren't your mob onto it? I'm supposed to be banished to Siberia, remember?'

A momentary uncomfortable silence, then Hutchens cleared his throat.

'Three are on suspension, two on sick leave, two on holiday. I'm scraping the bottom of the barrel. Thought of you immediately.'

'Cheers.'

The faintest whining hint of desperation crept into Hutchens' voice. 'Cato mate, I need you. For the next few days anyway.'

Cato couldn't shake the thought that there was more to this than met the eye. Was Hutchens really scraping the very bottom of the barrel before he thought of his old mate Cato? The sun scorched the back of his neck, flies worried his face, and the headless three-legged cow was starting to smell really bad. The road out of Katanning shimmered in the heat haze. Who was Cato Kwong to look a gift horse in the mouth?

'Tell me more.'

'Washed up this morning. Looks like a shark attack but the local doctor reckons our bloke might have been dead before he hit the water. He's a country quack so probably talking through his arse.' Same old Mick Hutchens, thought Cato, Zen master of the sweeping generalisation. 'I need you to take a look, confirm or deny. No hassle, no fuss. Fill out the paperwork and file it, Cato. Home by Friday.'

Cato had lost track of time – then he remembered, today was Wednesday. If it really was that simple and clean-cut he'd still be home in time for the weekend. It was his turn to have Jake. They could have a family weekend together, just the two of them. Yeah right.

'Who's the officer-in-charge down there?'

'Senior Sergeant Tess Maguire ...' Hutchens paused, no doubt for effect. Cato didn't miss a beat, didn't give Hutchens the reaction he wanted.

'Taser Tess?'

'The very same.'

After her ordeal at the hands of the mob up north, the Commissioner had made taser stun guns standard issue for all officers in the optimistic belief that the outcome might have been different had she been 'suitably equipped' with a fifty-thousand-volt zapper. Cato had his doubts about their effectiveness in that kind of situation, particularly if they fell into the wrong hands. Scepticism aside, it had made Tess something of a folk hero among her colleagues right around the state. She had been more than that to him, once.

'I thought she'd left the job.'

'Sent to Hopetoun. Same thing. Look, take Buckley with you to make up the numbers but mate ... keep him away from those sheep.'

Hutchens signed off with a 'baaaaaah'. Cato sighed and snapped his phone shut. Then it came to him, *Merit Cup for perfect roast.*

Merit Cup: an anagram, 'Prime Cut'. It was enough to turn a good man vegetarian.

Jim Buckley was hunched over by the wing mirror, mouth pursed, using a Kleenex baby wipe to try to get the bloodstains off his Stock Squad shirt. Cato coughed politely for attention.

'Sarge. Something just came up.'

They should have been in Hopetoun by early afternoon but Jim Buckley had insisted on backtracking to put the cow's head into storage in the freezer at the Katanning cop shop. The local boys weren't happy. They'd have to find somewhere else to store the snags and steaks meant for this Friday's sundowner barbie.

'Use some initiative,' Buckley had snapped at them, rather ungratefully.

Then they'd stopped along the way for a late lunch: two meat pies, a Mars Bar and a Coke for Buckley; for Cato just the one pie, a floury bruised apple and an orange juice, having caught sight of himself in a window and seen what just half a week on the road can do. Then there were the four smokos and two piss stops. Then they'd pulled up a couple of speeders and issued tickets, Buckley getting his stats up, Cato getting his blood pressure up. He was impatient to get to the body. He wondered if Buckley ever felt the thrill of stuff like this – a possible case, a mystery: was the body dead before it went into the water? That kind of thing. Probably not. He caught a glimpse of himself in the rear-view mirror – flecks of grey at the temples but, at two months short of thirty-eight, he was in as good a shape as he had been for years. The banishment to Stock Squad left him with extra time on his hands and he used some of it to get fitter. Swimming, cycling, and avoiding the kind of junk he'd eaten when he was doing normal cop hours – whatever they were.

Recently Cato didn't seem to be able to get enough sleep. There was a time when he buzzed along on four or five hours. Nowadays he usually got the full eight, often more, but still sometimes woke up exhausted and lethargic. Today? Today he saw a flicker of energy in his eyes that he hadn't seen for a long time.

It was midafternoon by the time they crested the rise that would drop them down into Hopetoun. The suffocating heat of the interior had eased as they neared the coast. The hot easterly had become a fresh south-westerly and Cato was beginning to feel halfway human again. As they rolled down the Hopetoun main drag – Veal Street it was called – Cato reflected they were having a big meat-themed day. Cows' heads, gift horses, barbies, pies, even the crossword solution. And now Veal Street; that's life in the Stock Squad.

Two telephone boxes stood outside a cafe where a handful of people drank coffee on a pine deck. In one of the booths was a man with his back to them, wearing dusty blue and fluoro-yellow work overalls and holding one hand over his free ear trying to block out the wind noise. He turned to face them and Cato saw that he was Chinese. Their eyes met for a moment as Cato rolled past.

'More than just the one of you in town then,' Buckley observed.

Cato continued looking at the man through his rear-vision mirror.

'Well spotted. That must be why you're the sergeant and I'm a mere constable.'

'*Senior* constable: don't put yourself down, mate,' Buckley corrected him.

Cato had phoned ahead and got through to Hopetoun second-in-command, Constable Greg Fisher. Greg told him to meet them at the Sea Rescue hut beside the skate park. He had forewarned them: the hut was the cop shop until the new whiz-bang multipurpose emergency services building was finished. It might take a while, he'd said, 'chronic labour shortage'. From what Cato could see – a big pile of sand inside a temporary wire fence – there was little evidence the new cop shop had even been started. He pulled up onto the rust-coloured gravel. The Sea Rescue hut was a faded and peeling olive green and about the size of a shipping container–but not quite as pleasing to the eye. The door was open so Cato walked in. Greg Fisher was sitting at a desk talking on the phone. He looked up and acknowledged the visitors with a wink. Senior Sergeant Tess Maguire stood by a recently cleaned whiteboard, the smell of cleaning fluid hung in the air. She had a red marker pen in her left hand and Cato noticed her bare ring finger. In the centre of the whiteboard she'd given the body a name, 'Flipper', and drawn a question mark beside it. Over to the right-hand side, a short list of names and telephone numbers.

She turned. At first glance she still looked the same Tess to Cato but, on closer inspection, her eyes seemed darker and sadder. She was using them to measure him up too. Cato sucked his stomach in a little bit and lifted his head to give his neck more of a chance but Tess seemed to be more focused on the bull's-head logo on his Stock Squad breast pocket. Cato winced inside; he really needed to change back into civvies at the first opportunity.

'Nice uniform; heard you were coming to town.' The light seemed to have gone out of her voice as well. 'How's things?' she inquired idly, like the answer didn't matter.

'Good. Good.' He said it twice as if to reassure himself.

Cato introduced Buckley who was, after all, the senior officer. Tess filled them in on what little she knew: teacher, sharks, torso, doctor, head (lack of).

'Why Flipper?' Cato nodded towards the whiteboard.

Greg Fisher failed to smother a grin. 'The teacher who found him thought it was a seal at first, thought the arm was a flipper.'

'Do you get many people dropping in here?'

Cato could see Tess bristling.

'There'll be a room divider up by tomorrow,' she said. 'No member of the public will see the board.'

Cato wondered how you could divide such a small space

any further. Callous nicknames aside, as the days went by there would be plenty of other reasons why the information board would need to be blocked from public view.

'So tell me about the doctor's take on this.'

Jim Buckley clearly thought it was about time he asserted his presence. 'Yeah, has he been watching a bit too much telly, or what?'

Tess summed up what she'd been told, finishing with the news that the body had been carted up to Ravensthorpe, fifty kilometres away, and put into cold storage in the hospital there.

Cato swore. They'd had to come through Ravensthorpe to get to Hopetoun; he could have checked out the body on his way through–if somebody had bothered to let him know. Now they'd have to waste time backtracking. Greg looked uncomfortable. Cato could see that Tess didn't give a hoot: this was her patch, her rules.

'A pathologist is coming over from Albany; he should be at Ravensthorpe in a few hours. You can meet him there. Anything else you want to do while you're waiting?'

She had addressed the question to Buckley, letting Cato know who was boss. Buckley looked over at Cato. Detective Kwong took his sunnies out of his Stock Squad shirt pocket.

'Let's go to the beach.'

The beach at Hopey didn't offer any major new insights but Cato enjoyed the squeak of the brilliant white grains under his Stock Squad blundies and the sparkling clarity of the water rolling and crashing onto the shore. For him it was as much about getting a feel for the place, the lie of the land and all that. First impressions? Small. The tour of the town had taken about five minutes; there seemed to be about half a dozen streets either side of the main drag. East of Veal Street were mainly older holiday shacks; to the west, the newly built Legoland–as Tess called it–courtesy of the mine. At the south end of Veal Street, the town centre–three shops, a couple of cafes, a park, a pub, the beach, the ocean. At the north end, Veal Street became the Hopetoun–Ravensthorpe Road. Hopetoun was the original one-horse town and, at first glance, a beautiful and peaceful place to die.

Cato had asked Tess and Greg to find out tide and weather conditions for the last few days to see if that would tell them where the body might have entered the water. He also suggested following up any missing person reports from the last few weeks or so. Tess had given him a 'No shit, Sherlock?' look. Obviously, in both instances, she was already on the case. Cato should have expected the hostility from her but it still bothered him. It was at least twelve or thirteen years ago but it was clearly a sore that had never properly healed. And why should it? Cato was fairly fresh out of the academy and four years her junior. They had been partnered up, working nights out of Midland, Perth's bandit country, in the souped-up unmarked Commodore. Cato Kwong–Prince of the Mean Streets. High-speed chases through the suburbs, domestics, prowlers, break-ins. Routine stuff but still usually more a thrill than not in those days. And the adrenaline had fed the spark between them. It all seemed natural and inevitable and it was good, great at times. All over each other like a rash. Until he walked out on her.

It was nearly dark as they drove into Ravensthorpe. Just a few pale strips of sky lay in the west, sandwiched between the silhouette of distant hills and a blanket of ink-black clouds. Ravy, as it was known locally, was bigger than Hopey, only just. The main street was dark and deserted except around the two-storey red brick Ravensthorpe Hotel where an array of utes and four-wheel drives were angle-parked in anticipation of the Wednesday night pool competition. Some of the utes bore mine company logos. Cato had seen the lights of the mine off in the eastern distance as they passed the airport turn-off halfway between the two towns. You couldn't miss it, a patch of brilliant daylight in the surrounding dim dusk. They'd had to pull into the side of the road while an ambulance, with lights flashing, sped past.

Cato pulled into the hospital car park and killed the radio. According to the eight o'clock news the Australian stock market just had its worst day in twenty years. Jim Buckley snorted and muttered something to the effect of 'Boo-fucking-hoo'. It was deadly quiet, not many lights on. Like many country hospitals, Ravensthorpe was little more than a glorified nursing post, kept open by the skin of its teeth, the marginality of the electorate or, as in this case, the persuasive power of the mining company. The ambulance, having deposited its patient, was swinging back out onto the road; the driver and Cato exchanged a relaxed hand-flick wave.

Cato and Buckley approached the front entrance expecting the automatic doors to slide open. They didn't. Except for emergencies, the hospital operating hours had recently been cut back to an eight to eight shift. 'Staff Shortages' said the handwritten notice blu-tacked to the door. It was 8.05. Cato rang the bell and they waited. And waited. Cato cupped his hands to the door and peered through the glare for any signs of life or movement inside. Nothing. He swore loudly and pressed the bell a tenth time. Finally an elderly woman in a pink dressing gown floated into view with a cup of something steaming. She almost dropped her mug as she saw Cato's face up against the glass. He pressed his ID against the door mouthing 'POLICE'. It didn't help; in fact she seemed even more determined to hurry back to her bed and hide under the covers.

Jim Buckley stepped forward with a kindly smile, a cheery wave, and a non-Asian face. That seemed to do the trick. The old woman poked a button on the inside and the doors slid open. With a bedside manner that was a complete revelation to Cato, Buckley got directions to the operating theatre at the rear of the hospital as well as learning all he needed to know about her hernia and cataracts.

'Thanks Deirdre, and you take care of yourself now, love.'

'Are you coming back tomorrow, Roger?'

'Yes love, 'course I am.'

Buckley gave her a last little wave and led Cato down the corridor. Cato wondered who was meant to be looking after Deirdre overnight when he spotted a grumpy-looking woman with angry red hair knotted up in a bun. She was coming out of the ladies. She didn't give either of the men a second glance, as if strangers wandering the hospital corridors at this hour was an everyday occurrence. Instead she thumped through a set of double doors behind which Cato could hear muffled cries and commotion. Dear Diary, remind me to avoid needing an overnight stay in Ravensthorpe General and to never whinge about city hospitals ever again.

The lights were at least on in the operating theatre, a good sign. They pushed open the doors and walked through. A short wiry man paused, scalpel in hand. Behind him an assistant sat on a stool at a steel bench in the corner taking notes with one hand and eating a sandwich with the other. She didn't pause or look up from behind her curtain of black hair. In the other corner stood Tess. She looked at her watch meaningfully and smiled mock-sweetly.

'So you found the place okay.'

Cato's patience was stretched paper-thin. 'Had a bit of trouble getting in.'

The man with the scalpel was obviously keen to get on with it. 'Evening gentlemen, you must be the detectives. I'm the pathologist. Harold Lewis, Harry to you. Forgive me for not shaking hands. Shall we proceed?'

All this addressed in a fey voice to Jim Buckley who nodded. His attention was elsewhere.

'That's Sally,' said Harry waving his scalpel in the general direction.

It was a kind of low-rent *Silent Witness*, silent except for Sally munching on the sandwich and the scratching of her biro on a notepad. The body lay on a shiny steel table. Cato edged closer. His eyes travelled over the skin, the wounds, the stumps and the handless arm. Flipper. It didn't look human any more. But it–correction, he–once was. This shapeless lump of meat had a family somewhere. Cato would try to hold on to that thought. The smell was like an extra presence in the room. Sally seemed oblivious to it, wiping a wholemeal crumb daintily from the corner of her lips.

Dr Lewis got to work. The subject was a medium-sized male probably in the twenty to forty age-range. No obvious indications of any disease or illness. No scars, tattoos, or distinguishing birthmarks, and no obvious indications of racial origin. 'Going by the general slippage and flesh deterioration I'd estimate he's been in the water for up to a week. Sorry I can't be more precise.'

Harry examined, and Sally listed, the various wounds, mainly teeth-marks and tears. With the sandwich out of the way, Sally hopped off her stool and took some photographs.

Dr Lewis held the pale arm up, quite gently. 'Pity about the missing hand; it might have had a wedding finger, something to help us along. No such luck.'

As far as he could tell, the missing hand, right arm, and legs were probably the work of sharks. Lewis turned his attention to the neck, dragging down the magnifier on its extension arm.

'The neck hasn't been snapped like you might expect from the wrenching movement of a shark's jaw. It has been cut, or more likely sawn, perhaps with a chainsaw? A handsaw would be a lot of effort and leave more jagged markings on the bone. Not exactly my specialty but we'll get it looked at in Perth.'

Cato certainly agreed with the 'handsaw effort' part. Was it only that morning they'd been decapitating a cow in Katanning?

Lewis continued. 'So my observant friend, Dr Terhorst, would appear to be on the ball. Speaking of which, I thought he might have been with us tonight?'

He looked around the room as if Terhorst might have been hiding somewhere.

Tess looked up from writing her own notes. 'He was booked

to give a talk at the Hopey Wine Club tonight. He gave his apologies, said he'd call you tomorrow.'

'A wine buff too. A man of many talents, our Dr Terhorst,' Lewis said, a touch insincerely. He made the 'Y' incision and opened the body up. Tess went pale. Cato made himself keep watching; it wasn't his first time, by any means, but it had been a while. Buckley was concentrating on Sally's calf muscles, oblivious to the carnage on the steel trolley. Lewis lifted the lungs out. Cato could see where the wiry muscularity came from. A few lung lifts every day would keep anyone in good shape.

'The lung contents rule out death by drowning,' Lewis confirmed.

He examined them further, probing with his scalpel, humming softly to himself. Cato tried to place the tune: it might have been a bit of Puccini, or Shirley Bassey. Finally Lewis glanced at Cato.

'I would say your friend was definitely dead before he went into the water.'

Cato and Tess shared a look; it seemed he was going to be around for a while longer. Lewis plucked out and squeezed what appeared to be a blood-soaked semi-deflated balloon into a plastic container. Stomach contents: pretty empty, but there were indications of rice and chicken in there. Blood, skin and tissue samples would be taken for further testing but Cato had seen enough for now. His neck prickled with something approaching excitement.

'Are you saying this is a murder, Dr Lewis?'

'Possibly; that's your job not mine. There could be any number of reasons for what we see here: accident, panic, cover-up, foul play. Anyway ...' he tapped Flipper's neck lightly with his scalpel and looked Cato straight in the eye, 'it's definitely a bit fishy.'

5

Thursday, October 9th. Dawn.

'Fuck.'

That was the considered response of DI Hutchens when Cato phoned his ex-boss early the following morning and told him about the preliminary pathology report. Cato was outside on the street, the sun was just up and birdsong filled the air. Magpies warbled sweetly like angels being drowned in a bathtub. A gentle breeze filtered through the gum trees. Cato was enjoying the peace and tranquillity.

'Fuck,' Hutchens said again.

Cato waited and kept his mouth shut. Hutchens had let it be known that he wanted an open-and-shut case with papers filed. He didn't have the manpower for a murder investigation, if that's what this was. And, gruesome as it might be, at this stage he did not see it as that high a priority. Right now the body was a nobody that nobody had reported missing. Nobody seemed to care. Maybe nobody would and it could quietly slip away into the ever-growing list of 'Unsolveds'.

Cato watched a magpie swoop a morning walker as he patiently listened to Hutchens rant. The bugger was that, already, there had been journo inquiries to Police Media in Perth. Crime or no crime, sharks were big enough news. Head office wanted it played down until they knew more about what they were dealing with. So far the media were being fobbed off with what appeared to be a 'drowning' and the probability that the so-called 'shark attack' was most likely post-mortem curiosity. In the meantime Hutchens had to be seen to be doing something just in case a grieving relative popped out of the woodwork. And now the pathologist was suggesting foul play.

Hutchens punctuated his monologue with another expletive.

One of his detective sergeants was due back on duty on Monday from a family holiday in New Zealand but had phoned in saying he'd slipped on a glacier and snapped his ankle.

'A fucking glacier. Prick.'

The next one due back was a week later and she'd cleverly kept her phone turned off while she no doubt partied hard in Bali. Everybody else was too fucking busy. There was a stagnant, ill-tempered pause. Cato wanted a crack at this so he let the silence hang. And hang. And was rewarded with an exasperated grunt.

'I hope I'm not going to regret this. Reckon you and Buckley can hold the fort for a week or so?'

Cato made sure nobody was looking, punched the air and grinned. Hutchens sucked in a breath as if he'd seen the gesture down the phone.

'Just look and act like real detectives but don't actually try to find anything out. We don't need it. Just walk the walk, okay? Then, a week Monday, walk away. I'll have someone else down there by then.'

'Won't let you down, boss.'

'Too right you won't.' Hutchens cleared his throat. 'In effect you run it, Cato. Work out whatever you need to with Buckley to keep him sweet. Any journos come sniffing, send them my way or just tell them to fuck off. Mate, keep your nose clean on this. Don't stuff up and I'll owe you one. I might even bring you back in from the cold.'

Cato didn't intend to hold his breath on that.

Hutchens made some scratching and rustling noises. 'Give me the number of that boss of yours. What's his name again?'

'Saunders. Brett Saunders.'

'Oh yeah, "Colonel" Saunders, Sheep-Shagging Squad. I hope he can spare two hotshots like you and Buckley.'

So did Cato.

Cato went back inside to get some breakfast. Miraculously two rooms had been free at the Fitzgerald River Motel, directly over the road from the police shipping container, now a de facto 'Murder HQ'. It was a miracle because everywhere, including the caravan park, had been full for the last two years. Life in a mining boomtown, apparently. Yet to Cato this place still seemed tiny, quiet and unspoilt. Mining boom to him conjured up the vivid red earth of the Pilbara and mile-long trains. If this was a boom then – first impressions anyway – it seemed to be a muted one.

The two rooms had become available because, according to Pam the bustling receptionist who seemed to know everything and didn't mind sharing it, the previous long-term resident, a middle-level accountant at the mine, had just been sacked for downloading extreme porn. Pam's lips pursed disapprovingly at that one. The second room had just come back into service after being trashed the previous month by a party of contractors 'celebrating' the end of their tour of duty. Either way it was a big relief to Cato. The idea of bunking in with Jim Buckley for the next week didn't appeal. Pam's eyes had widened when they presented their police ID and gave Albany CIB as the billing address.

'That'll be the body on the beach. They reckon he'd been involved in drugs.'

'That right?' said Cato.

'Oh yes, since that mine opened the dealers have been targeting this place. Eastern States cartels out to make a killing. You mark my words.' Pam gave a what's-the-world-coming-to shake of the head and disappeared out back.

Buckley was freshly showered and shaved and finishing off a big fry-up. Cato joined him at the cramped table overlooking Veal Street and Murder HQ. Buckley glanced up from the remnants of brekkie and mopped up some egg yolk with a corner of toast.

'What did your mate Hutchens say then?'

Cato thought he detected a note of resentment there. He savoured it for a second but almost immediately felt guilty. Maybe his soon-to-be ex-wife was right, he did have a mean streak and a chip on his shoulder. He tried to shake it off and stay bright and positive.

'We're on the case, temporarily seconded to Albany Detectives; they're over-stretched. We've got just over a week before Hutchens sends one of his regulars over to run things.'

Buckley didn't seem that excited, even less so when Cato told him just who Hutchens wanted in charge. Cato sweetened it so that it sounded like Buckley would maintain a 'managerial overview and inter-agency liaison role'.

All bullshit and they both knew it.

Buckley squinted out through the lace curtains. 'Go get 'em, Jackie Chan.'

Something was burning. There were blood spots in the sink. Stuart Miller muttered his third 'fucking hell' of the day, chucked the disposable Bic into the scummy water and rushed through to the kitchen to rescue his toast. The timer on the microwave read 8.20. Days when he woke up after The Dream were usually like this: accident-prone, out of sorts, pissed off. He hadn't had The Dream for months: just as well, too many mornings like this and he'd have topped himself by now. He tried scraping some of the black stuff off the toast. He didn't actually mind the taste that much but Jenny kept warning him he'd get cancer if he ate it. He gave up, binned it and slotted two more in the toaster.

Miller switched on the radio. Somebody was wittering on about the cost and quality of a cappuccino in Perth versus Fremantle. He usually preferred the ABC talk over the ads and crap music on the other stations but lately the chat seemed to get more and more trivial and giggly. Alien. Sometimes when he woke up from The Dream he felt as if he'd just landed like those poor wretched asylum-seekers in the leaky boats up north: desperate, unable to fully understand what was going on, isolated, not knowing what the day would bring. He went back to the bathroom and peeled his daily pills off their foil–blood pressure, cholesterol, blood thinner, beta blocker–chucked them down without the water and got back to shaving. Why shave? He no longer had a job to go to, no longer had appearances to keep up. Jenny had left him a list of things he might do to occupy his dotage, provide him with a meaningful and active retirement. The backyard needed weeding, a few things to be got from the shop, he could walk or cycle into town and back, and there was always retirees tennis for fun, fitness and friendship.

'Fucking hell.'

That was the fourth for the day.

Everyone was gathered at Murder HQ for the first official squad meeting on Operation Flipper. Cato had passed on the news from DI Hutchens and noted a raised eyebrow and half-smirk from Tess when he explained the operational arrangements and line of day-to-day command. He kept to himself the bit about Hutchens wanting them to just go through the motions and not actually achieve anything. He had a point to prove, if only to himself, that he could be a good cop. Just once more. He'd called Jane to let her know something had come up at work and that he wouldn't be able to have Jake this weekend. Jane sounded particularly bright and carefree. Cato got the message: she was already moving on.

He outlined, for Greg Fisher's benefit, the essence of the pathology findings so far. The body would be on its way to Perth in a cold box on the next flight out from the recently expanded airstrip at Ravensthorpe. In the absence of proper freight facilities the torso was in a sealed body bag, in an old chest fridge supplied by the Ravy butcher. In Perth it would undergo further examination and tests. Cato was well aware that the flight from Ravy to the Perth PathLab would be the only fast-moving thing about the investigation. This wasn't a high priority–an unidentified person who nobody seemed to be making any noise about. Meanwhile, in and around Perth, there were at least four murders, a handful of rapes and half a dozen violent home invasions ahead in the forensics queue. He pointed this out to the faces in front of him and told them not to hold their breath. Jim Buckley smiled benevolently and promised he wouldn't. Cato felt the need to explain himself.

'This might just seem like a lump of rotting meat to some people...'–as expected, Buckley held his gaze; he wasn't the backing-down type–'but he is somebody's son, or brother, or even father. And I'd like to think that, if he belonged to me, somebody would do their job and find out what happened to him.'

Buckley winked and mimed applause. Cato, point made, signalled it was time to move on.

Young Greg Fisher was like a puppy, almost widdling himself with excitement. His first murder, Cato surmised. Greg reported on the two jobs he'd been following up yesterday. There were three missing-person reports within the Great Southern and South-East Coastal districts over the last two weeks. None of them matched. The first, a thirteen year old girl from Albany, had returned home the next day having proved some point to her parents. Tess grimaced at that one. The second, a thirty-six year old farm labourer from nearby Jerdacuttup, had looked promising but he had been located by Kalgoorlie police three days later when they arrested him for disturbing the peace in a Hay Street knocking shop. He reckoned he hadn't got his money's worth. Finally, a seventy-three year old woman with Alzheimer's had gone walkabout the previous Saturday and been found the next morning under Esperance jetty, sleeping dangerously close to Sammy the Sea Lion.

'So we're no closer to finding out who Flipper is,' concluded Greg.

Tess looked daggers at him. 'Don't forget to pop over to the town hall and pick up those room dividers when we finish here, okay Greg?'

Cato pushed on.

'Let's widen the trawl through the mispers. Get the whole state, no time limit. Meanwhile what about the tides and weather, anything there?'

Greg was looking pleased with himself. 'The prevailing conditions around here are south-westerlies. Anything dropped in the ocean would tend to travel eastwards. But for the last four days it's been easterlies. As the body ended up that side of the groyne we can assume it was dropped in somewhere east of here in the last few days. The Sea Rescue guys have a chart on the wall over there.'

They all got up and gathered around it. Greg continued, rapt at being the centre of attention.

'It was mainly strong easterlies in the late mornings up to mid-arvo and then it moved around to the south and west by late arvo and evening. Dropping right off to practically nothing overnight. Averaging fifteen to twenty knots at the height.'

All of which meant very little to Cato. 'Where do you think the body went into the water?'

'After talking with Sea Rescue I'd say anywhere between Mason Bay and Starvation Bay.' Fisher pointed to dots on the map. 'Starvo's about forty kilometres from here, Mason's maybe halfway? There's a boat ramp at Starvo and easy beach access at Mason but my bet is Starvo.'

He looked over to Tess for approval. She nodded agreement. Cato was duly impressed. Not being a boatie or a local, he didn't know any better anyway.

'Good work, Greg. Can you follow up any unusual activity in those spots over the last week–any strangers, any boats going out at unusual times, stuff like that? We also need to check known shipping and other boat traffic. Our friend could have been dumped by a passing tanker or trawler for all we know. Let me know how you go.'

Greg beamed and reached for the phone.

Buckley and Tess both looked expectantly at Cato.

'We don't know much but let's look at what we do know,' said Cato.

'Dead,' shrugged Buckley.

'Thanks,' said Cato.

'No head,' mused Tess.

Cato nodded. 'Somebody wants to make it hard for us to work out who he is.'

Buckley sniffed. 'Detection 101, so that's what they teach you on the Golden Boy Fast Track these days.'

Cato ignored the dig and turned to Tess. 'Any Chinese restaurants in Hopetoun?'

Tess and Buckley looked at their watches and at each other. It was just gone nine o'clock in the morning.

Cato patted his stomach. 'Hungry as.'

The temperature hovered in the low thirties for the third day running. It was bloody October as well, unbelievable. In Sunderland this would be a 'Phew What a Scorcher' tabloid heatwave: riots in the streets, prisoners on the rooftops, questions in Parliament. In Busselton it was 'fine, sunny, temperatures slightly above average'. My arse. The only room in the house with air conditioning was the bedroom but he knew if he was caught in there he'd be in trouble. Stuart Miller had to put on a show of being an active and happy retiree and not laze around in a nice cool bedroom and read the paper like he really wanted to. He could hear Jenny's words now in the prim Edinburgh Miss Jean Brodie schoolteacher's voice she used for the bad kids: *You'll be a long time dead, plenty of time for sleeping then, Stuart Miller!* Stuart Miller was well over it: the heat, the healthy, active retirement. The lot.

He put the fan on full blast, sat down heavily at the kitchen table and opened up the day's *West Australian*. The headlines screamed global financial crisis and meltdown like they had for the past week or more. Then he turned to page four.

$200,000 reward for family's killer

Police today announced a $200,000 reward in a bid to catch a man who allegedly murdered his wife and three children in 1981. Homicide detectives have released a digitally enhanced photofit image, which aims to show how the prime suspect Derek Chapman would look 27 years after the killings.

A 1981 inquest found Chapman electrocuted and bashed his pregnant wife Maureen, 32, and their children Kevin, 6, Penny, 4, and Mark, 2, in their home in Norwood, Adelaide.

Miller's ears were roaring, his temples throbbing ... electrocuted and bashed. He looked at the photograph again: it hadn't registered at first, probably because it bore no resemblance to his Cup Final killer, Davey Arthurs. The face in the 1980 photograph was more groomed: hair short and styled, tinted glasses with big frames, a thick Ian Botham moustache, and the face fuller, fleshier. Miller wouldn't have picked it except for the MO. Could it be the same man, thirty-five years later, here in Australia? The one who still crept into his dreams at night with a bloody hammer and jump leads? He read on.

Chapman, now aged 63, placed the bodies in his Holden ute and left it parked in bushland in the Adelaide hills area. The bodies were found the next day ...

Homicide detectives flew to Perth yesterday following reports Chapman may be living there. Police Media have also released an image of Chapman, based on information from a woman who knew him and who reported a sighting of him in Bunbury in the state's South-West in 1998, 17 years after the murders.

He looked at the photofit of the way they thought the killer might look today. The Botham mo was gone, the glasses now had slim steel frames, the face was rounder and with a few more wrinkles, a bit less hair, and it was grey. Everybody's grandad: except he'd killed his pregnant wife and their eight-year-old son on Cup Final day in a dreary terraced redbrick in Sunderland. Then, eight years later, it seems he'd gone and done it again in Adelaide on the other side of the world. Derek Chapman–Davey Arthurs. Here in WA? The most recent sighting was in Bunbury just fifty kilometres down the road from Miller's Busselton home. The hairs fizzed on the back of his neck.

> *Detective Senior Constable Tim Delaney of the South Australia Police homicide squad said he hoped the reward and the image would produce the information police needed. 'There have been a number of sightings of Chapman over the years, which leads us to believe that he is still alive and living interstate,' he said. 'The fact we are revisiting this case shows how seriously we are treating the West Australian information.*
>
> *'We hope to encourage Chapman to give up. Twenty-seven years is a long time to live with such a crime hanging over your head. It would have to be weighing heavily on Chapman's conscience.'*

Miller smiled grimly at that one. 'You wish.'

> *'It's horrific that a father could slaughter his own wife and children in their own home. We really want to try to get closure on this.'*

'Wouldn't we all.' Stuart Miller reached for the phone.

6

Thursday, October 9th. Midmorning.

No. There weren't any Chinese restaurants in Hopetoun. There was a cafe, The Taste of the Toun, but it was closed. It was a squat, drab, brick thing, the last but one building in Veal Street. The last building was a pub, the Port Hotel, a one hundred year old two-storey sandstone fortress, also closed. After that it was all Southern Ocean as far as Antarctica. Cato took in the sweep of sparkling water and made a mental note to see if the Hopey shop sold bathers. Across the road from both buildings, a couple of toddlers rotated sleepily on a kiddie roundabout in McCulloch Park while their mums sipped Diet Coke at a picnic table. There was a shelter overlooking the beach. According to Tess it was a hangout for the disaffected youth of Hopetoun to do drugs and experiment sexually.

'Come to think of it, I haven't seen him for a while,' she said, frowning.

'Who?'

'The Disaffected Youth.'

'Just the one?'

'Since his big brother got a job at the mine, yeah.' She paused to consider the situation further. 'Well some of the teenagers get a bit excitable now and then but there's only the one kid in town who's shaping up to be a future statistic.'

'Particularly if he's sexually experimenting on his own,' observed Jim Buckley.

Cato pondered the career and psychological merits of Stock Squad versus a posting to Hopetoun. Touch and go.

'By the way, is that Hope'toon or 'town?' he asked.

'The older locals call it Hopet'n, lose the last vowel. But

they're outnumbered by the blow-ins these days and you can call it whatever you like as long as you're paying.'

There endeth lesson one from Tess Maguire. She added that the pub also did meals.

'Chicken and rice on the menu?' asked Cato, his mind on the last-known stomach contents of Flipper. They really had to find a better name for the poor bugger, preferably his real one.

'The pub and cafe are more your steak or fish and chips kind of places. Chicken, yeah, maybe for the girlfriends. Not much call for rice though.'

It seemed that in the relatively short time she'd been in Hopetoun, Tess could pretty well recite both menus off by heart – not a big ask. She'd never seen rice on either menu, ever. So there was no point in talking to the proprietors about any of their recent customers; Flipper's last meal didn't come from any of these salubrious Hopetoun eateries. He was most likely eating home-cooked, but where was home?

All this talk of food had them more than ready for their mid-morning break. They bought coffees from the mobile Snak-Attack, a caravan converted into a food kiosk and parked on a vacant block just up from the general store. A chocolate hedgehog for Jim Buckley was thrown in for free when he seemed to recognise the young guy behind the counter.

'On the house,' chirped the host with exaggerated bonhomie as he focused on spooning froth into the cardboard cups. Dark curls, blue eyes, used to being admired by his customers. His name was Justin, apparently.

'Been here long, Justin?' asked Buckley, conversationally.

'About six months; nice spot eh,' Justin replied with a ready smile.

'How about before that?' Buckley pressed.

Justin's smile was becoming more fixed by the minute.

'Freo, Margaret River; my girlfriend used to live in Margaret River. She owns this joint.'

The girlfriend rolled up. A stunner. She blessed them all

with a prim smile and a flick of her long dark locks.

Buckley beamed appreciatively. 'Looks like you're doing very well for yourself, Justin.' He winked and waved the hedgehog. 'Catch you around.'

Cato raised a questioning eyebrow at Buckley and got a second wink in reply.

They rolled down to the groyne in the Stock Squad four-wheel drive. Tess warily eyed the bull's-head logo on the car door. When Cato gunned the engine he thought he heard her go 'brrmm, brrmm' under her breath. Now they were looking out over Seal Rock, about three hundred metres offshore. The early morning stillness was long gone. The sun was still out but a stiff breeze had blown up from the southwest. It would only get stronger as the day wore on. On the rock three or four brown shapes huddled together against the wind and the spray from the whitecaps. Cato assumed they were seals. Buckley paced around outside having his smoko and talking on his mobile. The wind gusted in a different direction and Cato overheard a brief snatch of the conversation.

'Too busy for that, just tell me now for fuck's sake.'

Cato was in the driving seat, Tess in the back. Both were taking a great interest in the view. Spectacular. You couldn't fault it. Ocean, mountains, beaches. Ocean. Mountains. Beaches.

Ocean. Mountains. Beaches.

Cato broke the silence. 'Is it always this windy?'

'Pretty much.'

He looked in the mirror. Met her eyes. 'So how have you been? Since ... then.'

'Since when? Since you left me? Or since I nearly died?'

'Both.'

'Good. Thanks for asking.'

'No worries.'

Well that seemed to go well, Cato thought to himself.

Tess's mobile buzzed: a resident near the pub complaining

about beer bottles in his front yard, broken glass in the street, and the aerial and wing mirrors snapped off his car.

'And wondering when the police were going to do something about those bloody mongrel miners,' Tess relayed to Cato. 'Life goes on.'

She looked relieved to be getting out of the bull-mobile and into a proper police car. Cato suspected that was not all she was relieved about. Jim Buckley wrapped up his call, flicked his cigarette away and climbed back into the Land Cruiser with a troubled look.

'Everything okay?' Cato said.

'Yup. Where to now maestro?'

'Back to Murder HQ; let's see what Greg the Wonder Boy has been up to. Do a bit of thinking.'

'Suits me.'

'So when are you buggers going to put a stop to it?'

Donald Rundle glared up at Tess from behind bushy eyebrows. He had gone on for about five minutes and, despite her best efforts and her training, Tess still hadn't managed to get a word in edgeways. At one point she'd found her hand straying towards the taser stun gun clipped to her belt but she checked herself. Rundle shifted his weight on to the other foot, crunching more broken glass as if to prove his point. As far as he was concerned, an Englishman's home was his castle, blah blah blah. Jeez he was a Pom-and-a-half. Tess held up a hand to try to stem the torrent of whingeing.

'Okay Don, look, I'll make another report but you need to also talk to the pub and let them know.'

'Money-grubbing bastard, as long as he's making a quid he couldn't give a toss about the rest of us.'

'And put in a complaint to Liquor Licensing,' Tess said. 'I gave you the name and number last time. Do you want me to write it down again for you?'

Tess had adopted her slightly raised 'aged-care' voice and was trying to rustle up some semblance of sincerity. It didn't help.

'I'm old, not deaf or senile. There's a difference.' Rundle glowered. 'I came down here for a bit of peace and quiet and I had it until that bloody mine opened and that toerag took over the pub.'

Toerag? Tess was beginning to feel like she was in an old episode of *The Bill*. She glanced at Don Rundle's million-dollar view across the road to the Southern Ocean; yes she was still in Hopetoun, not Sun Hill. Don was off again pointing out his snapped wing mirror and aerial. Tess was saved by the trilling of her mobile: Greg wanting to know if she fancied a ride out bush. She put a hand up to halt Rundle's tirade.

'Sorry Don, got to go. Urgent police business.'

Stuart Miller's first call was to directory inquiries: Adelaide Police. He assumed Detective Tim Delaney would already be in WA but hopefully they'd be put in touch. They put him on hold; the hold music was AC/DC, 'Highway to Hell'. He hadn't heard that one for a while. A fragment of music trivia dislodged from deep in his cranium: didn't AC/DC now have a Geordie for their lead singer? Then again, he was from Newcastle, not Sunderland, and there was a world of difference in those twelve miles. He used to sing a ditty called 'Geordie's lost his Leggie' about a young lad losing his marble 'doon the netty', the toilet. Exactly. Miller wondered how the singer communicated to the rest of the band with a killer accent like that. Hand signals? Mind wandering on to anything but the task at hand, Miller felt rusty and awkward. This was no longer his world.

He'd left the police within two years of the Arthurs murders. As the case grew colder he felt less and less like staying. He drifted into private security, like many ex-cops, but didn't have the lack of imagination required to do the job properly. One blustery northern winter's day he was walking past Australia House near the Tyne Bridge in Newcastle and he once again saw the posters of Sydney Harbour Bridge bathed in sunshine.

This time he walked through the door. Jenny's younger sister Maggie, a nurse, had emigrated the previous year and kept on sending postcards peppered with words like 'sunny', 'warm', and 'beach'. The last one, just a fortnight before, had two new bits of information: 'boyfriend' and 'cop'. Jenny had rolled her eyes at that news. Anyway he and Jenny and Graeme, by then eleven, were on a plane to Perth within six months–landing on a cold, blustery Perth winter's day. He'd laughed out loud that day and never looked back.

Somebody finally decided to answer the phone in Adelaide. Miller told his story to the uppity little wanker in South Australian homicide who made it clear that he thought Miller was a crank; yes, the ULW promised, he would pass on the details to DSC Delaney as soon as he could. Miller slammed the phone down and glared at it. He looked at the clock on the wall, figuring out what time it would be in Sunderland. Four in the morning–wasn't that a line from a song? He dialled another number.

A 1981 inquest found he electrocuted and bashed ...

The same findings as in the Arthurs case.

Davey Arthurs had disappeared off the face of the earth. All they found out about him was that he was born in 1946, almost exactly nine months after VE Day, the original post-war baby boomer. He had worked in the shipyards as an electrician, had a couple of criminal convictions for drunk and disorderly, a self-drawn tattoo of the letters CK on his left forearm. His mother and younger brother were still alive and living in Sunderland and couldn't understand why he would do such a terrible thing, and his mother-in-law thought he was a nice enough lad. Considering he'd slaughtered her daughter and grandson. Nobody knew who 'CK' was; maybe an early girlfriend?

Electrocution, it took a good deal of cold calculation to do that. Bludgeoning someone to death, even your own child, seemed to have somewhere in it the hint of reason, however remote, however mad. Even losing control is a reason of sorts.

But fixing jump leads to your wife and child, positive and negative, negative and positive – was that what evil was? Stuart Miller had given up seeing a point to his work while somebody could do something like that and still at large, walking the streets. Free, to do it again. Nobody was answering at the other end but Miller couldn't bring himself to put the phone down. He just listened to the hypnotic ring-ring, ring-ring. Then came a click, a fumble, a rustle and a grunt.

'Lawton speaking, who's this?'

'Chris. It's Stuey Miller here.'

There was a slight delay or echo in the voices as they travelled across the world. They'd kept in touch over the years, Chris Lawton still seeing Miller as a bit of a mentor even after all this time and all those promotions. Now he was Assistant Chief Constable, Northumbria Police, and a shoo-in for the soon-to-be-vacant top job. Lawton dropped the big-boss tone when he heard who it was.

'Stu. What's up? It better be good at this time of morning ... Christ, 4.00 a.m.!'

'I think I might have found Davey Arthurs.'

Miller knew that placing Arthurs in WA meant placing him in a geographical area approximately the size of Western Europe before the Iron Curtain came down, but decided not to trouble Lawton with that little detail.

'Fucken hell. Where? You sure?'

Miller told him all he knew and took down a fax number to send the newspaper article through. Lawton had talked about scanning and emailing but Miller didn't know what he was on about. He promised to pass on Lawton's details to South Australian Homicide so they could liaise and compare notes. Speaking of which.

'Chris, what's the chance of me getting another look at the Arthurs case history?'

Lawton assumed his Assistant Chief Constable voice. 'You're retired and well out of it, Stuart. Let's keep it that way eh? Protocol and all that; we need to do these things by the book these days.'

Miller knew there was no chance of changing the man's mind; Lawton was headed for career greatness and wouldn't jeopardise that for anyone or anything. He summoned up a bright no-hard-feelings voice.

'No worries Chris, but keep me in the loop okay? It'd mean a lot. Old times' sake?' Miller almost pleaded, hating himself and Lawton as he did so.

'No worries? You're sounding more and more like an Aussie, mate. Yeah we'll stay in touch. And Stu, thanks for that.'

Miller put his phone down. So that was it. After thirty-five years he gives them a solid lead on Sunderland's most notorious unsolved, one that remained at least a smudge on Lawton's otherwise unblemished CV.

Yeah we'll stay in touch.

He recalled an image, an impression from the day: Detective Constable Chris Lawton dry-retching in the backyard of 11 Maud Street. The case that had killed a pregnant young woman and her little boy had also killed Miller's belief in the job and in himself. Damned if he'd be sidelined on this one.

Greg Fisher had left a note for Cato. He and Tess were off to the bays out at Starvo and Mason to talk to the boaties, they had their mobiles and the UHF switched on to take any routine calls. Greg had crosschecked the state mispers reports and a summary of 'possibles' was sitting in Cato's email inbox. Cato logged in. There were about a dozen males on the list fitting the age range. Some had disappeared up to ten years ago. Some were last seen standing in remote locations up north or on the outskirts of desert outposts or stumbling out of outback pubs at closing time. Travellers, station hands, mineworkers, waiting for a lift, waiting for help with broken-down vehicles, waiting for somebody to save them. Some had probably started walking and never came back. He crossed off four of these as doubtful. The times, distances and circumstances didn't add up. He opened up the photos of three others. They seemed either too big, too small, too old, too young or too pale. Too pale? Although Dr Harry Lewis wouldn't commit, Cato had already convinced himself that the dead man he saw was not Caucasian. Any more than that was purely guesswork. That left five on Greg's list. Out of the corner of his eye, Cato could see that Jim Buckley had his feet on the desk and was flicking through the day's newspaper with its lurid 'We're all doomed, doomed I tell ye' headlines. He didn't seem to be reading anything; he was miles away.

Cato returned to his list. A missing Perth businessman, thirty-eight; last seen in a gay nightclub in Northbridge about a year ago. It had been a bit of a surprise to his wife who was now grieving a little less than she might otherwise have been. Italian background, Carlo Donizetti, medium height and build; a possibility? He scanned further down. One leaped out at him. Two years ago, a Royal Australian Navy frigate had come into the south-coast port of Albany after picking up a sick harpoonist from a Japanese whaler in the Southern Ocean. Heart attack. Cato remembered it on the news at the time. Otherwise kindly humanitarian conservationists protesting loudly that they should have left the bastard to die. The navy ship had been on joint exercises with the Indonesian, Singaporean, Thai, and Malaysian forces. An Indonesian sailor had been seconded aboard the Australian frigate. Lieutenant Riri Yusala. Twenty-five years old. Medium height. Slim build. He'd jumped ship after two days in Albany. Since declared an illegal immigrant but authorities were also hedging their bets by expressing 'concern for his welfare'. Albany, a hop and skip from Hopetoun, west along the South Coast Highway. Cato studied the picture. Smooth complexion and boyish face; he looked well-fed and affluent. He had an education. He also had a wife and two young kids. Nothing concrete; it was pure instinct that had Cato's heart beating faster. Riri Yusala.

'Why did you jump ship and where did you go?' wondered Cato. 'And is that you in the cold box on the morning flight to Perth?'

7

Thursday, October 9th. Late morning.

Tess was in a filthy mood as Greg Fisher bumped the paddy wagon through another of the huge potholes left by the previous week's heavy rain and turned into the dogleg on Mason Bay Road. She had been silent and irritable the whole journey. It wasn't Don Rundle the whingeing Pom. It was Cato Kwong the infuriating ex. Swanning in like nothing had happened between them and everything was okay as long as you didn't face up to it. True, he had raised the subject when they were out on the groyne but it was obviously on his TO DO list between BUY TOOTHPASTE and SOLVE MURDER. Item 6: Make Tess Miraculously Forget that I'm a Bastard Because I Left Her and Still Haven't Told Her Why. Tick. Sorted. Then move back on to the business at hand with everybody la-la happy. She snorted and Greg gave her a funny look.

A construction team was working on a pipeline that stretched north through the low dusty scrub as far as the eye could see. She knew it snaked about twenty kilometres to the mine. In the other direction, south, it would finish its journey at Mason Bay at a fenced-off compound just along from the campsite. According to the sign by the side of the road, this was the pipeline for the new desalination plant which would deliver all of the nickel mine's substantial fresh water needs. Tess surveyed the landscape. Gently rolling coastal scrub topped by a huge blue sky.

'Bloody beautiful isn't it?' said Fisher, voicing her thoughts. She nodded and he obviously took it as a cue to expand.

'But most of the mob from these parts left about a hundred

years ago. They're Auntie Daisy's mob, on my mum's side. They were driven out by a massacre after one of your "pioneers" was speared. Auntie Daisy said it was to persuade the dirty little bugger to leave the young Nyungar girls alone.'

Tess had been only half-listening but she began to tune in; this was the first time she'd heard an alternative take on the local history since she'd come to town.

'Yeah, he died so they decided to teach us a lesson. "Civilising the natives" – that's what they call it.'

Greg knew all about that stuff, he told Tess, having been raised in Pinjarra, another famous massacre site, just south of Perth. His mum had warned him about taking the job down here.

'She said, "This country is just too sad, Gregory. Auntie Daisy's mob don't go there now and if they do they don't stop. They wind up the car windows, hold their noses, and keep driving to the other side."'

Tess looked at her young colleague. His family stories were filled with stuff she would never fathom.

'So how come you're here then?'

Greg lifted one hand from the wheel in a 'that's life' gesture. An early country posting was part of serving your time to get where you wanted to be and quicker, he said. Even with his fair skin he still knew he was up against the tinted glass ceiling so he had to learn to play the game.

'Look at Detective Kwong, he's up there.'

Apparently it had been Kwong's face staring out at him from the recruitment posters at the Careers Expo that encouraged him to sign up.

'Anyway if this country gets too hard to handle I'll just have to hold my breath like Auntie Daisy and shoot on through.'

Tess had been feeling vaguely sympathetic and more respectful of her baby-faced colleague until he cited Cato Kwong as his inspiration. Not good timing. She grunted. One look at her face told Greg to save the rest of the history lesson for another day.

One of the construction workers held up a red stop sign as a grader pulled out into the unsealed road ahead, sending up a choking dust cloud. Greg did as he was told. He recognised the stop-sign man, Travis Grant, a fellow member of the Hopetoun Southerners footy team, the Sharks. Travis had on the same fluoro overalls that just about everyone was wearing in town these days, and reflector surfie sunnies. His blond tinted hair was spiked, unruly, and matted in dust. He had a big wide smile; he was the spitting image of legendary leg-spinner Shane Warne, give or take a few kilos. He nodded through the open window, acknowledged Tess's presence and grinned at Fisher.

'Greg, how's it hanging?'

'Travis, good mate, how's the knee?'

'Getting there. Should be good for next season. Where you off to?'

'Just taking a run down to Mason's and Starvo.' Greg gestured towards the pipe. 'Looks like you're nearly there.'

'Yeah, another month maybe then it's the big switch-on. Just need these idle bastards to pull their fingers out.' Travis Grant thumbed over his shoulder at the vague human outlines in the dust cloud behind him. 'So what's up? Kane been doing doughnuts in the Starvo car park again? Or is it the mysterious case of the missing surf ski?'

Greg sat taller in his seat. 'Get fucked Trav. Serious business today, didn't you hear about the body?'

No, Travis said he hadn't heard about the body. 'Been camped out here since Sunday. What happened?'

'Washed up yesterday. Looks like sharks but we're keeping an open mind.'

Tess shot him a warning look. Too much information to the punters, too early. She nodded vaguely south across the landscape towards Mason Bay.

'Noticed anything unusual or suspicious the last few days, Travis?'

'Like what?'

'Strangers, boats coming and going at unusual times, anything strange or unusual, that's all.'

Travis squinted back over his shoulder to the ghostly shadows hovering in the dust.

'Most of these bastards are strange and unusual. Don't know most of them. Can't understand them. And they do lots of weird shit. You can round the whole fucken lot up if you like. Once the job's finished that is.'

'Thanks Travis, very helpful.' Tess was quickly tiring of the high-pissing Mr Grant.

Travis glanced casually over at the reversing grader. 'So what's Starvo and Mason's got to do with it?'

Greg Fisher redeemed himself with a cards-to-chest display. 'Don't know yet. Watch this space.'

The grader was out of the way now and even though Travis hadn't yet spun his sign around, Greg took it upon himself to go. In the rear-view mirror Tess caught a glimpse of Travis giving them the finger and his big Warnie smile before disappearing in the dust.

Stuart Miller was too hyped up to hang around the house waiting for a phone call that might never come. Senior Constable Tim Delaney could be anywhere in WA: up north in the red dust, driving around one of those soulless suburbs on the outskirts of Perth, or just down the road. Maybe he already had Davey Arthurs in custody. Davey Arthurs aka Derek Chapman. Stuart knew he shouldn't be thinking it but he was; he wanted Davey Arthurs still out there. He wanted to be the one to bring him in, even if it was thirty-odd years too late.

He went into the bathroom to splash water on his face, cool down and freshen up. The face in the mirror was tanned but sagging, too much of the good life, the brown hair receding a little but greying rapidly. A good thick head of hair – it ran in the family, along with high blood pressure. Had he taken his pills today? He couldn't remember. That was another family trait, Alzheimer's. Miller's mind was all over the place but it was his eyes that told him the truth about where he stood. Not the pale scar in the corner of the right one or the laugh lines radiating out from both. It was the weakness. He hadn't been able to cut it as a cop because he was too soft. Bring Arthurs in? Who was he kidding? He had no right to any claim on the Arthurs case. He'd walked away from it, away from the blood and slaughter. Defeated. A young mother with her head caved in, her little boy resting against her with his hand on her knee. He'd abandoned them. All he had to show for it was bad dreams and days like this.

'Get real,' he told the face in the mirror.

But he knew he couldn't let go of Arthurs. Or maybe Arthurs wouldn't let go of him. Was that what The Dream was about last night? A premonition?

Miller picked up a wide-brimmed floppy hat, sunnies and his mobile, and stepped outside into the heat. It was nearly enough to make him change his mind and head for the dark, air-conditioned bedroom. But he didn't. He walked along the foreshore footpath, heading west into town. Ahead to his right, the long wooden jetty stretched almost two kilometres out into Geographe Bay. The water was unnaturally blue and, on a day like this, probably infested with millions of little jellyfish. Always just below the surface of what seemed like a perfect paradise, a nasty sting to remind you of what else life had to offer.

It's horrific that a father could slaughter his own wife and children in their own home.

Davey Arthurs, Derek Chapman. Where are you?

The sweat was pouring off Miller and he was out of breath. He looked up and found he'd already walked the two kilometres into town. Where did the last fifteen minutes go? His eyes were stinging from the salty perspiration. His polo shirt stuck to him, back and front. He was at a roundabout. To his left, the Busselton coffee strip; to his right, the jetty and beach; straight ahead, not much. He stood there like a confused pensioner who'd forgotten who, where, and why. His head was all over the place, off the bloody planet. His hand was throbbing. It took him a moment to realise it was his mobile. He answered it.

'Hello?'

'Tim Delaney.'

No 'Hello, is that such and such?' On any other day Miller would have lectured the young upstart on good phone manners. But that would have been probably just a symptom of his low testosterone levels, his grumpy-old-man syndrome. Today? Today he was so fucked up he didn't even know which way to turn. Miller parked himself at a spare table outside a coffee shop and told Detective Delaney his story. It took a while; he realised he probably sounded like a silly, confused old codger. He certainly felt like one. Delaney obviously hadn't come to the call with a completely open mind either: his responses were cluttered with non-committal umms. Perhaps his ears were clogged as well. He kept asking Miller to repeat things. But then a penny must have dropped somewhere because all of a sudden Delaney seemed to be taking him seriously. Was it the similarity in the MO that Miller had described?

'Your accent,' Delaney interrupted, 'is that what you call Geordie?'

Obviously the thirty years in Australia hadn't quite transformed Stuart Miller into Slim Dusty.

'Aye, that's right.'

The voice at the other end brightened. 'Same as Derek Chapman, so you can't be completely bullshitting me if you both talk like that. Let's meet.'

Jim Buckley looked up from the entertainment and gossip section of the paper and grinned.

'Clocked him.'

Cato was still scrolling through the mispers, checking if he'd missed anything.

'Say something?'

'Justin Trousersnake. Snak-Van Boy. Clocked him.'

'And?'

'Three, four years ago, Perth Cup, I pulled him over. He had a looker with him in the car then too. Leggy blonde, private school type, a bit lippy. Didn't know when to shut up.'

'That what you arrested him for? Lippy, leggy blonde in his front seat instead of yours?'

'Would if I could. No. He had a big bag of eckies in the glove box and a Dockers rookie with his chick in the back. Simpson, his name was, the one that got de-listed last year for drinking too much. His chick was a bit of a donkey, now I come to think of it.'

Cato shook his head in wonder. 'Photographic memory, amazing. Was the donkey blonde or brunette?'

'Redhead. Nice bod but teeth too big for her mouth. Anyway Justin got off the ecky charge. Good lawyer; the same one who does the bikies and gangsters. Not cheap.'

Cato sat up and took more notice. 'Justin: supplier of ecstasy to the fairly rich-and-famous, now the supplier of coffee and burgers to Hopetoun. Bit of a step down in the world. I wonder what, or who, he's hiding from?'

Buckley folded his newspaper. 'Are you thinking what I'm thinking, B2?'

'Lunch time?' Cato nodded.

Buckley stood up and reached for his jacket, he paused briefly. 'How germane is it to your floater?'

Cato stopped and studied Buckley. 'Germane. Now that's a word I never thought I'd hear you use.'

Tess and Greg had no luck at Mason Bay. It was midweek and deserted, not even any grey nomads hanging around. They'd had a bit of a poke around some of the campsites near the water's edge and the short steep sandy tracks down to the beach. Not sure what they were looking for – a smoking gun, a bloody knife, a signed confession? They didn't find any of those or anything else for that matter. They'd pushed on another twenty kilometres or so to Starvation Bay. At least there were a few shacks here and a proper boat ramp. Greg was back on the history lesson and a thawed out Tess was more receptive now.

'Starvation Bay, called that in the early days by those whitefellas who couldn't see all that food in front of them because it didn't come served up on a plate with shiny cutlery and lovely white napkins.'

It seemed that all along this stretch of coast the names left by the white 'explorers' betrayed their ignorance: Starvation Bay, Mount Barren ... they'd called it 'worthless' when in fact it had more life than you could point a stick at in a thousand years.

They came to a halt and Tess unbuckled her seat belt. 'You're a font, Greg, do you know that?'

The water was flat and bright blue in the growing heat of the day. The bay was sheltered from the south-westerly and Tess could see the foaming whitecaps out beyond the headland. But here, tucked into a corner at the western end, all was calm. A green 1970s vintage Land Rover was parked halfway down the boat ramp with its trailer sitting empty in the water. Whoever it was, they weren't expecting to share the ramp that day, or didn't care if they were.

They heard the outboard before they saw it, a tinny rounding the headland. An old bearded salty-seadog type with a grubby, weathered Eagles cap, long-sleeved faded blue work shirt and khaki shorts waved briefly from the helm. He guided the boat in and Greg helped him get it on the trailer. Up close, Tess adjusted his age estimate downwards, figuring him to be nearer early sixties. He and Greg exchanged minimal greetings, trimmed smiles and guarded looks while they secured the dinghy. The old guy wasn't particularly inquisitive about his young helper. Greg opened the proceedings.

'Catch anything?'

'Few whiting, herring, skippy. Had better.'

The accent was Pommie. An Australian twang in there too so he was obviously not fresh off the boat. The seadog squinted out at Greg Fisher from under his cap.

'You a cop then?'

Greg looked down at his uniform, back at his paddy wagon and over at Tess. Obviously nothing much escaped this guy.

'Yeah that's right, Greg Fisher. Hopetoun. And this is Sergeant Maguire.'

They all shook hands. The old man kept his attention focused on Greg Fisher. Shy with women? Tess wondered. Old school? Gay? Well he was a Pom, so anything was possible. Tess was happy to let Greg run with it. Captain Barnacle scratched the back of his neck.

'New are you, son?'

'About three months.'

'Yeah, thought I hadn't seen you around. Then again I haven't really been over to Hopey much lately. Better variety in the Ravy shop. Better meat. Better vegies.'

Tess could see Greg Fisher's eyes were already glazing over, this was the kind of conversation nannas had.

'Anyway, er, sorry I didn't catch your name.'

'That's because I didn't give it to you son. It's Billy Mather.'

'Right, Bill, look we've had a body washed up at Hopey and we're trying to identify who it is and how it got there.'

Mather's eyes narrowed. 'Body?'

Tess restrained herself from stepping in again. Greg was in danger of crossing a fine line about how much information to provide to the punters while you're actually trying to get information out of them. What were they teaching at cop school these days? She'd have a word with him later.

'Have you noticed anything unusual around here the last few days, Mr Mather? Strangers, people coming and going at odd times?'

Mather rested one arm casually on the boat trailer and flicked his spare hand in the direction of the campsite.

'Couple of campervans been through last week, old farts blowing their super before they die.'

Greg had his notebook out. 'You didn't notice the kind of vans they were?'

Mather nodded. 'Aye, both Britz, I always remember them, being one meself,' he chuckled, inviting them to join him in the joke. Greg obliged with a brief and encouraging smile. Tess didn't.

'How many people in the Britz?'

'Two each, couples. Old. Couldn't describe them. All oldies look the same to us young'uns eh, son?'

Greg smiled again, patiently. 'When did they move on? Did you talk to them?'

'Nah, stuck up middle-class twats. Give you those waves that say hello but don't come any closer, smiles to match. They all left at the weekend. Been there two nights. Got through five bottles of Chardonnay between them. Check the bin,' he thumbed over his shoulder.

Tess reappraised the old bugger: not quite as laid back and simple-minded as he'd first seemed. Not averse to the old Pommie class warfare either.

'Anything else?' said Greg.

'Can't think of anything son.'

Greg looked annoyed at being called 'son'. He'd joined the force to get away from being treated like a kid. It wasn't working too well today.

'Well thanks Mr Mather ...'

'Billy.'

'Billy. And if we need to contact you where can we find you?'

Mather pointed to a caravan about a hundred metres back in the camping area.

'If I'm not there I'm either out fishing or somewhere about. I'd give you my email and mobile phone number son but they don't work too well out here.'

Greg and Tess thanked him again and left. The UHF

spluttered into life and Tess took the call. It was the kind she dreaded these days.

It was not quite lunchtime. A small gathering of mums, toddlers and prams had congregated around the picnic table at Justin's Snak-Attack. No sign of the girlfriend. Cato and Buckley smiled and nodded greetings to the mums as they approached the counter. Justin had his back to them as he spooned some milk and froth into a cup. He turned around and produced a smile.

'Back again gents; you must like the coffee.'

Buckley flashed his ID.

'Three years ago, Perth Cup. You, the Docker, some women, and a bag of eckies. Remember?'

The smile held. The mums were all ears. Justin snapped his fingers as if dredging up a long lost memory.

'Detective ...'

'Buckley,' said Buckley. 'And your surname ... Woodward?'

'Yeah that's right. I was cleared of course. Remember? Last time I'll loan my car out to any mates. You can't tell with people these days, can you?'

He winked over towards the mums. Cato thought he saw at least two of them blush.

Buckley was only just getting started. 'Can you step outside of there for a moment, Justin.'

'Why?'

'It's not easy conducting an interview with us down here and you up there in the dark, behind a flyscreen.'

'Interview?'

'We could all pop back to the office if you like?'

The mums were no longer even pretending not to listen. They were staring at Buckley and Cato, not in a very friendly way either. It was Justin who kept things calm. He stepped down out of the back of the van and came round the front to join them, big cheesy in place.

'Happy to, gents, now, what can I do for you?'

'Mind if we take a look over the van, Justin?' said Buckley already walking up the steps. Justin ran his hand through his curls and smiled patiently.

'Help yourself.'

While Buckley made a show of opening and shutting drawers and cupboards and unscrewing the lids off various containers, Cato nodded his head down the street to indicate that he and Justin should take a little stroll.

'So what's a guy like you doing in a place like this, Justin?'

'Is this a pick-up?'

Cato gave a thin, grim smile. 'How about answering the question?'

Woodward folded his arms and rocked on his heels. 'Sea change. And there's good money to be made with the mine and everything.'

'From what I hear you like the high life. Mixing it with the celebrities and the beautiful people, going to all the best parties, selling them all the best drugs. Hopetoun? Uh-uh.' Cato shook his head.

Woodward rolled his eyes. 'I've got a clean sheet. I haven't sold anybody anything except coffee.' He dropped his voice and opened his palms in a conciliatory gesture. 'Look, I admit I was a bit of a wild child in the past. I was younger then. People change. I'm ready to settle down.'

He fixed Cato with a steady look, no doubt aiming for honest and straightforward. Didn't quite pull it off. Buckley had finished his quick search. He came down out of the van and drew his finger across his throat. Neither had expected to find anything, they just wanted to start shaking a few trees. Cato met Woodward's wandering gaze and held it in place.

'Settling down, or keeping your head down? Have you upset anybody lately, Justin?'

The big cheesy returned. 'Not me, mate, I'm everybody's friend.'

Cato's mobile buzzed. He looked at the caller ID; it was Tess. He put up his hand for Justin to stay where he was and answered the call.

'We need you out at the mine,' said Tess. 'There's some trouble.'

'Trouble? What kind?'

'A brawl, up to twenty involved. Mine security can't handle it.'

'What's that got to do with me and Jim?'

Tess let rip. 'We need the numbers. Just get your fucking arse in gear and get out there now.'

She broke the connection. Cato looked at the phone like it had just burnt his hand. He signalled urgently to Buckley and they sprinted to the car. Justin watched them go. Cato looked through his rear-view mirror. He hadn't missed that look of relief on Justin's face.

8

Thursday, October 9th. Early afternoon.

Blood roared through Tess's ears as she raced the van into the centre of the compound, lights flashing and siren wailing. She felt like throwing up. It was always like this now before going into potentially violent situations: since Karratha, since Johnno Djukic.

By agreement she'd been met by her Ravensthorpe colleagues at the mine entrance. They would all go in together to maximise numbers and effect.

Tess's opposite number at Ravy, Sergeant Paul Abbott, had a big frame but the kind of fleshy insecure body language that marked him out as easy prey to those out there of a mind to take advantage. He was a nine-to-fiver. If crime happened outside of office hours he wasn't particularly interested. His offsider, Mitch Biddulph, a bullet-headed, barrel-chested farm boy, seemed a little more pumped up and enthusiastic for the fray but Tess was concerned by his thousand yard stare, the one that normally affects war veterans during or after the battle–not before. Greg just looked a bit pale. SWAT they were not. She dived in.

Three separate fights seemed to be in progress, grown men in fluoro overalls slugging it out in the big boys' playground. Psycho Teletubbies. Tess flicked out her baton and unclipped her taser with her free hand. They'd take care of each fight one at a time. She went for the nearest combatants, checking that Greg, Paul and Mitch were backing her. A large Maori was stomping on a smaller figure curled up on the ground while two other blokes hung on to his neck trying to pull him off. They hadn't done very well so far. Tess remembered seeing an international rugby game on TV a few years earlier, All Blacks Jonah Lomu running down the wing with four English players hanging off him like Lilliputians. She shouted the usual formal warning but nobody was listening. She stood directly in front and fired the taser darts into his chest from a metre away. He grunted and dropped. The boys moved in with the handcuffs. It was a quick result and had the desired effect on the other combatants; they stopped. What was the term the Americans used? Shock and awe.

Four mine security personnel hovered nervously. They were used to talking tough over a beer but had never really been tested until today. Checking passes at the gate was their strength. Their leader, who by the look of his gut had obviously done a lot of tough talking over a lot of beers in the past, helped his men to shepherd the gladiators a safe distance from each other. Tess called him over while her colleagues attended to the man on the ground.

'What happened here?'

The ID badge identified him as Karl Moore, Security Supervisor. Yeah right, good work, thought Tess. Moore cleared his throat to deliver the line he'd obviously worked out.

'An argument started and then all hell broke loose.'

Tess could probably have figured that one out for herself. 'Who between?'

'The regular shift and the contractors.'

'What?'

Moore looked at Tess as if she was a bit of an imbecile and helpfully pointed to the two groups. 'Orange fluoros versus yellow fluoros.'

Tess looked and saw it now: the Maori, dazed and handcuffed, in blue and yellow fluoros; the other guy, still flat out, blue and orange. And the other combatants, now turned spectators, two groups – yellow and orange – still glaring at each other and trading curses. The orange group were mainly Anglo. The yellow group a United Nations of Maoris, Filipinos,

Indians, Chinese and Africans, plus a few wild-eyed Braveheart rangas who looked like they owed allegiance to no one but themselves. Tess turned back to the Security Supervisor.

'What was the fight about?'

Moore shrugged his shoulders and gestured towards the Maori. 'Ask him.'

Tess crouched down by the big man, now securely handcuffed and facedown on the gravel. 'Well?'

His face bore traditional tattoos, a bloody nose and a gashed eye closing over nicely thankyou. He opened his good eye.

'Git fucked.'

Tess sighed and looked over towards his victim, curled up like a foetus and still not moving. 'How's he looking?'

Greg Fisher kept his face and voice neutral and suggested they call an ambulance. Karl the Security Supervisor let him know it had already been done–not as useless as he seemed then. Tess stepped over to get a closer look at the victim. He had a face like a dropped pie. Mashed as it was, she still recognised it: Kane Stevenson, Doughnut King.

Detective Senior Constable Tim Delaney wasn't as tall as he'd sounded on the phone. Stuart Miller figured he must have only just made the height requirements, if they still had them these days. Or maybe they weren't so fussy in Adelaide. He was certainly dapper; in spite of the fierce heat he had on a suit and tie and didn't look like it bothered him. He said he'd been in Bunbury, a rapidly expanding port city two hours south of Perth and forty minutes along the coast from where they were sitting in Busselton. The last known sighting of Derek Chapman had been there over ten years ago. Miller and Delaney were in the Equinox Cafe overlooking the Busselton Jetty, keeping their voices low so that the carefree tourists chattering around them would help mask their own conversation. Miller had all sorts of questions swirling inside his head; he reached for one.

'You said Arthurs, or Chapman, sounded like me. How do you know? When did you hear his voice? Wasn't this all way before your time?'

Detective Delaney twisted his mouth into a smile.

'Derek Chapman, a Royalist to the core. The Queen's visit to Adelaide, March 1977: he's there with the wife and kids, the same ones he topped a few years later. He's waving his little flag and he's picked up in a vox pop by local ABC news.'

Miller reminisced: 1977, Sex Pistols, 'Anarchy in the UK' and 'God Save the Queen'. Meanwhile Miller and his young family had just been through their first Perth summer: blue, blue skies and sand burning their feet, a world away from the pessimism, greyness and industrial decline of north-east England. And Davey Arthurs teasingly close all that time.

'The reporter dug the tape out of the archives after the 1981 murders. He'd seen the photo on the news and remembered the raving Pom with the weird accent. Apparently it wasn't used at the time because nobody could understand a fucking word he was saying, but they'd kept it for training purposes. Who not to interview.'

Miller shook his head, betraying the ghost of a smile; it was all too familiar. He'd registered that look of bewilderment on people's faces countless times during his own thirty years in exile. Stuart Miller and Davey Arthurs – both needed subtitles.

Delaney was part of a newly established Cold Case Unit, he explained, and they'd used this high-profile case with its gruesome details and old but, hopefully, workable leads to launch it. The digitally enhanced photofit helped sex it up for a twenty-first century public and the news media couldn't get enough of it. So, Miller wondered, was this just a publicity exercise for the SA police force and a nice distraction from reports of corruption and incompetence on the thin blue line? Delaney seemed to read his mind.

'It's not just a stunt. We do believe we can land him,' Delaney fixed Miller with a look to show he meant business.

Miller wasn't convinced.

'WA's a big place and your info is, what, ten years old? He could be anywhere. He could have moved on. He could be dead.'

'Hence the public appeal. The calls are already coming in to the 1800 number in Adelaide.'

'And?'

'Sightings in Port Hedland, Pannawonica, Perth, Fremantle, Bunbury, Albany, Kalgoorlie ...' Delaney smiled wryly, 'all dead-set certainties.'

'Any that ring true?'

'We're still processing it. We'll be following up the calls. My colleague is in Perth coordinating that now.'

Delaney leaned forward as if taking Miller into his confidence, letting slip the almost certainty that Chapman was very much alive and kicking. At least two of the reported sightings, admittedly still a year or more out of date, had also been 'hearings' and one of the witnesses, another Pom, had been able to do a very credible impersonation of the man he'd met in a roadhouse just before last Christmas; the accent was a real giveaway. Miller couldn't argue with that last point but he could tell from the body language that Delaney was still not being totally up-front. It was cat and mouse; the younger man wasn't going to write him off just yet because he might, for all he knew, come good. So he was offering the illusion of sharing and giving to keep the old fart in the fold. Miller had expected it; he used to be a cop after all and he knew only too well that instinct to play the cards close to the chest. No point in fighting it, he needed as much as he could get from Detective Delaney and this would possibly be his only chance.

'What can you tell me about the MO?'

'Seems like he wanted to make pretty sure they were dead. Caving their heads in should have been enough. But he was nothing if not thorough.'

Miller felt his jaw and neck muscles tighten and the

moisture disappear from his mouth. 'The news report mentioned electrocution. How?'

Delaney spun his phone almost absent-mindedly on the table.

'Jump leads, some gizmo, a plug into the mains. Very inventive.'

Miller nodded grimly. 'All sounds like the same man doesn't it?'

Delaney wanted something from Miller now. 'Any clues from yours as to the big Why?'

Miller curled his lip. 'No profilers in my day mate, no psychological claptrap. Just good and bad.' Yes, he was playing the elder statesman, dinosaur and proud of it, but he had to admit a psychological profile of Arthurs would have been bloody useful. He lobbed the ball back over the net.

'Did your psych take a look at the case notes?'

Delaney nodded.

Miller steepled his fingers. 'And?'

Delaney stopped spinning his phone and checked the time on it. 'She reckons he's fucking mad.'

Miller could sense a meeting being wound up. 'So how long have you got before they close up the purse strings and call you back home?'

Delaney's face hardened. 'That's my business.'

Not long, Miller guessed. Detective Senior Constable Tim Delaney: a man working to try to catch a killer but on a tight budget and a strict deadline. Under pressure to get a result: same as it ever was. All Davey Arthurs/Derek Chapman had to do was keep his head down for a fortnight and things would be back to normal.

'Anything I can do to help?'

'Like what?' To Miller's sensitised ears Delaney's reply was only a rung above a sneer. 'Look, I appreciate the contacts you've given us for the Northumbria Police, that should fill in a bit more background. But unless you've got a magic wand or you get the chance to rugby-tackle him in the street it's hard to see how you can help, Stuart.'

He'd obviously done his homework. Miller hadn't been a cop for thirty years. This was the case that destroyed him. He was already beaten, washed up, fat and comfortably retired. What could he possibly offer? Miller read the patronising look and averted his gaze.

'Yeah, right ... I don't know.'

Delaney stood up and put out his hand.

'Well, Stuart, thanks for the tip-off, very useful. Here's my card. Give me a call if anything else comes back to you, okay?'

And he was off, a smart young man in a suit, going places. Miller, a silly old codger in his baggy shorts and sticky polo shirt, didn't move.

The fat lady had sung by the time Cato and Buckley arrived at the mine. They'd passed an ambulance on the way in, its headlights flashing but no siren. Cato could see Tess, Greg and two other officers interviewing various people in separate clusters and taking notes and names. Some sheepish security guards were loitering, looking like spare parts and sharing a smoke. One of the police vans was occupied; swearing and kicking sounds echoing from the back. The accent sounded Kiwi. Jim Buckley went over, slapped the window a few times and told him to shut the fuck up. It didn't work. Tess's little group seemed to be nodding and smiling a lot. Cato figured them for management and PR people, he went over to stick his nose in.

Tess glowered at him. 'Glad you could join us.'

Cato smiled at her then shifted his gaze and extended his hand to her companions. 'Detective Senior Constable Philip Kwong.'

A man with nice, clean, ironed blue and orange fluoros, a managerial healthy tan, good teeth, firm jaw and piercing eyes stuck his hand out in return.

'Marnus Van der Kuyp, General Manager.'

South African and a half. His companion was slightly smaller, rounder, and it looked like his job was to be nice to people.

'Bruce Yelland, Community Relations.'

'Bit of trouble today?' Cato said, stating the obvious.

Yelland shrugged and smiled. 'Sorry to have dragged you out here, bit of a storm in a teacup.'

'A man has been hospitalised,' Tess reminded him.

Yelland didn't miss a beat. 'Yes, yes terrible. The guys responsible are finished here, that's for sure. Zero tolerance for this kind of behaviour, absolutely.'

Tess wasn't letting him off the hook. 'Well we've still got to get to the bottom of this. Charges will be laid. We may need to come back and talk to some of these people again. And yourselves of course.'

Cato played nice guy while Tess fixed her eyes on Yelland and Van der Kuyp; the latter gave her a curt nod and a quick smile. A few metres away in the paddy wagon there was another flurry of kicks and a 'Fucken bastards, let me out of here!' Bruce Yelland looked like he was having trouble sticking to his job description today. He forced another smile. The look said 'boys will be boys'.

'Of course, you have our full cooperation, Sergeant.' He turned to Cato. 'Good to meet you, Philip. You must come out here one day and we can give you the grand tour.'

'Love to,' said Cato with a big friendly grin.

The big cheeses rolled away. The Ravy reinforcements, having finished taking names, quickly introduced themselves to Cato and Buckley, then they too left with their noisy prisoner.

'Thank Christ,' said Buckley, taking out a cigarette and lighting up.

Cato nodded to Tess for them to take a short walk away from the smoke.

'What happened?'

'An argument between regular shiftworkers and contractors; got out of hand. The Maori in the van stomped on a kid. Knowing the kid, I wouldn't be surprised if he had it coming. He's a bit of a mess but he'll survive. He's gone to hospital for checks. Most other injuries are minor cuts and bruises.'

'What was it about?'

'From what we've heard so far, it's ongoing tension between locals versus incomers, Aussies versus foreigners, staff versus contractors. The usual tribal us-and-them crap.'

Cato nodded: same old, same old. Tribalism was the bread and butter of police work: that and grog. Oh and idiots. All three in fact.

Tess sighed and pinched the bridge of her nose. 'It seems to have come to a head in the last few days over health and safety. There was an accident yesterday, a chemical spill from one of the pipes. Apparently one of the contractors caused it and when they yelled at him to hit the emergency switch he couldn't understand them. Meanwhile the poor bastard still in the tank was getting his legs boiled by some corrosive.'

Cato remembered the ambulance he'd seen on his way to the Ravensthorpe post-mortem last night; so that's who was behind the double doors giving out the muffled cries. Cato hoped they'd managed to drum up enough medical staff from somewhere to help out at Tumbleweed General.

'But surely they should be taking all that up with management?'

Tess shrugged. 'They're all on individual contracts now. Not so easy to stick your head up and be counted these days. Easier to take it out on the bloke next to you.'

Jim Buckley had rejoined them. He frowned. 'So it was the Kiwi who caused the acid spill? I didn't think his English was that bad from what I could hear.'

Tess's mouth twitched into a smile. 'No, one of the Chinese, but the contractors are sticking up for each other. Apparently there's been enough bad blood generated over the last few months to make an injury to one an injury to all.'

'Bloody foreigners,' said Buckley, eyes sparkling with mischief.

Cato focused his attention on Tess. 'So where to from here, boss?'

By Cato's standards, this was an apology for him being less than helpful when she called for assistance earlier. Their eyes met and for the first time since he'd arrived Cato detected a glimmer of warmth in Tess's voice.

'Let's go and talk to our gladiators. You and Greg take Man-Mountain, he'll be at the Ravy lockup once the doctor has checked his cuts and bruises. I'll go to the hospital to see how the "victim" is shaping up.' Tess paused. 'Jim, could you help me out with that, please?'

Buckley looked up surprised and a bit worried. He was probably not used to being called by his other name, or people saying 'please' – and no doubt wondering why Tess wanted him along anyway. Cato was wondering the same thing.

9

Thursday, October 9th. Midafternoon.

Man-Mountain's name turned out to be David Tahere. He'd had his eye stitched, been booked and processed, and was sitting meekly in the Ravensthorpe cop shop interview room when Cato walked in. Cato had sent Greg Fisher back to Hopetoun to pursue their Flipper inquiries before the day turned into too much of a write-off. The chair under the Maori could have been from the local playgroup for all the dignity and comfort it afforded him. Tahere looked up at Cato with the eye that was still able to open properly.

'You a cop?'

'Yes. Detective Senior Constable Kwong.' Cato took a seat opposite him.

'Don't look like one.'

'Must be my cunning disguise. What happened out there today, David?'

'Got into a fight.'

'I gathered that. Now you're facing an assault charge.' Cato had run David Tahere through the computer system. 'Not your first time, you've got a bit of a record.'

'Wasn't my fault. He started it.'

'Original.'

'And tell that chick cop, she uses one of those zapper things on me again I'll shove it up her arse and light her up like a fucken Christmas tree.'

Knowing Tess, Cato didn't fancy his chances. 'Mate, there's a guy in hospital. This is serious. You're looking at doing time for this one. So tell me what happened, we need your side for the record.'

'I'll tell my story to Legal Aid.' Tahere looked around as if they might be playing hidey behind the door. 'Where are they anyway?'

'Might take a while down here mate. This is the country. We're talking days rather than hours.'

Not strictly true but Cato was keen to expedite the matter and get back to Operation Flipper. 'You know you've lost your job because of this don't you?'

Tahere sighed and shook his head. 'All because of that scrawny, motor-mouthed Pakeha cunt.'

Cato checked his notes. 'Stevenson?'

Man-Mountain growled. 'That's what I said wasn't it?'

'He doesn't look like the kind who'd go picking a fight with somebody your size.'

'He didn't. He and his two mates set about one of the little Chinks ... No offence ...'

'None taken.'

'And I've had a gutful. They've been giving us the shits for weeks. He had it coming.'

'Want to make a statement now, David?'

'Yeah.'

Cato readied his pen over his notepad. Tahere looked at him out of his good eye.

'Git fucked.'

Tess kept looking in the rear view on the way to Ravensthorpe. She had enjoyed her glimpses of a slightly perplexed Cato Kwong in the car behind. The afternoon sun was still high in the sky, and away from the coast the temperature had climbed by about ten degrees. Tess glanced over at Jim Buckley, filling the passenger seat and looking uncomfortable.

'How's it going with you and Cato in Stock Squad?'

'Yeah, good.'

'Keeping busy?'

'You know how it is.'

She had a pretty good idea; she was doing much the same thing most days in Hopetoun. Filling in time as easily as possible.

'How did you end up in Stock Squad then?'

Buckley fixed her with a back-off stare. 'I asked for it.'

Tess wondered if he realised that could be taken more than one way. 'Surprised to see Cato in there; I didn't think it was his cup of tea.'

Buckley visibly relaxed, the subject had moved away from him and on to Cato.

'I don't think he planned it.'

'No, not an obvious career move.' Tess realised too late it might not be what Buckley wanted to hear. 'I mean for somebody like Cato.'

'Meaning what?'

Buckley was on the front foot now, beginning to enjoy himself. Tess pushed on regardless.

'High-flyer. Fast track. That was Cato.'

Jim Buckley smirked. 'Want some other words? How about "fuck-up" or "corrupt" or "rotten apple"?'

Tess stared at the road ahead and gripped the wheel a little tighter.

'Cato? When was this? What happened?'

She found it hard to believe but the look in Buckley's eyes said it all.

'Remember that Cockburn newsagent murder?'

She couldn't fail to; it was high profile for all the wrong reasons. Jim Buckley reclined his seat a little, stretched his legs, and relaxed into his story.

'A woman got her head pulped during a robbery. They picked up the first poor bastard they saw on the street and pinned it on him. The big boys, like DI Mick Hutchens, got the "confession" out of him.'

Buckley waved his cigarette packet hopefully at Tess but she shook her head disapprovingly. He pressed on with his tale with added relish.

'Young Kwongie was an ambitious back-room boy, it was one of his first cases. His job was to make sure the witness statements fitted the confession Hutchens had conjured up. When the shit hit the fan and they found the real killer, by accident as fucking usual, the inquiry showed that the only strong paper trail had been left by Golden Boy.'

'His name didn't crop up in the news reports at the time,' Tess pointed out, unwilling to accept what she was hearing.

'Maybe the spin doctors put up a bamboo curtain.' Buckley sniffed. 'After all, he was the poster boy for the new multicultural Police Service, wouldn't want to taint that tasty image would we?'

Tess didn't bother responding.

'Maybe if he'd looked like the rest of us potato-nosed farm boys he'd have been hung out to dry. Anyway, long story short, Hutchens got moved sideways and downwards. Down all the way to Albany in fact. And your mate got demoted and dumped on us in Stock Squad. Bit of an insult to us I reckon.'

Cato. Dirty. Was it possible? Of course it was. Every day, cops were tempted to cross the line. Money. Results. Revenge. Laziness. There could be any number of reasons for it but no excuses, not in her book.

'I wonder why he didn't get out,' Tess said, as much to herself as to Buckley.

'Don't the Chinese have a thing about losing face?'

Tess switched on the air conditioning. 'Those cultural awareness classes have been the making of you, Jim.'

Kane Stevenson had been stitched up and cleaned up and just arrived back from X-ray. There was no apparent skull fracture or damage but he'd be kept in overnight for observation, if they could rustle up some suitably qualified night staff. He was half propped up in the bed with big pillows fluffed around him. Little boy lost. The big long-lashed brown eyes, which got him into and out of a lot of trouble, were closed over, his nose was broken and lips split. He had what looked like a footprint across his face. Odds on it would match David Tahere's right boot. Tess almost felt sorry for him; it didn't take much to bring back memories of her own time in hospital. The silver lining was that Kane Stevenson wouldn't be doing any more burnouts on the airport road for a while. Karma was the word that sprang to mind.

The nurse, a severely fit and severely blonde young woman, was looking forward to going off-duty in half an hour and heading to basketball practice. She had let it be known that she was determined to keep to her schedule. Her badge said 'Briony'. Tess reckoned it should have said 'Brunhilde'.

'He's still pretty groggy so just a few minutes please. He should be in better shape for questions tomorrow.'

On somebody else's shift, Brunhilde might have added. Tess wondered if she should salute but instead just nodded thanks. She noticed Jim Buckley checking out Brunhilde's calves as she left. Pathetic. Tess leaned down closer to Stevenson.

'Kane, are you awake?'

A half-moan, half-grunt escaped through the mashed mouth.

'Sergeant Tess Maguire here, mate. Can you talk?'

Same response with a gurgle thrown in. Tess looked up at Buckley.

'This is going nowhere fast. Leave it until tomorrow?'

A twitch in Stevenson's battered face. Buckley saw it.

'Kane. My name's Detective Sergeant Jim Buckley. I think you're pretending to be worse than you are. You don't want us here. Why's that, Kane?'

Kane went limp and started playing dead again.

Buckley pressed on. 'The word is that you started it. Been shooting your mouth off about the Asians, the foreigners. That's why the Maori kicked your arse. That what happened?'

Nothing. Buckley leaned in close to Stevenson's ear. 'Have a good night's rest, Kane, we'll pop back in to see you tomorrow.'

Stuart Miller had brooded all day. Detective Delaney had, gently but firmly, put him in his place and it rankled. Not least because Delaney probably had a point. What did he have to offer? Jenny had given up trying to have a conversation with him and retired to the office in the granny flat to write some school reports. He'd hopped on to the internet and googled news reports of the 1981 Adelaide murders. It was pretty much as the *West Australian* had summarised it: a mum and three young kids electrocuted and bludgeoned, packed into the Holden and left in the bush: a macabre family getaway. Derek Chapman, Davey Arthurs. Why had he done it again? Was there some psychological trigger or was he just, as Delaney put it, fucking mad? It also begged another question: how did he get the papers enabling him to change his identity and move to Australia? And, biggest question of all, had he killed yet again, before or since the Sunderland and Adelaide murders?

Miller was outside the loop. He needed more than Google to help him search for a killer. He needed to read the case notes from the Chapman murders, he needed the resources of the police force, but Delaney had patted him on the head and told him to leave it to the professionals, or words to that effect. The only person he knew inside the system, in the WA police at least, was his brother-in-law, Jenny's sister's bloke. Maggie had married the cop boyfriend from all those years ago. He was a brusque wanker and a bit of a clock-watcher but he was the only thing on offer. Jenny's sister had died just over two years ago and they had even less contact with the wanker-in-law these days. Outside, the neighbours' bairns were being summoned from their street games as the evening dimmed, called back into the safety of home and family. Miller's resolve hardened; beggars can't be choosers. He searched through the tattered address book and found the mobile number.

'Jim. It's Stuart ... Jenny's husband?'

There was a pause. Miller could almost hear the rusted memory-wheels grinding into motion at the other end.

'Stuart. Ey up lad, what can I do for you?' said Jim Buckley, caricaturing his brother-in-law's flat-vowelled, singsong accent.

Miller heard the forced brightness and effort at civility. He cleared his throat. 'Have you seen today's paper?'

Grand Final Day and the home team have lost, badly. No matter. The Karratha Hotel is pumping. Karratha, WA, the epicentre of the mining boom. The drink is flowing, music thumping; it's standing room only and just the two fights so far. Tess and Constable Peter Latham fix their smiles in place and walk in. On their way to the bar they are assailed by sweat, testosterone, and alcohol fumes plus a cocktail of greetings, 'G'day mate, have a beer' or 'Get fucked, fucken pigs'. Tess gives Pete a look, it says stick close. The manager, a squat barrel of a man in his late fifties, leans close to yell into Tess's ear.

'Is there a problem?'

No, we're here because we love this shit. Instead she says, 'Big night tonight, George?'

A whoop goes up as a barmaid, having lost a coin-toss, lifts her T-shirt for the crowd – a favourite mining town party trick, and theoretically banned. Tess gives George her stern schoolteacher look. He shrugs.

'Sometimes they get carried away. I'll have a word.'

Just then there is a surge in the crowd, a few stumbles, a flying middy of beer and Tess is soaked. She is beginning to get pissed off. A big bloke with a checked shirt and ginger mullet is in her face: Johnno Djukic, three previous for assault, each time putting his de facto in hospital for a few days. Nice guy.

'It was tails. I win. Show us your tits, missus.'

His breath could power a V8.

'Back off and behave yourself,' Tess snaps.

Djukic holds up his hands in mock fear and gives her a broad smile that never reaches his eyes. Big joke, the mates oooh, aaah and tsk-tsk. Tess cranes her neck to see where Pete is. From the raised, angry voices further down the bar she has her answer. He is engaged in a shouting match with a skinhead who, by the state of his eyeballs, has been consuming chemicals along with his grog. He is wired, beyond reason, and ready for blood. Tess has her hand on her baton as she tries to catch Pete's eye.

A glass smashes, the crowd surges again, a bar stool flies through the air. Tess feels an agonising wrenching jolt as someone grabs her by the hair, then she is lying on the floor curled up tight while they kick, and stomp, and spit. She looks up one last time trying to recognise faces for later – if there is a later. Johnno Djukic is in there, getting his two cents' worth, stomping with the best of them, so is her colleague Pete and Greg Fisher and Jim Buckley and Cato. She thinks it will never stop. She just knows she is going to die. In the distance a siren wails and wails. And wails.

Tess woke up fighting for breath, and crying again. Her alarm clock wailed. She turned it off.

10

Friday, October 10th. Early morning.

Murder HQ. Friday, 8.00 a.m. sharp. Cato wanted a quick catch-up with everybody. He felt like yesterday was a bit of a wasted day; rousting the Snak-Attack boy and breaking up fights at the mine kept them all nicely occupied but didn't get them any closer to solving the mystery of Flipper.

Cato had woken bright and early, determined to make progress. He wanted to chase up the missing Lieutenant Riri Yusala. Was he Flipper? He also wanted to do a bit of tree-shaking. Yesterday's little visit to Justin's coffee van might have been a distraction but it had also given him the idea. This was a small town – how hard could it be to set tongues wagging and see what happened? Who knew who, or what, might come scurrying out of the woodwork? Pam the All-Knowing All-Seeing All-Telling Receptionist was his best bet; he'd made a big show of being curt as he dropped his room key in on the way to breakfast. Clearly here was a man with a lot on his mind, a lot of secrets, and it had worked a treat. Pam hovered in her split role as receptionist and breakfast-server.

'How are your inquiries progressing, Inspector?'

Cato appreciated the promotion. 'Good, thanks.'

He'd laid on the absent-minded man-of-mystery thing with a trowel.

'I hear there's drugs involved. A syndicate.' Pam enunciated each syllable of the last word in hushed breathless tones, relishing the 'syn' part.

Cato pretended to look alarmed that she knew so much. He glanced around the almost empty dining room and made a soothing, shushing movement with his hands.

Pam nodded knowingly. 'Your colleague, will he be joining us for breakfast today?'

Cato made his expression unnaturally neutral. 'Not sure, he's making a few calls.' He checked his watch. 'Seven a.m. here.'

Cato looked like he was trying to calculate time zones. That was all Pam needed. It wasn't just a drug syndicate; it was an International Drug Syndicate, and these weren't just ordinary cops. She bustled away to get Cato his coffee. Cato smiled to himself, wondering how far it would spread around town by day's end. The downside was that the rumour mill would probably also find its way back to the news media, something Hutchens specifically didn't want right now. Cato was on a deadline; due to be shunted out by one of Hutchens' puppets in a few days anyway, he figured the career-benefits of a quick result would hopefully outweigh Hutchens' displeasure at his little game. He frowned. Quick results and little games, wasn't that what got him into trouble in the first place?

A polite cough from Jim Buckley brought him back into the moment and back into the Murder Room. Cato noticed that Buckley still had a distracted look about him. Constable Greg Fisher reported on the trip to Mason and Starvation bays and the chat with Billy Mather, none of which had generated anything of real interest except for the tip about the grey nomads who'd passed through. When he got back to Hopetoun after the ruckus at the mine he'd spent the rest of the afternoon following up on said grey nomads. He struck lucky quickly. Security video footage from the Hopetoun general store fuel pumps showed a Britz van filling up the previous Saturday; that fitted Billy Mather's time frame. Greg had noted the rego number and phoned the company.

'That produced a hirer's name and mobile contact: Mr Kevin Redmond from Newcastle, New South Wales, by this time plugged into a powered site in Esperance. Two hundred kilometres east along the coast,' he added for the benefit of the city slickers.

Mr Redmond had sounded like a Pom. Greg Fisher observed that you couldn't move for the bastards these days and Jim Buckley nodded sourly in agreement. Redmond confirmed that he and his wife had called through Starvation Bay last weekend and hadn't noticed anything unusual. The other campervan had been hired by his wife's sister and her husband, and Redmond doubted they'd noticed anything either or it would have helped the flagging conversations in the evenings. Redmond had put his brother-in-law on the phone and he'd confirmed as much.

'Except ...' teased Fisher.

'Except what?' said Cato impatiently.

'On the first night, that's last Thursday into Friday, he got up to take a piss. Prostate.'

'Yes?' Cato said.

'At around 2.15 a.m. – apparently he noticed the time on the microwave – he stepped outside to do the business and noticed some lights down near the boat ramp. Didn't give it any further thought. Too busy trying to piss and get back to bed.'

Greg Fisher sat back beaming.

'Late night lights on the boat ramp at Starvo,' said Jim Buckley cupping his chin thoughtfully in his right fist. 'That could be the turning point in this case.'

Greg Fisher nodded enthusiastically until he realised that Buckley was being sarcastic. Cato didn't want the meeting to sink into oblivion just yet.

'The old guy, the fisherman ...'

'Mather?' offered Greg.

'Yeah, he didn't mention any lights?'

Greg shrugged. 'Asleep? Bit deaf? Forgot?'

'Maybe, or, for all you know, lying, or hiding something. Can you get back to him and double-check?'

Fisher blushed. 'Sure.'

Fisher wrapped up his report and beat a hasty retreat. No,

he hadn't got around to checking out shipping movements yet but yes, he would get onto it now, talk to a few boaties around town, and get back to Mather about those lights.

Next it was Cato's turn. He told them about the mispers list and the two of interest to him – Riri Yusala and, to a lesser extent, the closet Italian gay Carlo Donizetti. That raised a smirk from an otherwise dour Jim Buckley. There were contact numbers for the case officers assigned to the two mispers, one in Perth for Donizetti, and Yusala's in Albany: DI Mick Hutchens' turf. Cato would follow up on that today. Tess Maguire met his eye. He couldn't read the look, it was as if she hardly knew him. Private. Keep Out.

'I'll be following up on the mine fight,' Tess said, 'Talking to Kane Stevenson and some of those other names we took. I'll be on that for most of the day.'

Tess's expression challenged Cato to say it ain't so. He didn't. Jim Buckley asked her if she wanted him there for the Stevenson interview. She didn't. He looked surprisingly disappointed.

Tess left for Ravensthorpe. Greg Fisher was already on the phone checking shipping. Cato gave Buckley the number for the Donizetti case officer, keeping Riri Yusala and the Albany office for himself. He rang the number.

'Julie Silvestri, Albany Detectives.'

The voice at the other end of the phone sounded like it was being channelled through a soggy mattress. Cato introduced himself and told her what he wanted. She took a moment to find the case on her computer; Cato could hear the clicking of the keyboard and heavy mouth-breathing. Julie Silvestri had a cold.

'Here it is,' she croaked, 'Riri Yusala, missing since ... February 2006. Looks like he jumped ship here at Albany ... naval exercises ... whaling ship ... I assume you've already read all this?'

Cato confirmed that he had and asked what else she could

tell him about the case.

'Wife and two kids back in ... Sulawesi?' Not easy to say with a head cold.

'Yes, I read that too,' said Cato.

A few more keyboard clicks. 'A couple of unconfirmed sightings: the first, a month or so after he disappeared. It was on a building site in Perth, a security guard with aspirations to be Sam Spade. Trawls mispers sites for a hobby, sad bastard. Anyway that's how he recognised him, or thought he did. Reckoned he was doing some labouring on the hush-hush. If it was him he'd moved on by the time we had it checked out and whoever it was also had a new name ... Freddy Sudhyono. The foreman couldn't confirm anything from the picture. "They all look the same," he said.'

'And the second sighting?'

'Fremantle Markets: another month later. Somebody reckoned they saw him working at the satay stall there. A bit more credence to that one.' Julie Silvestri snuffled and seemed to catch some mucous in her throat.

Cato winced at the noise. 'Why?'

'The guy who saw him was on leave from the Australian Navy, he'd been on the same ship as Yusala. He was sure it was him but he didn't report it until about six weeks later. He hadn't realised Yusala was deemed a missing person until he went into his local cop shop to collect his son who'd been picked up for underage drinking or something. Saw the Missing Persons poster while he was waiting.'

'So why the "concern for his welfare" if he was last seen alive and well?'

'Our Freo colleagues went back to the satay stall. It says here, quote, "The stall owner was terrified." A Vietnamese woman, Penny Nguyen, said she'd last seen Freddy – so he's still using the same name at that point anyway – she'd seen him arguing with two guys one night after work about a week earlier. They'd bundled him into a car and sped off. He hadn't been back since.'

Cato leaned forward and gripped the phone a little harder. 'Any description on the guys or the car?'

'Australian. White. Big. That's both the guys and the car. Otherwise it was too dark to see and it all happened too quickly, et cetera. No other witnesses, it seems.'

'Nothing since?'

'Nothing.'

'What about his family or the Indonesian Navy? Did they provide any information on him worth knowing?'

'Nothing on file. The Indonesian Navy doesn't seem to have made any waves about his disappearance.'

She snorted at her little joke, inviting Cato to join in. He gave a false chuckle and heard Silvestri blow her nose daintily, one nostril at a time, away from the phone – snorting at her own joke probably hadn't been a good idea.

'Think he's your floater?'

'Maybe. But we're a long way from Fremantle Markets, and a long time past that sighting,' Cato said.

'Maybe they took him for a ride to give him a warning of some kind and when he got his chance later he did a runner?'

'Maybe.'

'Maybe baby. Anything else I can do for you, darl?' Silvestri sneezed and the receiver exploded in Cato's ear.

'Have a nice hot lemon drink and some Panadol. Thanks Julie.'

'Can I have a Panadol?'

The voice was self-pitying and slightly distorted, coming as it did out of Kane Stevenson's smashed lips. But at least he was talking, which was good news for Tess. The nurse shook her head at Kane's request.

'Not for another four hours.'

It wasn't Brunhilde from the Nazi Women's League, Tess noted. Jim Buckley would have been disappointed. It was an older, some would say matronly, woman; her badge said 'Jill'. Jill left and Tess smiled a greeting towards Kane Stevenson's one half-open eye.

'Looking much better today Kane.'

A grunt. The good eye closed.

'Got a headache; that fucken Maori. Should be locked up.'

'He is. We'll be needing a statement from you, as victim, for the court case.'

The eye opened again. 'Court case?'

'Assault occasioning bodily harm: serious offence, the jailing type.'

'Good.'

Tess had her notebook and pen ready. 'So what happened?'

'The big fucken Maori kicked the shit out of me.'

'Why? What started it?'

'Dunno. Just minding my own business and he starts up.'

'We've got witnesses saying you'd been abusing the foreign workers, the contractors. That true?'

'Just looking after my team.'

Tess glanced idly at the medical chart at the end of his bed; it meant nothing to her.

'Your team?'

'Health and Safety. The Chinks haven't got a fucking clue, always accidents with them around. You try talking to them and they can't speak a word of English. Not even "Turn the fucking valve off". Mate of mine nearly died the other day cos of them useless cunts.'

'Did you assault any of the contractors, Kane?'

'Bit of pushing and shoving, can't remember who did what when. All I remember is the big ...'

'Maori, yeah Kane I get the picture. Soon as you're well enough we'll do a proper typed and signed statement for the court case, okay?'

'Too right. Get that bastard put in jail. Get rid of them one way or another eh?' Kane Stevenson smiled but winced when it cracked his sore lips.

Tess put her notebook away. 'That's the spirit. By the way, have you heard? Apparently you're fired as well. You won't need to worry about sticking up for your team anymore. Chin up Kane, keep smiling.'

Stuart Miller had woken in a foul mood. His brother-in-law had given him short shrift over his request to help find Arthurs. One, he was too busy and had more important things on his mind. Two, it was a needle-in-a-haystack job. Three, there were rules these days about unauthorised access of the police database. Thanks for nothing, you grumpy old time-serving bastard. Jim Buckley had never been one for taking the job home with him. Miller recalled family Christmases in the early days: Jenny and Maggie would clear off over to the beach with all the kids and he'd be left to make conversation with his semi-pissed and half-asleep wanker-in-law. Even though Stuart was out of the game now the obvious point of connection should have been The Job. Not a peep. No matter how many times Stuart would start the ball rolling with an anecdote, Jim would kick it into touch with a belch and the pop of a new can. The return of screaming kids and yet another plateful of turkey came to be seen as a relief. He'd tried relating all of this to Jenny over the usual rushed breakfast this morning but he could tell her mind was on the coming day at school. She summoned up a semi-concerned, 'Ach, ye poor wee sausage,' in her Edinburgh brogue then pecked him on the cheek, squeezed his bum, told him she loved him, and left another list of jobs that needed doing.

He plonked himself down at the kitchen table and flicked away the chores list irritably. Reaching for yesterday's paper he pored over the cold-case article again, willing it to give him some idea of what to do. After two or three re-reads and a second cup of tea he finally saw it.

> *Police Media have also released an image of Chapman, based on information from a woman who knew him and who reported a sighting of him in Bunbury in the state's South-West in 1998, 17 years after the murders.*

Who was she? How did she know him? What were the circumstances of the sighting? This was before their new publicity push because the photofit was based on what she had seen. So what led the SA Police to this woman in WA? What was Detective Tim Delaney holding back? Stuart Miller reached for his phone and the embossed business card of the young man in the suit.

Six down, twelve letters. *Fellow's glee takes your breath away.* Cato nodded to himself, clicked his biro, and filled in the answer. 'Manslaughter'. The coffees arrived. He furtively slipped the crossword pages out of the paper, folded them into his jacket pocket and put the newspaper back into the cafe's complimentary pile along with the glossies. Jim Buckley clapped his hands at a spot just above and behind Cato's head.

'Moth, got it, must have escaped from your wallet. Poor bastard was blinded by the daylight.'

Cato ignored the jibe and sized up his partner. 'Everything okay at home?'

He couldn't help himself, he had to stick his nose into Jim Buckley's business: curiosity rather than real concern. Since breakfast Buckley seemed to have spent every spare moment talking quietly but fiercely into his mobile. He had just done it again, pacing up and down outside, smoking and muttering into the phone while they waited for the coffees. They were sitting at a table at the top deck of the Taste of the Toun cafe. The view out over the Southern Ocean was magnificent. The day was fine and the wind was already up, it was an easterly but still cool as it came off the sea. In Perth an easterly came off the desert, hot and unforgiving. The top deck of the cafe was a bit claustrophobic with undersized tables and chairs and a roof that sloped down to below head height at its lowest point. Both Cato and Buckley had to stoop when standing in that space. If he'd been green, Buckley would have been a dead ringer for Shrek having unknowingly wandered into the seven dwarves' cottage.

'Fine,' said Buckley.

Cato took the hint. 'Great,' he said.

Buckley's call to the Donizetti case officer in Perth had drawn a blank. No sightings: Donizetti had disappeared without a trace, bank account untouched, no credit card transactions, nothing. Suspicion initially fell on a boyfriend who had previous for domestic violence but, while he remained a person of interest, it was hard to pursue without a body and without any forensics pointing the finger. There had also been a spate of gay bashings in the area in previous weeks. Take your pick.

Meanwhile Greg Fisher had been a busy little bee: he'd got back to the old man at Starvation Bay who had insisted he'd slept through and hadn't seen or heard anything to do with lights on the boat ramp and was sorry he couldn't be of any more help. Fisher had also left requests with the harbourmasters at Adelaide, Esperance, Albany and Fremantle to check shipping through their ports in the last few days with any notifications of missing personnel. He'd been in touch with fishing cooperatives at key points east and west to check if any fishers were reported lost overboard and he was now out on the groyne chatting with boaties at the town ramp.

Buckley slurped his coffee. 'Think this Indonesian is your man then?'

'Maybe,' Cato shrugged, not wanting the other to think he was getting too excited by the possibility.

'Long shot if you ask me.'

'Probably right,' Cato said, screwing up his face after a mouthful of the brew. 'Maybe we should go and say hello to

Justin; he may be a skanky drug-pusher but he knows how to do coffee.'

Buckley brightened. 'Well we do have unfinished business with him. You reckon he looked pretty relieved to see us go yesterday.'

Cato could tell that Buckley would be more than happy to be back on the kind of police work he understood. Hassling drug-pushers, retrieving stolen tractors, anything was better than trying to put a name to a piece of rotting flotsam that probably fell off a foreign fishing boat. Out on the street Greg Fisher had finished talking to the boaties on the groyne. He gestured up towards their window, thumbs down, no luck there. Cato decided to give Buckley what he wanted.

'Okay, take young Greg with you and have another chat with Justin. See if you can find out who or what he's hiding from. But Jim ...' Buckley had started to rise and was stooped under the low ceiling, cigarette packet in hand, 'no rough stuff, we don't want to give Greg any bad habits, eh?'

Cato smiled; he'd meant it as a joke, male bonding and all that. Buckley produced half a smirk. 'Reckon you're the one to be giving advice about how to be a good cop?'

Cato stopped smiling.

The ranger put the outboard into reverse as he approached the cave. The ocean was fairly calm at this side of Quoin Head, a secluded bay about forty kilometres west of Hopetoun in the Fitzgerald River National Park. A jutting headland sheltered it from the strengthening easterly which was whipping up white-caps further out to sea. His khaki park-ranger shirt was sodden from the sea spray he'd faced on the way out. The sea cave in the western side of the headland was about eight metres high and the same wide. He knew it went back about fifteen metres, gradually narrowing down to no more than the height and width of a child. And it was dark back there.

The report had come in from a fisherman the previous

afternoon: something bobbing around the mouth of the cave, maybe a seal or a dog? The angler hadn't gone down to investigate because the waves were building into kingies. Maybe the creature was injured by a shark, or tangled in a net or fishing line. Seal, schmeal, the ranger thought, they come, they go, they live, they die. But if it turned out to be someone's pet dog or, heaven forbid, a person, then that was a whole different matter. Anyway it was his job to check it out and it wasn't like he had much else on at the moment.

He flicked on his Dolphin torch, scanning the surface of the water as it lapped against the sides of the cave. The outboard chugged – he didn't want the tinny to be caught on the treacherous rocks around the cave mouth; it could be a real pain in the arse sourcing new prop parts down here. Another quick scan and he'd be out of there.

Something shimmered in the torchlight against the mossy cave wall further back. It was too small to be a seal, or a dog, although it could possibly be part of one. He turned the outboard off, allowing the boat to drift for a moment. He had a net attached to a two-metre pole but even at full stretch from the front of the dinghy he was still another two metres short of whatever it was. Outside the cave entrance the wind had moved south and conditions, even in the sheltered end of the bay, were chopping up. A wave surge sent the dinghy further into the darkness and clanging off a side wall. At full stretch out the front of the boat, he was bounced off a small jagged overhang. It scraped down the side of his face and hurt like hell.

'Fuck.'

The curse rebounded all round the cave and out on to the blue waters of the bay. He was now much nearer to the object and he focused his flashlight on it.

'Fuck,' he said again. Quieter this time.

11

Friday, October 10th. Early afternoon.

'Where's Quoin Head?' Cato asked Tess as they bumped westwards along the gravel road. The rugged rock-strewn Mount Barren reared up ahead to their right like it was auditioning for a location role in *Lord of the Rings*. It was somehow smaller close up than it seemed in the distance.

'About forty kilometres inside the national park. Nice camping spot, when it's not closed by bushfire or dieback,' said Tess. 'But we're meeting our bloke, his name's Steve Bell, at the ranger's house just up here.'

Jim Buckley was crunched up in the back seat looking thoughtful. Apparently the visit to Justin Woodward had been unproductive, the Snak-Attack was closed and the proprietor hadn't been at home. To their left, the wide sweep of blue foamy Southern Ocean and the hazy hint of some islands out on the edge of the known world. There were clouds out there too, a dark smudge on the distant horizon, but they looked like they would pass along the bottom of Australia and into the bight without troubling this stretch of coastline.

Tess turned left up a rough rutted driveway to a green wood and fibro house with a couple of sheds, a rainwater tank and a weather station on site. The view from the front porch was a million dollars, or probably more these days, across unspoilt low scrub to the ocean. The occasional royal hakea stood head and shoulders above the rest of the vegetation, lurid orange and red diamond-shaped wounds blistering the dark crusty skin. Spring had well and truly sprung and the air fairly hummed with its vibrations.

Steve Bell was already outside waiting for them, blood

on his ranger shirt and matting his blond sideburns, a big elastoplast barely covering the scrape down the right side of his face. Otherwise he had that perennially fit, rugged and healthy look of the outdoors type. 'It's in there.' He nodded towards an old rusty fridge up on the porch, the kind normally used to store beers and meat for the barbie.

Cato went up and opened the fridge door. There it was, the 'Quoin Head head'. It was in the biggest freezer bag Bell's wife had been able to find, he explained. She'd made herself scarce, it was nearly school's-out time and she intended to keep the kids away until both the police and the head had gone. No offence.

'None taken,' Cato assured him.

The head lay sideways on the top shelf. The eyes were missing, hair black, or dark anyway. Nose, ears and lips had been fish- or crab-nibbled and there was a strand of green mossy seaweed clinging to the chin. The head was male.

Jim Buckley peered over Cato's shoulder. 'Spitting image of you mate.'

Cato stared at the whiteboard in the Murder Room, at the name circled in the centre, Flipper. The head was on a flight to Perth to join the rest of the body. Both bits of Flipper had now moved a few steps up the priority ladder at the pathology lab and Cato had been told he could expect a preliminary report within forty-eight hours. That wasn't quick enough for him but it would have to do. Buckley had been right, the head definitely looked of Chinese origin. It certainly didn't look like Indonesian Navy Lieutenant Riri Yusala.

The only Chinese Cato had seen in the area had been the guy in the phone box on the main street on day one, and those working at the mine and getting into fights. Was that where he needed to look? Was that where he should have been looking all along? He reminded himself he'd only been in town for two days, although it felt longer. Nobody from the mine had reported anybody missing, but then again they hadn't been asked. Or maybe they hadn't even noticed. Apparently there were over two thousand people on site, most of them were fly-in fly-out, and that didn't include the contractors and subcontractors.

Somebody coughed and he realised that they were all sitting there waiting for him to say something–Greg Fisher, Tess Maguire, Jim Buckley. Patiently hanging out for some words of wisdom from Sherlock fucking Kwong.

'What now, Maestro?' asked Buckley, as if reading his mind.

Buckley's dig in the Taste of the Toun still rankled with Cato but only because, like all home truths, it was on target. He'd been busted for being lazy, sloppy, incompetent, arrogant and corrupt. He was a disgrace. Fair cop as they say. But how had it come to this? That first day on the detective squad: the try-hard handshakes, the surly nods and knowing looks. It wasn't unanimous but it was certainly widely believed, Cato Kwong was the new golden boy. He was a protected species, the modern face of WA policing, the one on the recruitment poster. He wanted them to know he was a good cop and he would show them all. Was that when the self-delusion started, on day one as a detective? Did he in his own heart of hearts also believe he was a protected species?

He certainly seemed bulletproof in those first few months out of uniform. DI Mick Hutchens taking him under his wing, showing him how it was done. An early result on a string of home invasions, Mick Hutchens puffing his chest out modestly for the news crew and Cato Kwong in the background putting the cuffed prisoner into the car, dark blue detective's bib proudly on display. Then a big hydroponic drugs bust: Cato Kwong gets the tip-off from suspicious neighbours and the Western Power electricity readout backs him up. This time Detective Senior Constable Philip Kwong gets to front the cameras and they like what they see.

Then one chill winter's morning, a Cockburn newsagent, Maria Lazzara, is found with her head smashed and the cash till empty. An opportunistic, tacky low-rent robbery accompanied by a savage bashing with a blunt instrument wielded by somebody who obviously had a taste for it. Fremantle Detectives caught the case, DI Mick Hutchens leading the investigation. Cato Kwong was put in charge of collating the handful of witness statements. The first was a nurse in a taxi on her way to the early shift at Freo Hospital. The cab stops at traffic lights and through the cold dawn drizzle she notices lights on in the shop and a man there: stocky, medium height and reddish hair. Why did she notice him? Something a bit scruffy about him and not quite right; he didn't seem like he belonged. Another witness, a student teacher on a moped, had to brake suddenly and nearly came off in the slippery conditions. A man had run out into the road in front of her: medium height, stocky build, reddish hair. It was just around the corner from the newsagent's. The timing corresponded. By late morning they had their man: Peter Beaton–a tall, thin rangy alcoholic no-hoper with a spider web tattoo on his neck and a record for opportunistic, tacky low-rent robberies. He had been picked up by a patrol who'd noticed him acting suspiciously. Beaton was just four streets away from the murder scene. Mick Hutchens and another senior detective went to work on him. After two days they had a confession. Nine months later a jury put him away for life.

How early did Cato Kwong know it was all bullshit? When the coalition of pushy journos and do-gooders secured an appeal for Peter Beaton after eight years of incarceration? Or was it when DI Hutchens pulled him to one side half an hour after the confession was signed and mentioned a couple of anomalies that needed straightening out? Like what? Like our man is tall, skinny, with darkish hair and a big fucking spider's web tattoo on his neck that nobody seems to have noticed, not medium height with reddish hair like the witnesses are saying. No worries. Cato Kwong was Mr Can-Do. The nurse in the taxi was contacted. She knew the score, been out with a few cops in her time. Yes, maybe the man she saw at a distance of thirty metres through the dawn drizzle was actually stooped over, that may account for the height thing. Pretty sure the hair was reddish though but yes it did all happen a bit quickly. Maybe darkish-reddish? The student teacher was pretty adamant that he was medium height, stocky build and reddish hair. She was up close and personal and he nearly made her come off her bike. She wasn't changing her statement.

Hutchens and Cato considered the matter. Maybe it was someone else who just happened to be in the area. Maybe best not to call her as a witness, bury the statement and just use the nurse and the confession instead. Maybe Detective Senior Constable Philip Kwong began to think right then that it was bullshit. If so he did nothing about it. Peter Beaton had put his hand up and now he was locked up. Case closed. Cato Kwong's star continued to rise and before long he was a detective sergeant with his eye on Mick Hutchens' job.

Over the years the 'Free Beaton' campaign intensified. They found an independent pathology expert who showed that the wounds inflicted on Maria Lazzara could not have been left by the weapon described in the confession. The shape and indentations were wrong. Hutchens had fumed. 'Wounds? Indentations? What the fuck would they know? Strawberry jam is fucking strawberry jam.'

An independent cold-case team is brought in to review the evidence. They concur with the expert on the murder weapon. They raise an eyebrow at the witness statements, particularly the one from the student teacher filed at the back and never produced in court. Then they run the scene fingerprints through the new whiz-bang computer. Bingo, a match on a known thug serving time in Bunbury Regional Prison for another opportunistic and tacky low-rent robbery, with violence. Medium height. Stocky build. Reddish hair. Peter Beaton, the very first murderer Cato Kwong helped put away, was the wrong man. Shit meets fan. Heads must roll but the only clear, concrete breach of protocol, the paper trail, the smoking gun, could be traced to Detective Sergeant Philip Kwong. Golden Boy. Protected Species. Those at the top of the food chain get a disapproving shake of the head and the dreaded tsk-tsk but they get to stay on the path to greatness. DI Mick Hutchens is invited to consider early retirement but digs his heels in and tells them to get fucked. He's moved to Albany instead. Cato Kwong, no longer on the protected species list, gets demoted and sent to Stock Squad in the sincere hope that he'll get the hint and quietly slip away into oblivion, career effectively over. He'd known for a long time now: it was a career founded on self-delusion and bullshit. Stock Squad was exactly the right place for him.

'Maestro?' Jim Buckley repeated.

Cato shook himself back through the time warp. 'The mine, the contractors, the subcontractors – we want a list of all Chinese nationals or Chinese-Australians on their books. Then we do a rollcall. Second thoughts, just get the full list of all employees from them. We're not just looking for a victim here, we'll also be looking for a perpetrator.'

Greg Fisher put up his hand like he was at school, then realised what he was doing and put it down again.

'It's not just the mine...' All faces turned towards Fisher and he blushed, bless him. 'There's a general labour shortage around here. The mine is sucking up any spare skilled labour so they're bringing in guest workers for construction, for plumbing, electrics, earthmoving, you name it.'

Cato nodded in agreement. 'Fair enough. Widen it, the building firm and contractors on the new housing estate, et cetera. You and Tess know the scene and the people better than we do. Can you do that Greg, Tess?' More nods. Cato looked over at Buckley. 'And we'll take that tour of the mine.'

Tess scanned the list provided to her by one of the bigger mine contractors, Dunstan Construction Industries in Ravensthorpe.

There were about twenty Chinese-looking names on the list, all accounted for at this stage. They'd all been paid yesterday and signed receipts to that effect. Tess and Greg were on their way back to Hopetoun to call on a smaller contractor supplying labour to the surrounding housing developments. The sun was dropping over to the west, the Barren Ranges lying on the horizon like a huge black sleeping dog. Friday afternoon. The pub would be starting to fill up. Her normal job would occupy her fully tonight: drunks in the pub, same as it ever was.

Tess felt her chest tighten, her stomach knot. On the list in front of her, a third of the way down, sandwiched between Kyle Dixon and Frank Duncan. John Djukic. Employed driving a water-truck at the mine. There he was, the man who'd tried to kick her to death and got away with it. According to the roster Johnno Djukic was commuting from Esperance, five days on four days off, and living part-time in a donga at the mine site village. Djukic: ginger mullet and coal-black eyes, bastard offspring of an alcoholic Scottish mother and a foul-tempered Serbian father. Ending up with the worst of all their genes. Djukic winking, grinning and blowing her kisses across the courtroom while his lawyer weaved a tale of chaos and confusion surrounding the events in the Karratha Hotel. Creating enough reasonable doubt to let Djukic walk free.

By the time the verdict came in she'd had her own doubts. Was it really him in the centre of the melee stomping and kicking her like it was personal? She knew there were others but she hadn't been able to identify them and that was part of the problem. 'Did she have something against gingers?' his lawyer had joked. Her young colleague Pete Latham had been invalided out of the force with half an ear bitten off, a fractured eye socket and partial loss of sight in the left eye. His career over before it really began. Johnno Djukic. Had he really tried to kill her? As far as Tess was concerned the answer was still yes.

'What's the matter?' It was Greg Fisher, in the driving seat, looking scared.

'What?'

'You're ... are you crying?'

She hadn't even realised she was. 'It's nothing. Focus on the driving.'

'Sure, boss. Sorry.'

Tess wiped her face, and kept on scanning the list. John Djukic was on a four-day break. He was due back on Monday. Three days' time.

'Bloody big,' Buckley agreed.

'State of the art,' Bruce Yelland informed them with a proud sweep of the arm.

'Hole in the ground,' Cato was thinking to himself.

The sun clipped the summit of Mount Barren. The dark clouds that he earlier thought would pass safely to the south had crept up behind the ranges and now boiled with the storm they carried within. Inky-purple cumulonimbus bubbled with pinks, oranges, greys and blues. The wind occasionally swelled into gusts that slapped the ute side-on. It was late in the day and extremely short notice, big boss Marnus van der Kuyp had pointed out through a fixed smile, but he was sure he could rustle something up. Yelland had been pulled out of a mine crisis-planning meeting to do the honours. No, he informed Cato tersely, holding on to his civil tongue like the true pro he was, they weren't actually planning to have a crisis. Cato was none the wiser. The tour would be the severely abridged version. Cato and Buckley let Bruce Yelland know they were duly appreciative.

Van der Kuyp had already instructed Human Resources to provide a list of all Western Minerals on-site and fly-in fly-out employees on the understanding that the list would be treated with confidentiality and employee privacy in mind. Cato had nodded and smiled that he understood, which wasn't the same as agreeing to comply. The tour was an optional extra, not immediately germane–that word again–to the investigation but Cato was beginning to get a gut feeling that the mine was central to uncovering what had happened to Flipper. The severely abridged version of the tour would suit him fine, for now. He just wanted to get his head around what was going on in this bloody big state-of-the-art hole in the ground. And whether it might have cost a man his life.

A huge three-hundred-tonne yellow tip truck rumbled past them in a dust cloud, a kids' Tonka toy on steroids. Bruce Yelland nodded towards it, uncurling a finger from the steering wheel in casual greeting. 'In its raw form the nickel in there is worth about twenty thousand dollars a tonne. In simplistic terms, and leaving out the processing and refining stages, each container on each roadtrain taking the nickel from here to Esperance port is worth about a quarter of a million. That's just one container on one day. Do the sums for a week, a month, a year.'

As far as Cato was concerned it was Monopoly money, currency of la-la land, too big to comprehend. It was those meaningless graphs and charts at the end of the evening news, when you're putting the kettle on before coming back for something that makes more sense, like the sport and the weather. Except those graphs and charts had all been pointing south the last few weeks while the experts slaughtered chickens, scrutinised their innards and confidently predicted financial apocalypse. Yelland obviously knew the apocalypse was meant for everyone everywhere else.

'This is a fifty-year mine. It cost two billion dollars to establish. That means Western Minerals Group is here for the long haul. Hopetoun's days as a collection of fishing shacks are well and truly over.'

'So the odd body here and there isn't likely to get in the way of business then?' Cato commented, not really expecting an answer.

Yelland shrugged, he didn't seem too sure of the point of the question. 'We've got mines all over the world. Africa,

North and South America, Asia, you name it. Of course we care about our employees and we always aim to do the best by them. But this is the real world, the show must go on. Death? All part of the circle of life, I think someone once said.'

'Simba,' said Jim Buckley.

'What?' Both Cato and Yelland turned to look at him.

'The Lion King,' he announced confidently.

Detective Tim Delaney didn't return Stuart Miller's messages or texts until close of business. Miller was nearly climbing the walls with frustration by the time the call came through. Delaney sounded far away and on the edge of mobile reception; he quickly got to the point.

'Why the interest in her?'

'The paper said she was the last to see Chapman; she gave you your photofit. So who is she, how does she know him, and how come you know her?'

'Stuart, are you playing games with me?'

'What?'

Miller didn't have a clue what he was on about but something had suddenly shifted and he needed to grab it before it slipped away again. He made a stab in the dark.

'She's the one that got away. When you dusted off the cold-case files a few weeks ago you finally got around to checking MOs in other states' crime lists. It's the kind of information resource and cooperation that didn't really exist back in 1981, not in a big way anyway. The best you were hoping for was another body but you hit jackpot – a survivor.'

'How long have you known?'

Well he'd had all afternoon to brood and speculate but it was about thirty seconds, truth be told. Instead he enigmatically said, 'I've got my contacts.'

'You didn't mention them before. Stuart, I don't need to be telling a man with your experience that this isn't a game.'

That's progress, thought Miller, he was no longer a silly old codger, he was 'a man with experience', even if he was making it up as he went along.

Delaney seemed to come to a decision.

'We're chasing our arses from Pannawonica to Paraburdoo up here ...' Hence the distant drop-out quality of the call, Miller realised, 'and you're going to stick your nose into this whatever I say, aren't you?'

'Yes.'

'So let's agree to go sharesies. If you come up with anything let me know first, okay?'

Miller nodded but if Delaney couldn't see it down the phone then maybe it didn't count. 'I need a name and a current contact number for her, the survivor.'

'Too late, she's dead.'

Miller gripped the phone tighter. 'When? How?'

'Eight years ago. Topped herself.'

'So where did you get the photofit from?'

'She gave one to Bunbury Detectives at the time. We've enhanced it. We decided to keep her death out of the papers so it wouldn't muddy the waters.'

Miller rubbed at his temples, trying to get a grasp on his thoughts. 'Any relatives?'

'Stuart, I don't want you bothering them just to satisfy your curiosity. They've been through enough already. How would that help find him?'

'Fair point. I just ... I don't know, they might say something which means nothing to them, or you, but makes absolute sense to me.' He gave an exasperated sigh. 'Look I really need to see the case notes. I'm working half-blind here.'

'No can do, mate. Not allowed.' Another thought pause from Delaney's end. 'There's a brother; I'll call him and see if he wants to talk to you. Don't hold your breath.'

Delaney rang off. Stuart Miller sat with the phone in his hand and a stupid smirk on his face. He hadn't pulled a stunt like that in over thirty years.

Friday evening in Hopetoun, nearly mid-October, summer just around the corner. In another couple of weeks the clocks would go backwards, or forwards, or whatever it was they did for daylight saving and it would still be light right now. Not dark, cold, windy, and pissing down. If Tess woke up this instant and somebody told her it was still mid-winter she wouldn't have been surprised. In fact it would come as a relief. It was really all a dream, no Flipper, no Cato. No Johnno Djukic.

'Want one?' Greg Fisher held out a bag of jelly dinosaurs.

'Thanks.'

She took a couple and stuffed both in her mouth: green and purple flavour. She washed them down with a gulp of thermos coffee. They were parked on the gravel by the new tennis courts, halfway along Veal Street, waiting for patrons to come driving up from the pub so they could breathalyse them. Simple pleasures, but in this weather nobody was going anywhere.

Tess had called in at home for a shower, a bite to eat, and to fill the thermos before joining Greg for the evening shift. Melissa had texted her to say she was at a friend's house and would probably sleep over. Tess hadn't met any of her daughter's friends properly yet but was relieved that Melissa had some. Greg crunched away absent-mindedly on a packet of chips. 'Thins,' it said on the packet, as if just saying it made it magically true. Cops: if the bad guys don't get you, the junk food surely will. Tess looked at her partner. Greg was already beginning to show evidence of the jowly, slack-gutted, forty year old he would become. Not that she could talk. It was a while since her figure showed the benefits of the regular netball she used to play, a long while.

Greg misread her look. 'Want one?'

He offered his packet of Thins up for inspection. Honey soy chicken, sort of. Tess dug her hand in and grabbed a few.

'Play time.' Greg chucked his chip packet onto the back seat, started the engine, flicked on the flashing lights and put the wipers up to full blast to clear the screen of driving rain.

A low-slung souped-up white Falcon ute was tearing up the road from the pub, veering a little from side to side and doof-doof-doofing at full blast. The lit-up police wagon could have been a pensioner on a gopher for all the notice the ute took as it passed in a rain-soaked blur. Tess held on to the sissy handle above her door and braced herself: the paddy wagon skidded on the gravel as they screeched away from their parking spot in hot pursuit. Ahead of them, at the top of the hill leading out of town, was the one and only roundabout. The ute sailed across it without slowing. Tess yelled at Greg not to do the same. He didn't, quite. Now it was open road for fifty kilometres to Ravensthorpe. If the ute felt so inclined, it could leave Tess and Greg behind; the paddy wagon would be no match for its speed, and visibility was so bad they were never going to get a fix on the rego number. Instead the ute slowed and stopped. Greg Fisher thumped the wheel with the palm of his hand.

'Fucking dickheads.'

It was a dangerous look in his eyes, the kind Tess had never seen before, not on him anyway.

'You stay here. I'll deal with this.'

She unclipped her seatbelt and got out. Greg stepped out of his side but stayed put with the door open and called in the ute rego for a check. Tess walked forward braced against the wind and rain, torch in one hand, breathalyser in the other. As she neared the driver's door the window rolled down, double-doofing the world outside.

'Turn the music off please.'

The driver: late twenties, three days' growth of stubble, and a strong smell of cigarettes, Jack Daniels and Coke. And BO. Nice.

'Sure mate. Any problem?'

'Speed and dangerous driving for one thing.'

'That's two isn't it?'

The ute erupted into hoarse cackling as if it was the wittiest line this century.

Tess held out her hand and snapped her fingers. 'Licence please.'

While the driver fumbled for it, Tess leaned down to look at his fellow travellers. In the front passenger seat a similar model: male, late twenties, grungy bogan. In the back another male: same vintage but slightly cleaner cut, verging on a pretty-boy, what she could see of him. He was flanked by two females, maybe he was the bait. One of the women seemed to be conjoined to the pretty-boy's face and was tugging at his zipper, oblivious to the audience. Tess ahemmed and shone her torch on to the happy couple. They disentangled and heads turned.

'Oh, hi Mum,' said Melissa, as if she'd just come home from school.

12

Friday, October 10th. Nearly midnight.

Amphetamines, ecstasy and GHB–fantasy, the so-called date-rape drug–all in small amounts, for personal use, and enough grog to fuel the First Fleet. That was the haul from the souped-up Falcon ute and the cashed-up mine contractors. Plus a video camera and some stick mags. Melissa and her mate Stacey were both high as kites on the eckies and at least half a dozen alcopops. The men all stone cold sober according to the blood tests. Tess shuddered at the thought of where and how the night might have ended. The men were in custody at the Ravensthorpe lockup. Given what they had in the car, their apparent intentions, and superior horsepower, Tess still wondered why they stopped, and why, once busted, they remained calm and compliant with just the two cops on a dark and stormy night with no one around. Maybe it was just that they were old hands, they'd been there before and knew that the odds were in favour of them being back on the streets tomorrow.

Melissa's friend Stacey was back in the bosom of her family. No gushing thanks from her parents for rescuing their daughter from the clutches of evil intent, just dirty looks for Tess and Greg as if they somehow were responsible for their wayward child. Finally Melissa too was back in the bosom of her family, Tess Maguire. Tess sitting at the kitchen table at midnight with a lukewarm Lemon Ruski and her fourteen year old daughter down the hallway sleeping off a big sesh. Senior Sergeant Tess Maguire in her government-issue kitchen that was yet to feel like a home. Maybe if she put some photos on display instead of always leaving them in the tattered envelopes now in front of her on the kitchen table. Outside the wind was howling as if in terminal pain. Rain pounded the tin roof. Somewhere nearby a loose gate banged with each gust and a dog barked itself hoarse. Tess's throat and chest felt so tight she thought she might never breathe again. What scared her much more though was the realisation that she wished it so. She could quite readily go to sleep and not wake up.

The photos: a wedding in Broome at Cable Beach, her first posting after Cato; flowers in her hair, a simple dress. Slim. Barefoot. Her new husband, Mike, with his arms around her, looking down into her eyes. Another one where he's standing behind her, his arms crossed over her shoulders and resting low on her stomach, Melissa already in there kicking to be free. Tess looking straight at the camera, challenging it to contradict this happy day and the camera obliging, catching Mike looking elsewhere. In the direction of that woman from the bank.

More photos. Mike no longer there. Tess with Melissa, now four: a birthday party, pink everywhere. Still in Broome, in the backyard, Tess waiting for Mr Right. He was a no-show. Then another: Melissa, a pre-teen beginning to discover black, both in her dress and her moods. Another backyard party, Tess's fortieth? Another posting; another town; another government-issue house; yet another school for Melissa for year seven, Karratha Primary.

John Djukic. He had tried to take her life away, she was sure of it. He'd failed. Or had he? Tess had felt utterly hopeless and powerless as those boots and fists rained down on her. She had been completely violated. It was a shock that still numbed, long after the fractured bones, ruptured organs, cuts and bruises had healed. Something was broken in there and it would never mend. Melissa had picked up on it. How could she not? Melissa had picked it up and taken a portion of it into her own fragile young soul, a darkness shared. Tess took a gulp of the Ruski; it tasted sickly sweet. Where had she picked up the taste for this crap? Mike? The Pilbara? The Force? She was well rid of all three–except she hadn't left the Force, yet. She flushed the remains of the drink down the kitchen sink and flopped on to her unmade bed. Tess needed to sleep but knew it wouldn't come quickly. It never did. She looked at the bottle of prescription sleeping pills on her bedside table. Looked for longer than she usually did, then turned off the light and lay there.

The rain drumming on the air-conditioning unit outside his motel room was loud enough to wake the dead. Cato Kwong was already wide awake and it was nothing to do with the full cup of instant coffee in his hand. He sat on the bed with the lists of names from the mine and the contractors collated by Greg Fisher at the end of the day. Also strewn across the floral-patterned doona, the photographs of Flipper taken at the post-mortem. Was that only two nights ago? Dr Harry Lewis's preliminary findings had been typed up into a hard copy. That and the photographs were waiting for him in an envelope at motel reception when he got back from the tour of the mine. Pam the inquisitive receptionist had reluctantly handed it over with curiosity creasing her face.

'Package for you, Inspector.'

Cato wondered how his game of Chinese Whispers was going, what twisted form his little rumour had assumed by now, and whether anything would come of it. Already, news of the floating head had sparked an inquiry from the Esperance Express and Cato had flick-passed the journo over to DI Hutchens for a snow job. It was only a matter of time before he'd be fielding more calls. He estimated another day at most before the goalposts shifted on the Flipper inquiry.

Jim Buckley had headed out to the pub to grab a meal and, by the determined look on his face, a skinful of drink. Cato bought takeaway fish and chips from the Taste of the Toun and watched some TV in his room. Friday night crime, solved in an hour–if only. He'd phoned Jane, hoping to talk to Jake, and talked instead to an answering machine. Maybe that wasn't the worst thing that could have happened. He and Jane were running out of civility. She hid hers behind a mask of determined happiness. Fair enough. She'd borne the brunt of his bitterness and disappointment at being hung out to dry by the corruption inquiry. Who would want to continue living with that? Jake was somebody he hadn't really got to know yet, his own son. He wondered if it was already too late for that now.

Around mid evening a vehicle had gone thundering past Cato's window with the kind of doof-doof racket he hadn't heard since he left the city at the beginning of the week. It almost made him homesick. Almost. Friday night in Hopetoun had rolled over into Saturday and here was Cato Kwong sitting on his bed thinking about a dead man, a dead Chinaman. He'd seen that look on their faces. Buckley. Tess. Greg. The ranger. A dead Chinaman, should be right up your street. Like a dead whitey should be right up theirs? He'd had it in Perth as well. Gang fights in Northbridge; he'd been part of the Gang Squad for a while. They figured he'd have an insight into the Vietnamese street thugs and their way of thinking. Sure. Insight. It comes with the shape of the eyes.

There were times when Cato forgot he was of Chinese descent. He didn't know the language; the last person to speak it in his family was a great-grandparent over in Victoria, a survivor of a goldfields pogrom. But now his little sister, Susan, was combining study of Mandarin with her MBA, aiming to cash in big time on the mining boom and the voracious Chinese appetite for Australian red dust. Chinese-ness had not been a significant part of their upbringing. Indeed, his parents, in particular his father, seemed at pains to make it not so. Cato Kwong didn't feel Chinese, however that was meant to feel. He could go for hours and hours, even days, forgetting that he was Chinese. But usually, as the song goes, there was always something there to remind him.

Cato looked at a photo of Flipper lying on the steel table at Ravensthorpe Hospital, then at the list of names. All accounted for, all present and correct. So who was Flipper? Cato thought back to day one and the Chinaman he'd seen in the phone booth as he drove into town. He remembered now the fluoro overalls the man was wearing, yellow and blue. Tess had filled him in on the boomtown colour code: so he was a contractor, not the orange of mine staff. Cato scanned the contractor lists. There were four major contractors and a couple of minor subcontractors. Four of the lists had no Chinese-sounding names on them at all. That left Dunstan Industries and SaS Personnel, twenty Chinese on the first and sixteen on the second. He grabbed a pen and notebook and jotted down a to-do list for the following day.

Jim Buckley terminated the call and put the mobile in his jacket pocket. He stood on the short fishing jetty at the end of the groyne, did a long loud satisfying piss into the Southern Ocean and belched a bourbon and Coke concoction. The rain had eased to a spiteful persistent drizzle that sent cold rivulets down the back of his neck. The wind was still blustery but had done its worst; in another few hours it would be as weak as a kitten. In another few hours it would be dawn. A gust lifted the lid on the rubbish bin and added a pungent mix of fish bait and beer to the salty breeze. Shadows flitted across the spill of yellow lamplight and a jittery seagull took flight from its perch on a mooring post. The clouds were already breaking up; a half-moon and a million brilliant stars that would never be seen in the city shimmered through.

Jim Buckley saw none of the stars and felt not one whisper of the wind. The cold drops of rain running off his face and down his neck might have been the soft warm breath of a lover for all he was aware. Jim Buckley had cancer. It was eating away at his colon and secondaries were spreading through the rest of his body. The biopsy results had confirmed it. Game over. He should have been given the results at a face-to-face but his GP had finally relented, they went back a long way, and over the phone late today he'd at last been prepared to confirm what Buckley had known and denied to himself for the last two months. Jim Buckley, widower at fifty, grandad at fifty-two, would most likely be dead at fifty-three.

Buckley thought about his parting words to his brother-in-law and smiled grimly at the idea that he might have done one last good thing before he kicked the bucket. In the morning he'd get Kwong, Tess, and Greg Fisher and together they'd wrap up a last little bit of business. Real police business, not this fucking ghost-chasing bullshit. He flicked his cigarette into the churning water below him and belched some more Jim Beam into the cold night air. He was sick of Hopetoun, he was going to pack his bags and go home to die.

The gravel crunched softly behind him. When it came, the blow to his head felt like a sweet release.

13

Saturday, October 11th. Dawn.

The way the body was lying, it was obvious he hadn't seen it coming. Dark blood stained the old wooden planks of the jetty. Jim Buckley's legs were twisted at a grotesque angle. Cato Kwong rose from his crouching position and rubbed his eyes with the palms of both hands. He wished he could erase the image, rub out the day and start again.

The call had come at about 5.00 from a fisherman, keen to get out early to take advantage of the calmer conditions and clear skies. He'd rung Tess and she had passed the news on to Cato and Greg Fisher. They were all together now in a stunned silent circle around Jim Buckley. Dr Terhorst had been roused from his bed and was concluding his preliminary examination but the results were plain to see. Jim Buckley's skull had been caved in by a soccer ball–sized rock which lay about a metre away spattered with hair and blood. Cato shook his head trying to clear it; he already felt out of his depth with the Flipper case. Now this.

The rain had only ceased in the last hour or so. They might get a partial or full footprint from the soggy gravel but Cato wasn't feeling optimistic this morning. CSI Hopetoun, good luck. He snapped on some crime-scene gloves and crouched down again, reaching under Buckley and into his jacket pocket. A mobile phone, still turned on. Cato checked the recent call lists, outward and received, and made a note of the numbers. The trouser pockets yielded keys, loose change, and a wallet. Cato flipped it open: credit cards, a Medicare card and eighty-five dollars in notes. An ATM receipt timed for mid evening the previous night. Driver's licence, police ID, a Perth video store membership, a photo of a toddler. All seemed present and correct. Cato passed everything to Tess for bagging.

It was close to six now. The town was beginning to wake up to a blue sky with a few wispy trailing white clouds and the fresh smell that a good downpour brought. Even though it was a Saturday, shift workers would still be heading out to the mine either under their own steam or on the bus that picked them up outside the general store. Some of the fishermen were also early starters plus there were the early-morning joggers and walkers. Tess had parked her wagon across the entry road to the groyne, effectively blocking any traffic from coming near but pedestrians were still able to get through. Already some curious ghouls were making their way over. Tess nodded to Greg Fisher who snapped out of his daze and into action, spreading his arms wide in shepherding fashion. Dr Terhorst was telling Cato what he already knew but at least it was now official.

'Do you know who would do such a thing?'

'If I did I wouldn't be standing here, Doctor.'

'Quite so, do you think it's connected to your other inquiry?'

Cato shrugged. 'I doubt it, we weren't getting anywhere.'

Terhorst patted Cato's shoulder and walked towards his car. 'I'll arrange for Harry Lewis to come back to Ravensthorpe then?'

Cato nodded, flipped open his phone, scrolled the number for DI Mick Hutchens and took a deep breath.

Hutchens was due in Hopetoun by late morning, midday at the latest. He'd instructed Cato to say nothing to any news media; they were expected to be all over it within hours. They'd been able to hold back the tide on Flipper but nobody doubted that this story was going to spread, and quickly. Besides, this was now a real job and a priority. Cato knew Hutchens well enough by now; the man would be at battle stations and relishing a major high-profile inquiry. If anyone was to front the cameras it would be him. He would be bringing a handful of his team from Albany and half a dozen others were flying down from Perth Major Crime later today.

'We'll fingerprint, DNA, and flog the whole fucking town if we have to.'

His last words as he slammed the phone down on Cato. A dead cop, all stops would be pulled out, even for a bloke that Hutchens himself had called a useless fuckwit only two days earlier. But now it was different; Buckley was family. This was going to be a circus, Cato realised gloomily as he snapped his phone shut.

Seven-thirty. The locus was now taped off and secured. Greg and Tess were erecting a tarpaulin over that part of the jetty with the help of the two uniforms from Ravensthorpe: Biddulph and Abbott. Entry to and from the whole groyne area was now blocked by Tess's car and a couple of the hapless security men borrowed from the mine. A statement had been taken from the fisherman who found the body. The motel had been instructed not to clean Jim Buckley's room and to keep it locked until further notice. There was no more to do until the Mick Hutchens Circus hit town. Cato knew his chances of having any further connection with either the Flipper or Buckley cases were practically zero. Jim Buckley, no longer just a gruff, frustrating pain in the arse. He glanced down at the lifeless body: Jim Buckley, now a murder inquiry.

'Not small is it?' Greg Fisher observed as he secured the last tarpaulin guy rope to a railing.

'What?' said Cato, coming out of his deep, dark place.

'The rock.'

Cato looked at it, thought about Buckley's height and size. 'No.'

'They'd have to be reasonably strong.'

Cato turned away from him. 'Let's leave the detecting to the grown-ups, mate. They'll be here soon enough.'

Greg appeared hurt. Cato felt guilty for a moment but thought better of it. This wasn't a job for fragile egos, you couldn't afford that until you got into management. Tess finished tying up her corner of the tarp and gave Cato a reproachful look. She looked like shit.

'Big night last night?' Cato asked, cupping his hand to his mouth in a drinking gesture.

Then Tess's hands were at his throat and she was in his face, tears welling in her eyes.

'Shut your hole you smug bastard. You've failed here. Why don't you just fuck off home.' Greg tried to tug her away but she shook him off. 'Tell your mate Hutchens and all the other bent mongrels from Perth: we don't need your kind of help.'

Cato walked away, face as dark as yesterday's clouds.

Greg caught up with him at The Deck Cafe, the one place left that he and Buckley had not got around to trying. Cato didn't need the coffee from the Taste of the Toun; he already had a bitter taste in his mouth and Justin's Snak-Attack was closed. Normally it would have been open by now for the mine managers' early shift takeaway cappuccinos, but not today. So it was The Deck. Cato was at a table outside, his face lifted to the early morning sun and his eyes closed. If he left them that way, and didn't think too much, he could almost be in paradise. When he opened them he saw Greg Fisher studying him.

'Yes?' he said irritably.

'I used to dream about you.'

Cato wasn't sure where this was going. 'Yes?' he said again.

'You were on the recruitment poster at the Careers Expo. When all me mates were saying, "Fisher's joining the monarch" and calling me "coconut" and "sellout" I'd think about you on that poster. Even in my sleep. You'd talk to me, say, "Don't listen to them dickheads, Gregory".'

Cato smiled for the first time that day.

Greg was still standing up, looking down at him. '"Step Forward". That's what it says on the recruitment poster. "Step Forward". But on the day we need you to take charge you walk away. What's going on?'

Cato swallowed his first smile of the day. Greg nodded to himself, point made.

'Tess is having trouble with her daughter, Melissa. We pulled over a car last night. Melissa was in it. She's fourteen.'

Cato was all ears, he didn't even know Tess had a daughter, never mind a troublesome one. But then again why would he? They hadn't spoken meaningfully since he left her. 'Go on.'

'She was with a mate and three blokes, high as a kite on eckies and alcopops. The blokes had GHB, eckies, grog, and a video camera. They had plans.'

Cato's blood thumped in his ears. 'Is she okay?'

'Yeah, Tess got a fright though.'

'Where are they now?'

'Ravy lockup.'

'Charges?'

Greg shrugged impotently. 'Possession. Dangerous driving. You know the score, it's hard to keep people locked up on something as vague as "Evil Intent". Likely to be released this morning.'

'Not before I have a word with them. Stay here. You and Tess keep the scene secure and wait for Hutchens. I'll be back later.'

Cato took his coffee with him and jumped into the Stock Squad four-wheel drive.

He didn't know why he was tearing up to Ravensthorpe to confront the sleazebags. It had nothing to do with him. Maybe he wanted to do something to show he cared about someone other than himself. Do something? Like what? Maybe he just wanted to hit somebody. Maybe he just wanted to get out of town for a while, away from Tess Maguire, away from Jim Buckley, and away from his own failures. Maybe he couldn't stop thinking about his damn self after all. He switched on the radio as a distraction and hit the search button until he got some reception. The Four Tops–'Walk Away Renée'.

Step Forward–Walk Away.

Young Fisher had landed one on him. He found Classic FM and settled into some cello. The sun rose higher over waves of yellow-flowered canola, cabbage-whites danced on the soft morning breeze. The sky was now virtually cloudless. Wagtails, wattlebirds and currawongs flitted and swooped among the roadside gums. It was a great day to be alive. Had Jim Buckley made an enemy in the pub? Not hard to these days: too many drinks, a nudge, a wrong look, winning at pool when you weren't meant to, being in the wrong place at the wrong time. This was the golden age of the one-punch killer. Buckley stuck out like a sore thumb as a cop; he knew he did and thrived on it. Put him in a tutu and pink wig and you'd still clock him for a walloper. Had someone recognised him, somebody with an old grudge? Buckley had a reputation. He never backed down, never shirked a fight, sometimes happy to start one if he thought it necessary, or if he was in the mood. Cato needed to speak to the pub manager and patrons. He stopped himself. DI Hutchens and his team would have all that well covered.

Was it anything to do with the last few days? They weren't getting anywhere with Flipper as far as they could tell. What else? They hadn't been involved in the fight at the mine, that was all over by the time they arrived. Tess had taken him off in her car, what was that all about? Was that where she got the oil on his past, from Buckley? Maybe, probably, but was it germane? Cato smiled, Buckley's word. Germane. Then it hit him.

I've clocked him.

Justin. Snak-Attack.

Is it germane to your floater?

A face from the past, dealing in speed and ecstasy. That's what was found in the car last night with Tess's daughter. And GHB: was Justin back in business and branching out into the date-rape drug? Justin Woodward. Closed for business this morning and yesterday morning, missing the trade from the early shift. Why? Big night? Lie in? Done a runner? Woodward, not answering Cato's question about who or what he was hiding from. Justin's look of relief when they were called away to the fight at the mine. They hadn't had a chance to revisit Woodward to find out what all that was about. Was he connected to the sleazebags and the car full of drugs? Was that what got Jim Buckley killed? Cato was looking forward to his chat with the boys in the Ravy lockup.

Stuart Miller hadn't slept a wink. Jim Buckley's midnight call was a bolt from the blue. Jim had been convinced that Davey Arthurs was there in Hopetoun. He would do a bit of checking this morning and then they'd bring Arthurs in. The worst he could be was wrong. Miller had tossed and turned all night; Jenny had finally given up on him and retreated to the spare room for some quality sleep. His gut was churning; what if it really was Arthurs after all this time? He chuckled at the irony of a plodding time-serving old bastard like Jim Buckley nabbing the prize. Miller checked his watch; heading for midmorning. Had they made their move on the man who might be Arthurs? He texted through to Buckley: trying not to sound too desperate and readying himself for disappointment.

how's it going? stu

In the meantime he was en route to Bunbury, a forty-minute drive away. Detective Tim Delaney had phoned back with a number for a Brian Munro, the brother of the woman who had survived an Arthurs attack only to commit suicide a few years later. Stuart had rung the number, still not knowing the name of the dead woman; Brian Munro had provided it anyway – Vicki. They were due to meet in half an hour. Munro's wife would be out shopping and the kids had long since left home. Point taken; this was just between the two of them.

Brian Munro lived in a spacious two-storey new building overlooking the Indian Ocean. The house had been designed so that the bedrooms were downstairs and the kitchen and family room were upstairs, opening out on to a wide balcony equipped with a huge barbecue. It was a house designed around the view and the lifestyle afforded to its inhabitants. It was probably worth not much short of two million. The temperature had dropped from its uncomfortable midweek highs, freshened by overnight rain. Out on the choppy sea a couple of kite surfers skimmed across the spray. Munro stepped out on to the balcony from the kitchen bearing a tray with cups, milk and a coffee plunger. He was around forty-five with a slight build and the bookish look of a librarian or academic. In fact, according to Tim Delaney, he was a sharp businessman with half a dozen hospitality companies dotted around the South-West. And, Delaney had added unnecessarily, not to be underestimated.

Munro quickly got to the point. 'So what do you want to know and why?'

Miller wasn't sure how much ignorance he should come clean with, so he gave Munro a bit of his own history dating back to that day in May 1973. As his story unfolded he could see Munro relaxing and accepting him for what he said he was.

'You sound a lot like him. The way you talk. Of course we didn't know him as Davey or Derek. To us he was Bob.'

'Bob?' This was a new one to Miller.

Munro nodded. 'Bob Kerr.'

Miller nearly choked on his coffee. Arthurs had adopted the name of Bobby Kerr, Sunderland FA Cup captain. The sentimental little sadist, talk about tarnishing a fond memory. He explained away his splutter as a mistimed cough.

Munro took a sip from his own cup. 'Do you want to see a photo of Vicki?'

'Sure.'

They put down their coffees and went into the open-plan living area. On a shelf unit, housing mainly home entertainment gizmos and DVDs, there was a row of photographs. Miller spotted her immediately: the twenty-something year old in her graduation gown in a photo taken in 1986, before she met 'Bob'. Long blonde hair and a knowing smile, a dead ringer for the girl on the mantelpiece in Sunderland. Arthurs himself was no catalogue model and a good ten to fifteen years her senior. What did she see in him?

'Vicki's first marriage had fizzled out. No spark. She said Bob made her laugh, not just the funny accent, apparently he had a great sense of humour.'

Munro gave a short bitter laugh. He pulled out a heavy thick binder with more photos and flicked through the pages.

'This is her after that bastard finished with her.'

Miller tried not to flinch. The upper right hand side of her head had required major reconstructive surgery. It had left her horribly disfigured and, by the look of the photo, blinded on that side too. Miller drew in his breath sharply.

'When did this happen?'

'Nineteen ninety-eight, February, they'd been together about four years by then. They were talking of finally getting married later that year. They already had a child at that point. Shelley, three.'

Miller didn't want to but he knew he had to ask, 'Did she ... the little girl ...?'

Munro's sad shake of the head and brimming eyes said enough.

Miller pushed on, hating himself for it but determined to know. 'How come Vicki survived?'

Munro pulled himself back together. 'The bastard didn't hit her hard enough and his little electric gizmo didn't work. Must have blown a fuse or something. Who knows? The police at the time also speculated that he may have been interrupted, a knock at the door maybe.' Munro closed the photo album and put it back on the shelf. 'It destroyed her. She pretty well died then anyway, the day he took away Shelley. Vicki was half blind, disfigured, brain-damaged. She could no longer talk or walk properly. That nasty mad fucker needs to be put down.'

Miller nodded. 'The newspaper mentioned a sighting of him in 1998?'

'We gave the police a description at the time. We did have photographs of him, well Vicki did, but he took them, along with the negatives.'

Clearing up after himself, learning from the Sunderland and Adelaide crimes.

'The sighting?' Miller pressed.

'It was towards the end of that year. Vicki was still in hospital, she spent nearly nine months in there one way or another. One day she looked out of her ward window and there he was down in the car park, just standing and staring. Maybe looking for a chance to finish what he started. She told the police but they weren't able to find any trace of him. One even suggested she might have imagined it.'

'The description you gave, that's what's been in the papers recently?'

'Pretty much. We gave more detail at the time but I suppose the main thing they're interested in now is what they need to make up the photofit.'

'Anything that you thought was important that didn't appear in the recent press reports?'

Munro scratched his chin then fingered the sleeve of his shirt. 'There was this tattoo, a crude thing he'd done himself, the letters "CK". As he told us his name was Bob Kerr we assumed it was a family member.'

Miller grimaced; that at least nailed for him that Arthurs and Chapman and Kerr were the same man. But who was CK?

'Anything else?'

Munro shook his head. 'I remember Vicki saying something strange to me one day after it all happened. She said she used to try to ask him about his past, his early life as a kid. And he used to always say he didn't have a past. But that's not really useful for identifying him is it?'

Miller didn't know what to make of it. Munro was looking at his watch; maybe Mrs Munro was due home soon. Miller had one last thing he needed to know.

'Vicki's suicide, when was that, what happened?'

'It was just over a year later, early in 2000. One night she climbed up the lookout tower just back up the hill there and jumped off. We found her the following morning.' He choked on his words. 'I didn't even know she'd gone out.'

'No doubts about the cause of death? Definitely suicide?'

Munro looked pained at the very idea. 'As I said, she died inside the day her daughter was taken. She was an empty shell after that. Besides, she pinned a note to herself.'

'What did it say?'

Munro shrugged irritably and checked his watch again. 'It said, "Had enough. Vicki." Speaking of which ...'

It was time to go. As Munro ushered him out the front door he murmured, 'I said it to Delaney and I'll say it to you. We don't want to talk to you people again. Either do your jobs and find him or close the book, so we can too.'

They shook hands and Miller turned to leave.

'But ...' Munro breathed deeply and Miller turned back. 'If you do find him, do me a favour and kill the bastard. Or God help me, I will.'

The scenic lookout tower atop Marlston Hill stood twenty-five metres high. From it you could see Brian Munro's house, Bunbury port, Koombana Bay, most of the city, and the Indian Ocean. The spiral concrete staircase left Miller straining for breath after the climb. The parapet was nearly chest height on him. He looked down at the concrete car park below. How and why would a half-blind, brain-damaged and movement-impaired woman come all the way up here one night, clamber over the high parapet and chuck herself to her death? There must be easier ways of topping yourself. Or did she have help from Davey Arthurs? It wouldn't have been beyond Arthurs to squeeze a suicide note out of her or forge her handwriting, nobody was going to be looking too closely at it.

Maybe Vicki Munro did do it all by herself but if she didn't and Arthurs was involved it raised two new issues about him. First, he was becoming very meticulous at covering his tracks and second, he was no longer restricting himself to his usual method of killing.

'They've gone.'

'What?'

'Gone. We let them go about an hour ago. Bailed for a court appearance at a later date. Got their IDs and driving licences and all that. Well-behaved, polite blokes, considering.'

The Ravy desk sergeant, Bernie Tilbrook, was fresh back off a week's holiday, fishing and camping over at Bremer Bay on the far side of the national park. He had a farmer's red tan and a well-fed face, ripe for impending retirement. He liked to see a bit of good in everybody, generally. All this Cato gleaned from a bit of introductory Stock Squad–style country banter.

Cato growled. 'Considering what?'

'Considering what they were suspected of possibly planning to do. All speculation of course, could have been just planning a party, all consensual and that.' Tilbrook winked.

'With two fourteen year old kids? And they're all what, pushing twenty-five, thirty?'

'The girls had told them they were eighteen. You can't tell these days can you?'

Cato shook his head, he wasn't going to buy into this. 'Their papers?'

'What?'

'Their process papers, you did process them? Photograph them?'

Bernie Tilbrook was beginning to lose his post-vacation joie de vivre. 'A bit of civility wouldn't go amiss. Yes we did process them and photograph them. We are capable of doing things just like you do them up in Perth. Sometimes better.'

'That's not the first time I've heard that today.' Cato smiled thinly, belatedly attempting a soothing manner.

'Doubt it'll be the last either,' said Tilbrook. 'The book's over there.'

Cato opened the file and looked at the names and charges. He read them out loud to himself. 'Jonah Silver, twenty-seven; Bevan Tuckey, twenty-eight. Neither seems to have any previous. Both work at the mine.'

'Doesn't everybody these days?' muttered Tilbrook, without looking up.

The last name grabbed his attention. 'Freddy Bataam, twenty-six.'

Cato turned the pages and found the photo. Hair a bit longer, but still without a doubt it was the handsome, youthful clean-cut face of Lieutenant Riri Yusala, Indonesian Navy.

14

Saturday, October 11th. Late morning.

'Pretty-Boy.'

Tess recognised him straight away, but not as Riri Yusala. She knew the name from Cato's meeting updates but had not got around to digesting the Flipper file so she had not seen the photo from the Missing Persons website. She knew him as Pretty-Boy, the one his daughter had been pawing in the back seat of the sleazebags' doof-doof ute. No wonder they'd been so well behaved: they weren't just smart about the likelihood of quick release, at least one of them really had something to hide.

'Last seen heading west,' confirmed Cato grimly.

Tess kept staring at the photograph. 'Shit.'

Cato couldn't have put it better himself. He'd asked Bernie Tilbrook, nicely, to put out an alert on the vehicle but it could be anywhere in a radius of two to three hundred kilometres by now. Cato and Tess were on their way to Justin Woodward's home. The coffee van remained firmly closed, much to the consternation of the Hopetoun yummy mummies group. Greg Fisher and the Ravy uniforms were in charge of the crime scene. DI Hutchens had texted an update: he was due in the next hour or so. If Woodward really was a contender for Jim Buckley's murder then Cato wasn't going to wait for the cavalry before checking it out. This could be his first and last chance of a sniff on this case.

Cato cast a sideways glance at Tess. 'Sorry for earlier.'

'Yeah.' She didn't meet his look, instead she pointed out of the front windscreen over towards the left. 'That's it there, just past the blue Hyundai.'

The Woodward abode was a cream-coloured fibro in

Barnett Street, running parallel with Hopetoun's main drag. They rolled to a stop outside the house. No sign of life. No car in the drive. A dirt bike leaned against a gnarled peppermint tree in the front yard. Its stand had snapped and there was mud and rust on the wheels. A tasselled and striped hammock was slung between two posts on the front porch, weighed down by a hardback book and cushion. The book was *Moby Dick*, a page corner folded over about a quarter of the way through. Further than he'd ever got, noted Cato. He rapped on the front door; a dog yapped from inside. No answer from any humans. He tried the door: locked.

They made their way down the side to a gate that would take them into the backyard. Wind chimes hung from a low-roofed pergola over the back patio, the breeze not yet strong enough to produce a sound. The dog was still yapping away but at least it was a yap rather than a big, boofy attack-dog kind of bark. The dog bowl was outside on the patio, one of those double ones with biscuits in one side and water in the other. There was no sign of a dog flap. Why had the dog been left in the house if they had gone out somewhere? Had they left in a hurry? Cato stepped towards the French doors to peer inside. There was a scraping noise behind him. He froze.

'Anything?' Tess whispered.

'No,' he hissed, heart racing.

'So why are we whispering?' she whispered again.

There was a sudden frenzy of scratches and thumps. Both Cato and Tess jumped backwards, she reaching for her gun and he stumbling and falling over an aloe vera plant. It was the dog, yapping, tail wagging, pawing at the French window.

'Fuck,' Cato barked.

He held the thumb of his left hand, it was throbbing. He'd fallen on it. Dislocated it by the looks.

Tess barely suppressed a giggle as she put her gun back into the holster. 'You okay?'

'No.' He nursed his hand between his arm and his side. 'It

looks like there's no one at home and we haven't got authority to go breaking and entering. Yet. Let's go.'

'What about the dog?'

'What?'

'The dog. It's inside, but the food and water is out here.'

'Boo hoo,' said Cato, uncharitably.

Another hundred-kilometre round trip to Tumbleweed General just to look at a dislocated thumb seemed a bit extreme. It was tempting to be anywhere else but Hopetoun when DI Hutchens and the A-team arrived, but that would be running away and Cato was sick of doing that. So he sat in the Murder Hut with half a bag of Tess's frozen peas tied to his thumb with a handkerchief. Tess looked deep in thought. The whiteboard hadn't changed much since day one. Just a few names and phone numbers and the word Flipper in the centre, ringed and question-marked.

Tess broke the silence. 'What do we do about Woodward and the rest?'

Cato shrugged. 'Pass the information on to Hutchens when he gets here. He's in charge now.'

'And Flipper and the lists of Chinese?' She prodded the piece of paper in front of her.

'Same. It's Hutchens' call from here on in.'

'Roll over and play dead, huh?'

Cato just shrugged again. It was about as articulate as he was going to be today. He could see that Tess was itching to do something and it wasn't necessarily going to be something constructive. He remembered her in his face earlier that morning. He had to admit to himself, he'd been scared of her. It wasn't as if it was the first time he'd come up against anger and potential violence but it was always from the punters and he could switch off with them. Us and Them: easy. 'Us and Us' was a little more complex and unsettling.

Tess found some paperwork to hide behind, her pen stabbed at an official form. After a few more minutes at the sharp end of her body language, Cato picked up his bag of frozen peas and headed for the door.

On the way back down to the groyne Cato passed the Snak-Attack, still closed. There was a small collection of Stepford mums, prams and toddlers resolutely gathered around Justin's picnic table as if just by their loyalty and presence they could will him to show up and make them their morning lattes. One of them recognised Cato from that day when he and Buckley had paid Justin a visit. She glared at him; clearly he was to blame for her coffee morning being ruined yet again. Maybe she was right about that.

The sun was high in the sky and had picked up strength, along with the breeze. Constable Greg Fisher was leaning against the bonnet of his paddy wagon, parked across the access road. Inquisitive souls hovered nearby, peering towards the tarp and crime-scene tape over on the jetty and trying to get a response from Fisher. He'd obviously dispensed with his public relations training and now relied upon his glare to send them packing. One resourceful ghoul had managed to evade Fisher's roadblock and kayaked straight out from the beach to inquire with a bright smile what was going on. Ravy Sergeant Paul Abbott leaned down from the jetty and crooked his finger towards her. As she edged closer, slapping the water with her bright yellow paddles, he fixed her with a stare.

'None of your fucking business, now fuck off before I arrest you.'

Abbott informed Cato that Buckley's mobile had beeped midmorning. Cato checked the message through the transparent evidence bag: a friend who didn't know yet.

how's it going? stu

Not good, mate, not good. He noted the incoming message number and added it to his list. Cato circled Buckley's body slowly. It had already changed shape, seemed to have sunk and shrunk a little. The smell was getting stronger. DI Hutchens needed to be here soon before things really started getting unpleasant.

'Speak of the devil,' Cato said under his breath.

Two unmarked white Commodores rolled up to Greg Fisher's roadblock. A short sharp exchange of words followed and Greg backed the paddy wagon out of their way. The cars bumped across the potholes and gravel to within a metre of Cato's feet, the passenger door opening on the front car before it had come to a stop. Detective Inspector Mick Hutchens: grey forward-comb fringing a grim chubby face and piercing blue eyes. Half a head shorter than Cato, he made up for it with belligerence and attitude.

'Can't trust you to do a simple fucking job. Unbelievable.'

'I'm good thanks. We're all bearing up well after the tragedy.'

Cato couldn't help himself, he had to give some lip. Somebody was in his face for the second time that day.

'Don't you fucking dare,' Hutchens hissed, sour traveller's breath blasting Cato from point blank.

He brushed past Cato and knelt down beside Buckley. Just looking, that's all he could do. Hutchens' fellow passenger was now out of the car. She seemed too young to be a detective, or was Cato just getting old? Tall. Brown hair pulled back in a businesslike ponytail, a clear-complexioned look of confidence that said Perth private school and good at sports. She stuck out her hand towards Cato.

'Lara ...'

Croft? wondered Cato.

'Sumich.'

They shook. Her grip was firm enough to let you know she was present but not trying to prove anything.

A man stepped out of the second Commodore, same vintage as Lara. He sported an overly firm handshake and a loud tie.

'DC Mark McGowan.'

'Hi Mark,' said Cato.

Lara Sumich donned some paper overshoes and set to work with a video camera, recording the scene and adding a low, soft commentary as she circled the body. McGowan followed her tracks, clicking away on the stills Nikon. With nothing to add from his own appraisal of the scene, Hutchens asked for an ambulance to be brought to take Buckley away as soon as Lara was finished. The body had lain there for four hours more than necessary, but at least it had now been perused by a real detective.

'Family?' Hutchens nodded towards Buckley.

They all looked at Cato. He realised he knew absolutely nothing about Jim Buckley because he'd never really shown any interest, until the last few days, and even that was more idle curiosity than interest. What had made Jim act so strange and troubled these last forty-eight hours? Was it anything to do with this?

'I don't know. We never really ...'

'Two grown-up sons, wife died year before last. Aneurysm. He became a grandad last year. Little girl. Samantha.'

They all looked around. It was the voice of Greg Fisher, fresh from replacing the paddy wagon at the roadblock.

A forensics team was among the squad flying down from Perth that afternoon. Hutchens had taken one look at the Hopetoun Police donga and snorted. He'd commandeered the town hall next to the telecentre and waved away the protests of the Bootscooters Club, due to hold their practice that very afternoon. The Bootscooters president, a tall woman with a five-paddock voice, would be reporting him to the shire president, she promised.

'I think you just broke her achy-breaky heart, boss,' Lara Sumich had commented out of the corner of her mouth.

The Sea Rescue whiteboard had been scrubbed of the few Flipper notes and trundled the fifty metres or so up to the town hall. Folding tables and stacks of chairs had been dragged off the stage. Hutchens saw to it that the crime-fighting tableau was arranged exactly 'just so'. For now they would use their mobiles and laptops until a fully equipped mobile command post arrived tomorrow. The room was huge, dingy, cold and echoing. And it beat the donga hands down. In the far corner of the hall sat an old upright piano, coated in dust and flaking white paint. It looked like it hadn't given out a tune in years. Cato trailed his finger along the dusty lid absent-mindedly. Hearing Hutchens bark out his orders reminded him of crime scenes past when he was still on his upward trajectory and the DI's little protégé. He glanced over at the self-assured head girl, Lara Sumich. Was she the new golden one?

The uniforms were still guarding the locus for forensics. The detectives had been joined in the hall by Tess Maguire. Hutchens said hello and flicked a glance towards Cato who pretended he hadn't seen it. Now Hutchens wanted a briefing before they started, as he put it, kicking down doors. Lovely. Cato filled them in on who had found the body and when, the doctor's preliminary findings, and the circumstances under which they'd last seen Jim Buckley. He held back on the bit about Justin Woodward; in his mind it was pure speculation so far. He didn't want Hutchens jumping the gun, they'd already been down that disastrous path once before. Besides, Cato harboured hopes of pulling a rabbit out of a hat.

Hutchens snapped out some orders. 'Lara, you talk to the fisherman again, the one who found the body. Take the uniform with you, the one who took the original statement ... Greg? That him?' Tess Maguire nodded confirmation. Exit Lara. Hutchens twisted his head. 'Mark?'

DC McGowan raised an eyebrow, he must have seen it on a TV cop show somewhere. 'Boss?'

'Get down the pub. See if they've got any CCTV footage there. If so seize it.'

'Done.'

'Before you go ...'

McGowan halted mid-stride, keen as mustard. 'Yes, boss?'

'Organise some coffee and milk and biscuits and stuff. Tim Tams, they're always nice.'

McGowan glowered. Cato stifled a cough.

'Soon as you can mate,' Hutchens prompted him with an encouraging smile. McGowan stalked from the room, face like thunder. That left just Tess, Cato and Hutchens.

'Now then ...' Hutchens said, smile disappearing, eyes locking with Cato's. 'Tell me what it is you're holding back.'

Bang goes the rabbit, thought Cato glumly.

15

Sunday, October 12th. Just after midnight.

The dog started yapping again. It was a still and silent night, dog notwithstanding. The moon was bright, just a few days off full. The stars alone seemed to give off enough light to see by; one of them died in front of Cato's eyes: millions more where that came from.

They had surrounded Justin Woodward's fibro cottage in Barnett Street. The Perth contingent arrived midafternoon. Three of them split from the main group to do the scene-of-crime forensics. After a briefing from Hutchens, the remaining half-dozen spent the evening interviewing the pub staff and patrons to try to get a picture of Jim Buckley's last hours. A pre-raid squad meeting filled out more of the picture. Apparently there were no fights, no arguments, no spilled drinks. And Buckley hadn't won at pool. He'd just quietly sat eating his bar meal – steak and chips, the barmaid seemed to recall – and drinking and staring into space. He'd chatted to people here and there but nothing out of the ordinary. He had disappeared for a short while, mid evening, but returned and then he was there until closing time, around midnight. Yes, said the barmaid, Justin Woodward and his girlfriend had been in the pub earlier in the evening before Buckley arrived. They left soon after he came in.

Lara Sumich and Mark McGowan had passed the afternoon and evening sitting in a squad car a stone's throw from Woodward's house. McGowan was sullen and uncommunicative about the Tim Tams thing. Sumich did the quick crossword and sent a few dirty text messages to her sometimes boyfriend, setting herself the challenge of photographing her pierced left nipple with her mobile without McGowan noticing. She succeeded. Justin Woodward and his girlfriend had rolled back into their driveway just after 9.50 p.m.

Cato glanced at the driveway. The car was still there now, one of those little jeeps that roll over if you take the corner too fast and crumple like wet cardboard when you hit the tree. It was early nineties vintage, black with playful pastel splashes of colour along the flanks. The canvas roof was brittle-dry, discoloured and torn above the passenger side. A fishing rod poked out of the hole in the roof. They now knew that the car was registered in the name of the girlfriend, Angelique. According to the records she was originally from France, arrived about two years ago and now here she was, living in Hopetoun with her boyfriend. Woodward's records, official and unofficial, were also dusted off. Nothing had been pinned on him so far but he had, in the not so distant past, kept some very bad company in the drug world.

Cato, on hearing that, developed a cold, sick feeling in his stomach. Had his little rumour game unwittingly intersected with the activities of a real-life drug syn-di-cate, as Pam the Gossip would have put it? Had he set up the hapless Jim Buckley as a hotshot drug enforcement specialist to be assassinated? Cato refused to believe it; this was Hopetoun, not Mexico or Colombia. Yap. Yap. Yap. Nobody had done a background check on whether or not the dog was registered.

DI Hutchens nodded, McGowan swung the battering ram and the door flew inwards, rebounding off an inner wall. There was a squeal and the yapping stopped. McGowan, Hutchens and Lara Sumich raced through the house, guns drawn and yelling the usual warnings. Cato, as ordered, stayed with Tess and Greg Fisher in the front yard and listened to it all. There was a lot of banging and crashing, a female scream, raised male voices, some thuds and bumps, a grunt and a groan. Then crying.

Justin Woodward was brought out by McGowan and Sumich. He was handcuffed and it looked like his nose was broken. Mark McGowan had a relaxed, smug look on his face. Clearly he'd been able to take the Tim Tams out on someone. Lara Sumich wasn't so easy to read. She handed Woodward a tissue to stem the blood flow. The raiding party was now over and the guests began to leave. That was when Angelique found the dog, a small black thing, between the front door and the wall. Neck snapped.

'Lily.' She sank to her knees and sobbed, hands cradling the limp, lifeless black bundle of fur. McGowan sniggered, DI Hutchens tutted. Justin Woodward looked at Cato as he was led away.

Cato Kwong couldn't sleep. The Perth–Albany contingent had taken over half of the motel. A few disgruntled guests had been relocated to the caravan park cabins or the prefabricated workers village just outside town, to make room for Cato's new noisy neighbours. Hutchens had waved the words 'murder inquiry' around to good effect since he'd arrived. Only one room remained vacant: Jim Buckley's. That had been taped off and would be examined further in the morning for any clues to his demise. Cato checked the crimson display on the radio alarm clock again. Three-twenty. There was chatter, laughter, music, and glass sounds in the room next door. Detectives on tour, detectives on overtime. Cato knew he couldn't and wouldn't get them to turn it down. They were already giving him strange looks during the day. They knew who he was. They knew his history, or the rumour-mill version of it anyway, and they knew his apparent status in this investigation. Nobody. Official.

Justin Woodward was locked up and interviewed without any Cato input whatsoever. Cato's work was done once he'd informed DI Hutchens of his suspicions. Suspicions? Speculation, guesswork, Cato had wanted to say at the time, but DI Hutchens wasn't listening. Cato wasn't really listening himself. He wondered how long it would take for the rumour he'd started to come back round and bite him. Not long he guessed. Door-to-doors were starting in the morning. Once they got to Motel Pam's door, attention would swing back on to Cato. Had he stupidly gone and provided a spurious motive for a killer? If he hadn't started the drug operation rumour would Jim Buckley still be alive? It didn't bear thinking about. Nor did it detract from Justin Woodward's status as a suspect, or from the notion of drugs being behind it. It just made a mountain out of a stupid molehill. Face facts: Cato Kwong probably had blood on his hands. A quick result with Woodward wouldn't be a bad thing for all concerned.

DI Hutchens and Lara Sumich had taken Snak-Attack boy to the Ravensthorpe lockup. Hutchens had fumed at the absurdity of no secure police facilities in Hopetoun: a hundred-kilometre round trip just to lock somebody up, fuck's sake.

A glass broke next door and there was a surge of laughter and thuds. Cato cursed. He got up, splashed water on his face and put on some shorts and a T-shirt. He switched on the kettle, tore open a sachet of instant coffee, and opened the bar fridge in search of a mini-milk. None, black would have to do. The Flipper file was on his bedside table. Hutchens hadn't brought the matter up yet: not high on his list obviously. Cato poured scalding water into his cup, flicked the file open and sat down to read.

Names. Chinese names. Anglo names. Some looked Spanish, Filipino, African, Dutch, or were they South African? East European names, a smattering of Arabic and Indian, all in tiny Hopetoun, a regular United Nations. The global movement of labour: in some places, like here, it seemed that a man or woman's skills were a prime commodity, in short supply and able to command top dollar. In other parts of the world, labour was so cheap and replaceable it was easier to use a hundred people to do the work of one tractor.

Hopetoun. One general store, a pub, a real estate agent

offering beach shacks at breathtaking boomtown prices, a bakery, two coffee shops and Justin Woodward's snack van–temporarily closed due to unforeseen circumstances. All had at least slightly inflated prices but this was still not an easy place to spend wages which apparently averaged two to three thousand a week. Still, there was plenty of evidence of consumption: expensive four-wheel drives that looked like they never went off-road, jet skis, quad bikes, boats–big ones. Indulgence. Stuff. The tiny town was full of it, and a look that seemed to go with it all. Was it only four, now five, days since he'd arrived in town? Yes, but already it had got to him, insinuated itself under his skin. Images, sounds, sensations he'd absorbed unconsciously over the last few days. That self-assuredness. Smugness? A solid belief that this inflated prosperity was right, proper and here to stay. While the stock markets of the world crashed and burned, this little town on the south coast of WA was a beacon of hope on an island of unwavering confidence. This was a fifty-year mine; it was part of an industry that made, what was it Bruce Yelland had said, fifty billion last year alone? It was run by one of the biggest players in the world, WMG, Western Minerals Group, net worth the equivalent of some smaller nation's GDP. The Boom, god bless her and all who sail in her. WMG, and what were the other names on the headed lists of employees? Dunstan Construction Industries, SaS Personnel, suppliers of labour and services to the boom. He now knew a little more about WMG, courtesy of Bruce Yelland. The others?

Cato dragged his laptop out of its case, plugged it in, connected to the telephone line and logged on. No wireless connection in the motel yet but he was sure it would only be a matter of time. Next door there was movement, it sounded like the party was breaking up at last. Dunstan's had their own website: *Dunstan Industries–construction, industrial and domestic–Think Global, Act Local.* Cute. Based in Ravensthorpe, proprietor James Dunstan. In the top right-hand corner a passport-sized photo of a smiling middle-aged man; the type you'd be happy to leave your kids with. Current projects: Barren Pastures housing development, Hopetoun Emergency Services Centre, WMG Desalination Plant, WMG Nickel Workers Village and so on and so forth. What Halliburton is to the Iraq War, Dunstan's is to the Hopetoun boom, guessed Cato.

SaS Personnel. The website was for a company based in Hertfordshire near London, specialising in security guards. No mention of Australia. No, it had to be a different company. He tried again, limiting the search to Australia. Nothing. He tried a company search through government tax and industry regulation websites. Then he had it, Stevenson and Sons Personnel trading as SaS Personnel, labour recruitment services. Director, Secretary, and sole shareholder, was one Grace Stevenson. CEO, Keith Stevenson, registered office, Dempster Street, Esperance. Cato thought of Kane Stevenson lying in Ravensthorpe Hospital: any relation? He'd follow up tomorrow. Cato logged off and put his laptop to sleep. If only he could do the same for himself.

16

Sunday, October 12th. Early morning.

Sunday morning. Hopetoun slept in. It was too blustery even for the keenest of fishermen to venture out. Cato Kwong zipped up his jacket and shivered as he stepped out of his room. Deep in thought, he didn't notice Lara Sumich exit the room next door. They collided. He winced. Cato lifted his dislocated thumb for inspection: it looked like it might have been knocked back into position. Lara Sumich said sorry, smiled absent-mindedly and started to walk away.

'Find anything?'

'What?'

Cato nodded towards the door she'd just come through. 'Buckley's room, anything of interest?'

Lara looked behind her as if to make sure they were talking about the same room. 'No, no we haven't started on it yet. I was just checking it was still secure. I'm next door, I thought I heard someone in there.'

'And?'

'Looked okay to me.'

Cato nodded. 'So how'd it go with Woodward last night?'

'Good.'

'Full confession, signed and everything?'

'Not yet.'

'Had breakfast?'

'Not yet.'

'Want to join me?'

Lara responded with an eye twinkle and a seductive curl of the lip. Cato felt himself flush like a teenager.

'Can't. Sorry. Meeting the boss for another round with

Woodward ...' she pointed towards the sign on the door across the courtyard. 'Anyway the restaurant is closed.'

In Hopetoun it seemed the early bird had to wait until the worm had finished his lie-in.

DI Mick Hutchens emerged from his room two doors down, freshly combed and shaved and with a crisp clean white shirt and dark-red power tie: he was expecting to field some media today, albeit second-rankers from regional TV. The glamour squad from the city was due on the Monday morning flight, first thing.

'Morning, Cato. Lara, ready to rock and roll?'

'Boss.'

Lara zapped the remote at the Commodore, its locks thudded open and sidelights flashed.

Cato asked Hutchens the same question he'd asked Lara. 'How'd it go with Woodward?'

'Good,' said Hutchens.

'What's his story?' Cato persisted.

'Says it wasn't him.'

Cato put up his hands in surrender. The shutters were down and he was locked out. 'Okay, message received and understood.'

'Good,' said Hutchens as he slammed the car door shut.

Lara revved and gave Cato a little wave on the way out.

Cato watched them leave and waited for the heat to go out of his face, and elsewhere. Lara Sumich could switch from Head Girl to Super Vixen in the curl of a lip and the flare of an iris. Awesome. Anyway, another day – another day and he still hadn't been kicked off the Flipper case. He flicked open his mobile and keyed in a number.

'Where do you live?'

'Why?' Tess sounded half-asleep and grumpy.

Cato checked his watch, it was just past seven, on a Sunday morning. He was losing track of normal time, how other people lived. He'd been awake most of the night and was raring to go. Why wasn't everybody else?

Tess's voice hardened, she must have just checked her own clock. 'Do you realise what time it is?'

'About five past seven?'

'Cato?'

'Yes?'

'Fuck off.'

The phone went dead. He re-dialled.

'What?' There was violence in the voice.

'SaS Personnel, Stevenson and Sons: Director, Grace Stevenson; CEO, Keith Stevenson. Any relation to Kane?'

Tess was wide awake now. 'Keith is the dad. Don't know Grace. I always thought the mother was called Kerry. Grace ... Grace. Aunty? Sister?'

'So where do you live?'

'Why?'

'Have you ever tried to get a good cup of coffee around here on a Sunday morning?'

'I've never worried about where to get a good cup of coffee anywhere, any time of any day. You need to get a life, coffee snob.'

But she told him her address anyway.

'Currawong Gardens,' said Cato.

That was the given address for Grace Stevenson. They were poring over Tess's home laptop, looking at the company details again. They had to crunch up close at the kitchen table to both be able to read it, a bit too close for comfort for Tess, and yet not. It brought back memories of a kind of intimacy she hadn't known in years. He still smelt the same; the memory was unsettling and dangerous, another thing in her life putting her on the edge of abandon. Melissa was asleep. Teenager, she wouldn't surface until at least ten. Two and a half hours. Tess realised she was plotting and scheming lasciviously and mentally slapped herself.

Cato had walked from the motel to Tess's home on a hill in the half-built new housing development at Mary Ann Waters, allowing her ten minutes to make herself look respectable. Not easy. Her hair stuck out like Cat Lady in The Simpsons, a crease ran down the side of her face from a crunched up pillow and her breath didn't bear thinking about. A five-minute shower, a toothbrush, and a pair of clean trackie daks later, she felt a whole lot better. She'd rescued her favourite T-shirt from the laundry basket, sniffed it–not too bad.

'Currawong Gardens, Hopetoun,' Cato repeated.

'It's an independent-living aged-care complex.'

'A what?'

'Old folks home, it's out the back of town, the old part, the road out to Starvation Bay. They reported a break-in there a few weeks ago. It turned out she'd put her wedding ring down to do some washing up and forgot.'

'Grace?' asked Cato, perplexed.

'No, some old love.'

Cato looked at Tess like she was a batty old duffer only a finger-click away from Currawong Gardens herself. With Cato assuming the driver's seat, the train of thought left the siding and choo-chooed back on to the track.

'Grace is listed as Director, Secretary, and sole shareholder.'

Tess picked up the phone and rang Currawong Gardens. She asked if they had a Grace Stevenson working or living there. The woman at the other end said they did but she was otherwise engaged.

'In what way?' said Tess, identifying herself and putting on her senior sergeant's voice.

'She's being cleaned up. Had a bit of an accident last night.'

Too much information this early on a Sunday morning.

'How old is Mrs Stevenson?'

'Eighty-six last week; didn't know much about it though, poor love.'

Tess took a punt. 'Does the son Keith visit very often?'

There was a tutting sound. 'He hasn't been in since he dropped her off here three years ago. The grandson visits now and again though. Lovely boy.'

'Kane?'

Another tut. 'No, Jai, the little one, he's still at school. A real sweetie.'

Tess frowned then thanked her and put the phone down. She filled Cato in on what she'd gleaned but left out some of the unsavoury detail. He refilled their coffee cups. The brew obviously met his exacting standards if he was going back for more.

'Doesn't sound like your typical high-powered company director in charge of what must be a very profitable enterprise.'

Tess shrugged: it turned into a neck stretch then a yawn, arms reaching for the ceiling. Out of the corner of her eye she caught Cato admiring the stretching of fabric across her chest but trying to make it look like he wasn't looking. Sometimes he was an open book. Tess smiled to herself. Time to get out the scalpel.

'How's the wife?'

'Jane? Fine. Good.' Cato's smile was forced, the voice unnaturally light.

'Been married long?'

'Seven years.'

Cue itch.

'Kids?'

'A boy, six, Jacob.'

'Missing him I expect.'

'Yes I am.'

He sounded like he meant it, plain as day, but also looked a bit surprised at the fact.

'And Jane too, no doubt,' prompted Tess.

'Sure. Of course.'

'So why aren't you home with them?'

'What?'

'DI Hutchens is going to want to run both cases. Your work is pretty well finished here. You can go back to your family. That's what you want isn't it?'

Cato nodded unconvincingly.

Tess weighed up all she had gleaned – but then she wondered why the hell she was so interested anyway. A flashback popped into her mind of a steamy Sunday morning between the sheets with Cato Kwong long, long ago and far, far away. She steadied her beating heart and hopped back on to that train of thought.

'Let's pay Keith Stevenson a visit.'

Clearly relieved at the change of tack, Cato put his cup down expectantly.

Tess held up her hand. 'Wait. I need to change out of my Desperate Housewife outfit first. So relax, finish your coffee.'

'Sleep well, Justin?'

DI Hutchens slapped his file and notebook down on to the table and scraped back a chair. Lara Sumich had taken up position just behind and at the edge of Woodward's field of vision. The interview room was standard police issue, four walls, a table and three chairs. The clock behind Woodward told everybody it was 8.20. A small colonial-era window high on another wall offered a glimpse of blue sky, scudding clouds and the branch of a gumtree shaking in the wind. A video camera was perched up in one corner, a modern addition. Hutchens was full of beans this morning and wanted Woodward to know it. The response from the primed suspect was a snort and a curl of the lip.

'I'll take that as a no,' Hutchens beamed.

He had left instructions with the nightshift: plenty of whistling, loud conversations, banging, jarring mobile phone ring tones, that sort of thing. It was only five hours since the last round of questioning had finished. Woodward would have been lucky if he'd managed a full hour's sleep. Hutchens had also made sure that the breakfast served would be as unappetising as possible. The nightshift had grimly assured him that was the way the local roadhouse served stuff up anyway.

Woodward ran a hand through his dark curls. He had bags under his eyes and needed a shave. His nose was red and swollen but not broken. He rustled in the police-issue blue paper forensic suit; his own clothes now under a microscope somewhere. Hutchens flipped the lid off his takeaway cappuccino, sniffed over-appreciatively and took a sip.

Woodward made the first move. 'Where's my lawyer?'

'This is Sunday, the country. We're trying our best. Hope you'll help us out in the meantime, Justin.'

'Or else what?'

'Or we'll just wait for him, or her, to arrive and continue tomorrow.'

No reply. Hutchens took that as consent.

'Must have ruined your day, Justin.'

Woodward raised a middle finger and used it to scratch sleep out of the corner of his eye.

Hutchens persisted. 'Detective Sergeant Buckley, turning up like a bad penny.'

A shrug.

'Here you are nicely set up with your girlfriend ...' Hutchens pretended to check his notes, 'Angelique. Lovely girl.'

Woodward kept his gaze fixed on the tabletop.

'French?'

Tabletop.

'Tourist visa, due to expire in a few weeks, I see.'

Tabletop plus a derisive shake of the head. It seemed to say, 'Is that the best you can do?'

'And Big Jim Buckley rolls up to rain on your parade.'

Tabletop and feigning bored.

'Did Angelique know about your drug-pushing past?'

'Why would she? I don't have one. I haven't been convicted

of anything.'

'It speaks!'

Hutchens sat back in his chair and folded his arms. Change of tack.

'Where did you and your girlfriend go when you left the pub?'

'Home.'

'Why?'

'To fuck.'

'Left your drinks half-finished,' said Hutchens, like it was sacrilege.

'Some things are more important.'

Lara Sumich nodded in agreement. Hutchens gave her a little glare.

'Jim Buckley had just come in. Is that why you left?'

'I already told you why we left. We were horny. She was gagging for it.'

He turned his head to look at Lara like she would understand and Hutchens wouldn't. Probably not wrong. Another warning glare from Hutchens.

'How do you know Freddy Sudhyono?'

'Who?'

'Freddy Bataam, also known as Riri Yusala, Indonesian bloke.'

A twist of the hands and a stifled yawn.

'Must be a mint to be made these days in your line.'

'Coffee? Yeah we're doing okay,' Woodward agreed.

Hutchens leaned forward and hardened his look.

'Ecstasy. Amphetamines. GHB. Miners with money to burn.'

An exasperated look, a hurt look. 'I don't do that kind of stuff, Inspector. Caffeine. That's where the smart drug money is. Hopetoun is crying out for good coffee. The stuff the others make tastes like shit.'

Hutchens took another sip of his own cappuccino. 'You're not wrong on that point anyway.'

Lara put hers back down unopened.

Hutchens paused and made a show of flicking through the file, checking notes. 'What did Jim Buckley miss when he searched your van?'

An eyelid flicker and an over-relaxed shrug this time. 'Nothing. He had a look. Couldn't find anything because there was nothing to find.'

'Why did Jim Buckley have your mobile number in his phone?'

Another eyelid flicker and another shrug, a bit more exaggerated, eyes resting again on the tabletop.

'He called you Friday afternoon, about four. You spoke for nearly three minutes. What about?'

Tabletop. Tic over right eye.

'What about, Justin?'

'I don't know.'

'What the fuck do you mean by that?' Hutchens slapped his hand down on the table at the spot Justin seemed to find so interesting.

Woodward sat back and folded his arms. 'I think I'll wait for that lawyer now.'

17

Sunday, October 12th. Midmorning.

Cato and Tess didn't have far to go. The Stevensons lived about twelve doors up from Tess and over on the expensive side of the street. It was a two-storey McMansion with views of the Southern Ocean. A nine-metre fishing boat, *Kerry*, sat on a trailer on the steep, sloping driveway. There was a shiny new blue quad bike on the front lawn and a basketball hoop over the carport. A new model silver Prado occupied one of the parking spots and a dusty SaS Personnel four-wheel drive Hilux occupied the other. All in all, it was a fairly typical Hopetoun boomtown home. The front door opened before they got to it.

'You charged that fucken Maori bastard yet?'

Kerry Stevenson, loving mother of a son that could obviously do no wrong. She had big brown eyes, a sweep of dyed black hair to her shoulders and a junk-food body in a shapeless tracksuit. Cato estimated she could have been anything from forty to sixty years old, her skin tanned and lined from many years' exposure to the Australian elements. She took a long drag on her cigarette and waited for an answer. Her gaze ignored Cato, it was fixed on Tess and the uniform. Tess smiled.

'Hi Kerry. How's Kane?'

'Sufferin'.'

'Is he out of hospital yet?'

'Tomorrow. How come you lot don't know all this already? So what about that fucken Maori?'

'All in hand,' Tess assured Mrs Stevenson.

'Well what are you here for then?'

'Keith. We'd like a word. Is he in?'

Kerry turned her back and barked down the hallway. 'Keith.

Fucken cops. For you.'

Keith Stevenson was built like a pit bull yet had that affable farm-boy look that many men wore in these parts. As if it was only yesterday their hair had turned grey and the gut had started to go its own way, and only the day before that they were playing good-natured rough and tumble games in the schoolyard. Good-natured but determined to win. He wiped his hands on his Born to Fish T-shirt and stuck one out towards Cato.

'This about Kane?'

Sincere. Genuine. Concerned. Matey. He ushered them back down the hall to the kitchen. Kerry seemed less enthusiastic about having Cato over her threshold.

The Stevenson kitchen had all the gadgets known to humankind on display, yet it looked eerily underused. On the benchtop sat the remains of a fried breakfast and two cups of coffee. Cato's stomach rumbled. In the adjoining open-plan dining area a plasma TV dominated the scene. On the floor in front of it a boy, maybe ten or eleven, clicking furiously on a game console: Jai, he presumed, the lovely little boy who visited his granny at Currawong Gardens. Jai was busy shooting everyone and everything in his line of vision; blood gushed, bodies disintegrated. He didn't turn his head to check out the visitors. Tess mouthed 'Disaffected Youth' at Cato, nodding her head in Jai's direction. So this was him. Explosions and gunfire echoed around the room until Keith found the remote and pressed mute.

'Sorry mate,' said dad with a nervous appeasing grin and a wink.

The boy turned around for a second and glowered out of dark eyes that were just like his mum's. He had a scar on his upper lip from an operation to fix a cleft palate. He noticed Cato noticing, put his hand to it self-consciously then doubled the darkness in his stare for Cato's benefit. He obviously had an alternative persona for his visits to granny in the nursing home.

Keith held his coffee mug up and raised a questioning

eyebrow. The prospects were good; they had an espresso and cappuccino machine on display. Cato nodded eagerly. Keith Stevenson beamed and reached into a wall cupboard for a jar of instant. Tess buried a smile and declined the same offer.

'So. Kane?' Keith Stevenson nudged.

'Actually we're here about another matter.'

Even muted, the huge flickering plasma was distracting. Little Jai sat staring at it, game console clicking double-time and making mayhem.

'What's that then?' Keith spooned some Blend 49 into a mug.

Cato shook his head at the sugar bowl but nodded at the carton of milk. 'SaS Personnel.'

Keith focused on pouring the milk. 'Yes?'

'Your company.'

'That's right.'

'But in your mother's name.'

Kerry Stevenson snorted and lit up another cigarette from the embers of the first. She exchanged a look with her husband. He returned the milk to the fridge.

'That's right. She's a ... silent partner.'

'Very.' Tess agreed. 'So why do you have the company registered in the name of a woman in her eighties who, according to the staff at Currawong Gardens, can hardly even care for herself?'

Keith Stevenson paused with a kettle full of boiling water in his hand. 'Is there a law against that? What's this all about?'

No longer concerned and affable. Cato could forget the coffee now. Small mercies.

'If there is a law against that I'll find out and let you know. In the meantime we are conducting a possible murder investigation.' Cato's voice was as cold as the glares of his hosts.

'The cop? What's that got to do with us for fuck's sake?' Keith Stevenson laughed humourlessly. 'Fucking pathetic, a bloke has a past and you won't let him forget it. Now you want to pin this one on me.'

Cato grimaced inwardly. They'd neglected to run Keith Stevenson's name through the system before paying him a visit, so they didn't know what that past was. Fools rush in.

'No, not yesterday's incident, this is about the body on the beach a few days ago. We believe it to be a Chinese male. Possibly one of the workers around these parts.'

Stevenson stirred his coffee. 'Yes and we gave you the list didn't we? Everybody signed in, present and correct for their wages on Thursday. Nobody missing.'

'How do they get their wages? Do they all line up?' asked Tess.

'They come in throughout the day according to their shifts, sign the form and take the pay slip. The wages are paid direct into bank accounts.'

'What if somebody is off sick that day?'

'Usually they'll arrange for somebody to sign for them.'

'Did that happen this week?' said Cato.

'I'll check with the foreman.'

'Thanks.'

Cato couldn't help himself; having just been done a favour, he had to push it a little too far. 'By the way, you still haven't answered the question.'

Stevenson bristled. 'Which one?'

'Why you have legal ownership of your company vested in an elderly, infirm woman in a nursing home.'

Keith Stevenson gestured towards the front door. 'None of your business, mate. Time you left.'

Jai took that as a cue to unmute his game. Automatic gunfire erupted in the Stevenson kitchen and some dude got his, big time.

Miller was back on the old Google again. He had locked himself in the study while Jenny pottered around in the backyard weeding, planting, pruning and enjoying the spring sunshine. There was still no word from Jim Buckley and he wasn't answering his phone. Probably another bullshit wind-up. Davey Arthurs in a pub in Hopetoun under the watchful eye of his brother-in-law? It had seemed too good to be true, and it was. Stuart's meeting with Brian Munro had nagged at him all night. Something Arthurs had said to Vicki Munro about his past. He didn't have one. What did that mean? Miller had already trawled the Adelaide murder reports but now he wanted to go back to Sunderland, May 1973. Would that stuff be on the internet? Only one way to find out.

A search on the *Sunderland Echo* site showed its online records didn't go back far enough. He could order copies of the real thing if he was happy to wait a week or two. He wasn't. He tried the national papers; the murders had been gruesome enough to warrant their interest. He read their take on it, stomach churning at his own memories, but nothing there that he didn't already know. His internet skills were rudimentary; he knew how to search but not necessarily where, or how to wade through the ocean of rubbish that was offered up on every click. He was drowning in trivia. He remembered a TV documentary he'd seen recently, a baby-boomer Rock God searching his family tree. Master of the guitar solo but a real nanna on the computer – they'd had to beep his string of curses. Miller knew the feeling.

The Census. The Rock God had managed to find the Census online, or at least the film crew had shown him how. Would the records of the Arthurs family and who was living at 11 Maud Street during that time throw up anything new? Maybe CK was in there somewhere? He tapped on the keyboard. The 1971 Census had David, Christine and Stephen Arthurs in situ at 11 Maud Street.Davey's occupation: shipyard electrician. So far, so good. He trawled backwards, following Arthurs to the previous Census in 1961 – aged fifteen. He found him living with mother Elizabeth and little brother Andrew in Southwick, not far from the shipyards. Mother's occupation: shop assistant. So during the ten years to 1971 they'd moved up a little bit in the world, from Southwick to Fulwell. A mini-notch on the register of social class that permeated everything in those days, probably still did and that was one of the reasons Miller had got the hell out. Davey, his mother and little brother ... but where was dad? Dead? Done a runner?

The 1951 Census. David, Andrew, Elizabeth, and William (father) living in the same house in Southwick. Davey was five, Andrew two, mother was a housewife, and father a labourer at the shipyard. End of story? There was no 1941 Census because of the war. No CK in the picture over the two decades. Miller sat back and rubbed his eyes. Where to next? He thought back to his own childhood: in 1951 he was eight years old. He'd been conceived in 1943 when his father went AWOL ahead of a posting to North Africa, a last conjugal visit before a hellish two years in the desert. Miller fingered the scar by his right eye: there had been times when he'd wished the vicious old bastard had copped a German bullet. When the old man had come back after the war, that's when the nightmare started for them. After demob his father had been given a skilled job in one of the heavy engineering plants that serviced the shipyards and coalmines. It was relatively well paid: he was never short of money for a drink. By contrast Arthurs' dad's wages as a shipyard labourer wouldn't have gone far. Were those hard times the start of it all for Davey Arthurs? Miller didn't buy it. Plenty of people had it tough. Very very few of them turned into serial killers. No, it was something else. But what?

Miller skipped back to the 1931 Census, switching the search to Davey Arthurs' father. William John Arthurs aged twelve, living with his mother and father and sisters in Seaburn. Just down the hill from Fulwell. One of the big semidetached houses two streets back from the beach. His father was a bank manager. So Davey Arthurs' father is born into prosperity and privilege and ends up in a shitty low-paid job just after the war living in a grimy two-up, two-down terrace. How did that happen? And where did dad disappear to between the 1951 and

1961 census?

Jenny signalled through the window for him to get the kettle on. He gave her the thumbs up.

'A busy boy,' Cato agreed.

They were logged on in the Murder Hut, looking at the record of Keith John Stevenson, DOB 26th April 1956. Early years were spent around the northern suburbs of Perth. He had teenage convictions for shoplifting, car theft, assault, drunk and disorderly. Perth in the '60s, early '70s, limited entertainment options. Keith graduated in his twenties and thirties to hanging out with known standover men around the nightclubs of Northbridge and picking up the kind of convictions that go with the territory: serious assaults, possession of weapons and drugs. Perth in the '80s: WA Inc and cash to splash. Then he upped the ante: charged with manslaughter in the early '90s. He'd king-hit an American sailor, a father of three from Alabama, during an altercation in a pub in Fremantle. The sailor was in a coma for six weeks before they pulled the plug. Stevenson was acquitted of manslaughter but served a year on a lesser assault charge.

'Since then, not a peep, he's kept his nose clean for over fifteen years,' Tess said.

'Reformed character?' said Cato.

Tess shook her head. 'No such thing.'

'Prejudices like that won't get you far in the modern WA police service.'

'Hopetoun's far enough I reckon.' Tess tapped her finger on the employee lists. 'So when do we do the rollcall?'

Cato yawned, the sleepless night was finally catching up with him.

'It'll wait until tomorrow. Start of the new working week. Okay with you?'

She was surprised both at his willingness to wait and that he cared what she thought.

'Sure,' she shrugged, already turning her mind to the rest of her Sunday: washing, tidying and trying to communicate with Melissa. Wondering what she would do about Johnno Djukic, due back at work tomorrow.

Cato looked at her. 'You okay?'

'Fine,' said Tess. 'Yeah, fine.'

Over their midmorning cuppa, Stuart Miller told his wife what he'd been up to, locking himself in the study all morning. At least he hadn't been surfing porn sites, he joked.

'Maybe you should, hen. It might spark things up a wee bit around here,' she retorted gloomily. But she'd been drawn in too.

Davey Arthurs was part of their shared history; he'd blighted both of their lives. And she was intrigued by the dangling questions. How did Arthurs senior go from being a well-off middle-class boy before the war to relative penury in later years? And what happened to dad between Davey's fifth and fifteenth birthdays?

Jenny was more computer savvy than Stuart and, as part of a social sciences project, had taught the kids at school how to research their family trees. First things first: William Arthurs' death record.

Stuart Miller marvelled at his wife's dexterity as she whizzed around cyberspace. He was also dumbfounded by the amount of online information there was in the field of genealogy. Thank god for anoraks and train-spotters. Finally she had it: William John Arthurs, date of death 19th September 1953, age thirty-three. Cause of death: asphyxia. Though not required to, the doctor had helpfully added 'hanging' in brackets. Place of death: the two-up, two-down in Southwick. When Davey Arthurs was just seven years old his father had, it seemed, committed suicide. That's where dad disappeared to, but why did he do it?

Jenny then looked up the war record of William John Arthurs. The Imperial War Museum database listed him as a lieutenant in the Durham Light Infantry, as befits the son of a bank manager–seeing action at Dunkirk, North Africa and the Salerno landings in Italy. Medical discharge February 1945, a few months before the war ended. Severe depression and catatonia. Read shell shock. Davey's dad probably wouldn't have been in any fit state to hold down a responsible, better paying job; even labourer in the shipyards would have been a bit of a stretch for Billy Arthurs. Siring Davey and Andy must have been about all he was good for. For some reason his middle-class family had abandoned him to his fate; nobody had invited the homecoming hero back to the big house by the beach in Seaburn to recuperate from his wartime traumas. Charming.

Jenny Miller sat back, a triumphant gleam in her eye. 'That what you're after?'

Miller nodded, impressed. 'All very interesting but what does it have to do with his son Davey turning into a nasty, vicious little bastard?'

Jenny stretched and yawned. 'Yeah well I've had enough of this, I've got some marking to do.' Her hand hovered over the mouse, she winked and dug her elbow playfully into his side. 'Unless you want to take one of your wee blue pills and look at some porn?'

18

Monday, October 13th. Early morning.

Guan Yu stepped out of his caravan into the half-light of dawn. He shivered and cupped both hands to a mug of tea and lifted it to his mouth. The high cirrus clouds to the east were streaked pink and red with the approaching sunrise, fanning out across a sky bigger than he could ever get used to. This was the best time of day, when he could have a few moments to himself to relish the peace, quiet, clean air and space: so much space. He slapped his hand three times loudly against the side of the van. Three workmates inside, slow to get out of bed. With four adults snoring and farting in a van barely big enough for two, the best place to be was outside in the fresh morning air.

The caravan was in a clearing in bush on the south-eastern corner of a huge and neglected block they called Paddy's Field. Guan Yu had no idea who Paddy was. As far as he knew, this land was owned by their employer but they never saw him: big man, too busy. Too busy to look after his land and his animals, thought Guan, as a handful of bony, bedraggled sheep bleated pathetically from a respectful distance. He slapped his hand on the van three more times. The sheep skedaddled, his workmates stirred, cursed, and farted. One began to clear his nose and throat and the others joined in the morning chorus. Guan swilled the dregs of his tea around the bottom of the cup and flicked it towards a small pile of mallee roots. It reminded him to restock for the evening fire.

Twenty metres away, another caravan door was flung open and more sleepy Chinese faces emerged as the sun broke the distant tree line. They added to the dawn chorus, now a snorting cacophony. Three men in a van meant for four; they had a bit more room to move now that Chen was gone. Across the paddock the minibus came into view. Bumping over the rutted track it creaked to a stop between the two caravans. The window rolled down and Travis Grant poked his head out, cigarette in the corner of his mouth and reflector sunglasses perched up top.

'Wakey-wakey. Chop-chop. Ready go workee?'

Guan Yu nodded and smiled like he was expected to. He wondered why Mr Grant spoke such strange English and never asked where Chen was. Ever.

Justin Woodward could stew for another half-hour at least. DI Mick Hutchens had commandeered Sergeant Bernie Tilbrook's office at Ravensthorpe cop shop. That hadn't gone down well but Hutchens couldn't give a shit. He had the preliminary autopsy results back from Dr Harry Lewis who'd delayed his examination of Buckley until late Sunday morning. It hadn't done much for Hutchens' mood; he'd also just heard that the extra officers and the mobile command post were to be delayed another twenty-four hours. Hutchens held his tongue during the post-mortem examination. He'd nail the jumped-up little twerp later, once the job was done.

Jim Buckley had not one but two major head wounds. It looked like the killer had first bounced the rock off the back of Buckley's skull from a short distance behind, maybe less than a metre, to incapacitate him. Once he'd gone down they, he, or she, had followed up by dropping it on his head again. In fact it was done with such force the second time that it must have been lifted high and hurled down. That was the one that killed him. Hardly elegant but certainly effective, was Lewis's redundant observation. There had been no apparent struggle, no apparent physical contact between victim and assailant. But there was every chance the killer had been splashed with Jim Buckley's blood.

Buckley had a bellyful of steak, chips, salad, bourbon and

Coke. No unusual drugs in the system–he was on medication for blood pressure and cholesterol. One thing they hadn't expected and which further analysis confirmed–Buckley's guts were riddled with cancer. If he hadn't been murdered he probably would have been dead in about six months anyway. Dr Lewis had no objection to the body being released to the family. Hutchens could see no particular merit in having Buckley looked over again by a Perth boffin; they had the relevant organ, blood and tissue samples anyway. Buckley's oldest son had been notified. Hutchens didn't want to think too much about what the family was going through right now. He knew they needed to be able to bury or cremate the poor bastard and he wasn't about to stand in their way. The Commissioner too was keen for this to be expedited; a cop's funeral was always a good opportunity to consolidate hearts and minds and budget submissions.

Forensics hadn't been able to get much from the locus. Rain and other contamination had turned prints, fibres, and any other potentially useful particles into a murky broth, according to Hutchens' officer-in-charge DS Duncan Goldflam. The motel room also had too many prints and fibres from previous occupants and staff for that avenue to be really worth pursuing, although diligence dictated that he must. Buckley's belongings and laptop were examined but nothing jumped out. Anything that put Justin Woodward in the frame would do nicely but so far, nada. All they had on the pub CCTV was Buckley at the bar–drinking, eating, staring at the TV, staring at the barmaid, staring into space, and occasionally sharing a few casual words with people over the course of the evening. Buckley was seen leaving and returning mid evening for about a ten-minute interval. Justin Woodward and girlfriend were seen leaving early, abandoning half-finished drinks. The alert on the white turbo ute owned by the probable Woodward associates–the Indonesian and his two sleazy mates–had produced zilch. The phone records had thrown up Woodward, which was a plus, but the only other numbers seemed to be a doctors surgery and another private number, a family member in Busselton. All in all, Hutchens knew it, they had nothing.

Justin Woodward knew it too, as did his lawyer. He'd flown in yesterday on the late afternoon flight from Perth. Henry Hurley: short, pixie-faced and surprisingly muscular. He worked out to make up for the height thing. Hooray Henry. A city brief well known to Hutchens and his colleagues from Major Crime. He normally represented the gangsters and bikies and didn't come cheap; Justin's daddy was paying. Too busy to be able to come down himself to support his son, he was nevertheless pulling out all the stops, and his chequebook, to help. Word had already drifted back to Hutchens from higher in the police food chain that entrepreneur and socialite Patrick Woodward was using his connections, chewing ears in the police, legal, and political fraternities about harassment of his son. The message to Hutchens was charge him or release him by day's end. Henry Hurley had already voiced his outrage at the rough and unwarranted treatment meted out to his client and let them know he'd be making it official. Hutchens nodded and smiled at the little tosspot. He didn't give two hoots.

Henry and Justin sat on one side of the table, Hutchens and Lara Sumich on the other. Lara knew the score, the lack-of-compelling-evidence thing; she looked like she wanted to be somewhere else. Hutchens introduced everybody and announced the time and date for the record. He knew this was probably the last run with Woodward and they'd have to let him go unless somebody crashed into the room with a smoking gun or he broke down and confessed all; neither were likely. Woodward hadn't volunteered any more since Sunday morning when he'd decided he wanted his lawyer. Before that he seemed to be cool, relaxed and have an answer for everything he could be bothered responding to. Everything but the phone call between Buckley's mobile and his at around four on Friday – that had rattled him. Hutchens would bet his overtime that Hurley and Justin would have plugged that hole by now. It didn't stop him trying though. After a leisurely stroll through the preliminaries and over old ground to make sure Woodward was sticking to his story – and he was – Hutchens got around to the nub of the issue.

'The phone call, Justin, the one from the deceased to you on Friday afternoon; we still need to get to the bottom of that.'

Woodward nodded helpfully, he'd remembered now. 'Yes, Mr Buckley did phone me ...' Mr Buckley, nice touch. 'He said that he'd mislaid something when he was searching the van. A bunch of keys.'

'And you spent ...' Hutchens made a show of checking his notes, 'three minutes and forty-six seconds talking about that?'

'Yes, he described them to me and we were trying to picture where he might have left them.'

'Describe them for me.'

An eyelid flicker, the lie had become unnecessarily elaborate. Time to backtrack. 'I didn't really take it in to tell you the truth. I was getting ready to go out with Angelique. We talked about where he'd been looking, where he might have put them down. But I hadn't noticed anything when I locked up that day.'

'And that was it?'

'That was it.'

'Why couldn't you tell me this yesterday?'

Justin nodded again, ready, willing and eager. 'I'd had a terrible night's sleep. I didn't get to bed until after three, as you'll know.' A glance this time for Lara, implicating her. 'I'd just reached my limit, the end of my tether. Sleep deprivation. Does terrible things to you, you know.'

Henry Hurley patted his client's hand consolingly and served DI Hutchens a half-reproachful, half-pitying look. 'Was there anything else you wanted us to help you with, Inspector?

The coach rolled into the roadhouse forecourt and pulled up at the Dunstan Industries demountable where a fleet of minibuses waited to whisk groups of contract workers away to various sites. The brakes hissed and the doors eased open. A parade of sleepy men and women in fluoro overalls emerged into the sunshine. Tess Maguire checked her watch, 8.30. Most of the coach passengers had already been awake for at least two hours for the drive from Esperance to Ravensthorpe and were only just about to start their ten-hour shift now. After another sleep-deprived night of her own, Tess knew exactly how they felt. She was in her private car, an eight year old grey Subaru, and out of uniform; this wasn't strictly police business. Then he appeared in the coach doorway.

John Djukic. The mullet had gone but his hair was still the same rust colour. He was clean-shaven. He'd put on a bit of weight. Drive-in drive-out work patterns took as much of a toll on the body as fly-in fly-out, maybe more. Roadhouse food and work-camp life takes no prisoners. Djukic and his band of brothers, and a few sisters, trudged past within a few metres of Tess's Subaru. She didn't make any attempt to hide herself. She almost willed him to notice her. He didn't. He walked straight past and boarded a minibus which, according to the handwritten card in the windscreen, was headed out to the mine. The minibuses buzzed away with their cargoes of worker bees. Tess realised she'd forgotten to breathe for the last minute or so. She opened her window and gulped deeply of the country air which was bitter with the blue smoke of hastily snatched cigarettes and crackling with dust from the swirl of vehicles. She gunned her engine and followed the convoy down the road.

It was the strangest feeling. Midmorning on a dusty unsealed road just outside of Hopetoun. A still and steadily warming day. Cato Kwong shielded his eyes from the glare of the mini-cluster of white demountables marking the entrance to what would be Barren Pastures housing estate by the end of the year. No sea views here but the new residents would be able to look forward to glorious sunsets over the brooding Barren Ranges a few kilometres west. East and north were acres and acres of canola as far as the eye could see. South, the creeping expanse of Hopetoun reaching towards the peace and serenity of country life, as fetchingly represented on the advertising hoarding which reared above them: Live the dream in Barren Pastures.

Very strange: sixteen Chinamen summoned to line up before Cato Kwong. He imagined it from a bird's-eye view. It could have been the stage for a set-piece kung fu spectacle except they were all wearing blue and yellow fluoro overalls and looked not ready for battle but totally bemused by his appearance and role, Zen Master Kwong. The initial low murmur as they were herded into the Barren Pastures car park had subsided. Now they were just watching and waiting.

Greg Fisher accompanied Cato today. Tess had phoned to say she had some other business first thing. Fisher seemed to know the foreman, Travis Grant, he nudged Grant who then gave Cato the nod to proceed. Cato started reading aloud the list of names. There were chuckles and sniggers at some of the pronunciations but while he might not have landed a job as a newsreader at SBS, he was a vast improvement on Travis Grant's pidgin-for-deaf-foreigners. As each recognised his name he stepped forward, waved, smiled, and nodded like he was being introduced for the hundred metres backstroke final.

'Hai Chen.'

Nothing. Nobody stepped forward.

Cato read it again. Still nothing. Some of the Chinese coughed or looked anywhere but at Cato.

Travis Grant lifted his reflector sunnies and looked around a bit. 'Anyone seen Hai Chen? Hai Chen?' Grant repeated loudly.

Nothing.

Cato decided to push on, get all the others ticked off, and then come back to that one. He continued with the names until the last of the men stepped forward. Cato studied the list again.

'Hai Chen?' he said uncertainly, then repeated it.

Travis Grant shrugged. 'Must have done a runner. It happens.'

'Where does he live?'

'China?'

Cato fixed his gaze on Grant. 'I'm not really in the mood for pissing around, mate. Take me to where he's been living, this ... Hai Chen.'

Cato felt a tap on his shoulder. He turned. One of the Chinese was there, he took half a step back and bowed towards Cato. The face looked vaguely familiar, or was it just that they all looked the same to him? Then he remembered, day one in Hopetoun, the man in the phone booth on the main street.

'Chen dead. I kill him.'

The man nodded eagerly and put his hands forward, fists clenched, wrists together. Cato wasn't sure what to do. He hadn't actually brought any handcuffs with him.

19

Monday, October 13th. Late morning.

Guan Yu was in custody at Ravensthorpe Police Station. He occupied the cell recently vacated by Justin Woodward. Apparently the place hadn't seen so much business since the Hopey Easter Fish-Off four years ago when celebrations got so out of hand that reinforcements had been summoned from Albany and Esperance. Cato was buzzing like a toaster in a bathtub; this time yesterday, Flipper was still unidentified prime cut, albeit with a likely country of origin–China. Now Flipper had a name, Hai Chen, apparently killed by his compatriot Guan Yu. Dizzying.

The story of how, when, where and why would have to wait until an interpreter arrived from Perth. That would be late afternoon at the earliest. Work was suspended for the day and the Chinese entourage was under instructions to stay on site until somebody worked out what to do next. In the meantime Cato and Greg Fisher were part of a mini convoy, led by Travis Grant, heading out to Paddy's Field where both Hai Chen and Guan Yu lived in caravans courtesy of their generous employer, SaS Personnel. Keith Stevenson had been summoned to meet them there. Proprietor and Director Grace Stevenson was apparently indisposed.

Cato wanted to see if there were any personal belongings of Hai Chen. He needed DNA, or some other forensic links, to confirm that Flipper and Chen were one and the same. In the ute in front, Travis Grant was accompanied by one of the Chinese who, with better English than the others, acted as a go-between on the job. In writing, the man's name looked unpronounceable, Xi Xue, but it approximated to 'She Shway'.

Cato's inability to conjure up any fluent and credible Mandarin continued to be a source of merriment. He wasn't going to even try to explain. You see it's like this – I'm not really as Chinese as I look, it all began with my great-great-grandad in Bendigo, et cetera, et cetera. His mobile beeped feebly, low battery; he'd forgotten to plug it in overnight. He checked the signal. Dead. Good excuse for not phoning DI Hutchens and appraising him of developments.

Paddy's Field was at the corner of a thousand-acre property owned by Keith Stevenson. It sat halfway between Hopetoun and Ravensthorpe and just south of the airstrip. Handy. The land had been cleared of trees and vegetation six decades ago by descendants of one of the region's founding squatter barons; 'a million acres a year' had been the catchcry. The result: vast waves of grain and earth choked with salt. The squatter barons had diversified and, along the way, sold off parcels of useless land like this to the likes of Keith Stevenson. Nobody knew at the time why he wanted it; he clearly wasn't the farming gentry type. But the proximity to the airstrip servicing a new multi-billion-dollar nickel mine was a bit of a clue.

All this local history was courtesy of Greg Fisher who'd made it his business to get a grasp on the people, the history and the land he now called his patch. He said it was his way of showing respect. It was the same character trait that led him to chat to Jim Buckley in spare moments and find out in two days what Cato had failed to learn in six months of working with the man. Cato was both chastened and impressed and, by the smug look on his face, Fisher knew it. The ute ahead signalled and turned right down a rutted farm track.

'What do you know about the foreman, Grant?' asked Cato.

'Trav? Play footy with him. He likes a drink, likes a bit of biff at a game. Gets the chicks. Needs to mind his manners around blackfellas a bit more but, apart from that, sound.'

'Trust him?'

Fisher turned to look at Cato. 'Sure. Think so. Why?'

Cato shrugged, he didn't know yet. Grant, to all intents and purposes, was nothing more than Stevenson's right-hand man at SaS. Maybe Cato just didn't like Travis Grant's manner or the company he kept.

Ahead he could see a collection of ramshackle sheds and a half-demolished barn with rotting support timbers and a rusted corrugated tin roof. Another fifty metres or so beyond, a copse of tea-trees shimmered in the heat haze. In the centre of them was a clearing and two caravans. Skeletal grey sheep wandered in clusters bleating mournfully in the hot still air. They were gathered hopefully around a rusted water trough but all it offered was a few centimetres of green stagnant sludge. Flies hung in a thick cloud above the deflated carcass of what might have been a lamb. Cato exchanged a look with Greg Fisher who wrinkled his nose in disgust. On any other day this place was a prime candidate for some Stock Squad attention.

Travis Grant's ute pulled up by the nearest caravan. Cato and Fisher halted alongside. Grant hopped out and slipped his sunnies down to his eyes. He lit up a cigarette then opened his arms wide in mock welcome.

'Home sweet home.'

Xi Xue stepped around from the passenger side smiling nervously.

'How many live here?' Cato's question was addressed to Grant.

'Eight ... usually.'

Cato took in the scene; the caravans were little, round, 1960s-vintage Sunbeam cruisers. They reminded him of childhood holidays and simpler, happier times. In their heyday they might have been comfortable for a couple, as long as they got on. Now, rusted, battered and propped up on bricks, they were each meant to be home for four men.

In the centre of the clearing were the smoking embers of a campfire surrounded by small boulders and bricks. Propped at an angle against the bricks, a fire-blackened hotplate. A collection of cheap plastic chairs and picnic benches were scattered around the fire's perimeter and, just beyond them, a pile of mallee roots to fuel the fire. Under one chair, a plastic draining rack with plates, cutlery, mugs, and pans all neatly stacked and covered by a red-and-white chequered tea towel. The place might well have seemed rundown but the residents did have some pride in their Spartan domain. There was no rubbish anywhere.

'Water?' Greg Fisher asked, barely hiding his disgust at what he saw as Third World conditions.

Travis Grant thumbed over his shoulder towards the sheds and barn fifty metres back. 'Tap over there.'

'Toilets? Showers?' Fisher pressed.

'Dunny and a shower in one of them sheds and there's showers on most of the worksites. This a union inspection or something?'

Cato leaned in close to Grant's ear, keeping his voice low and steady. 'Pull your head in and lose the backchat. Now show me Hai Chen's van.'

Grant coloured slightly but recovered quickly. He turned to Xi Xue, speaking over-loudly in his cartoon pidgin.

'Hai Chen, which van? Where he live?'

'He lives in this one.' Xi Xue gestured to the other side of the campfire.

They walked over, Cato wondering whether or not Xi's use of the present tense was a language thing or a gentle rebuke of Grant and his patronising manners.

Mick Hutchens was back to square one. He'd let Justin Woodward walk, as ordered from above. So far he had nothing on him except a gut feeling that he was a slimy little bastard. Unfortunately the jury would need more than that. The fucker certainly had friends in high places. Even though this was a murder inquiry–on a cop for Christ's sake–they'd been influential enough to get him released, very prematurely in

Hutchens' view. The lawyer, Henry Hurley, had buggered off back to Perth leaving Hutchens his card and a smug smile. Mick Hutchens knew it wouldn't be the last time they'd meet. He intended to win the next round.

A squad meeting was scheduled for five that evening. By then everyone and everything should be in place. A media conference would be held at six providing a live feed to evening news bulletins. After a weekend of relying on news feeds from the stringers in regional, the city editors had swung into action. The glamourati had descended and were prowling around Hopetoun desperate for quotes and complaining about what the wind was doing to their hair. The motel was full, the caravan park was full, the demountable workers village was full. It was a media circus and Hutchens was the designated ringmaster.

The police mobile command post had arrived and now sat on the gravel outside the town hall. Until the IT nerds descended on the afternoon flight to plug everything in, it was about as useful as a chocolate fireguard. Some civilians and spare uniformed officers had been freed up from Esperance and would drive over this afternoon to take up the dogsbody stuff. And come to that, where the fuck was Cato Kwong? He'd expected him to be hanging around like a bad smell and nagging to get a piece of the investigative action. Sulking? It wouldn't be the first time. Cato, Tess Maguire, and that Fisher kid represented spare hands that he could use right now and they'd all just disappeared like cockroaches with the light on. Hutchens made a note to himself to chase them down.

Lara Sumich and Mark McGowan were trawling through witness statements looking for patterns or inconsistencies. Some of the door-to-door interviews had thrown up a cock-and-bull story about an international drug sting, undercover cops, and the body on the beach. Wrong murder. Small towns and their rumours for fuck's sake, Hutchens shook his head in disgust. That reminded him, he needed to get a grasp on what was happening with the headless torso now that Woodward had dropped off the boil. Another good reason to get Cato Kwong in here. He tried the mobile. A recorded message, switched off or out of range. Hutchens tossed his phone into the in-tray and looked daggers at it.

A couple of DCs from Major Crime were keeping Woodward and his girlfriend under none-too-subtle surveillance. They'd received a cheeky little wave from her and the finger from him. The happy couple had moved in with friends across the road until their house was back in order and their seized belongings returned. So far forensics had picked up nothing of immediate consequence from the murder scene, Jim Buckley's motel room, or the Woodward house and car. However, clothes, shoes and the washing machine filter were being examined for blood traces, as was the Woodward wheelie bin. The coffee van was under guard in an enclosed courtyard at the rear of the town hall and undergoing the fine-toothcomb treatment. The van had been promised back to Woodward by the end of yesterday but Hutchens had drummed up an excuse to keep it overnight. The two things that had made Woodward twitch were Buckley's phone call and his search of the coffee van.

The Forensics OIC Duncan Goldflam eased his six-foot bulk gingerly down into the flimsy folding chair in front of Hutchens' desk. He looked glum.

'Whatcha got?' Hutchens muttered, already knowing the answer.

'Nothing much.'

'What's that mean?'

'Exactly that, boss, no traces of blood anywhere. Still a few things to check to see if they warrant further analysis. Then we're done.'

'What things?'

Goldflam shrugged, 'Stuff from the coffee van. Kitchen gloves, some empty Tupperware boxes, the filter from the sink, a couple of unopened cartons of coffee.'

'Who's on it?'

'Robertson and Hamlyn.'

They were two Perth scenes-of-crime officers with plenty of runs on the board. At that moment the younger of the two, Mark Hamlyn, sauntered through the door still dressed in his paper suit, overshoes, and facemask. He lowered the mask to reveal a mouth surrounded by nerdy acne but lit up by a big smile.

'Got something for you, boss.'

The Sunbeam caravan was dingy and carried a sour smell of men's sweat, unwashed clothes, cigarettes and fish sauce. No wonder they seemed to spend as much time as possible around the campfire. Every spare centimetre of space was used. Clothes, food, a TV, DVDs, CD player, a pack of cards, a chess set and some knick-knacks all competing for room that just wasn't there. Xi Xue and Cato stooped in the dark, tiny, acrid space. Travis Grant and Greg Fisher had parked themselves outside. Normally they might have been passing banter about footy or town gossip; now they were uncomfortably silent, Fisher studying his team-mate with suspicion.

Inside the van, Cato gestured around him. 'Hai Chen lived here?'

A nod from Xi Xue.

'Anything here belong to him?'

A shake of the head, Xi led Cato back outside. He bent down and pulled a dusty and cram-packed holdall out from under the caravan. Obviously they hadn't wasted time making use of available space. Cato snapped on some gloves, crouched down and started to go through the bag. Fisher spread out a sheet of plastic and readied variously sized evidence bags for itemising the contents. Grant sat himself on one of the plastic camp chairs, lit another cigarette, and made a big show of being disinterested. Xi hovered around the perimeter of Cato's vision, a slightly sad look on his face.

Cato began to speak into Buckley's digital recorder. The last entry was something about the head of a cow long, long ago and far, far away. He announced the time, date, location, and those present.

'Work overalls–trousers and shirt–dark blue and fluoro yellow. Unwashed.'

He passed them to Fisher who labelled and bagged them. The list continued: footwear, socks, underwear, casual shirts, trousers, a jacket. Cato pulled out the next item.

'Small black bag containing ...' he undid the zip, 'toiletries–toothpaste, toothbrush, two razors, soap, nail clippers, shampoo, comb.'

From this Cato was confident they would get the DNA sample they needed to confirm or deny that Hai Chen was Flipper. He dug further into the holdall: a tattered, yellow A4 envelope. Cato removed the contents one by one.

'A Chinese passport ...' he flicked through the pages, 'in the name of Hai Chen. Date of birth, 1st October, 1976.'

Thirty-two years old. Cato looked at the photo; it bore enough of a resemblance to the head he'd seen in the ranger's fridge a few days ago. Also in the envelope, some letters and visa forms; he'd study them later. Remaining items, some photographs: one showed Chen with a woman standing beside him smiling, a toddler on his shoulders, a baby in her arms–a picnic somewhere in China. Greg Fisher labelled and bagged it.

DC Mark Hamlyn waved a Tupperware box at DI Hutchens.

'Ice. Crystal meth,' he added unnecessarily for Hutchens' benefit.

Hutchens smiled. 'Well, well, well.'

'Minute dust traces only; a bag's been in here, a leaky one.'

'Lovely.' Hutchens beamed.

Goldflam and Hamlyn joined him. They all beamed. It was a beamfest.

'And there's more.' Mark Hamlyn pointed inside a cardboard box emitting a rich aroma of filter coffee. Tucked between two layers of coffee bags was a flat transparent envelope. 'Ecstasy.'

An estimated two hundred tabs. Was this what Jim Buckley found during his search of Justin Woodward's van? Was this what he chose to keep to himself? Was this what got him killed?

Hutchens' eyes twinkled. 'We're on to you, you little prick and when we bring you in next time we're going to have you fucking giftwrapped.'

Guan Yu's caravan, across the other side of the campfire, was a carbon copy of Chen's. There was the same dark, pungent claustrophobia, heightened perhaps because four people still occupied this one. If Guan had shared Chen's home maybe that was motive enough for murder: a bit more elbow room, one too many farts or loud snores. But he didn't live with Chen so it must have been something else. Still, the man seemed ready to confess all, so hopefully the full story would be known once the interpreter arrived. In the meantime, Guan Yu's belongings were to be bagged to help with any forensics to support the confession.

A low rumble in the distance signalled a new arrival. A silver Prado four-wheel drive roared across the paddock, skidding to a halt alongside Greg Fisher's paddy wagon. Keith Stevenson emerged, not happy.

'What the fuck is all this about?'

Travis Grant jumped up out of his camp chair, trying hard to look purposeful. Xi Xue tried to be invisible. Greg Fisher was busy bagging some of Guan Yu's clothes. Cato Kwong stood up slowly from his crouch over a battered suitcase that had served as Guan's wardrobe.

'Mr Stevenson, glad you could make it.'

Stevenson ignored Cato; he turned and addressed the uniformed Fisher. The snub was deliberate and provocative.

'This is private property. I hope you have a warrant?'

Cato struggled to control himself. 'This is a murder inquiry. We'd appreciate your cooperation, Mr Stevenson.'

Stevenson decided to pay Cato some attention. 'Or else what?'

'Or else I'll have detectives all over this place, all over your office, your home, your accounts. We'll turn you inside out and take our time about it.'

Stevenson snorted, 'Good luck, Jackie Chan. You'll need it.' He turned his spittle and wrath on to Travis Grant. 'Soon as he's gone, close the place down. I want all these Chinks off the payroll and off my property. Send them back ...' He brushed past Cato on the way back to his car. 'Every last one.'

'You'll have to wait until we're good and ready, Mr Stevenson. I'm declaring this property a crime scene. Nothing comes or goes from here without my say-so.'

'Well I came and I'm going. Be seeing you.'

Stevenson slammed his door and the engine roared into life. Cato gave him a wave.

'Count on it,' he murmured.

20

Monday, October 13th. Midafternoon.

'Thanks for telling me.'

DI Hutchens wasn't being sarcastic, he seemed strangely calm. Cato had been expecting an explosion. They were seated in the cramped confines of the Sea Rescue hut rather than the luxury of the town hall. Cato Kwong had wanted his bollocking to be as private as possible.

He'd been running the Flipper inquiry on the basis of seeming lack of interest from Hutchens rather than any given authority. He'd pissed off a local businessman and pillar of the community. He'd used personnel to conduct a search of the caravans without official sanction from his boss. He'd told Greg Fisher to take all the evidence bags from Paddy's Field and unload them on to Hutchens' forensic team; they were now waiting on word from the boss before touching said evidence with a barge pole. Cato had a man in custody facing a charge of murder. Finally, he'd summoned an interpreter from Perth at God knows what cost and without any authorisation. This was the first Hutchens was hearing any of this. Meanwhile the word was that the Buckley case was in trouble. All in all, Cato expected volcanics.

Tess Maguire had been called over to an incident at the primary school. She seemed subdued but Cato had also caught a half-mad gleam in her eye. He had too much on his own plate to give it any further thought. Coincidentally, behind Hutchens' strange calm, Cato thought he detected a mad eye-gleam here too. Maybe there was something in the water. Maybe he should check a mirror in case he had a crazed glimmer of his own: it wouldn't surprise him.

Cato had gone through it all behind the closed door of the Sea Rescue hut: the floating head in the cave, the Chinese connection, SaS Personnel aka Keith Stevenson and the granny director. Then there was Guan Yu putting his hand up for murder, Hai Chen, the caravans, the need for forensics to confirm that Chen really was Flipper. All through it Hutchens nodded, jotting notes here and there. Listening, not exploding.

Hutchens got on the mobile and gave a nod to Forensics to get to work on this new job as long as everything on the Buckley case was under control.

'The interpreter, when's he due?'

'He's a she. Afternoon flight.'

Ravensthorpe Airport was a runway, a shed, and a paddock. The flights were all Western Minerals fly-in fly-out charters with public access restricted–usually to fill out any spare capacity. These last few days the blue and orange-fluoro brigade was outnumbered by police, journalists, lawyers, and now interpreters. At this rate WMG were going to have to organise extra planes just to get their own workers to and from the mine. Hutchens let Cato know that he had already fielded one grumpy call from somebody in HR, whose cooperation was hanging by a thread.

'Bit rude you authorising that ahead of me.'

Hutchens was trying to look surly but couldn't quite pull it off. It was written all over his face, he was as happy as a pig in shit. It probably didn't get any better than this. Two murders on his patch, one of them a cop: a good quick result on one and significant progress to report on the other and all in time for the evening news.

'Sorry, boss. So, where to from here, sir?' Cato's feeble attempts at remorse and obedience were transparent but Hutchens clearly had other fish to fry. He looked at his watch, then at Cato.

'You stick with the Chinaman. Do a first-run interview with him as soon as the interpreter is here. We'll see how we go from there.'

Cato failed to smother his pleasure.

Hutchens wasn't giving it all away. 'I want one of my crew in there with you.' Cato nodded warily. 'Mark McGowan's not too busy. Take him.'

Cato forced a smile and a nod of thanks, too caught up in his own world to ask how it was going with the Jim Buckley case. Hutchens told him anyway. In another day or two he hoped to have enough to bring Justin Woodward back in and bury him. This was news to Cato.

'Really? I thought he was off the hook?'

'Released pending further inquiries. There's a difference, remember?'

'So what's the progress?'

'Forensics in the coffee van, drug traces.'

Cato nodded slowly, expression neutral. Hutchens looked him in the eye.

'There's a bullshit story going around town about an undercover drug sting, linking it to the carcass on the beach. Heard that one?'

Cato shook his head and shrugged.

Hutchens didn't let up. 'Stupid bumpkins got their murders mixed up. Buckley's the one that has the drug connection. What's his name, Flipper, nothing to do with it. That's right isn't it?'

Cato couldn't stand it anymore, he wasn't in the mood for cat and mouse games. 'I started the rumour, a bit of tree-shaking. We didn't have anything else at that point.'

Hutchens sat back and put his hands behind his head. 'Get the result you were after?'

Cato averted his gaze, his eyes blurred, his chest tightened. But he held it all together, just. The thought he'd been trying to bury for the last few days was now jumping around in front of him waving its arms frantically.

'Jim Buckley's dead. I think I might have caused it.' His

breath shuddered. 'I don't know what to say or do about that.'

Hutchens sighed. 'Neither do I, Cato mate.'

According to the phone call, Jai Stevenson had been held back after school to have a chat about the cackling, the disruptive behaviour and the animal noises. Tess had nodded down the line like she knew exactly what Kate McLernon was talking about. Poor love, first she finds a headless torso on her morning run then she has a mad kid threatening self-harm. Don't waste any money on a lottery ticket right now, Tess had joked, letting her know she was on her way.

When Tess arrived she found Jai sitting on a high stack of chairs in a corner beside the broad beans that were germinating in recycled milk cartons. He was pressing a pocketknife against his own throat. Most of the kids had gone home apart from a handful galloping around the playground just outside. They were making more acceptable after-school animal noises, oblivious to Jai and his knife and his throat. He was humming and swinging his legs. He seemed unaware that he'd pricked himself and that a tiny trickle of blood ran down his neck. His eyes never left the teacher's and he was trying hard not to smile but couldn't help himself.

Tess nodded towards the teacher and walked in. Outside, Greg Fisher was shooing the kids away from the playground and off home. Other teachers, unaware of what was going on, were wondering about the sudden police presence. Fisher shooed them away too. Tess sat on the corner of a desk a couple of metres away from Jai. Behind his head, blutacked to the window, the class photo – a mixed mob of kids squinting at the camera. There he was, second row, third from left, the dark red vertical scar on his upper lip helping to mark him out from the crowd. The Disaffected Youth of Hopetoun. On a good day you could read him as a shy kid desperately in need of friends, fun and a fair go. On a bad day, like today, he looked dark and malevolent, an ugly stain on the childhood innocence around him.

'Hello Jai, what's happenin'?'

He rolled his eyes and gestured towards the knife. 'Duh. What do you think?'

Tess acted like she'd only just noticed it. 'Oh yeah, the knife. So, what's this all about Jai? What's going on?'

'Her.' He chin-pointed in the direction of the teacher.

'Mrs McLernon?'

'She prefers Muzz.'

Tess grinned and rolled her eyes too, co-conspirator with Jai. 'Okay then, Muzz. What's Muzz McLernon been doin'?'

'Givin' me the shits.'

Ms McLernon looked out the window, expression unreadable.

'Not again.' Tess turned an accusing eye on the teacher. 'What's she gone and done this time?'

'Said I was making noises. Disruptin', shit like that. She's a fucking bitch. Always pickin' on me.'

Ms McLernon sniffed and drummed her fingers on the desk.

Tess nodded in apparent agreement. 'I reckon. So what's with the knife? How does that help?'

'Gonna kill meself. Sick of this shit.'

'Yeah?'

'Yeah.'

You and me both, thought Tess, there had to be better ways of spending your day than dealing with dipsticks like the Stevensons. Like, for instance, stalking your former tormentor. She'd tailed the Djukic minibus convoy all the way down the Hopetoun–Ravensthorpe Road until the mine turnoff. There they'd parted company, for the time being. John Djukic occupied all her waking moments (and too many of her sleeping ones) and she wished he didn't. A soft breeze rustled a photocopied word-sleuth from a nearby desk; it fluttered to the floor at Tess's feet. It looked like it was about the weather. She could make out some of the words ringed in yellow highlighter: THUNDER and LIGHTNING.

'I've got a better idea.'

'What?' His dark little eyes narrowing.

'Remember that time I took you kids for a ride in the van? Siren, all that stuff?'

Jai sneered, that was obviously for little kids. Three months ago he'd been rapt, a bit of hearts-and-minds stuff from the new cop in town, but not good enough, not any more. Jai found the monotone he was looking for.

'Wow. Cool.' He gave her the finger.

Tess was losing patience; eleven years old and already she could see the man he would become, a vicious, manipulative coward, like bloody John Djukic.

'Have you seen how these work?' She took the taser off her belt and held it out towards him.

Jai's eyes widened. He said it again but this time he meant it. 'Wow. Cool.' Hypnotised, he leaned forward.

Tess pulled it back from him. 'You need to put the knife down first though, Jai. Hand it to me, eh?'

Jai lowered the knife and reached out for the stun gun. 'Can I have it now?'

'Sure.'

Tess started to pass it over. He snatched at it and there was a brief clumsy struggle as Tess tried to hold on to the taser and get the knife off him. Then Jai Stevenson yelped and dropped like a stone.

Greg Fisher popped his head round the door and took in the scene: a little boy groaning on the floor, Tess clipping the taser back on to her belt.

'Shit Sis, did you just do what I think you just did?'

'You did what?' DI Hutchens' good day was turning bad.

'Tasered him, sir.' Tess Maguire looked down at her feet. She wondered vaguely about the chances of an earthquake in Hopetoun tearing open the floor in the town hall and swallowing her up.

'He's eleven fucking years old.'

No. Hutchens was the one tearing up the floor and swallowing people whole. Tess scratched her nose, she didn't know whether to burst out giggling or break down sobbing.

'Twelve next month, sir.'

'He's still a fucking kid,' hissed Hutchens.

'He had a knife, he was a danger to himself and others. It just kind of went off accidentally. Anyway I only had it on warp factor two.'

Hutchens breathed deeply. 'Why today, Tess? Why today?'

She studied a spot high on the wall behind him.

Hutchens closed his eyes and pinched the bridge of his nose. 'Is he okay? Up and about again?'

Tess brightened. 'Oh yeah. His mother came to fetch him. Right as rain now, bit shaken maybe.'

'Well he would be. Fifty thousand volts.'

Hutchens mobile trilled, a Hawaii Five-O ring tone. He listened for a moment.

'No fucking comment.' He snapped the phone shut. 'Channel Nine wants to know if the tasering of this eleven year old kid had anything to do with the murder of Jim Buckley.'

Cato looked up from his file. 'Are we ready?'

Suspect and interpreter nodded in unison. Cato announced names, times, dates and places for the recording. It was 5.30, the sky outside still bright. Guan Yu had been cautioned and had confirmed through the interpreter that, for the moment anyway, he was waiving his right to have a lawyer present. The interpreter, Jessica Tan, had stepped off the plane an hour ago and was sharp, efficient and ready to roll. Cato knew the type, he'd gone to school with lots of them. Confession time: he was one of them. Conscientious, always did their piano practice, always did their homework. Always did everything very, very well–except in his case. Jessica Tan looked about ten years younger than Cato. He wondered idly if she was related to the Tans from down the street where he grew up. Probably not;

anything less than doctor, dentist, or lawyer was abject failure for those Tans. Interpreter? Not a chance.

They went through the basics about Guan Yu. Age twenty-eight and married with one child, a daughter. A home address in Chengdu, Sichuan Province, China. A welder by trade, he had been in Australia for about six months. His contract was for a year. He had been recruited to come to work in Australia by Hai Chen who was also from Chengdu.

'Mr Guan, today you told me you killed Hai Chen.'

Jessica repeated it to Guan Yu who already half-understood. He nodded his confirmation, adding a clear 'Yes' for the recording at Cato's insistence.

'Tell me what happened.'

A deep, shaky inhaling of breath from the other side of the table, Guan speaking, Jessica almost simultaneously translating.

'It was Thursday. We had all been working on the pipeline again.'

Cato thought back to the projects lists on the contractors' websites, the desalination plant pipeline for the mine.

'Ten days without rest, long hours. Dawn to nearly dark.'

Cato nodded at him to go on.

'We were sitting around the fire. Eating. Tired. Ready to sleep. It was already dark.'

'Who is we? How many? Their names?' prodded McGowan.

Guan Yu obliged: five people, the rest at the toilet block or already asleep. He gave their names and they were written down with spell-checks courtesy of Jessica Tan. Cato cursed silently. He was quite happy to leave this nailing of detail for a later run-through. He didn't want Guan's train of thought derailed. He whispered to that effect in McGowan's ear and was answered with a curt nod.

It transpired that Thursday night was dues-paying night. That figured, Thursday being payday. Hai Chen was the gangmaster. He had organised the Chinese end of the hiring in return for a commission from the contracting company, SaS, and a percentage fee agreed with each of the hired men individually. Chen had the best English, acting as a go-between from day one. On Thursday nights he collected fifty dollars cash from each of his fifteen Chinese workmates.

Mark McGowan frowned. 'Fifteen? But there are only seven or eight people in the Paddy's Field vans. Where are the rest?'

Jessica translated. 'They live in two more vans at Barren Pastures.'

McGowan did the mental maths. Seven hundred and fifty a week on top of Chen's own wages. He whistled softly. 'Not bad.'

Cato gazed at Guan Yu. 'How much do you make in a week?'

'Five hundred.' Guan nodded, sticking his thumbs up. 'Good, yes?'

McGowan snorted. 'McBurger's wages.'

Cato glared at him and turned back to look across the table. 'So you were giving Chen ten per cent every week?'

'Yes.'

'Go on. Thursday night was pay night for Mr Chen.'

'I did not have the money.' Guan Yu looked down at the table.

'Why not?' McGowan again, sitting back low in his chair, arms folded.

'I don't know.'

'What kind of answer is that?' McGowan snapped.

'I needed it for my family.' Guan's eyes were filling up.

Cato leaned forward, a picture of sympathy. 'So what happened then?'

'He chastised me, loudly, in front of the other men. He slapped me.'

Jessica Tan finished the translation by mimicking the slapping gesture they had all seen already from Guan. The clock ticked on the wall. A phone rang in an office nearby. Cato waited for Guan's breathing to steady.

'What next?'

'He was walking away from me, laughing and insulting me, waving his money in the air ...'

Jessica Tan flicked her wrist back and forth, a loads-a-money gesture. Guan Yu said something and flicked his finger across his throat. Jessica Tan provided the translation.

'I cut his throat. I bled the fat greedy pig.'

21

Monday, October 13th. Late afternoon.

Tess Maguire stood outside at the window for a moment and surveyed the scene. Melissa lay on the couch staring at *Deal or No Deal* without seeming to take any of it in. The TV volume was way up, it wasn't like it was a quiet show anyway, and Tess had heard it halfway down the street. iPod wires trailed out of her daughter's ears and four bottles of Lemon Ruski lay dead on the floor at her feet. The kitchen screen door rattled open.

'What the hell is this?'

Tess was home relatively early by her standards. It had been a short if tumultuous day. She'd stalked Johnno Djukic; tasered an eleven year old and probably would face assault charges from his parents; been carpeted by some fuckwit from Albany and ordered to take the rest of the week off and, quote, 'Sort your bloody self out.' They seemed to think she had a problem with anger management, that maybe she wasn't completely rehabilitated, would perhaps benefit from some more counselling. Anger-fucking-management? Dickheads. She looked over at her daughter. Now this.

'Turn that crap off. Put those bottles in the bin. Have a shower and smarten your bloody self up. I want you back out here in ten minutes. We need to talk.'

Melissa rolled her eyes. Didn't bother moving anything else.

Tess tried again, louder. 'Did you hear me?'

Not even a shrug.

Tess stormed over and stabbed the TV off then turned on her daughter who was busily feigning boredom and indifference. Tess wanted to punch her. She leaned forward with her hand out, Melissa flinched. Tess yanked the earphones out, grabbed the alcopop bottles and flung them in the bin.

'Okay we'll talk here. Now, what's going on?'

'Nothing. Leave me alone.'

Melissa finally moved. She jumped up and stormed into her room, slamming the door behind her.

'Melissa. Come back here.'

A shriek, sounding like it emanated from the depths of hell, came from the other side of the door.

'Fuck. Off.'

The door flew open and Tess was astride her daughter on the bed, face crimson with rage, head roaring and a hot mist fogging her vision. One hand was bunched around Melissa's collar, the other pulled back in a fist.

'Mum!' Melissa's eyes were wide with terror. 'Mum, stop!'

The spell broke. Tess looked down at the terrified face below her. She lowered her fist. 'Oh God, Mel. I'm so sorry.'

Melissa's face crumpled. She looked about four. 'Get out. Please just get out.'

Tess got up and left, utterly desolate; not knowing how to come back from what she'd just done.

'Show me how you cut him. Which hand was the knife in?'

Guan Yu waited for the translation, he looked at Jessica Tan, seeking guidance. She flicked her hands uncertainly, she was an interpreter not a lawyer. Cato stood up and got Mark McGowan to join him. He stood behind McGowan, reaching around with his left arm to secure him, then bringing his right hand across the neck in a slicing motion.

'Like this?'

Guan Yu shook his head. Cato released his victim.

'So show me. Here. Mr McGowan is Hai Chen.'

McGowan crooked his finger at Guan encouragingly. Guan Yu rose to his feet giggling nervously and went to stand behind McGowan. Cato gestured for him to proceed. The self-confessed killer stepped forward reaching with his left hand to grab McGowan by the hair, gently.

'This man very big, tall, Chen not so big.' Guan let go of McGowan's head.

Cato asked his colleague to crouch a little. 'Better?'

Guan nodded, 'Yes, a little more please. Good.'

Guan stepped forward again, grabbing the back of McGowan's head with his left hand and driving the thumb side of his right fist into a spot just below McGowan's right ear. He mimicked the withdrawal of the blade and another stabbing motion into the front of the neck and a wrench back towards the original wound. If Guan Yu was having any scary flashbacks to that night of blood and terror, his face didn't reveal anything: he could have been slicing Peking duck on a slow night in Chinatown. Mark McGowan crossed his eyes, clutched his throat and poked his tongue out in schlock horror. Jessica Tan couldn't suppress a nervous titter. Guan Yu joined in the macabre mirthfest with a high-pitched hee-hee of his own. Cato calmed them all down. He kept Guan and McGowan in their positions.

'What happened then?'

'He fell down. Dead.' Guan Yu was coping remarkably well without the interpreter.

'How do you know he was dead?'

This time Guan waited for Jessica to translate, and Cato waited for the response.

'Maybe he didn't die immediately. He made noises. Gurgling. Moaning. Maybe it took a few minutes. A lot of blood.'

'Did anybody see this?' McGowan, with pen poised over his notepad.

'Of course, everyone must have seen it.'

'What did they do?'

'Nothing.'

'Nothing?' Cato double-checked with Jessica.

'Nothing.'

'Nobody tried to help him?'

'No,' said Jessica for Guan Yu. 'We all hated him, we all watched him die.'

Cato Kwong checked his watch. It was dark outside now, just the wrong side of eight. It was clear that everyone was getting tired. Jessica Tan's translations were taking longer, brains were seizing up, McGowan was yawning for Australia. An infusion of the disgusting coffee from the cafe down the road had done nothing for anyone's spirits or tastebuds. Pushing on would be counterproductive but Cato was desperate to know, at least in brief, how Hai Chen went from being dead in a field twenty kilometres inland to dismembered flotsam on Hopetoun beach. As far as he could tell, Guan Yu appeared not to have any ready access to a car, never mind a boat. Cato smiled encouragingly at Guan and the interpreter.

'We will take a break very soon. Just a few more questions for today.'

They nodded for Cato to proceed. Guan's nod looked less enthusiastic, he seemed to be getting bored with confessing to murder.

'So you watched him die. What happened to the body after that?'

'We covered him with a...' Guan and the interpreter struggled for the word, 'a tent sheet...'

'A tarpaulin?'

'Yes, tarpaulin, and we left him for the night. I was going to bury him in the morning.'

'So you left it overnight. Covered in tarpaulin?' Nods. 'Then what, you went to sleep?'

'No, we sat around the fire and drank whisky. Lots of whisky.'

As you would, with a dead body a few feet away, thought Cato.

'And in the morning you buried the body?'

Cato tensed; if the answer was yes then how did it end up on the beach? Guan Yu shook his head. Did he magically conjure up a four-wheel drive and a boat? Did somebody help him? Was Cato on the verge of wrapping up the mystery of Flipper?

'No.'

'No? Why not?'

Guan Yu scratched his neck and gave a little embarrassed cough. 'Hai Chen was gone.'

No room at the inn. Stuart Miller smiled wearily at Pam the Fitzgerald River Motel receptionist and flicked his wallet shut. He couldn't believe how long the drive had been: hours and hours, nearly nine of them in fact. Admittedly he had got lost on the back roads of the southern wheatbelt taking what–he had been assured by the guy at the Albany Highway roadhouse–would be a really good short cut. It had turned out to be a winding, sign-less, kangaroo-strewn nightmare. Now he was here, it was dark and he was exhausted and hungry. The motel was full and the cafe was shut. Welcome to Hopetoun.

Jenny had taken the call late last night, Sunday. It was from her nephew Tony, Jim Buckley's eldest. Apparently it had taken them the whole weekend to recover enough from their news to remember to phone their Auntie Jenny. Just in case she wanted to know, Tony had said. No wonder Jim hadn't been answering his phone and text messages. The funeral was a few days off yet. At this point they hadn't even released Jim's body. Apparently it had happened very late Friday night or very early Saturday morning. Miller already knew it to be the latter. Jim had been talking to him on the phone at just after midnight; voice slurred, wind noise in the background, and water. Waves? How much longer did he have to live then? A minute? An hour?

Miller started the car, a new model Statesman, and pulled out of the motel car park. He headed for where he thought the sea might be. Opposite the pub he could see and hear waves breaking on the beach, a milky-white froth in the moonlight. Off left from the main street, the slip-road led down to a wide groyne lit at the far end by a single lamppost. The pub looked empty, on the verge of closing. The lights were off in the cafe next door. He drove on to the groyne, crunching across the rutted, potholed gravel, and came to a stop under the light near the small wooden jetty.

He knew he'd agreed to pass on any developments to Detective Tim Delaney but somehow he hadn't got around to it yet. He felt a tad guilty, particularly as Delaney had come good and phoned through with an answer to something that had been nagging him. How Arthurs, a simple shipyard worker from Sunderland, had managed to get a new ID to travel abroad. Delaney had the Immigration Department run a check on incoming passengers circa 1973. No computerisation back then but a visa record in Sydney did flag an overstayer. Andrew Arthurs, Sunderland, UK. Davey's younger brother, same height and as alike as made no difference. Davey had used his little brother's passport, simple.

'So he's not The Jackal,' said Delaney. 'He's just a nasty, scabby, opportunistic little mongrel.'

'True enough,' Miller had concurred, 'but both still have a lot of animal cunning.'

Would he ever let Delaney know he had a red hot lead on the south coast? Maybe. Maybe not. Miller still harboured the fantasy of bringing Arthurs in, the Mountie getting his man. He reclined his seat, grabbed his jacket from the back as a makeshift blanket, and tried to sleep.

Cato Kwong knew he probably shouldn't be doing this, but he couldn't sleep and the urge was too strong. The town hall Major Incident Room, as it was now called, stood squat, silent, and dark. Thin moonlight filtered through the roadside gums and a soft breeze tugged at their leaves. There was not a soul about. Cato slid a key into the lock on the flimsy plywood door and turned the handle. It was a spare that McGowan, as part of the official team, had been issued. On the drive back from

Ravensthorpe, Cato convinced him he'd left his own official-issue key at the lockup and just wanted to access the database to check something out. The younger man had yawned, accepted the lie, and handed over the key.

The door opened with a rusty squeak, he left the lights off. He knew where he was going and made immediately for the far corner of the hall. He sat down on the stool and lifted the lid. The peeling white gloss coat on the old upright piano seemed to glow in the moonlight beaming through the windows. Cato pressed down on the pedals; the left one was particularly stiff. He ran his fingers up and down the keyboard. Most of the lower register was out of tune. That would make for a very dodgy left-hand arpeggio.

He started playing–Chopin's Nocturne in B-Flat Minor, Opus 9, Number 1. It was one of his three selected pieces for the performance exam he sat when he was fifteen, still young enough to be a child prodigy although pushing it a bit. The other two were Bartok's gypsy songs and a Schubert impromptu. But the Chopin was his favourite: haunting, melancholic and passionate, according to his piano teacher Miss Grabowski who, to her eternal chagrin, was born a hundred years too late and lived in Fremantle instead of Warsaw. She was old-school and spat derisively when he mentioned that most of his little friends were learning by the Suzuki method.

'We are artistes, Philip; we don't do painting by numbers here.'

After five years with her, his knees had grown hairy, his thighs muscular, his hands big yet still nimble enough to skip through the cantilena.

He played it now, cascading down through the keys. After tripping over it so many times and with Miss Grabowski's trembling hand lingering on his to guide him, she had finally announced one day, with perspiration on her upper lip and an accent she'd conjured from her family tree, 'You are ready.'

But in the examination room under the steely gaze of the

Board he realised he wasn't. He froze. So many of his 'little friends' in their Suzuki classes had sailed through this moment because regular performances before an audience were a staple of their teaching. He stumbled over the Chopin cantilena and killed his child-prodigy prospects stone dead. Humiliated, head boiling and eyes brimming, he'd stormed out of the examination room and flung his music books into the nearest bin. Out on the street the first thing he saw was two cops chasing a young guy down the road before beating the crap out of him in broad daylight. That's when Philip Kwong realised what he wanted to do with his life.

It had taken a long time for him to retrieve the joy of playing piano for himself, the calming meditative pleasure. And he'd since learned that there was more to policing than what he'd witnessed after his piano exam. Failed child prodigy, failed police poster boy and failed ace detective. He brought the nocturne to a close with a clunk on the off-key low notes. Cato Kwong was relatively calm and at peace with the world. The applause from the shadows scared the living daylights out of him. Lara Sumich sauntered through a shaft of moonlight with a playful half-smile and sat down on the stool next to him.

'Bravo,' she whispered.

Her shoulder brushed his, so did her hip, thigh, and knee. Her perfume was discreet, musky and probably very expensive. The moonlight on her neck revealed a sheen of perspiration. Come to think of it the temperature did seem to have risen a touch.

'How's the case going?' she inquired casually.

'I'm thinking of finding a proper job. Maybe Cato the Carpenter.'

'Elder or Younger?'

'What?'

'Isn't that where you got it from? The ancient Roman lawmaker? I can't remember whether it was Cato the Elder or Younger but one of them was a byword for incorruptibility.'

'That education of yours was worth every cent.'

Lara pursed her lips. 'Mind you he was also known as an uptight, austere bigot.'

'That's sounding more like me I must admit.'

Lara tinkled a couple of bars from 'Für Elise'.

'Fancy a duet?'

They played a rollicking plinking-plonking exuberant round of 'Chopsticks' before collapsing into adolescent giggles. Then, with the echoes still dying around the old gyprock walls, Lara placed her hand high on Cato Kwong's thigh and planted a long wet kiss hard on his mouth, allowing her fingers to flutter across his zipper as she broke contact.

'Good night, Detective Kwong.'

And she was gone, leaving him flushed, flustered and with a throbbing groin. It wasn't until later that he realised he'd neglected to ask her what the hell she was doing there at that time of night anyway.

Tess Maguire was halfway through a bottle of gin, Mother's Ruin some called it. Melissa hadn't come out of her room, the offer of dinner was ignored. Tess had left her own plate pretty well untouched too. It sat there in the middle of the kitchen table, pasta shells doused unceremoniously with a jar of ready-made bolognaise sauce, congealing now under a sixty-watt bulb. It was dark outside, still and cool, a cloudless night with millions of stars.

The radio murmured low in the background, a late-night talk show discussing the global financial meltdown and when and if it was going to wash up on the shores of this wide brown land. Given the so-called turmoil, the voices were calm and reasonable, verging on the soporific. Tess had been dwelling on her own personal meltdown and was contemplating possible remedies. There they stood lined up on the table ready for inspection. Sleeping tablets, tranquillisers, antidepressants. Up. Down. Up. Down. The doctor had prescribed like he owned the pill company. None of it had worked. None of those pills had managed to purge Johnno Djukic from her system. Tess Maguire unscrewed the caps, one by one, spilling the contents out onto the table in front of her and mixing them up like Scrabble tiles.

22

Tuesday, October 14th. Early morning.

'Bullshit.'

That was DI Mick Hutchens' succinct reaction to the news that Hai Chen's body had disappeared into thin air according to Guan Yu. Cato Kwong flipped his palms upwards; he had run out of answers. In fact, he was running out of questions too. His brain felt like it was coated in sump oil. They were at Hutchens' desk in the town hall. The sun was just up, bursting over the treetops. Outside there were hammerings, rattlings and cursings as the Mobile Command Centre was being lowered from the trailer to its new home in the town hall car park. The way things were going there was every chance that both murders would be solved before it was ever open for business.

'Dead set, that's what he's saying.' Cato was standing up, too tense to sit. He hovered near the dusty old upright piano and lifted the lid to glance abstractedly at the yellowing ivories and the hot, troubling mental snapshot of his midnight tryst with Lara Sumich.

'Bullshit,' Hutchens repeated. 'Keep at him. He's spinning a line.'

'Why? He's already admitting to murder. What's to be gained from disowning the body?'

'Fuck knows how his mind works but stick with him. We want his whole story to fit, right through to the lump of meat on the beach.'

Cato sighed and nodded. He took a swig of coffee, and relished the rich smooth taste. The Major Incident Room was now equipped with a plunger and several bags of boomtown-priced Brazilian blend from the general store. Things were looking up but what they really needed, thought Cato, was for Justin Woodward to be out of the frame for Buckley's murder so the bloke could get back to doing what he did best, strong flat white. With his free hand Cato tinkled a two-fingered version of the opening bars of 'I don't like Mondays', The Boomtown Rats.

Hutchens was impressed. 'Good job it's Tuesday. Didn't know you played piano.'

'Chinese,' Cato pointed to his own face. 'So, where are you at with Woodward?'

An upward twist at the corner of Hutchens' mouth. 'The drug traces in the coffee van, confirmed as eckies and ice.'

Cato whistled. 'Nice. Anything else?'

Hutchens shook his head. 'We're trawling the phone records, bank accounts, witness statements. Talking to intelligence in Perth about any whispers on Woodward.'

Or Jim Buckley, thought Cato, loath to speak ill of the dead. But he voiced his thoughts anyway. Hutchens met his eye.

'Yes. That too.'

Lara Sumich appeared in the doorway, bright-eyed and bushy-tailed. 'This private?'

'No,' they said in choirboy unison.

She graced them both with a smile, throwing in a free iris-flare for Cato, and strode across to the small kitchen at the back of the hall, footsteps echoing on the jarrah floorboards. She flicked on the kettle and dropped a tea bag into a cup, Hutchens enjoying her every move, Cato idly watching Hutchens and waiting for his blood to subside. What was he these days, fifteen? He needed to get a grip; he was technically old enough to be her father.

He ahemmed to get Hutchens' attention. 'I'll get on up to Ravensthorpe. Any chance of any forensics on Hai Chen's stuff today? Something to keep us ticking over?'

Cato inwardly winced at the almost pleading tone he'd adopted. Hutchens had already moved on from Flipper, his mind was probably on Lara, or the Buckley case, or plotting his next career move.

'I'll talk to Duncan, I'll get him to call you.'

Mark McGowan hovered at the door, recently showered and shaved. He lifted his chin in Cato's direction. 'Ready to put the screws on Mr Yu?'

'Mum. Wake up.'

Tess Maguire stirred and opened one eye. She'd fallen asleep in the armchair and her neck had seized up, leaving her head to one side with the chin slightly raised like she was deep in thought.

'Mum.' Melissa's voice; a bit more urgent, a hint of panic.

Tess's temples throbbed and her neck felt like it was encased in freshly poured concrete. Then there was her stomach. She lurched out of the chair, dizzy with the pain of the hangover, rushed to the toilet and chucked her guts up. She was there seven long minutes until her belly was empty and only bitter bile remained. That and the thumping migraine.

'Disgusting,' Melissa sniffed, handing her mother a cup of tea.

Tess eyed the tea suspiciously, then decided she had nothing to lose. It tasted wonderful.

'Shouldn't you be at school?' she croaked.

'Shouldn't you be at work?'

'I'm on stress leave.'

'Me too.'

Tess mustered a smile: Melissa, a sharp answer for everything, wonder where she got that from? She looked outside, it was shaping up as a glorious spring day.

'Fancy a swim?'

Melissa shook her head. 'No. Thought I'd have a shower. Maybe clean my room. Go for a walk.'

Tess nodded slowly. 'Want company?'

'No. Not right now. Thanks.'

Melissa looked like she was about to say something else. Tess waited for it, Melissa obliged.

'I thought I was meant to be the reckless out-of-control one around here.'

Told, by a fourteen year old. The upside was it was the longest conversation they'd had in weeks.

A rap on the windscreen. 'Mate, wake up. You okay in there?'

Stuart Miller snapped his eyes open and jerked upright. A spasm shot down his neck and along his right shoulder from cramped and seized-up muscles. Miller wound down his window, squinted and smiled at the concerned, weather-beaten face bent towards him.

'Yeah, thanks ...' Miller thumbed over his shoulder back towards town, 'no room at the inn. I arrived late.'

The fisherman grinned and gave him a relieved thumbs-up. 'No worries, thought you might be another dead'un. Dropping like flies around here.'

Miller wiped some sleep dribble off his chin and pretended ignorance. 'What do you mean?'

'A cop murdered, right here. At the weekend.'

'Jeez,' Miller whistled and shook his head. 'Did they get the bloke that did it?'

'Nothing announced but I heard they lifted somebody on Sunday. Drugs they reckon: a Colombian syndicate. Probably supplying the miners.' He nodded sagely then stuck his hand through the open window. 'Davo.'

'Stuart.'

They shook.

Miller cocked his head, he couldn't do much else, it seemed to be stuck in that position. 'You said, dropping like flies, sounds like more than one?'

'Yeah, a few days before that, a body on the beach. Well, bits of one apparently. No head they say.' Davo grimaced.

'Are the two cases connected?' Miller pulled the lever to bring his seat upright.

'Who knows?' Davo patted the side of his nose with his

index finger. 'This town has gone to the dogs since that mine opened. Anyway, need to see if those fish are biting. Glad you're not another dead'un. Catch ya later.' Davo waved ta-ta and strolled down to the end of the jetty, unfolded his chair, and opened his tackle box.

Stuart Miller yawned, stretched, cracked a few vertebrae and started the car. The sun was up and the ocean was calm and blue. It was already shaping up to be a lovely day in Hopetoun. Miller's stomach rumbled; he went in search of breakfast.

Tess Maguire reached forward, clawing the water and dragging it back before lifting her elbow high for the next lazy long stroke. The ocean was crystal clear, bracingly cool and flat as a sheet of glass. There was not a breath of wind. The sun glinted through the droplets from each stroke, dripping diamonds. All you could hear was the movement and splash of water made by one person – her. Under the surface, clumps of brown weed hovered above the sand, a curtain of tiny baitfish lifted and parted, terrorised by a gang of herring. Tess focused on her stroke, cupping the water and drawing back, kick regular but strong. She had the beach to herself. Hugging the shoreline, she headed west from the groyne over towards the boat ramp with the pontoons floating twenty metres out to her left. Ahead in the far distance, Mount Barren and the hills of the national park as clear and sharp as a photograph. Something stirred and lifted in the sand ahead of her, a stingray, maybe a metre wide. Black wings and a whip-like tail flicking as it glided away out to the depths.

Another movement, a darting shadow over to her left in the deeper water. Was it still the stingray? Her heart raced. It was less than a week since a pair of sharks had deposited Flipper in the shallows on the far side of the groyne. Even though he now apparently had a name, it was Flipper that stuck. There it was again, over to her right this time. Tess stopped, trod water, and looked around. What did they always say? You never see the one that gets you. Why did every moment of beauty in this place seem to come with an edge of terror? There, again, in front this time, coming her way. It swam into clear vision before her, a baby sea lion, sleek, fawn, with deep, dark-brown patches. Consummately graceful under the water, it darted around behind Tess and then appeared right under her, swimming in the same direction. It turned on its back, still swimming along and now looking directly up at her. The bugger was smiling. Tess snorted and laughed, swallowing seawater, coughing, spluttering and laughing some more. She was back in her own depth now. Planting her feet in the sand but keeping her head under water she followed the sea lion's movements as it darted here and there and round and round while she blubbed her heart out.

Cato had checked his emails before he left for Ravensthorpe. The Perth pathologists' reports on the torso formerly known as Flipper and the Quoin Head head sat in his inbox. He'd printed them out to read in the car on the way up. Reading in the car gave him travel sickness so he braced himself, scanned the report and tried to ingest the details as quickly as possible. They were in one of the Albany CIB Commodores. McGowan had slotted in a CD of something repetitive and not too lyrically challenging. He seemed happy enough to nod his head in rhythm, admire the view, and not chat. That suited Cato.

The good news was that the head and the torso were from the same body. That helped. There were also similar cutting marks on the head end of the spinal column corresponding to those on the torso end. The teeth were in reasonably good shape so, depending on the efficiency of the Chinese dental profession, it should be possible to get a match if the records exist. All good so far. Cato could taste the beginning of the salty bile of travel nausea. He looked up from reading and fixed his eyes on the road ahead to steady his churning stomach. McGowan stopped nodding to the music.

'Everything okay?'

'Yeah. Sure. Just thinking.'

'Don't strain yourself. You look a bit peaky.'

The inner turmoil receded. Cato risked another skim of the report: nothing about Guan Yu's graphic description of slitting Hai Chen's throat. Would time in the water have erased traces of that? He noted a mobile contact number at the end. He rang it.

'Stephanie Kennedy.'

One of Perth's leading pathologists. And, by the sound of her voice, one of the tiredest too. Cato checked the clock on the dashboard, 7.05. He winced.

'Sorry for disturbing you so early.'

Cato introduced himself and referred her to the case. 'Dr Kennedy ...'

'Professor,' she corrected him.

'Professor. Do you recall seeing anything resembling knife wounds in the neck?'

'Is it in the report?'

'No.'

'Then obviously I did not.'

Cato outlined the scenario Guan Yu had described and raised the issue of whether or not immersion in sea water for a few days might affect things.

'Undoubtedly it would, but those kind of wounds should still have been detectable.'

'So as far as you're concerned there was no indication of knife wounds to the neck?'

'That's correct.'

'So how did he die?'

There was an exasperated sigh at the end of the line. 'Have you actually read my report, Mr Kwong?'

He could feel a self-inflicted ambush coming on. 'I'm just going through it now.'

'Well maybe you should have read the whole thing before bothering me. Page two towards the bottom: there was a bullet lodged in the skull. He was shot.'

Cato shook his head and looked again. Yes, there it was, in plain English.

'Shot,' said Cato dumbly.

McGowan winked at him.

Professor Kennedy mmmed patronisingly at her end of the line. 'That's right. And the two other things to note: a very recently broken nose and a gash on the back of the head. Will that be all Mr Kwong?'

'Yes, thanks Professor.'

She tutted and ended the connection.

'Somebody's been telling us fairytales,' said Mark McGowan.

Cato released a little belch to help settle his tummy.

23

Tuesday, October 14th. Midmorning.

'So the next morning you wake up planning to do something about the body.'

Cato Kwong kept his voice and face neutral. Inscrutable, that was the word they always used. The Inscrutable Mr Kwong.

'Yes, but he was gone.' Guan Yu nodded, eager to please.

Jessica the interpreter looked as bright and crisp as it's possible to be after a night in the Ravensthorpe Motel – situated a cosy thirty paces from the main bar of the Ravensthorpe Hotel.

They'd gone through the whole story again and Guan Yu was sticking to the script he'd produced yesterday, including the bull-dust about slitting Hai Chen's throat. Mark McGowan was playing out the rope and Guan Yu was winding it around his neck.

'As you say, he was gone, but we'd like to take it a step at a time and get as much detail as possible.' McGowan's voice was soothing. They'd decided to switch roles for the day: McGowan good, Cato bad. They didn't expect Guan to fall for it, they just fancied a bit of variety. 'So what time did you wake up?' McGowan pressed, gently inquisitive.

'Five a.m.'

McGowan wrote himself a note. 'Five. And where did you plan to bury him?'

'He was gone,' insisted Guan through Jessica Tan, who was clearly beginning to share his confusion as to why they were pursuing the matter of the burial that didn't happen of the body that wasn't there.

'Yes, later he was gone. But you didn't know that at the time.

You had a plan to wake up at five and do something about Hai Chen before work started?' McGowan smiled, encouragingly.

Guan Yu's eyebrows creased in a frown then he shrugged. 'Bury him.'

'How. Where.' Cato–curt, bad Cato.

'With a spade, away in the bush behind the sheds.'

'Show me.'

Cato drew a little mud map with the caravans and the sheds. He passed the notepad and pen across the table. Guan hesitated and then he chose a spot. X marked it.

'Just you? Or did you have help?' Cato keeping his gaze cold.

'He was gone. We did not do it.' Guan Yu, and Jessica interpreting his exasperation.

'We?' snapped Cato.

'Me,' said Guan Yu.

McGowan changed tack slightly. 'So what were your thoughts when you saw the body was gone?'

'What?'

'What did you think? Did you think it was strange? Did you look for it? Did you ask your friends if they'd seen it anywhere?'

McGowan and that encouraging smile again. Cato was beginning to warm to him.

So was Guan Yu; he produced a look of shared bewilderment, bringing DC Mark McGowan into his confidence. 'Yes, very strange, I thought to myself, how can this be? I looked around the area but nothing.' He opened his eyes wide and lifted his palms to illustrate his words, Jessica the interpreter aping the gesture.

'Weird.' McGowan shook his head slowly, sympathetically. 'And then you just had your breakfast and sat and waited for the work bus to arrive, yeah?'

Guan Yu nodded and added a 'Yes' for the recording.

'And did you think about it anymore? Where it could have gone? Who might have taken Chen's dead body?' said McGowan.

Guan shrugged. 'Mystery.'

'Yes, sure is. And what about Mr Grant, Travis, he didn't ask where Chen was?'

Guan shook his head emphatically.

Cato leaned in close across the table and spoke low and menacing. 'Bullshit. All bullshit. Now let's try again. This time I want the truth.'

Guan waited for Jessica Tan to translate even though it was clear that he already understood.

Cato tapped his finger on the manila file in front of him. 'Maybe I need to explain to you. We have the head and body of Hai Chen. We have done medical tests. We know he was not stabbed, he was shot. So tell me where you put the gun after you killed him.'

As Jessica translated, Guan Yu's face changed to genuine bewilderment and now fear.

'Gun? No. No gun.'

'Bingo.'

Lara Sumich flipped shut her mobile. DI Hutchens checked his watch, gritted his teeth, and gestured for her to continue their rudely interrupted conversation. Lara took a sip of herbal tea and smiled appreciatively like they had all morning to chat. Was she deliberately winding him up or what?

'That was OCU,' she said.

The intelligence section of the Organised Crime Unit in Perth had just joined some dots between Justin Woodward and Freddy Bataam aka Freddy Sudhyono aka Riri Yusala. Admittedly the dots were faint and a bit scattered, based on grudge-bearing dobbers, scuttlebutt, and supposition. But wasn't that the basis of most intelligence? Countries had gone to war on less and in police work there was no such thing as coincidence. It seems Freddy Etcetera kept very bad company in skanky-druggie land, continually running up debts and getting on the wrong side of the wrong people. He should really have been picked up and deported as an overstayer but he kept on being useful to the OCU; apparently he dobbed at the drop of a hat. What with the dobbing and the drug debts he obviously liked living dangerously. OCU had him down as a friend of a friend of a friend of Woodward's.

Hutchens frowned. On its own the intel was less than impressive but taken as part of a bigger picture it was, well, a bit better. Stay positive.

'The case against his nibs is building nicely,' he murmured. 'Keep digging Lara. Go fetch.'

Hutchens had spent most of the morning snarling down the phone at reporters who seemed more interested in the tasering of a little brat than the murder of a cop. Lara dismissed, he got back into the swing of his bad temper.

'Where's Tess Maguire?' he barked.

Greg Fisher hovered uncertainly near the whiteboard with a sheaf of papers. He'd been drafted in as a dogsbody. 'She's at home, sir. Apparently you told her ...'

'Get her in here. Now.'

Greg Fisher picked up a phone.

DS Duncan Goldflam popped his head around the door. 'Something you need to see, boss.'

Lara Sumich glanced over her shoulder.

'What now?' Hutchens growled.

'I think you'll like it.'

Goldflam winked at his boss and crooked his finger. It was the kind of thing you only dared do if you'd worked with Hutchens for long enough and knew him well enough. Goldflam ticked both boxes. Hutchens followed him outside. They clumped up the three steps into the forensics van.

Goldflam closed the door and lowered his voice. 'We've got a match.'

'A match of what, for fuck's sake.'

'Jim Buckley's hair on the jeans Woodward was wearing the night of the murder.'

'I thought you'd already run all those tests on day one?'

'We went over them again in case we missed anything. After we found the drug traces it just seemed worth doing a due diligence.'

Hutchens studied Goldflam and his little band of eager beavers for a moment.

'Bingo,' he said approvingly.

Tess Maguire nodded at RSL Russell at his usual table outside the general store. He looked through her like she was a wisp of smoke and returned to studying the day's *West Australian*, RSL raffle tickets and collecting tin temporarily demoted while he caught up on the news of the world. Tess shook her head and smiled to herself. Grumpy old bugger. She wondered how long she'd have to live in town before he acknowledged her existence. In the shop she picked up some milk, bread, tea bags and filter coffee. The latter a sop to Cato, she was an instant girl from way back. Pandering to Cato the coffee snob? Why? She shrugged to herself and got a few funny looks in the checkout queue. Shrugging to yourself, that was only a short step to talking to yourself. At the checkout, the operator, a gravelly voiced, hard-faced woman, beamed at her.

'Morning Tess, how ya goin?'

Tess was taken aback, she almost looked behind her in case there was another Tess hiding back there. The checkout woman was usually a female version of RSL Russell–not the effusive type.

'Good thanks, you?'

'Good yeah.'

Tess did some detective work and checked out the badge on the woman's uniform. It said Margie; it meant nothing.

'Great.'

Tess nodded and beamed, packing her things into a shopping bag. Margie gave Tess her change and winked. Tess wasn't sure what to do so she winked back.

'See ya darl,' said Margie brightly.

Tess's mobile trilled: Greg Fisher.

'DI Hutchens wants to see you.'

'Yeah?'

'Yeah. Urgent.'

'Okay. Won't be long.' Tess closed her phone, the swim and the sea lion already ebbing into the distance.

As she dropped her shopping bag into the car boot a silver Prado screeched to a halt in the angle-park next to her. The driver-side door slammed shut on a fug of cigarette smoke. In the back seat was Jai Stevenson, looking sorry for himself.

'You fucking animal.' Kerry Stevenson planted herself in front of Tess.

'Hi Kerry,' said Tess.

'You could have killed him.'

It had been a while since there'd been a stand-up row in Veal Street. The handful of shoppers and passers-by had a ringside seat and were not even pretending not to stickybeak. Tess's new best mate Margie had stepped outside for a smoko. Even RSL Russell had ventured out from behind his card table and stood beside Margie, arms folded. Tess thought she detected a glint in his eye.

'This probably isn't the time or place, Kerry.'

'Bit too public for ya,' she growled. 'Prefer to torture ya kids in private?'

Tess pushed past and got into her car.

'You haven't heard the last of this,' snarled Kerry.

A nicotine-yellowed finger prodded Tess's driver-side window. While his mum continued raving, Tess could see Jai in the back seat with his little Gollum smile. As Tess crunched her car into gear, RSL Russell winked at her. Did he really just do that? Then Margie the checkout chick gave a thumbs-up, mimed tasering Russell beside her, crossed her eyes and stuck out her tongue, grinned and gave the thumbs-up sign again. Tess was finally accepted in Hopetoun. She looked up into the Prado. Jai's smile had evaporated.

Stuart Miller tapped Greg Fisher on the shoulder.

'Got a moment?'

The young copper didn't seem too impressed at the physical contact. 'What can I do for you, sir?'

Miller offered his hand. 'Stuart.'

Greg Fisher gave his name and shook the hand. 'Yes, Stuart?'

'Jim Buckley, he was my brother-in-law.'

Fisher visibly relaxed. 'Oh right, yeah. Sorry about Jim. Terrible thing to happen, terrible.'

'What exactly did happen?'

'Maybe you should have a chat with the senior officer, Inspector Hutchens, he's just inside.'

'Yeah I will, sure, but he'll be a very busy man. Maybe you could just give me the bottled version.'

Stuart Miller smiled reassuringly, Greg Fisher didn't buy it.

'Do you have any ID, Mr ...?'

'Miller.' He showed him some.

'Thanks Stuart. Look I really think the best person for you to talk to is Inspector Hutchens.' Greg Fisher gestured towards the door of the town hall.

Miller sighed, smiled and followed him.

The young cop opened the door and gallantly waved him through. 'You know, Stuart, that accent of yours. You sound just like a bloke I was talking to recently.'

'If he's willingly confessing to murder does it matter if the story's a bit rubbery? Maybe he just needs his memory jogged.' Mark McGowan slurped on a strawberry milkshake.

Cato didn't want to tell him he'd been down that path before and been burnt. Badly. McGowan probably knew anyway. 'It needs to add up in court or we'll look like idiots. Or worse ...'

They were taking a break in the Country Cafe down the hill from Ravensthorpe cop shop. Cato had ordered a pot of tea; he was increasingly wary of coffee in these parts. McGowan had the bright pink milkshake and an energy bar. Must be a gym thing, mused Cato. Jessica Tan was getting increasingly perplexed by the turn of events. She had advised Guan Yu urgently that he really should go no further without a proper lawyer. He had readily agreed. One was on the way now from Albany, due by midafternoon.

'So what's it all about? What's he playing at?' McGowan slurped some more pink stuff up through a long black straw.

Cato didn't know. Nothing made sense. On the verge of a confession, an easy win in the Flipper case had suddenly been snatched away from him. Maybe that was the point: it wasn't meant to be an easy win. Karma–one of Jane's favourite concepts. So-called easy wins had been his undoing in the past. Now he had to pay in some way.

'He's either making it up as he goes along ...'

'Yes but why?' said McGowan.

'He wants the attention? It wouldn't be the first time some sad bastard has copped to a murder he didn't commit.'

McGowan's eyes met Cato's briefly then moved on to a faraway spot out the window.

'Or he's covering for somebody else?' McGowan crumpled up his energy-bar wrapper.

'Same question you raised. Why?' Cato squeezed the last bit of flavour out of his tea bag.

'He owes somebody? He's scared of them?'

'Scared enough that he prefers a long prison stretch for murder?'

McGowan noisily drained the last of his milkshake. 'As you said, he wouldn't be the first sad bastard to see it that way.'

DI Mick Hutchens shook Stuart Miller's hand and offered condolences and reassurances about how they were doing everything they possibly could and yes they would follow up on that cold-case connection with SA Homicide, blah blah blah. He could see that Miller didn't believe a single word of it. Miller had explained how Jim Buckley had called him at midnight on

Friday convinced that he'd seen this Davey Arthurs aka Derek Whatsisname in the pub. Within an hour he was dead.

Hutchens nodded his head patiently. 'Yes, yes maybe but Jim had been drinking heavily, he couldn't be sure if it was your man. If he was then why didn't he challenge the guy? He didn't. So surely this Davey Arthurs bloke, if it was him, would have no reason to attack him, would he?'

Miller shifted his balance to the other foot and exhaled sharply. Not happy. Hutchens was on a roll.

'At the most it's a coincidence, Stuart. But my money is on mistaken identity.' He made a show of taking Miller into his confidence, two old cops together. 'Between you and me, mate, we've got someone in the frame for this. We just need to tidy up some loose ends. Give us a few days.'

He patted Miller's arm, an off-you-go-now gesture. Off Miller went.

Hutchens' phone rang. He listened for a moment, a grin spreading across his face. 'Right, cheers, we'll get someone over straight away.' He thanked the caller, put the phone down and smiled at Lara. 'Fancy a drive? Albany. They've got a Freddy Bataam sitting in the lockup. They're wondering if we'd like to talk to him.'

Freddy Bataam, hopefully the last nail in Justin Woodward's coffin. Lara Sumich picked up her car keys and almost skipped out of the room, ponytail bouncing with joy. Hutchens knew the feeling.

24

Tuesday, October 14th. Midafternoon.

'This is totally unacceptable.'

Amrita Desai shook her head in disgust. Jessica Tan nodded hers in grave agreement. Cato Kwong and Mark McGowan served up a pair of benevolent smiles. Guan Yu absorbed everything and gave little away. It was getting crowded in the interview room, and hot; the air conditioning was on the blink. A freestanding fan had been brought in but it was playing havoc with the paperwork on the table. Through the small, high window a shaft of light from the late afternoon sun fell across the scene: two on one side of the table, three on the other. Cato had just done the preliminaries for the interview and the young, bright-as-a-button Legal Aid lawyer from Albany had immediately put her protest on the record.

'I repeat, this is totally unacceptable.'

She was referring to the previous interviews with Guan Yu, conducted without legal representation.

'Shall we proceed?' DC Mark McGowan clicked his biro tetchily and raised his eyebrows to the assembled company. He was outnumbered: he was the only Anglo in the room and he probably wasn't used to it.

Guan nodded eagerly in response. He was sandwiched between the two women. He wouldn't have had such proximity to the female of the species in months. The heady aroma of the women's perfumes charged the air in the small stuffy room. For all the perversity of the situation, Guan Yu looked like he was beginning to enjoy himself. Cato took stock of the situation, sensing the day slipping out of his grasp.

He took them back to the beginning of Guan's story and

asked him, yet again, to talk about that Thursday night, Hai Chen's payday, and what went on around the campfire. Again Guan stuck to the script. When he got to the part about the description of how he killed Chen, the lawyer stepped in.

'No, no, no. We need to stop. I need to consult with my client.'

Cato gritted his teeth. 'Haven't you already discussed this? You had two hours with him before we commenced the interview.'

'Two hours consultation and preparation for an interview that could result in a murder charge? Really, Detective Kwong.'

'But he's already described this scene to us at least twice.'

'Without any legal advice.' Amrita Desai tapped her pen on the tabletop for emphasis.

'He declined it.'

'He's Chinese. He hardly speaks any English.'

'He had an interpreter,' McGowan chipped in.

'That doesn't mean he, or she ...' a finger flick towards Jessica Tan, 'understood his legal rights.'

'They were read to him before we started.' McGowan's voice was rising.

'Legalese. How can you know whether he really understood the meaning and implication of the words Ms Tan translated to him?'

Cato glanced at Jessica Tan. She was looking a bit miffed. She probably thought she'd done an okay job, now her ability as an interpreter was being questioned by this ... lawyer.

'Interview suspended, 5.12 p.m.' Cato nodded to McGowan. They picked up their things and headed for the door.

'As I've said before, we believe the taser was accidentally discharged during a struggle and I must stress the officer involved was following procedure. There was a clear indication that the young man presented a danger to himself and to others.'

DI Mick Hutchens had been ambushed by the media pack outside the Major Incident Room at Hopetoun town hall, the camera lights casting an eerie glow on his hunted face.

A question from the crowd: 'Was it not possible for two adult police officers to subdue him in any other way? Did the situation really require the use of something capable of giving a fifty-thousand volt electric shock to the little boy?'

Mick Hutchens held out his hands and gestured downwards trying to calm the throng. 'The matter is being investigated and the officer has been transferred to other duties. Until we have all the facts I am unable to comment any further.'

'So Sergeant Maguire is being disciplined then?'

'That's not what I said.'

Tess Maguire picked up the remote and killed the TV. Whatever weasel words Mick Hutchens used, the reality was that, yes, Sergeant Maguire was being disciplined. Stood down from normal duties pending the outcome of the inquiry; that was the upshot of her summons to the town hall today. Tess had remained calm and surprisingly untroubled when Mick Hutchens informed her that Sergeant Paul Abbott would share his week between Ravensthorpe and Hopetoun to plug any gaps in Tess's routine duties. Given that Hopey was crawling with cops anyway you wouldn't get away with dropping a lolly wrapper these days. A part-time replacement for a full-time Tess, that pretty well summed up how useful she was in the job right now.

She felt good. The morning swim had reinvigorated her in more ways than one. The job sucked and she didn't need it. The kerbside confrontation with Kerry was also revealing. She was now flavour of the month around town because she'd fulfilled their deep craving for rough justice–on a little kid, for Christ's sake. Much as he might have deserved it over the years, zapping kids wasn't actually her job. Tess was aware that she was part of a creeping fashion for using the taser as a first resort of domination and punishment rather than as a means to defuse genuinely dangerous situations. No, Senior Sergeant Tess Maguire wasn't fit for duty and she was the first to admit it. Working out a healthier relationship with her daughter was infinitely more important right now. Working out a healthier relationship with herself came even before that. She would never be able to do so until, one way or another, she got Johnno Djukic out from under her skin. Now she had all the time in the world to think about how to do exactly that. Suspended. Perfect timing.

'Doesn't look like Billy Mather to me.'

Greg Fisher peered at the newspaper clipping Stuart Miller had given him. He'd remembered the story from the previous week. The picture hadn't registered then and didn't now. They were sitting in Stuart Miller's car parked out on the groyne in the same spot he'd spent his cramped and uncomfortable night. Miller had gone in search of the young plod immediately after leaving the town hall; the kid had mentioned something about funny accents. Fisher wasn't available until late afternoon so Miller spent the intervening hours bringing his notebook up to date. The record of his inquiries and observations was a backup. If he had the heart attack that had been threatening these last few years he didn't want this work wasted and yet another chance lost to nail Davey Arthurs, even if it meant Detective Tim Delaney getting all the credit. The notebook was in the glove box, next to his heart pills.

The sun was dropping over the Barren Ranges in the national park, casting an orange and pink glow over the world. The sea rippled in the soft evening breeze. A handful of anglers cast hopefully off the end of the jetty for a feed of herring. Further in the hazy distance, tiny silhouetted figures fished for bigger prey from the beach. It was as peaceful as a postcard. Both men ignored it. They were mesmerised by the horror perpetrated by Derek Chapman aka Davey Arthurs aka Bobby Kerr. But was he also Billy Mather?

Greg Fisher shook his head and handed the clipping back to Miller. 'I can't see it.'

'But you said he had an accent like mine and Jim Buckley said he'd spoken to someone that night in the pub, he thought it was Arthurs. Look again, go on, please.' Miller pushed the clipping back at Fisher.

'Mate, I'm sorry, I don't think they're the same man.' Fisher was losing patience. Miller asked him again to describe Billy Mather. He sighed heavily and did so. 'About one seventy-five tall, grey close-cropped hair and beard, blue eyes, skinny.'

Miller double-checked his mental maths; centimetres to feet and inches, the height still fitted Arthurs, and the eyes. Even if the photofit had made him plump instead of skinny, why couldn't Fisher see it?

'The nose ...' Greg pointed out, 'Billy Mather's nose isn't that big. His ears don't stick out. The whole shape of the face.' Fisher tapped the photograph and shook his head emphatically. 'If it's him he looks nothing like he looked thirty years ago.'

Miller folded the newspaper shut. 'Neither does Michael-fucking-Jackson. Where does Mather live? I want to see him for myself.'

Greg Fisher checked the clock on the dashboard. 'Six-forty, I'm off duty.'

Miller looked up and grinned. 'So what are we waiting for?'

'My client has prepared a statement which I have been instructed to read on his behalf.'

Cato Kwong closed his eyes, folded his arms and sat back in his chair. The confession and miracle result on the Flipper case was about to disappear into thin air. Mark McGowan glowered across the table. Amrita Desai moistened her crimson lips and commenced reading. Cato nodded slowly; in many ways he'd seen it coming as soon as she walked through the door. Her client was a simple man, she was saying, his command of English was severely limited, he was not adequately informed of his legal rights nor appropriately cautioned about the implications of anything he might say. Consequently he now retracted his previous statements. The lawyer handed a copy to Cato.

Mark McGowan exploded. 'The fucker admitted to it twice. He walked out of the crowd and asked to be cuffed. Nobody forced him. Nobody tricked him. This is fucking bullshit.' He slammed his hand down on the desk.

Guan Yu and Jessica Tan jumped. Amrita Desai looked slightly disapproving.

Cato added his own warning glance before turning back to face Desai. 'Is your client prepared to answer any further questions?'

'Of course, he is willing to assist in any way he can.'

Cato turned to Guan Yu. 'Tell me what happened on the Thursday night when Hai Chen collected his money. Tell me how he died.'

'I do not recall,' came the translation.

25

Tuesday, October 14th. Mid evening.

'Likes his bloody peace and quiet doesn't he.'

Stuart Miller had been in Hopetoun for just under twenty-four hours. He hadn't showered or shaved for nearly two days. His face was grizzled by grey stubble. His clothes were beginning to assume a life of their own. They had called in at Greg Fisher's house so the younger man could change out of his uniform and marked car and into jeans, T-shirt and an unmarked, battered fifteen-year-old Hilux. Miller had noticed a beautifully maintained 1970s Land Rover glide by while Fisher was inside getting changed. A real classic, unlike this rust bucket.

The ute's suspension was shot to hell but at least it was, if required, four-wheel drive. According to the lad, some sections of the gravel road out to Starvation Bay could develop axle-shearing potholes almost overnight from a good rain. Potholes or not, the journey was playing havoc with an arthritic trapped nerve in the small of Miller's back. He hadn't expected Billy Mather to be living forty kilometres away along an unsealed road. He was tired, smelly, hungry and in pain.

Greg Fisher swerved as a roo crashed through the bush and across their path.

'Bit of a hermit our Billy. Free spirit. The outback is full of them.'

He was clearly enjoying himself. And why not, maybe he was about to be a key player in unlocking a thirty-odd year old murder mystery. Does a young lad's career prospects no end of good. And if not? Well it was a nice night for a drive, clear and still – but bloody bumpy. Miller grimaced as the ute fishtailed round the turnoff to Starvation Bay.

A nearly full moon flickered across the surface of the Southern Ocean. There was a gentle breeze punctuated by the scratchings and twitterings of animal nightlife. The light was on in Billy Mather's caravan. They pulled up and hopped out, Miller standing tall and arching his back to ease out the kinks, cramps, and aches. A washing line fluttered gently. A folding card table and a frayed, old-fashioned canvas deckchair sat under a makeshift tarpaulin awning strung between the caravan and an adjacent gum tree. The card table was marked with coffee cup rings, a pair of well-worn thongs beneath the deckchair. There was a smell of recent cooking: meat, eggs. Something else, Miller couldn't place it.

He was uneasy but not sure why. Was it just that he was out of practice? He glanced around and then through the trees just a few metres away he noticed it: the classic old Land Rover he'd seen earlier in town was parked nearby. Coincidence–or had Mather been following them? Owt or nowt? His unease grew. There was no sign of any other life in the camping area. No campervans, no grey nomads. Billy Mather obviously had the place to himself. So why hadn't he appeared at the approach of Greg Fisher's rumbling and wheezing out-of-condition ute?

Greg called out. 'Billy. You in? It's Greg Fisher. The cop from Hopey, remember?'

Nothing. Maybe he was asleep. Miller tapped on the door. They waited. No reply. Fisher looked at Miller and shrugged. The curtains were drawn in the windows. Miller tried to look through a gap. He could see a stove and sink, some plates and cups, unwashed. No sign of Billy Mather. A mournful bird sound rose from the trees followed by a rustle and flutter. That smell teased his nostrils again, what was it?

'Try the door?' said Greg.

Miller turned the handle. As the door swung open there was a rasping, scraping sound and the smell got stronger. Miller realised too late what it was. Gas. The caravan exploded.

Miller lay on his back, paralysed. His clothes were on fire, his face raw. Flames crackled and spat in the darkness. His eyes felt gummed together, everything blurred. He couldn't hear or see Greg Fisher. He became aware of a presence near him, the scraping of a foot, somebody crouching down, breath warm in his ear.

'You know mate you seem very familiar. I never forget a face, me.'

A clicking noise, it was the snapping of fingers, the sound of remembering.

'Detective Sergeant Miller? That it? Aye, thought so. Saw your picture in the *Sunderland Echo*; kept it in me scrapbook for yonks afterwards.'

Miller tried to speak.

'Sorry, didn't catch that, bonny lad. Hey that's a lovely car you've got by the way. Sticks out like a sore thumb around here though. You can spot a stranger a mile off.'

Miller could smell burning flesh and realised that it was him.

'So how did you find me? Was it all down to Wonder Boy over there? Him and his trick questions about the lights on the boat ramp? They were none of my business, that's why I said nowt. That's what people never learn. Mind your own business and you canna gan wrang.'

Miller didn't have a clue what he was talking about. He just wanted the pain to stop. There was the noise of an engine in the distance. Davey Arthurs started to move away. Miller clawed at his arm. He felt a pat on his shoulder.

'No marra, you just rest yourself there. I'll be back in a minute.'

26

Wednesday, October 15th. Dawn.

Cato wrinkled his nose. The air was acrid with the stench of smoke, melted rubber and plastic. Charred clothes hung from a bizarrely intact washing line in a grotesque mockery of the devastated scene. DI Mick Hutchens and his forensics man, Duncan Goldflam, were deep in conversation. A tie-less and shirt-sleeved Mark McGowan was taking notes from a bewildered grey nomad and his distressed wife. Lara Sumich looked like she hadn't slept; she'd driven the three or four hours from Albany and gone straight to the scene. For all that, she seemed to be buzzing. Now and then she would catch Cato's glance and lock on for an unsettling second too long. Lara was interviewing the caravan's owner, a shell-shocked, grizzled old hermit called Billy. Blue and white tape secured the area around the still-smouldering remains of the caravan. Cato Kwong didn't really know what he was doing there. As far as he could tell he was surplus to requirements. Maybe they wanted him to help with a grid search or to make the coffee.

Across the millpond serenity of Starvation Bay, wispy orange and pink-tinged clouds fanned across the brightening sky, heralding sunrise over the carnage. A fire truck tended by Hopetoun volunteers was damping down. Recent heavy rains had helped ensure that the flames hadn't spread. Such a conflagration didn't bear thinking about. A fire investigator was on the way from Albany and more were on standby in Perth if required. Arc lights still illuminated the scene for the photographers and forensics team. The ambulances were long gone: one was headed for the airstrip to meet the Flying Doctor for emergency airlift to Perth, the other to Esperance Hospital, a two-hour drive east. Tess Maguire was accompanying the patient in the Esperance-bound ambulance. DI Hutchens had hardly paid her or Cato any attention. He clearly already had plenty on his plate.

Cato surveyed the scene from beyond the tape and tried to make sense of the little he knew. Greg Fisher and an older man, Jim Buckley's brother-in-law and apparently a Pommie ex-cop according to Hutchens, had been found seriously injured on the ground in front of a burnt-out caravan owned by one William John Mather. That was him over there, being interviewed by Lara. Cato knew him as the one Fisher had interviewed about boat movements in connection with the Flipper case. The stalled Flipper case that would have to revert to the hard slog of painstaking investigation now that Guan Yu's confession was withdrawn. History was repeating itself and Cato was not learning from it.

Greg Fisher wasn't in uniform when he was found. It was his heat-blistered ute, not his police wagon, that was parked a short distance away on the other side of the flame-singed gum tree. So their visit didn't appear to be official police business. Jim Buckley's brother-in-law and young Greg Fisher, what were they doing calling on this hermit on a dark night in the middle of nowhere? There had been an explosion, probably gas. The men had been found by Billy Mather at around 10.00 p.m. when he returned from an evening fishing trip. He had prevailed upon a couple of grey nomads arriving late in their campervan to drive back to within mobile phone coverage to report it while he tended as best he could to the injured.

It was touch and go. Greg Fisher, en route to Esperance Hospital, had second-degree burns to the upper body. The other man was in a much more serious condition; somebody said he was likely to lose his sight. Cato could see the markings where Fisher and Miller had been found. Forensics were wrapping up the video and photography side of things, flicking off the arc lights. Lara Sumich finished talking to Billy

Mather; somebody had rustled up a cup of tea for him from a thermos. He now sat dazed, in a folding chair outside the taped perimeter, staring into space and cradling the warm cup in both hands. Hutchens and Goldflam were also winding up their chat.

The boss summoned them all before him with a casual wave, mustering them away from earshot of the witnesses. Goldflam's forensics team continued their analysis of the site. Hutchens nodded briskly towards Lara.

'The old boy, what's his story?'

She scanned her notes. 'As per the initial call-out, he got back from fishing around ten-ish– couldn't be exact, time's not really his thing– saw the flames and found Fisher and Miller. At the same time the couple in the campervan rolled up. He got them to phone triple zero and he stayed and tried to help ...'

'Yeah we know all that already. Why were they visiting him?'

Lara shrugged. 'He doesn't know. He recognised Greg Fisher from previous meetings in connection with the beach torso ...' her eyes connected with Cato's, 'but he didn't know the other man, Stuart Miller.'

'He had no idea why these two men should drive all the way out here at night-time to visit him?'

'No, boss.'

'Jim Buckley's brother-in-law, an ex-cop himself, takes an interest in Herman the Hermit here and enlists Greg Fisher's help. Nobody knows why?'

Shrugs and blank faces. Hutchens looked sceptical but whatever he was thinking, Cato noted, he kept it to himself. The DI shifted his attention to Mark McGowan.

'What have you got?'

McGowan flicked through his notepad. 'Mr and Mrs Hale: him Peter, her Nancy, from Toowoomba. Doing the "See Australia Before You Die" thing; arrived late last night, around 10.00, 10.30 They'd taken a wrong-turn and got bogged. Got in here, flames, et cetera, the old guy ...' he thumbed over his shoulder towards Billy Mather who was still staring into space – or trying to listen in, Cato couldn't be sure – 'running around like a madman. He got them to try to phone for help, they were out of range so he told them where to go, so to speak.' McGowan smiled at his little joke. Nobody joined him.

'Once they got back from making the call what did they do, what did they see?' Hutchens pressed.

'They tended to them as best they could until help arrived about an hour later. They also tried chucking a few buckets of water at the flames but it was no use.'

Hutchens checked his watch. 'Anything else?'

'No, sir, nothing.'

'Did he catch anything?' Cato to Lara.

'What?'

'He was out fishing. Catch anything?'

She yawned. 'I'll check if you like. Want to know what bait he was using?'

'No need, I'll take a look for myself later thanks.'

Cato got a funny look from Hutchens who then took up where he'd left off, barking instructions to all and sundry.

'Mark can you put in a call to the ambulance guys and Tess Maguire? I want an update on the patients. If Greg Fisher is able to talk, get her to ask him what he was doing here last night.'

McGowan yessirred and Hutchens switched to Paul Abbott, acting Hopetoun sergeant.

'Organise for a couple of uniforms from Ravensthorpe or Esperance to get out here to mind the place once forensics is finished. Then get Mr Mather to the motel in Ravy, soon as the hospital has checked him over. Organise some clothes and stuff and get somebody to stay with him for a while to make sure he's okay. We'll have him in for a chat later.'

Next it was the turn of Lara Sumich.

'Lara, you can drive back with me ...' he tossed her the car keys, 'and tell me about your trip to Albany.'

All boxes ticked, Hutchens squinted at Cato, 'I'll see you back at the ranch. We need to have a talk.'

Cato watched them go, wondering what the talk with Hutchens was going to be about. Apart from the terse exchange at the end, Hutchens hadn't paid him any attention. He hadn't been interested in an update on Guan Yu. He hadn't given Cato any specific task at the fire scene. He hadn't said goodbye nicely. What was he trying to say? This is what you're missing out on? Welcome to your world'–'the margins. Was Hutchens that spiteful that he'd get a man out of bed for the night to let him know he's as useless as a cheap Chinese import? Yes, he was. But Cato suspected there was something else at play. Was he being tested or auditioned in some way? Was he being deliberately kept at the margins because Hutchens knew that was his favourite stamping ground? Cato shook his head; too deep, too meaningful, too early in the day.

An old green Land Rover and trailer were parked on the boat ramp. Cato glanced in the windows. There was the usual paraphernalia: map book, lolly packets, a baseball cap, and a packed holdall on the floor space behind the driver's seat. The old man must have been planning a trip before his world turned upside down. Behind the car and trailer, Mather's tinny lay half-in and half-out of the water. With an incoming tide it was on the verge of floating off again of its own accord. He must have seen the flames and jumped out giving it a cursory pull up onto the ramp to try to secure it. Cato kicked off his shoes and socks, rolled the bottoms of his jeans up, and pulled the boat further out of the water. The cool ocean felt good around his feet and between his toes. He looked inside the dinghy: a fishing rod, a half-bag of berley and another of bait; squid bits, sealed with a rubber band and resting at the bottom of a red plastic bucket. No water in the bucket and no fish. A poor result for the night. A thermos, it felt full. He twisted the cap and sniffed the contents. Coffee. The aroma was rich and warm. Had Mather forgotten to drink it in all the excitement, or was his thermos full and his bucket empty because he hadn't yet gone fishing? If the latter, then why say that he had? Cato stifled a yawn. Let Hutchens and his Ace Detectives work it out. Last on the inventory: a rolled up and slightly damp edition of yesterday's newspaper. He weighed the options and consequences. Would he be tainting evidence if he drank the coffee and stole the crossword? Possibly. Probably. He poured some coffee into the flask-top cup and sipped. He'd had worse.

'Need a lift?'

It was McGowan calling down from the campsite. Billy Mather had paused with the back door of the car half-open. Paul Abbott was already in the driving seat looking expectantly at McGowan. The police contingent had commandeered the two four-wheel drive paddy wagons and a Prado borrowed from the motel owner. The detectives' Commodores would have been useless on the potholed road.

'No thanks.' Cato called back, holding up the keys to the Stock Squad vehicle. McGowan nodded, waved, said something to Mather and hopped in the paddy wagon next to Abbott. Billy Mather looked a little longer down at Cato before getting in the back. Cato realised he had a cup of Mather's coffee in his hand and the newspaper under his arm. The poor old bugger had lost his home, his thermos, and his *West* in one fell swoop. Cato Kwong, Mr Sensitivity.

Cato strolled back up the boat ramp to the blackened ruin of Mather's home. He approached the blue and white cordon tape and nodded a greeting to Duncan Goldflam. Goldflam was a diehard Hutchens man. The response was a surly, suspicious, and barely perceptible head twitch.

Cato ignored the snub. He gestured over towards the van. 'What do you reckon?'

'About what?'

'The van, was it an accident?'

'Who wants to know?'

Cato shrugged nonchalantly; what he really wanted to do was jump up and down on Goldflam's head, teach the nerdy fucker a lesson in civility. Cato Kwong, born-again aggro boy; where did that come from?

'The boss just asked me to take a look. Second opinion,' he lied.

Goldflam obviously didn't know whether to believe him or not, then must have decided it didn't matter anyway. 'Seems kosher enough to me. Help yourself. Look but don't touch.'

The fire crew, ambulance, Mather and the grey nomads, along with Fisher and Miller had all left prints in the sand and gravel. Water from the fire hoses and buckets had saturated everything in sight. There was no real need to tiptoe through the tulips here. Besides, it looked like an accident, not a crime scene. Cato approached the epicentre of the blast.

The van was now little more than a blackened shell. Three of the walls and most of the roof had disintegrated in the fierce heat, as had most of the floor. Half of the wall on which the stove sat had survived. The blast had radiated out from that point. The tyres on the trailer base had melted but the metal components and base-frame remained. There was little evidence of any of Mather's personal belongings surviving the inferno. Cato caught sight of something fluttering on the ground. He knelt down to examine it, a charred fragment of what looked like brown packing tape stuck to the edge of what remained of the caravan door. It was about ten centimetres up from where the door handle used to be.

'Did you see this?'

Goldflam came over and crouched down beside him. Peering closely he could see there were small dots of red paper or paint stuck to the tape. He appraised Cato with a sidelong glance.

'Could be something. Could be nothing. I'll take it away for a closer look.' Goldflam photographed and bagged the buckled, smoke-blackened section of the door. 'If you see anything else, Sherlock, give me a hoy.'

'Poor bastard,' Cato muttered.

'Say something?'

'The old boy, nothing left.' Cato waved his newly acquired newspaper at the devastation.

Goldflam snapped shut his equipment case. 'Looks like his simple life just got simpler then.'

'No shit?'

'That's what he said.'

They were in the motel Prado and Lara Sumich was in the driving seat. She'd just delivered Justin Woodward up to Hutchens courtesy of Freddy Bataam aka Riri Yusala. They were back on the sealed section of the road about ten kilometres east of Hopetoun. To their left the Southern Ocean shone blue to the horizon. Out there a distant smudge of dark cloud hovered; it may or may not make landfall, the weather jury was still out. Overhead a hawk hung in the soft morning breeze before swooping for its breakfast. A couple of crows feasted on a recent roadkill, leaving it until the last possible second before hopping out of the path of the car, flicking their wings and shaking their heads contemptuously.

Hutchens shook his head too and smiled. 'Justin Woodward killed Jim Buckley because he was being blackmailed by him?'

Lara kept her eyes on the road. 'Makes sense, boss. Jim did find drugs in the coffee van but kept schtum to Cato. Then he phoned Woodward later and demanded a slice for his silence. Woodward, after talking it over with his associates, takes care of business, his way.'

Hutchens tapped the passenger-side window absent-mindedly with his index finger. 'Beautiful. Lovely story. And Bataam, Yusala, whatever the fuck he's called, he's signed up to it?'

'He will, boss, dotted line.'

Hutchens fixed her with a steady eye. 'Everything's falling into place nicely then.'

She gifted him a coy, admiring smile and credit where it was due. 'You've cracked it, boss. Shall we bring him in?'

Hutchens nodded. 'Get Woodward, but gentle on him this time, nice and civilised please. Leave McGowan in the office.'

Cato mixed himself a double sachet of coffee and finished drying his hair. After a sleepless and, for him, wasted night out at Starvation Bay, a shower and a further caffeine fix was a prerequisite for making it through the rest of the day. He wrapped the towel around his waist, took a sip of coffee and scanned Billy Mather's crossword but his brain was all crypticked out. All was obviously not what it seemed at the accident scene–first and foremost what were Greg Fisher and the Pom doing there anyway? Looking out of his motel window on to the morning quiet of Veal Street he saw Lara Sumich returning from a run. A mad dash to Albany and back and a sleepless night had clearly not taken too much of a toll on her. What was she on? She saw him through the window and waved. Cato felt a stirring below as he remembered their late night encounter in the town hall. He started counting downwards from fifty to make it go away.

There was a knock on the door. He opened it. It was Lara, flushed from her run, dark sweat patches between her breasts and under her arms. All the usual places.

'Morning,' she said, using her bottom lip to blow some cooling air up her face.

'No rest for the wicked?' said Cato.

Too late, he realised the tent in his towel was on display. Lara smiled and stepped across the threshold, kicking the door closed with her heel.

'No, no rest, not yet.'

She peeled off her top and shorts, kicked off her running shoes and pushed Cato on to the bed loosening his towel on the way. Straddling, she lowered herself onto him. The movement was slow and deep.

She leaned forward, hair brushing his face and placed her nipple in his mouth. His tongue jiggled at the ring. He'd expected something like that to be erotic but really it felt like discovering a plastic toy in your cornflakes. Still, Lara seemed happy enough.

'No rest for the wicked.' She closed her eyes and gripped him tighter, her breath quickening.

After several months of celibacy Cato was no longer able to contain himself. Some time later Lara shuddered and collapsed on him.

'Well and truly fucked,' she murmured, a sob escaping her throat as she came.

'Me too,' groaned Cato.

Lara opened her eyes, slightly startled, like she'd forgotten he was there.

27

Wednesday, October 15th. Late morning.

'So what's your next move?'

DI Mick Hutchens folded his arms, sat back, watched and waited. Cato's attention was miles away. He was consumed with guilt even though his marriage was over. At the same time he hadn't realised how much he'd needed a good seeing to. Hutchens coughed him back into the moment. Cato collected his thoughts and spread them out on the table.

'Interview the remaining occupants of those two caravans. We'll need more interpreters.'

'How many?'

'Three or four would be good. Two would help.'

Hutchens made a note and nodded for Cato to proceed. So far it had been relatively painless. Cato suspected that Mark McGowan had already briefed his boss. He'd outlined the change in Guan Yu's story since the arrival of Amrita Desai; the quick result on Flipper had evaporated and the case had collapsed.

'We need to go through the dead man's belongings with a fine toothcomb, along with Guan Yu's, declare the caravans an official crime scene and get Duncan Goldflam in there to take a proper look. It's been a bit half-arsed so far because of ...' he chose his words carefully, 'competing resource priorities.' He ignored Hutchens' frown. 'We also need a more thorough search of that area for a murder weapon and to pin down the means of transporting the body to the ocean. Somebody has to have seen something.'

'Who do you need to help you?'

Cato bit his lower lip, bemused. Hutchens was meant to

have hung him out to dry by now. Who was there? In terms of local knowledge, Greg Fisher had been useful but he was out of action and Tess Maguire was suspended. Jim Buckley was dead. A lot had happened in the week since they'd taken that phone call on a hot, dusty road outside Katanning.

'Mark McGowan is up to speed if you can continue to spare him …' said Cato. Hutchens raised an eyebrow and smiled to himself as he made more notes.

'And Tess Maguire knows the area.'

Hutchens shot him a warning look. 'Give it a few days and we'll see. Meantime use some of the Ravensthorpe crew.'

Cato nodded and pushed on. 'Some urgent forensic, admin support, uniforms or volunteers for the wider search, but really …' Cato sized Hutchens up: in for a penny. 'I need a few more detectives. This thing needs to be done properly or not at all.'

Hutchens didn't explode. He nodded, shrugged, smiled. 'We should have some spares for you from the Buckley case in another day or two.'

'Really? What's happened?' The last Cato heard Hutchens and he were comparing brick walls.

'Lara Sumich's detective work, some forensics, and a witness putting Justin Woodward firmly back in the frame. We're bringing him back in today.'

That explained a buzzing, bewitching, bewildering Lara. Cato tried to stifle a blush by coughing and asking a businesslike question. 'Witness?'

Hutchens gave him one of his funny looks. 'Your mate from the Indonesian Navy, Yusala. He says Justin's our man. Swears blind.'

Miraculous, thought Cato.

Tess Maguire sat at the end of Greg Fisher's bed. He'd been given his own room in a side ward at Esperance District Hospital. He was hooked up to a drip and monitors, there were the usual tubes, wires and beeps. The right side of his face and chest, his right shoulder and right arm were swathed in gauze and light bandages. Most of the dark crew-cut hair on the right side of his head had been singed and here too were patches of gauze. This area had caught the brunt of the blast. He was sedated, he was on heavy-duty painkillers and he was lucky to be alive. The burns weren't as serious as first thought but there was still a chance of some grafting being required on his shoulder, chest, ear and cheek. He wouldn't be quite so youthful and fresh-faced when he emerged from this ordeal. That was the upshot of the conversation witnessed between the doctor, a solemn-faced girl who seemed to Tess to be hardly older than her own daughter, and Greg's teary mum.

Vanessa Fisher had driven from Pinjarra to Perth and taken a direct flight down to Esperance, arriving midmorning. It got her there quicker and it meant she didn't have to drive through the cursed Ravensthorpe area. She saw Greg's injuries as a direct result of him taking up that job in such a sad and evil place. He should have listened to their warnings. Tess couldn't argue with that.

She encouraged Greg's mum to go and have a coffee break and a spot of lunch while her son slept, promising faithfully to call her on the mobile if he woke in the meantime. Tess studied his face, asleep behind the oxygen mask, long curling eyelashes, and so young. She choked back a sob she never realised she had in her. What was he doing out at Billy Mather's camp last night, miles from anywhere? DI Hutchens wasn't the only one who wanted to know; Tess was curious too. Greg was her partner. Over the months since he'd started his probationary posting she'd got to know him and was beginning to like him and care about him. He was enthusiastic, energetic and ambitious. She remembered the feeling. They were meant to be partners but she knew nothing of this. Was he learning already to keep secrets, to have his own agenda? Or was she just too nuts to talk to these days?

Greg shifted a little in his sleep, his eyes and forehead furrowed in a frown. He had been with Jim Buckley's brother-in-law, Stuart Miller, an ex-cop from way back, according to McGowan who'd phoned her on Hutchens' behalf. What was their interest in Mather? Tess didn't know enough to speculate. Once he woke she might be wiser. In the meantime she picked up one of a small bundle of glossy gossip mags left by the well-meaning nurse. A fading teen pop star was still in and out of rehab and banned from seeing her kids, a Hollywood A-list super couple were pregnant again, and there'd been some dreadful wardrobe decisions at a recent red carpet event. All reassuringly divorced from the daily reality of Tess's life in Hopetoun. Greg stirred and snored. Tess willed him to wake up and then almost immediately felt guilty about it. Okay, so her motives for accompanying him in the ambulance to Esperance were not entirely altruistic. She had other things to do here in town and was hoping to get on with it sooner rather than later.

Greg snuffled, opened an eye. 'Tess?' The voice was parched, croaking.

She put down the mag, poured a cup of water for him and held it to his lips. 'You look like shit.'

'Thanks.'

'Your mum's just popped out for a break. Back soon.'

'Yeah fine.' He looked exhausted, like he might drop straight back off to sleep again.

'What happened out there, Greg?'

'Hoped you might tell me.' Then he frowned, remembering something. 'How's Stuart?'

'He's been taken to Perth. Still waiting to hear.'

'Bad?'

Tess nodded. 'Why were you out there, Greg? Why the visit to Billy Mather?'

'Stuart thought he might be some guy wanted for murder, an old Pommie case. I couldn't see the likeness myself.'

'Likeness?'

'Photo. In the *West* one day last week.'

'What made Stuart think it could be Mather?'

Greg croaked again and took another sip of water. 'I told him they had the same funny accent, Stuart and Mather. Plus Jim Buckley had phoned Stuart the night he died. He was convinced he'd seen the guy from the paper in the Hopey pub that night.'

'Mather?'

'That's what we were going to check. Stuart wanted to meet him to see if he was the same bloke.'

'And was he?'

Greg shifted position and winced. 'We still don't know. The caravan exploded. As far as I know, Stuart still hasn't seen him yet.'

Tess kept to herself the news from the hospital in Perth that, in all probability, Stuart Miller would never get to see Billy Mather.

Cato Kwong and Mark McGowan had retired to the peace and seclusion of the Sea Rescue hut. The town hall was heading for fever pitch. The media contingent had got wind of some significant development and were milling on the gravel outside. Some had also heard about the explosion out at Starvation Bay and were putting two and two together to make nonsense. DI Hutchens seemed happy to let them speculate away to their heart's content. He and Lara Sumich had already left for the Ravensthorpe lockup in a three-car convoy. The other cars contained Justin Woodward and his girlfriend Angelique, each in separate vehicles and accompanied by stony-faced detectives who looked like they'd been specially bred in an Orc factory on the outskirts of Albany. The suspect and his girlfriend would stew in Ravensthorpe until the arrival of Woodward's solicitor, hastily summoned from Perth. Cato couldn't help but smile when he'd caught sight of a freshly dapper Hutchens and his big wide grin on the way out the door. The pugnacious little prick was in his element.

McGowan, with the personnel list in front of him, was on the phone to Keith Stevenson, arranging to link up with the residents of the two caravans. Keith's previous threats to evict the Chinese workers and send them back home were, of course, all hot air for Cato's benefit. In fact they were still on the payroll, still living in their less than salubrious surroundings and still doing their ten-hour days. McGowan had the phone on speaker so Cato could enjoy the show. Stevenson hadn't lost the bluster.

'Why don't you bastards just leave me alone? This is harassment, plain and simple.'

McGowan tried his soothing voice. 'Keith. Mate. I'm just trying to do my job. Just like you.'

'Don't call me mate,' he growled.

McGowan abandoned soothing. 'Have them at your office by three, Mr Stevenson, or we'll come looking for them. Obstruct us any further and we'll close down your operations while we carry out our lawful business. You won't make another cent until we're good and ready. See you at three.' He flicked his phone shut.

Cato mimed applause.

McGowan looked a bit flustered. 'So where do we put all these ... people?'

'Let's commandeer one of Stevenson's portacabins. Least he can do.'

McGowan smiled. 'I'm beginning to like your style, Cato mate.'

Cato returned to the tagged belongings of Guan Yu and Hai Chen. He'd already dispatched around half a dozen uniforms from Ravensthorpe, Ongerup, and Lake Grace to comb Paddy's Field under the supervision of Duncan Goldflam. The geographical radius of cop reinforcements was growing exponentially to the twists and turns in each of the cases. Cato cursed the fact that he hadn't nailed Paddy's Field earlier, thus allowing even more time for any evidence to be removed, or destroyed by the elements. He'd also made an appointment for a chat with the foreman, Travis Grant, later that afternoon. Grant picked these blokes up and dropped them off at Paddy's Field every day. Had he noticed anything unusual? He must have. For one thing a key worker hadn't shown up for work that morning. By all accounts Chen was the gangmaster of the Chinese, the main conduit between employer and employees, yet Grant was lumping him in with the rest of the faceless hordes just pulling another sickie. Bullshit, and Cato Kwong had let it flow, unchecked.

He opened the first plastic Ziploc envelope: Guan Yu's contract of employment with SaS Personnel. Cato remembered the man's cheerful thumbs-up as he proudly told them about his weekly pay packet of five hundred dollars. On paper it all looked reasonable enough. His employer was sponsoring him as a temporary skilled migrant for the duration of the contract up to a maximum of two years. Travel expenses from China to Australia, and back again, would be covered by the employer. He would be paid the minimum award wage, just over forty-three thousand dollars a year. Cato did the sums: just over eight hundred a week coming down to about five hundred after tax and other deductions. So far so good, Guan Yu hadn't been lying about that part anyway.

What were the deductions? Accommodation, uniform, agency fees, daily travel to and from the worksite. Cato snorted. The rickety ancient caravans were the accommodation, Travis Grant and his minibus were the travel expenses, SaS agency commission, et cetera, et cetera. He began to see where Keith Stevenson was taking his substantial slice. Then there was Guan's mention of Chen taking his weekly cut of fifty dollars per man. How much cash in hand did that leave them? The official deductions, taxes and such, would account for the drop from eight hundred to five. The SaS deductions would reduce it even further. But Guan believed he was getting five hundred in his hand. Is that what happened? Did he find out he wasn't getting what he expected and blame Chen?

Cato dug out an envelope from Hai Chen's belongings. He had a similar contract to Guan except that as gangmaster his rate of pay was higher, nearer to fifty thousand per annum. He was also paid a one-off lump sum commission from SaS Personnel for organising the Chinese end of the recruitment. Five thousand dollars from SaS, plus his weekly rake-off of fifty dollars per man; seven colleagues in Paddy's Field plus another eight dossing in a donga at Barren Pastures. Fifteen lots of fifty per week over the course of up to two years. In terms of the la-la land currency floating around mining towns these days it was mere loose change but, relatively speaking, Chen was definitely doing all right.

Hai Chen's bank statements told a very different story: there were direct weekly credits of just over four thousand five hundred dollars. He was receiving the pay for himself and all of his colleagues into his account – no doubt an administrative convenience for all concerned. Maybe his mates believed he was holding their money in trust for them. In fact he was creaming off a further hundred bucks per week per man with weekly transfers of around one thousand five hundred to another account in his name. They were paying Chen a 'commission' of around a hundred and fifty dollars a week, not fifty; that made it thirty per cent instead of ten per cent. Chen's current balance on the linked account was just under sixty-five thousand dollars. He was well and truly cashed-up. Cato flicked through the rest of the papers in Chen's collection. Nothing else jumped out. But if Guan Yu somehow got wind of this rip-off then it was obviously a motive for murder. Men had certainly died for much less.

He checked another envelope: Chen's personal effects. Letters home, photos of kids, wife, a family wedding. Nothing. Cato looked again. Something had caught his eye in one of the wedding photos. It was a big team shot: Hai Chen and his bride in the centre surrounded by parents, grandparents, in-laws, everyone. He'd noticed the photo in his first brief trawl through the belongings out at Paddy's Field and not paid too much attention to the detail, but now he could see it. Over to one side, dressed to the nines in Chen's wedding album, wearing a bow tie and a big cheesy. Guan Yu.

28

Wednesday, October 15th. Midafternoon.

The hire car was hardly the most discreet of surveillance vehicles. Powder blue, Hyundai Getz, big rental stickers in side and back windows. A secretary's car, good lippy mirror though. Tess Maguire checked her reflection. She'd been awake most of the night and hadn't had time for a shower before the call-out to Starvation Bay. She needed more than a smear of lippy to look presentable.

Esperance, the Bay of Isles–she was looking at them right now. The Getz was angle-parked, pointing out to the Southern Ocean. To her immediate left the long jetty curved out into the sparkling blue bay. Away to her right was the port which serviced the lead and nickel ships, carriers of the poisonous pixie dust that had been sprinkled on the tourist town for the last three or four years. What was it the Buddhists or Taoists or whatever, called it? Yin and Yang? Those beautiful islands out in the bay, once the haunt of pirates, cutthroats and rapists. Greg Fisher had told her stories about the sealers who used to come to the mainland, kidnap Nyungar women and girls, and take them back to their island camps never to be seen again. A vision of beauty masking a scene of horror. Yin and Yang. The young woman strolling along the jetty with her toddler tottering unsteadily beside her. A young mum and her lovely little tacker: wife and child of stompin' Johnno Djukic; Yin and Yang.

Tess sipped her cappuccino from the Coffee Cat takeaway van, a favourite foreshore drawcard. The coffee was great, Cato would approve. She thought about phoning him, to see how he was going, to see why he hadn't gone back to his family yet.

Cato the mystery man. Cato could wait-o; Tess had work to do. Greg Fisher was now sleeping peacefully, watched over by his distraught mum. Tess had made her excuses and left. She'd made straight for the Bay of Isles car-hire depot and taken what was available. Then she'd parked the Getz outside the address given for Djukic and waited for something to happen. An hour or so later, something did.

She'd followed mother and child from their compact fibro home a few blocks back from the foreshore. Mrs Djukic had no reason to think the Hyundai behind her rusting white Datsun was in fact following her. She didn't inhabit that kind of world, very few do. Tess didn't know why she was doing this; John Djukic was two hundred kilometres away on the mine site. Tess gave it some thought: she figured she wanted to know as much about him as possible. Know thine enemy. This seemed like as good a place to start as any. Mrs Djukic and baby Djukic, both as cute as buttons, Johnno's pride and joy. Tess decided to have a word.

'Beautiful day.'

The young woman smiled and nodded in reply, picking up the little kid for a protective cuddle. Shy? Wary of a stranger? Wary of Tess herself, she of the sleepless night, the haggard look, the ungroomed hair? The young mum was Asian, Thai maybe? The little boy was about a year old. Some European features mixed in but no sign of Johnno's mad black eyes or red hair, yet. He was chuckling away, playing with his mother's bead necklace. The sea breeze was strengthening. Tess pulled her windcheater jacket closer around her, aware of the weight of her service issue gun in an inside pocket. She looked down from the jetty as the sea lion broke the surface of the water, nodding its whiskered head up at the spectators. It was a beautiful creature with a sleek shiny body and big brown eyes. Tess remembered her swim with the baby seal. The purity and beauty of the moment that had left her laughing and crying at the same time. Yin and Yang? Or just the symptom of an unbalanced mind?

'I'm Tess.'

Tess smiled, gave the baby a little wave and made a funny face. The young woman nodded and smiled back and clutched her child a little closer.

'Gorgeous kid.' Tess gestured casually at the infant.

The woman smiled again, this time in apology. 'Sorry. English not good.'

Tess nodded and smiled in understanding, lots of nodding and smiling today. She leaned on the top of the guardrail which kept people from falling the five or six metres into the choppy sea.

'Where you from?'

'Thailand.'

'Ah. Holiday?'

'No, no. Live here.'

'Tess,' Tess said again, pointing at herself.

'Koo. And this one, Johnny,' she patted the baby on the back gently.

'Cute.'

'Thank you.'

Tess sniffed the salt breeze and smiled again. There was nobody within two hundred metres or more. Koo and baby Johnny; she turned and faced them. One shove and they'd be in the drink; Tess was pretty confident the mother couldn't swim.

'Husband working?'

'Yes. Away at the mine.' She patted the baby again. 'Johnny miss his dad.'

Tess looked at them both. They were from a different world. They were innocent and had nothing to do with the history between her and Johnno Djukic. History, dead right. Push them in the water and watch them drown. Sure, that would solve everything. Not. Suicidal, beating up on kids and now harbouring homicidal thoughts towards strangers: is this what madness is? What the hell did she think she was doing here?

Her daughter's words came back to her.

I'm meant to be the reckless out of control one around here.

She turned away, wondering what to do to ease the bursting in her chest.

'Well, must go now. Nice to meet you, Koo.'

'Okay, bye-bye.' Koo lifted baby Johnny's hand and helped him wave at Tess, his face lit up with an uncertain smile.

Tess gave the kid a little wave back and pulled another funny face. 'Bye-bye.'

It was well and truly time to move on.

'Who's your mate, Trav?'

Travis Grant nodded tersely towards his cronies at the bar, winked, and tried his best to look casual. It wasn't working. Meeting in the Port Hotel in front of all the mates had been Cato Kwong's idea. No, really, Cato had insisted, his shout. They had retreated to a dark corner near the back door, Travis trying his best to merge into the peeling, scuffed wall behind him. Cato, for his part, making every effort to stand tall and stick out like a big sore Chinese thumb.

'Cheers.' Cato lifted his glass: a lurid-green lemon, lime and soda and a straw. He savoured the younger man's obvious discomfort, clinked Travis's middy loudly and sucked noisily on his straw. It was late afternoon, Wednesday, only a handful of punters, but they all knew Trav. An afternoon soap was playing on the twin plasmas with sound muted. A game of pool was in progress. Outside, across the road, the Southern Ocean had been whipped up by the afternoon breeze. The Hopetoun main drag looked like a Hollywood scenery backlot for a ghost town. Travis Grant certainly had a haunted look about him.

Cato took a sip from his bright green drink and put it back on the tall table. He sighed loudly and smacked his lips in satisfaction. 'SaS. Stevenson and Sons, that right?'

'Yeah, what about it?'

'Is that Keith and Kane?'

Grant snorted. 'Way off, mate. Stevenson's the nanna in the old folk's home. Keith's the son.'

Cato nodded like he hadn't already worked it out for himself. 'Why's the nanna down as a company director?'

Grant studied the beer mat. 'None of my business.'

'And you're Keith's right-hand man, you pretty well run things day to day, that right?'

A slight inflation of the Grant chest: 'Pretty much, he runs around making the deals and shouting at people and I keep the wheels of industry turning, mate.'

Cato nodded again then made a show of seeming to remember something. 'But Kane's out of a job now, the mine sacked him. He's the son and heir to the family business. So are you just keeping his seat warm or what?'

Another snort and a shake of the head: 'Little Lord Liability? Fucking joke. Keith wouldn't trust him to go to the shops.'

'No? How come?'

Travis Grant started counting off on his fingers. 'Can't keep his mouth shut, can't keep out of trouble, can't even hold down a piss-easy, well-paying job at the mine.'

'No love lost then,' Cato observed.

'Fucking idiot,' confirmed Grant. 'They made him a Team Leader, extra fifteen grand. All he had to do was shut up and stay out of the way of the blokes who really knew what they were doing. He even fucked that up. Picking a fight with a Maori that could eat two of him for breakfast, for fuck's sake.' Grant shook his head in disgust. 'He thought they really meant the Team Leader thing, started believing in his own publicity. In fact it was all a favour to Daddy–keep Kane out of everybody's way. Moron.'

Cato had a thought, he followed it for curiosity. 'What about Junior?'

'The Incredible Sulk? He's the runt of the litter. Kerry had him when she was too old. He came out munted.' Grant curled his top lip upwards Elvis-like and crossed his eyes to illustrate his point. 'They want to make it up to him by letting him do whatever he wants.'

'Special is he?'

'That's what he reckons and it's what they keep telling him. He can't handle the fact that nobody else sees it that way. Keeps chucking tanties. That zapping your police sheila gave him was the best news I've had all week. You lot can't be all bad, eh?' Grant sipped thoughtfully from his beer and smiled to himself. 'Pisses Kane off, big time. Dad takes the little runt out shooting most nights: rabbits, roos, emus, cats – never did that with Kane.'

Cato had enough family background, he changed the subject. 'Friday before last, remember it?'

Travis made a show of thinking back. 'What about it?'

'The early morning pick-up at Paddy's Field, what time do you do that?'

Travis studied the bottom of his drink. 'Depends on how far away the worksite is on any given day. They can be working one place one day, another place the next.'

'And that day?'

'Five-thirty, six-ish.'

'Still dark was it?'

'Don't think so. Sun would have been just about up, it's usually light enough by then.'

'Light enough for what?' Cato cocked his head.

'To see by, without the headlights.' Travis Grant was catching on. The conversation had moved back into dangerous territory.

'See anything that morning?' said Cato.

'Couple of caravans, sheep ...' Travis smiled slyly to himself. 'Some Chinks.'

'Anything different, unusual, unexpected?'

'Like what?' Travis held Cato's gaze for a second then scanned the room lazily.

'You tell me.'

'No. Nothing.' Travis took a good long pull from the middy and emptied it. 'We finished?'

Cato shook his head and signalled for another round. The barmaid looked at Travis as if seeking his permission. Grant winked reassuringly.

Cato checked the clock on the wall, 4.30. A news update on the plasmas: by the look of the graphics, today it was the banks and miners that were dragging the stock market down into the murky depths of hell. Nobody gave it a second glance. By now Mark McGowan, with the help of Ravy Sergeant Paul Abbott and Jessica Tan, would have started talking to the other occupants of the two caravans. So far nothing had come back from Duncan Goldflam and the search team in Paddy's Field.

Cato gestured for Travis to lean closer, share a confidence. 'Why are you protecting them?'

'Who?'

Cato thumbed over his shoulder in the general direction of Paddy's Field, a good twenty-odd kilometres away. 'The Chinese, one of them's already put his hand up for it. What's it to you? I thought you would have been far more helpful, Travis.'

The drinks arrived. Grant gave the barmaid another wink and smile. More than just friends, Cato surmised.

Travis took a long pull, wiped the froth from his lips with the back of his hand and blessed the room with a gassy belch. 'I'm not protecting anybody, mate. Do what the fuck you like with them. None of my business.'

'So there was nothing different about that morning?'

'Nothing, mate.'

'What about the fact that one of them didn't show up for work? Didn't you wonder where he was?'

A theatrical shrug, 'Pulled a sickie. Wouldn't be the first time.'

'And you didn't look in the caravan, check him out?'

'What for? No workee, no payee. Not getting me into one of those fleapits, who knows what you'd catch.'

'Chen's meant to be your gangmaster and he doesn't show up for work. You're telling me you're not in the least bit curious? Wouldn't Keith want to know something like that?'

It was only a quick flicker but Cato had seen it. Uncertainty. Fear? Something to probe later; he tried a different angle.

'Say somebody wants to call in sick, how do they contact you?'

'What?'

'I assume you'd want as much notice as possible if anyone is sick, so you can organise replacements?'

'Maybe.' Grant gave another sly smile. 'Or maybe we'd just get the ones who do show up to work harder.'

Cato tried a stab in the dark. 'Chen, your gangmaster, he had a phone, didn't he?'

'Yeah, wouldn't have worked out there though. No signal.'

And no phone among the collected belongings of Hai Chen, noted Cato.

'What's his phone number?'

'What?'

'Chen. You'd have him in your address book wouldn't you?'

Travis nodded, reached into his pocket and scrolled through his mobile. Cato wrote down the number for record-tracking later.

'Not much use out there then?'

'No, but if he walks north about a kilometre, that brings you out near the airstrip. There's a signal there.'

'All heart, you guys.'

'Keeps them fit,' Travis smirked.

The late afternoon sun had disappeared behind scudding clouds, casting a sudden extra gloom on the bar room tableau. Cato could see that Travis was running out of patience and cooperation: no eye contact, putting on bored, checking the watch.

'Where were they going to be working that day?'

Travis pretended to be thinking again. 'Friday before last

you say?'

Cato nodded.

'That team would have been on the desal pipeline. Out Mason Bay Road.'

'How far is that from where they live?'

'As the crow flies, maybe thirty k?'

'And the only way they can get there, or anywhere else for that matter, is if you drive them?'

'That's right, just a glorified chauffeur really, that's me.'

'At a price.'

Travis looked across the rim of his glass. 'Dog eat dog, sunshine. We all need to earn a crust. They're doing okay, your mates, don't worry. Lot better off than back home I reckon.'

'Keith giving you your fair share of the pie?'

A frown and another uncertain, suspicious, flicker.

Cato hopscotched around the questions, not giving Travis enough time to settle. 'So they have no access to a vehicle at all except through you?'

'Far as I know.' Travis nodded irritably, he was finding it hard to concentrate.

'So if, as Guan Yu says, he killed a man out there last Thursday week and the body was gone by the Friday morning, then he must have had help. And the only guy he knows with a vehicle is you, Travis.'

Grant slammed his drink down on the table and put both hands up defensively. 'No way mate. What those fuckers did is their business. I had nothing to do with it.'

The pub went quiet the way they sometimes do in the movies. The barmaid reached for the remote and unmuted *The Bold and the Beautiful*. Somebody was finding out they'd just been pashing with their long-lost illegitimate sister. Cato scanned the faces of some of the hardened afternoon drinkers, no longer bold, never had been beautiful. No wonder they preferred it with the sound down; too much like real life. One of Travis's mates looked up from his pool game, slapping the cue in his palm.

'Everything okay, Trav?'

Cato was aware that another crony had quietly planted himself behind and to the right of where he was sitting. Cato's hand gripped the glass of lime soda, not the coolest of weapons but his gun was locked in the bull-mobile. He figured if he limesoda'd the guy holding the pool cue first, then rushed Travis and smacked his face on the edge of the table, he might get the upper hand. Trouble was he couldn't see what the other crony was holding, maybe a shandy.

Travis came to a decision but not before letting Cato know who had the numbers. 'Yeah, no worries.'

The handful of drinkers resumed their conversations and the balls clicked again on the pool table.

Cato's voice was hardly a murmur. 'What did those fuckers do, Travis?' No reply. 'So if it wasn't you that helped them, then who was it?'

Travis shook his head and stared into the depths of his drink. 'Don't ask me, you're the detective and, unless you're going to arrest me, I'm finished here. Thanks for the beer.'

Travis hopped off his stool, car keys jangling in his hand.

Cato nodded towards them. 'Leave the keys with me.'

'I've only had the two, breath test me if you like.' Travis kept walking towards the door.

Cato's voice hardened. 'Leave them. Forensics will want to take a look at the car.'

'Make it official. Get the paperwork, or get fucked.'

Travis said the last line loud enough for everyone to hear. The door swung closed behind him. A whoop went up from the pool table. The barmaid looked flushed.

Cato found him outside across the road, angle-parked. Faces milled at the pub windows. Travis Grant had opened the minibus driver's side door and was climbing into his seat. Cato kick-slammed the door with maximum force onto Travis's exposed right leg, arm and shoulder. There was a muffled yelp of pain and a string of curses. Cato wrenched the door open again, hauled Travis out and pushed his face down into the gravel, making sure it got a bit of a scrape. He pocketed the car keys. Kneeling on the prone man's back, Cato cuffed him then hauled him to his feet.

'Let's go and take care of that paperwork shall we?'

Travis's mates had left the pub and were walking purposefully over the road towards them. Cato Kwong found a roar within him.

'Back off!'

They did. Cato frogmarched Travis the hundred or so metres up the centre of Veal Street to the police station in the Sea Rescue hut.

29

Wednesday, October 15th. Early evening.

'This is absolutely outrageous.'

Henry Hurley had arrived. DI Mick Hutchens made a soothing gesture with his hands. At least, he probably thought it was soothing. To the casual observer it may well have seemed threatening. They were boxer's hands, hard and surprisingly big, betraying the street-fighting origins of the squat, dapper detective. He had allowed Hooray Henry two minutes for his predictable tirade. Time was now up for the Pinstriped Pixie.

Justin Woodward had affected a raffish, supercilious look. Lara whispered to Hutchens that he reminded her of Hugh Grant.

'Who?' Hutchens whispered back, sneaking a look down her shirt.

Of course he knew who Hugh Grant was. He was the Pommie actor who got picked up in the US midway through a blowjob from a street hooker. Class act.

Lara began shuffling papers in a folder and looking impatient. They'd agreed on the way up: it was her turn to play bad cop this time. Hutchens had experienced a little shiver of excitement at the thought. Next door the girlfriend, Angelique, was being calmly and patiently worn down by a couple of B-grade detective constables with cold eyes and dull voices. They were looking for cracks in the alibi. It would be like an excruciating audit with the taxmen from hell. If she didn't crack under the unrelenting questioning, she'd probably fold with the unremitting boredom of looking at those two for hours on end. Hutchens cleared his throat, a cue for them all to get on with it.

'New evidence has come to light, Mr Hurley. We need your client's help to answer questions arising from these developments.'

'Is he at liberty to leave at any time?'

'Of course,' Hutchens lied.

They'd already worked out their strategy. Either way, DI Hutchens intended to formally charge Justin Woodward with murder today. If he answered some more questions willingly, then fine. If he clammed up now, Hutchens was still confident of his case. Woodward was history, dead and buried. It was Jim Buckley's funeral in Perth the day after next. As far as he was concerned, this would be the best fucking eulogy the poor bastard could have wished for. Hurley and Woodward had finished whispering. The lawyer gave a curt nod. Game on.

Lara finished shuffling her papers. The recording was underway, formalities done. 'Tell me about Freddy Bataam.'

'Who?' Justin Woodward did the Hugh Grant eyebrow thing again.

'Freddy Bataam, Indonesian guy, aka Freddy Sudhyono, real name Riri Yusala.'

'You asked me about him last time. Like I said then, I've never heard of him.'

'No?'

'No.'

'Funny. He knows you.'

Woodward looked up at Lara with his bedroom eyes and shrugged.

'A shrug doesn't answer the question, Mr Woodward.'

'What question?'

'Freddy Bataam claims to know you. Are you still saying that you don't know him?'

'That's right.'

'He claims he is your supplier.'

Woodward rolled his eyes and shook his head.

His lawyer gave an exasperated sigh. 'Is this your new

evidence Mr Hutchens? The word of a criminal?'

'Who said he was a criminal?' Hutchens: butter not melting in mouth.

Hurley flapped his hand dismissively at Lara, the subspecies in the room. 'Your colleague did. She said "supplier".'

Lara picked a sheet of paper out of her folder. 'Actually Mr Yusala, or Freddy Bataam, does not have a criminal record.'

And as a result of their little chat in Albany he still didn't. The car full of drugs and underage girls was going to disappear in a puff of smoke. That's what she'd told him anyway. Hutchens had smiled approvingly on hearing that one, it was the same kind of bullshit line he would have fed the bastard too.

Henry Hurley was shaking his head. 'If this is all you have, we'll call a halt to this farce right now.'

Hutchens did the soothing-threatening boxer's hands thing again. 'There are a couple of other matters still to consider.'

Justin Woodward patted his lawyer's arm confidently and twinkled at Hutchens. 'Humour me.'

Travis Grant had been booked for obstruction and sent home, on foot. His minibus was impounded and a tired, grumpy DS Duncan Goldflam had delegated his spotty offsider Mark Hamlyn to give it a cursory forensic once-over. Cato would have preferred a bit less of the cursory but didn't want to push his luck. The minibus was unlikely to be the vehicle that transported the body; it needed to be four-wheel drive to be sure of getting all the way to Starvation Bay with a boat in tow. Besides, there was no towbar on the back–but who knew what else it might throw up forensically. At the very least it would be out of action for a day or so and hopefully further disrupt the operations of SaS Personnel. Anything that made life difficult for Keith Stevenson and Travis Grant was a bonus for Cato. That reminded him, he still needed to put in a call to the RSPCA about those scrawny sheep in Paddy's Field.

The search of the sheep paddock had produced nothing. No

murder weapon, no missing limbs, no freshly turned earth, no bloodbath. McGowan's little inquiry team was still working their way through the residents of Paddy's Field but no word back yet. Cato checked his watch: gone 7.00. He decided to call it a day, he was stuffed. Sure, they'd all been up all night at the exploded caravan but the drained feeling had only come on in the last hour or two. Had it all just caught up with him? No. The violence he'd inflicted on Travis Grant, that's what had drained him. Oh, and Lara Sumich. He'd noticed something else too. He was tired, yes, but the knotted tension had disappeared from his neck and shoulders. Was that all it took? A good root and a bit of biff? Pathetic. Still, whatever it takes.

He switched off the computer and looked for a key to lock up the Sea Rescue hut. Greg Fisher had one, no doubt Tess Maguire had the other. He idly wondered where she was. He assumed she would have finished in Esperance by now and be on her way back. Cato snicked the yale and closed the door behind him. He'd worry about getting back in when the time came. The breeze had dropped off again. It was still light outside, a perfect evening for a barbie if he had any family or friends, or even colleagues. He wondered how Lara Sumich was going. Already the morning encounter was fading into a distant unreality. He was trying to shake off the nagging feeling that they hadn't actually fucked each other, rather that he had been fucked.

That reminded him. Guiltily, he debated phoning Jane and Jake, juggling the mobile in his palm. He took out his wallet and looked at the photo inside. It was taken in happier times at Little Salmon Bay, Rottnest. Cato behind the camera, Jane tanned and smiling in her red swimsuit, yellow flippers, and blue snorkelling gear. Jake looking happier than Cato remembered him ever being. It was taken three days before he was called to the internal inquiry. He stopped juggling his mobile; he didn't know what he could say to them that would even begin to undo the damage he had done. He wandered down to the Taste of the Toun to check out the menu.

Justin Woodward had gone pale. He looked like he wanted to throw up. He was shaking his head slowly from side to side, eyes fixed on his favourite spot on the tabletop. Henry Hurley was furiously taking notes on his yellow legal pad. DI Mick Hutchens leaned forward, eyebrows raised as if hearing all of this for the first time. Lara was counting points off on her fingers.

'So we've got you leaving the pub, drinks unfinished, just as Jim Buckley arrives. We've got a lengthy phone conversation between the two of you the previous day. We've got Freddy Bataam, your supplier, telling us that he'd been talking to you in the pub earlier that day and that you were going to, quote, sort Buckley out. We've got CCTV footage in the pub confirming you and Freddy Bataam were there at the same time ...'

Unfortunately the camera didn't actually catch them in conversation but it hopefully added to the weight of evidence.

'We've got tabs of ecstasy and traces of crystal meth in your coffee van, and we've got Jim Buckley's hairs on your jeans.' Lara pointed the last finger in his direction.

Woodward stared at the tabletop. 'You're mad. This is not happening.'

'Yes it is, Justin. Shall I tell you what I think actually did happen?'

Woodward shook his head again. If his answer was no, Lara ignored him.

'You've set up a new life down here with your girlfriend – coffee and cakes, doing nicely, and a side order of eckies and ice for the cashed-up miners. Detective Sergeant Jim Buckley comes to town, a face from the past, he recognises you. The van gets searched and Jim Buckley doesn't seem to find the drugs. Big relief. Then he calls you. In fact he did find them and he wants money from you to keep quiet ...'

Woodward snorted and shook his head firmly, pursing his lips. 'This is bullshit. The call from Buckley was about his keys. The only difference in the story is that Angelique took the call, not me, that's why I was worried. I didn't know about the call until later when she told me. I wanted to keep her out of all this.'

Lara sighed and pushed on. 'Freddy Bataam comes to town to drop off his supplies. You tell him about Buckley, your lucrative little operation is looking shaky. He wants to know what you're going to do about it. You still owe him money from the last drop off. He's getting impatient, he knows some nasty people. You tell him you'll sort it out. Later, Jim Buckley comes into the pub. Looking for an answer from you? Looking for his money maybe? You leave. You go home. You brood. You think about what you need to do. You work up courage ...'

'Fucking fairytales. I'm leaving.' Woodward made as if to stand up.

Hutchens leaned across the table and gently pushed him back into his seat. 'Nearly finished, mate.'

Lara was on a roll. 'You return later. You see he's still in there. You wait for him to leave. You follow him down to the groyne. He's preoccupied, he's talking on the mobile, having a smoke. He doesn't hear you come up behind. You pick up one of those big lumps of rock they've used to make the groyne. You bounce it off the back of his head. He's down but not out. You finish him off. Not elegant, not subtle, but job done.'

Justin Woodward was out of his chair, across the table, clawing at Lara's throat. Her chair sailed backwards and they landed on the floor still locked together. Hutchens watched with interest. Mr Smooth-as-Fuck wasn't quite as handsome right now. Spittle flecked his lips, a bubble of snot hung from the end of his nose, the bedroom eyes were bulging and bloodshot. His hands were tight around Lara's neck, thumbs pressing into her windpipe.

Henry Hurley was hopping from foot to foot and flapping his hands like an infant duck forced into premature flight. A couple of uniforms burst through the door and looked to Hutchens for guidance. He unclipped a gun from the nearest one's belt, knelt down and pressed it into Justin Woodward's neck.

'That's enough mate,' he said gently as if to his own son.

Woodward slumped. Defeated. He began to sob quietly. Lara Sumich shoved him off and set about regaining her composure.

Hurley was still flapping. 'I really must protest.'

Hutchens handed the gun back to the uniform and turned to Hooray Henry. 'You go ahead mate. Go for your life. Lara, charge Mr Woodward with murder and lock him up.'

30

Thursday, October 16th. Dawn.

Jenny Miller shuddered. This pink, pathetic gauze-wrapped figure hooked up to tubes, monitors and drips couldn't be Stuart. His hair was burnt off the right side of his head. From there to about midway down his chest and right arm it was pinky-red, raw meat. The right ear was a misshapen lump. The right eye was gone. There was a smell in the air, not just of hospital chemicals. Cooking. Maybe it was just the breakfast trolley doing the rounds. He would require reconstructive surgery on the ear and right side of his face. Skin grafts everywhere else. The doctor said they were talking about months and years of treatment and therapy. Gradually he would begin to look halfway human again but he would never be the man he once was. Apparently the doctor was a world leader in her field of specialist burns treatment. So why couldn't she make him into Stuart again?

Jenny had been at his bedside all night. He was out cold on a cocktail of sedatives and painkillers and god knows what else. She'd been offered some drugs too for her own pain but she'd refused. It wasn't her way. She'd thought about their years together during the fitful night: the early days in Sunderland, Stuart still with the Force, and she in her first job out from college in Edinburgh, teaching snotty Sassenachs in Geordieland. Stuart was driven, passionate, and absent most of the time. Still, there had been plenty of laughs and good times, good friends. Then the Cup Final Murders, casting a shadow over the town, over their family, and most of all over Stuart. Like something deep inside him had been bludgeoned to a pulp that day. Shell-shocked, like Davey Arthurs' dad.

Australia, a new beginning. Sunshine, beaches, flies. It was all strange and unfamiliar, yet not. They settled, they grew, they prospered, they moved to Busselton and the kids moved out. Graeme, their oldest, had conceded Busselton was a pretty little town but to him it felt like an open prison for retirees. 'Halfway to Paradise' he'd called it. To all intents and purposes she and Stuart were happy. Well, content anyway. Comfortable. Together. She'd taken that for granted until she nearly lost him just two years earlier: the chest pains, the heart scare, and now the pill regime. At the time she'd surprised herself at how much she didn't want to lose him. It was a powerful feeling. She needed it back, now more than ever.

Jenny Miller looked at her sleeping husband. They were two weeks off their fortieth wedding anniversary. She prayed she would have the strength to stick with him through all of this. She prayed that she could and would be there for him, in sickness and in health, like she'd vowed. She prayed she would still be able to look at his raw, scarred face and see the man she married. A cold panic welled up inside. She was terrified. She felt already that she wasn't up to it.

Davey Arthurs, the Cup Final Murderer. Stuart was convinced it was Davey in the newspaper. Then he'd had a phone call from Jim Buckley, a sighting down on the south coast. Stuart was fired up like he hadn't been since she married him. She'd even got caught up in it, briefly. Helping him with his bloody googling, spoonfeeding his obsession. Then came the dreadful news of Jim's death the very next day and Stuart packing his bags first thing Monday, a wild look in his eyes. Now Stuart had been given back to her, blinded, burnt alive and scarred for life. Not for the first time, Jenny Miller wished Davey Arthurs had been strangled at birth.

Mick Hutchens emerged from the town hall Major Incident Room into the early morning sunlight, flanked by Lara Sumich and some uniformed officers for colour and effect. Cameras swung on to shoulders, mikes were thrust forward. Hutchens arranged his features into something resembling gravitas.

'This morning I am able to announce that a man has been charged with the murder of Detective Sergeant James Buckley ...'

Lara Sumich smiled briefly; she was wearing a brightly coloured silk scarf around her neck that served only to draw attention to the bruises half-hidden beneath.

Hutchens hadn't finished yet. 'Justin Anthony Woodward has been taken to Albany and will appear before a magistrate later today ...'

A question from the mob. 'You arrested him previously and released him. What changed?'

'New evidence came to light which will be presented in due course.'

'Have Mr Buckley's family been informed?' It was Belinda Thingy from Channel Nine, solicitous and silky.

'Yes, they have been informed. Sergeant Buckley's funeral is tomorrow and of course our thoughts are primarily with his family at this time.'

Hutchens was winding up, he fielded a few more questions but his body language said time to go. The media entourage were left to do their stand-up pieces to camera and join the mass exodus over to Albany.

Tess Maguire slurped on her mug of tea and turned the radio off. Snak-Attack Justin, nailed by Hutchens for murdering Jim Buckley. Hard to believe, but she had long since stopped being surprised by what human beings are capable of. It went with the job. Hopefully the Hutchens circus would break camp soon and they could all get back to normal–tasering allegations notwithstanding. Of course there was still Cato and Flipper. Maybe she should phone him and find out how he was going–Cato that is. Melissa waved on her way out to catch the school bus, not exactly happy, more like determined, self-contained.

Tess waved back, 'Have a great day. See you this arvo.'

The Waltons on Walton's Mountain, almost.

Tess felt rested and well. She had arrived back from Esperance early the previous evening. She'd eaten properly, chatted briefly and non-confrontationally with Melissa and got an early night. She hadn't worked out what to do with the powder-blue Getz yet. It needed to be returned to the hire yard in Esperance eventually. Koo and baby Johnny: what were they doing with a monster like Djukic? Should she warn Koo, tell her what he was really like? Tell her to get out while she still could? No, she'd had the chance to do that in Esperance and hadn't taken it. Interfering in Djukic's life would only prolong her own agony. She drained her tea and headed for the shower.

'Congratulations.' Cato meant it.

Mick Hutchens feigned humility for a second and then accepted full credit where it was due. He waved a hand magnanimously in the direction of Lara Sumich who was seated at a nearby desk, phoning ahead to Albany to double-check arrangements for Justin Woodward's appearance in court.

'Lara did a lot of the groundwork of course, a real diamond. She'll go far, if I'm not careful.'

She smiled demurely in reply. Hutchens switched his benign gaze back to Cato. 'Now we'll be winding down a bit on that investigation. So tell me where you're at.'

Cato did so, happy to be forced to concentrate on work rather than that spot where Lara's neck met her shoulder. He hadn't heard anything yet from forensics on the minibus or any more on Paddy's Field and was still waiting for any developments from Mark McGowan on the interviews with Chen's and Guan's housemates. Travis Grant knew more than he was telling and was probably protecting his boss, Keith Stevenson, from further scrutiny. The contracts and bank statements seemed to suggest major financial rip-offs and exploitation in the mix. Cato would be chasing Hai Chen's mobile phone records now he had the number. Last but not least, Guan Yu's murder confession had been scientifically proven to be complete bullshit.

Hutchens sniffed. 'It's a fucking dog's breakfast.'

'Nicely summarised, sir.'

'What's to say you're not just chasing shadows here?'

Cato pretended he didn't understand. 'How do you mean?'

'Exploitation, unscrupulous bosses, missing mobile phones, bullshit confessions. Nobody gives a toss about Chen-bloody-thingo except you. Why don't we just send the lying squabbling bastards back home and close the book on it?'

Cato couldn't think of an answer that didn't involve airy-fairy notions like truth, justice, right and wrong. He got the distinct impression that, job done and mission accomplished, Mick Hutchens was looking to clear his desk and ship out back to Albany. Cato didn't want to hold him up and arguing too much would do exactly that.

'How about I see the current action list through to its conclusion and if nothing emerges – and it probably won't –' he added to reassure his boss, 'I tie it all up and close it by the weekend?'

Hutchens did some calculations. Today was Thursday, Woodward in court and in custody; Buckley's funeral tomorrow. Yes, closing everything down by the weekend was fine by him. Cato didn't push him on whether he meant the beginning or end of the weekend. He decided to use his initiative on that one.

Hutchens seemed distracted. 'Are you going to the funeral?'

Cato hadn't really thought about it. 'What do you think, sir?'

'You were his colleague, his partner, I'm surprised you're asking.'

Cato nodded. 'Yes. I'll go.'

'There's a flight tonight at eight, I'll organise a seat for you. See you then.'

Apparently dismissed, Cato got up to leave but Hutchens

wasn't finished.

'That business with the exploding caravan, what did you make of it?'

Cato shrugged. 'Bit strange. Duncan Goldflam seems to think it was probably a kosher accident. But why were they out there in the first place?'

Hutchens went into bad-poker-face mode. 'Wild-goose chase according to young Fisher. Tess Maguire talked to him in hospital. Apparently Stuart Miller thought some bloke in the paper, an old murder case, could be our man Herman the Hermit. Miller spoke to me earlier that day, he told me about a case he worked on thirty-odd years back in Pommieland, same MO. Nasty.'

Hence the bad poker face, Cato guessed. Hutchens knew more about Miller's reason for being there than he'd been letting on and he was seriously rattled.

Hutchens unfolded a nicely ironed hankie and blew his nose. 'Anyway Fisher reckons the photofit looked nothing like Mather.'

Lara Sumich finished her call and strolled back towards the hall kitchen. No doubt to get herself another herbal tea, deduced Cato. Mick Hutchens admired the view for a moment then turned back to Cato, voice lowered. 'Thing is, the Pom gets a phone call from Jim Buckley the night he dies, telling him this cold-case suspect is here in Hopetoun. It's probably mistaken identity, and certainly coincidental to Woodward killing Buckley, but I don't like loose ends. You neither, I imagine.'

They shared a look that went back years.

'So how about you nose around for me over the next couple of days? If you need the time maybe we could let that Chinese thing run a few extra days if you like ...'

Cato smiled. So was this what the testing and auditions had been about? Cato the lone wolf stepping in once again to cover his boss's arse? Hutchens opened his desk drawer and handed Cato an A5 envelope.

'This was recovered from Miller's car yesterday. It had been parked at Fisher's house. So much else going on, it fell through the cracks.'

Cato opened it. Inside was a spiral bound notebook.

Hutchens flicked his fingers at it. 'I had a bit of a scan last night. Most of it's gobbledegook but he clearly had a bee in his bonnet about something. You're a bright spark, maybe you can make sense of it.'

Cato was not to be sidetracked from what he saw as his main game, Flipper. He struck while the iron was hot. 'Maybe you could leave me a bit of support until the end of the weekend. McGowan? Some forensic?'

Hutchens pretended to think about it for a moment, then nodded. 'Okay, keep McGowan, saves me looking at his sulky face on the drive back to Albany. I'll also talk to Goldflam and his team about staying on a day or two.'

'Thanks.'

Dismissed, Cato made a bee-line for the kitchen. It was a narrow poky little room. Lara was busy rinsing out a cup, the kettle heading for boiling point.

'Morning,' Cato said.

'Hi.' That smile of hers again, half-mocking.

'I was wondering if you fancied catching up later?'

'What?'

'Later. A drink or something?'

Steam rose from the kettle as it bubbled and shuddered on the benchtop. Lara placed her hand on Cato's.

'Look you're a nice guy and not a bad fuck.' The kettle switched itself off. 'And there and then that's exactly what I wanted.'

Uh-oh. Cato broke eye contact and studied the floral pattern on Lara's mug as she squeezed the last bit of her tea bag dry.

'But when it comes to ...' she paused, 'boyfriends,' she looked almost apologetic, 'I kind of prefer my own age group.'

She gave him a consoling pat on the shoulder as she squeezed past on her way out.

'He's gone.'

This was turning into a habit. First Riri Yusala and the aspiring date-rape boys, now this. Desk Sergeant Bernie Tilbrook had been next door to the Ravy Motel to check on the welfare of Billy Mather. Apparently nobody had looked in on him since shortly after he arrived. The room was empty and the bed didn't look like it had been slept in. He was indeed gone, without a trace and with anything up to twenty-four hours' head start.

Cato gritted his teeth and stayed calm, resisting the temptation to chuck his mobile out the car window. 'Do you reckon you could get a couple of your blokes to drive around town? He might have just popped out for a walk or a bag of lollies or something.' Cato didn't believe it himself. 'In the meantime maybe you could put out an alert on the network?'

Tilbrook sighed like he was snowed under and this really was the last straw. 'Yeah I can organise that I reckon.'

'Thanks Bernie.'

'No worries, Constable.'

Cato snapped his phone shut and pressed down on the accelerator. A copy of the Buckley case notes sat on the empty passenger seat of the Stock Squad Land Cruiser, along with the pub security camera footage from the night of the murder; all courtesy of Hutchens, who had commandeered them from his underlings under the guise of due diligence as team leader and then promptly and quietly handed them over to Cato.

Hutchens obviously had some misgivings about Lara Sumich. Why? What was going on? He clearly had the hots for her; Cato could understand that, absolutely. Hutchens had a reputation, the odd whisper here and there of sexual harassment that never went any further. Was that it? Looking for leverage over Lara and getting Cato to do the dirty work? Or was it really a noble search for the truth about who killed Jim Buckley? Noble? Truth? Not words he normally associated with Mick Hutchens. Anyway, Billy Mather had gone AWOL, so he, the files and the disks could wait. Cato turned the car around. A man can only chase one wild goose at a time.

'Guan Yu did not kill Hai Chen with a knife. He broke his head with a stick.'

Jessica Tan finished off her translation with an appropriate miming gesture. Picture this, stick on head. Cato sighed impatiently. This was turning into bloody Cluedo. Was it Guan Yu in the paddock with the dagger, or by the campfire with the lump of four-by-two? Neither. Somebody shot the bastard but nobody was owning up to it. Mark McGowan was cracking his knuckles in an absent-minded yet vaguely sinister fashion.

Xi Xue looked to Jessica for some explanation of what the policemen thought of his revelation. Not very much.

McGowan glowered. 'This is bullshit. We know he was shot.'

'Shot?' Xi Xue speaking, no need for the translation this time.

'Shot,' said Mark McGowan, 'so how about giving us the truth and cutting the crap.'

That took a bit of creative interpreting but Xi got the message. He was adamant. 'No gun, no shooting. They argued. Guan hit Chen with the wood. He told us he killed him. We sat and got drunk by the fire. In the morning Chen's body was gone.'

At least parts of Xi Xue's story seemed to correspond with Guan's version: Chen demanding his weekly subs, an argument between him and Guan, Guan killing him, although the method differed both between the two stories and from the official pathology report. Then the correspondence of events again: yes, they got drunk by the fire, callously ignoring Hai Chen's dead body, and in the morning he was gone. So what was the bullshit with the stabbing and now the 'stick on head'?

'Chen was shot,' insisted Cato.

Xi Xue was equally insistent. 'No. Not by Guan Yu. Guan hit

him, he did not shoot him.'

Cato called a break and stepped outside with McGowan into a blustery sunny morning on the Stevenson and Sons' worksite. Trucks rumbled back and forth sending up dust clouds whipped into willy-willies by the gusting breeze. Bobcats, earthmovers, fluoro overalls, hard hats, water tankers, the crackle of two-ways, the trilling of mobiles: the symphony of a boomtown. Over at his office, standing at the window and staring out at the two policemen, was the maestro and choreographer, Keith Stevenson. Cato met his stare. The maestro gave him the finger and turned away.

'Doesn't like you, does he?' McGowan observed.

'I'll survive.'

Cato thumbed over his shoulder back in the direction of the demountable where Xi Xue and Jessica Tan were sitting on the top step sipping from water bottles, Xi seizing the opportunity for a nicotine fix.

'How does his story fit with the others you've talked to?'

'He's the first one to be helpful. The others have completely zipped up. Three monkeys routine.'

Cato nodded in the direction of Xi. 'So why is he any different?'

McGowan shivered, the breeze cool despite the climbing sun. 'Not afraid like the others? Too stupid to keep quiet? Spinning a line because in fact he's the real murderer? Take your pick.'

Cato squinted as a truck rumbled by sending dust into his face. 'Run him through it once more, then get Jessica Tan back up to Ravensthorpe. Call Amrita back in too. I want to talk to Guan again this afternoon.'

They agreed on a time and Cato hopped back into the Land Cruiser.

McGowan scuffed his heels in the gravel. 'Good result on Buckley I hear.'

'Yeah. Hutchens is pleased.'

'Yeah, he told me. He also told me to stay on this one with you for a few more days.'

Cato nodded. 'That'd be good.'

'Yeah?' McGowan looked inordinately pleased at being wanted.

Cato nodded. 'Couldn't do it without you, mate.'

'Reckon we'll get any result here?'

Cato surprised himself with his confidence. 'Yes, I do.'

He didn't yet know why, but he was beginning to believe it.

31

Thursday, October 16th. Early afternoon.

She hadn't seen anything quite as bad as this for years. The smell was revolting. Clouds of flies hovered above the corpses. She'd lost count. There were so many, all those sightless eyes, staring at nothing. The wind ruffled the gum trees, providing momentary relief from the stench of death. When it dropped there was only heat and silence. The silence of the lambs, at least thirty so far.

She wiped her brow with the back of her hand and plucked at her RSPCA uniform shirt where it stuck to her skin. Her name was embroidered below the logo – Cheryl. She nodded grimly to her colleague, a braided and nose-studded uni student on placement. This was grim enough for an old hand like Cheryl; it must be a vision of hell for a spring chicken like Brittany. Where do they find these names? Brittany was about fifty metres downwind, clicking away on her counter and camera with each gruesome discovery. She was near an empty water trough and the body count was higher there.

'Aw, yuk.' Brittany screwed up her face in disgust.

The Albany office had received an anonymous tip-off and flick-passed it to Cheryl in Esperance, an hour's drive nearer. The student placement was going too quietly so Cheryl, sick of watching the younger woman yawning and playing with her mobile, decided they should have a nice day out. Nice. Somebody had made a half-hearted attempt to pile some of the corpses together in a heap, perhaps with a view to disposing of them eventually. A couple of old but obviously inhabited caravans stood about a hundred metres away. She shuddered at the thought of living near such rotting carnage. As she drew near to the stinking heap of carcasses she could see something protruding from the far side. A few centimetres of stick, the end coated in what appeared to be blood. Cheryl shook her head in despair. Some sick bastard had been bludgeoning the sheep to death.

'Too cheap to even waste a bullet to put them out of their misery: bastards.'

Something fluttered on the end of the stick and she bent closer. She expected it to be wool but it was a tuft of what looked like human hair.

'How was the wedding?'

'What?'

Cato slid the photo across the table to Guan Yu, once again flanked by Jessica the Interpreter and Amrita the Lawyer. 'Hai Chen's wedding. That's you isn't it?' Cato tapped the photo with his finger.

Mark McGowan leaned forward next to Cato. They both had their arms crossed, resting on the table. Expectant. Waiting. Cato had briefed him in the car on the way over. Today they were going to sort Guan's fairy stories out once and for all. Guan looked at Jessica and Amrita for guidance but there was no need for translation and it was a simple enough question.

'That is you, isn't it?' Cato repeated, less conversationally this time.

'Yes.'

'Let me guess. The photo looks like it's the family of the bride or groom but the bride looks a little bit like you. So, Chen's your brother-in-law right?'

'Yes.'

'And you didn't think to tell us this before?'

Guan conferred with Jessica and she turned to face Cato. 'You did not ask.'

Mark McGowan put his finger to his lips as if he'd just worked something out.

'Ah, so is that why you argued? He wasn't just ripping off his co-workers, he was ripping off family.'

Guan played blank.

Amrita Desai leaned forward, hands clasped. 'I'll remind you that my client is under no obligation to answer any of these questions.'

'And I'll remind you that he has confessed to murder, whether you wish to withdraw that confession or not, and we have every right to ask these questions if we're going to get to the bottom of this.' McGowan tapped his pen on the table for emphasis.

Cato studied Guan Yu for a moment and decided to take a punt. One he hadn't warned Mark McGowan about. 'Interview suspended.' He gave a time and flicked off the recording switch. 'I don't really believe your client killed anyone, Miss Desai.'

McGowan turned to his colleague, perplexed. This was not how he imagined they were going to nail Guan Yu once and for all.

Cato ignored him. 'I believe he had an argument, he may even have had a fight. And I believe that Hai Chen's body disappeared. But this bullshit about cutting his throat doesn't get us anywhere. Chen was shot. Your client is making stuff up as he goes along. Why?'

Amrita Desai cleared her throat as if to speak but he cut her off.

'Have a word with him. If he's protecting somebody we'll look after him. If he genuinely doesn't know what really happened he should tell us, but he should know that I'm happy to walk away from all of this time-wasting bullshit today. We can still put him in front of a jury: even with his withdrawn confession, the witnesses to a violent argument and Chen's dodgy financial records. I've seen juries convict on less. Your client is looking at serious time in an Australian jail. I personally don't think he, or his wife and kids, really deserve that.'

Cato stood up out of his chair and nodded towards a watchful Guan Yu. 'It's a simple choice. Help us, or I walk away and leave you in the mess you've made for yourself.'

Jim Buckley looked deep in thought. He'd just finished his bar-top dinner and ordered another Jim Beam and Coke. He was at a high table near the window in the long, narrow bar room, juke box to his left and shark jaws mounted on the wall to his right. The security camera high up behind the bar just caught him at the top of its frame. It captured only every other second, so his movements and those around him were jerky. The time code showed it was still early evening, just after seven. He occasionally stared off up to his right. The pub plasma, the news would have been on.

Cato was filling in time watching the video while he waited for Amrita Desai and her client to either call his bluff or play ball. Mark McGowan was chasing Duncan Goldflam for any forensic developments. Cato had borrowed a spare office and video equipment from an ever-unhelpful Bernie Tilbrook but something about Cato's manner today stopped the desk jockey from pushing his luck. Justin Woodward and his girlfriend had left their drinks unfinished and walked out of the picture without so much as a sideways glance at Jim Buckley. Cato wasn't sure from the size and quality of the video image but he thought he'd seen Buckley smile at their departure. Figures passed in front of the camera: the after-work drinkers leaving and the night-time revellers arriving. Some, like Buckley, just stayed put. How much of this had the Buckley squad watched? Had they stopped after Justin and his girlfriend had walked out because that's where their focus was?

There were two disks with about three hours of footage on each. Cato didn't know what he was meant to be looking for and couldn't risk fast-forwarding. Six hours staring at a screen was more than he had the time or patience for. He scrolled through his mobile and found the number he needed. Tess Maguire answered on the first ring.

'Hello stranger,' said Cato.

'No stranger than you.'

It was a shared greeting from the old days, shifts passing in the night. There was a smile in her voice, nice change.

'Busy?' he inquired.

'Flat out, on the sofa. I'm watching Dr Phil, he's telling me how to relate to my kids.'

'Sounds like you're suitably qualified for the job I have in mind.'

Cato explained his situation and found Tess to be willing and able to trawl through the Buckley footage. He would arrange for a Ravy minion to drop the disks off to her.

'I thought I was persona non grata. The mad woman in the attic?'

'Always were and always will be. Hutchens is cool, he's leaving town and so are the media. Long as you're out of sight, you're out of mind.'

'I'm definitely the latter.'

'I owe you one.'

'I'll keep you to it.' Tess severed the connection.

The door to Cato's cramped office squeaked open and Bernie Tilbrook popped his head through.

'That Indian lady wants to speak to you.'

'Me first ...' McGowan squeezed in behind Tilbrook, ushered the sergeant out with a smile and closed the door. 'Couple of developments from Goldflam.'

'Yes?' Cato couldn't read McGowan's expression, perhaps because McGowan himself didn't know what to make of it.

'The red paper you guys found at Mather's caravan turns out to be part of a matchbox. Redheads.'

Cato nodded to himself, a matchbox and the sticky tape they found. Tape the striking strip to one edge of the door, and a bundle of matches to the other, and hey presto – a crude, not entirely reliable, but potentially very effective booby trap when the door is opened and the gas taps are left on. But such a trap would have to be set from the inside. How did he get out? Window? Roof vent? Most likely, unless he was a phantom shape-shifter. Cato realised he needed a coffee, a good big one.

'Anything else?'

'Duncan was on his way out to Paddy's Field. A call came in from the RSPCA about a stick with what looked like blood and human hair on it. He said watch this space.'

'Looks like we've found our lump of four-by-two,' said Cato.

'And I hit him hard with the wood and he fell down. Dead.'

Jessica Tan finished off with another of her action mimes. So far Guan Yu's new story and Xi Xue's tallied – an argument, a lump of wood, no knife and no gun. It was progress of sorts. Guan was a changed man, helpful as anything. The campfire drinking and the missing body in the morning also tallied. So how did Hai Chen end up shot? Where did the body go? And what made Guan own up to murder and then spin this bullshit yarn about slitting throats?

'Mr Stevenson.'

'What?' Cato and McGowan both leaned forward.

'Mr Stevenson said Chen was dead.' Guan made the finger-across-the-throat gesture and Jessica copied him.

'He knows I need money to send home for my daughter. She's sick.'

Guan Yu and Jessica Tan conferred for a moment looking for the right translation for the sickness. Finally Jessica turned back to face Cato.

'Leukaemia.'

Guan nodded and continued as if he'd just mentioned chicken pox. 'Mr Stevenson said he would keep on sending money. He would make everything right. Not to worry.'

Cato still didn't get the picture. 'Why did he come to you? How did he know about the fight? How did he know that Chen was dead?'

'I told Travis. I said we fought and Chen was dead but he disappeared.'

Cato frowned. Travis had neglected to mention that. 'So did Travis and Mr Stevenson dispose of the body?'

Guan shrugged. 'They must have.'

Cato shook his head, it still didn't add up. 'The body is gone by the time you wake up. How would they know to come out and do that?'

Guan shrugged again, he really was trying to be helpful. 'Mr Stevenson said I should not worry. Police not interested in Chinaman, especially a bad man like Hai Chen. Police not interested if he's dead. Just to keep my mouth shut.'

'And if you didn't?'

'He would send me back without money. No more medication for my daughter.'

'So why did you confess? All you needed to do was keep quiet.'

'Everybody saw us fight. Mr Stevenson said I would be the one you would want to talk to if you were interested in Chen. If so then he would take care of everything.' Guan Yu smiled sadly while Jessica finished her translation. 'And you were interested in a dead Chinaman, Mr Stevenson was wrong. He did not expect a Chinese policeman maybe?'

Mark McGowan sat back and folded his arms, a sceptical and belligerent look in his eyes. 'Did you get your money back then?'

'What?'

'Chen had just taken his weekly cut off each of you. He was dead. He didn't need it any more.'

Guan flushed and looked down at the floor. 'Yes, we took it back.'

That explained the three monkeys routine from all of them. They'd taken money from a dead man, even if it was their money in the first place. Cato remembered something from his conversation with Travis Grant.

'Chen's mobile phone, did you take that too?'

'No. It did not belong to us. We took only what was ours.'

'And the wallet, what did you do with that?'

'Back in the pocket also.'

Phone and wallet missing, probably sitting in forty metres of Southern Ocean by now. Cato was running out of brain space, he needed a break.

'One more question: what was all that rubbish about the knife and throat-slitting?'

Guan looked at Cato like he was an idiot. 'It's what Mr Stevenson said. Hai Chen dead.'

Guan made the finger-across-throat gesture again. That was it. Stevenson's generalised gesture for death or ending had been taken literally by Guan Yu. He really believed he was meant to confess to slitting Chen's throat.

At last it was becoming as clear as mud but now Cato had even more questions: how did Hai Chen's body get from Paddy's Field to the Southern Ocean? Who shot him and why? And where did Keith Stevenson and Travis Grant fit into it?

32

Thursday, October 16th. Early evening.

Coloured lights were strung across the first-floor balcony at the front of the Stevenson McMansion. From the rear came the hubbub of voices, clinking glasses, the low thump of music and the aroma of barbecued meat. The sun was dying in the west in a garish splash of blood-red sky. From the high ground of Millionaire's Row in Wilkinson Street the view across the Barren Ranges was stunning. Cato Kwong ignored the scenery, his mind was elsewhere. He lifted the catch on the side gate and joined the party out back.

There were about thirty guests in clusters of threes and fours on the spacious limestone patio and expansive well-kept lawn. Cato recognised Travis Grant bending over an esky, scowling when he noticed the gatecrasher. Beside him, Kane Stevenson, face healing nicely. They were in the company of a couple of the barmaids from the pub. Otherwise that was it as far as familiar faces go. The music was baby-boomer stuff: Daddy Cool, 'Eagle Rock'. A few heads turned briefly as Cato made his entrance, returning to their conversations once they realised they didn't know him. One or two did subtle double takes; they hadn't expected to see any of the Chinese labourers in Keith's backyard but realised it was probably rude to stare. Keith Stevenson, on the other hand, just stood and stared.

His squat powerful body strained against an Eagles footy top. The millionaire businessman completed the ensemble with board shorts and thongs. Daddy Cool himself. A sweating Corona poked out the top of his clenched fist. In the other hand, barbie tongs. Stevenson was turning thick lumps of meat on a hotplate and grill that seemed, to Cato's untrained eye, about the size of a ping-pong table. The host was mid-conversation with a tall, tanned, distinguished-looking man: mid-fifties, close-cropped grey hair, looked like he kept in shape from regular tennis or running. He oozed money and he eyed Cato with detached curiosity. It was mutual; the face was vaguely familiar to Cato but he couldn't place it, yet. Keith Stevenson made up his mind to try being hospitable.

'Mr Kwong, Philip isn't it? Can I get you a beer mate?'

Stevenson had chosen not to use any words suggesting police.

Cato helped him out in clear confident tones. 'No thanks, Mr Stevenson, this is business, not pleasure. Police business.' He flashed his ID card to underline his point.

The nearest conversations stuttered and stalled. Heads which had ignored Cato a few minutes ago now turned to study him.

Keith Stevenson smiled wearily at his tall, elegant companion: the trials of life and leadership. He gestured towards the open French doors and the kitchen beyond. 'Maybe we should step inside the house, Mr Kwong.'

'No. I'm good here, thanks.'

The meat smelled glorious. There was a marinade and Cato caught whiffs of garlic, soy sauce, lemon and chilli. He realised he was starving.

It didn't look like the host was about to offer him anything any time soon. 'So state your business,' Keith said.

Kerry Stevenson made a grand entrance through the French doors. She'd made an effort for the party. Tracky-dacks had been replaced by ironed slacks and a glittery T-shirt. She stared one-eyed at Cato through a blue curl of cigarette smoke.

'What's he want, Keith?'

Keith rustled up a smile for the benefit of his guests. 'Just a quick word love, and then he'll be on his way. So how can I help you, Officer?'

The last word pronounced with an added "H" prefixed for comic effect.

Cato was in no hurry, he lazily surveyed his surroundings. 'Nice place, Keith. Doing well for yourself.'

Stevenson served up a smug shrug. 'Work hard, play hard; reap the rewards.'

Cato nodded. 'Not bad for an ex-thug and standover man. It is "ex" isn't it?'

Stevenson's fixed smile hardened, the remaining party conversations fizzled out. They now had everyone's attention. 'Fair play mate, is this what you call "police business"? You're on my property, insulting me in front of my guests. It's just not on.'

The tall, smooth, rich guy stepped forward, hand outstretched. 'I don't think we've been introduced. I'm Jim Dunstan.'

Cato remembered now: the man from the Dunstan Industries website. Dunstan Industries, the Halliburton of Hopetoun. Cato shook the hand; it was a grip that wasn't trying to prove anything. It didn't have to, but it still failed as a circuit breaker. Cato Kwong and Keith Stevenson weren't to be diverted from the path they'd set themselves on.

Cato made the next move. 'Your employees, the ones who live in the caravans in Paddy's Field, how much do you charge them to live in that squalor?'

Stevenson flipped a lump of meat with the tongs, pressed it down and made it sizzle. 'If they choose to live like pigs that's their business, I'm just a landlord doing them a favour. This is a boom-town, accommodation is at a premium.'

Cato looked skywards and squinted in apparent concentration. 'A hundred and fifty per man, per week: four men to a caravan half the size of your kitchen. That's six hundred bucks a week. That would get you a fair-sized house even at inflated Hopetoun prices. How am I doing?'

'You sure you're a cop? You sound like a shop steward for your mates.'

There were a couple of snorts and chuckles from the audience.

Cato was undeterred, counting off on his fingers. 'Then fifty bucks a week each for transport; that's Travis and the minibus. A one-off payment for the overalls, two sets, a hundred each. Then there's the return airfare from China, agent's commission, et cetera, et cetera.'

Stevenson theatrically checked his watch. 'Well nice as it is to chat ...'

'They think they're on a good thing getting five hundred a week in the hand, but they're not even getting that are they? After all of your deductions they'll be lucky to scrape two, two-fifty. For ten hours a day, six days a week. That's what, about four bucks an hour? They'd be better off working at a fast food joint.'

There were a few embarrassed coughs from the audience.

'And if they complain you can just send them back and get another batch.'

'Have you finished?'

It was a low growl; Stevenson had taken a couple of steps closer. No, Cato hadn't finished. He had also noticed something in Jimmy Dunstan's face: a look of revulsion but also a bit of guilt in there too. He was doing the same with his foreign workers, perhaps not quite so venal but maybe on a grander scale? Bigger projects, more workers, a thinner skim but a wider spread. More subtle, more class.

Cato pressed home his point. 'And the really pathetic thing is that you don't even need their money. The value of the contracts on your books makes you a rich man either way, but you have to have it all because you can. Meanwhile, you hide your business affairs behind an off-the-shelf company with your decrepit old mum as the legally responsible office-bearer. Charming.'

Stevenson was clenching and unclenching his fists.

Cato took a step closer. 'Once a standover man, always one; is that why Chen was killed? The others found out about the extra deductions? They thought it was Chen ripping them off. But it was you all along.'

Stevenson was fast. In one fluid movement he launched himself forward, head-butting Cato, breaking his nose and momentarily blinding him with the pain. Cato reached out for a weapon, any weapon. His hand closed around a jar of Dijon mustard. He crunched it into the side of Stevenson's head. Stevenson kept coming. Cato's arm was pushed halfway up his back to snapping point, the way cops usually do to bad guys. Stevenson had his spare hand on the back of Cato's head, bending him over the searing barbecue, pushing his face down towards the hotplate, the very hot plate. Cato's free hand waved about, unable to get any purchase except on scalding metal. He was powerless, absolutely at Stevenson's mercy. There was a throaty chuckle from the back of the audience: probably Travis, the Master's Apprentice, getting his revenge by proxy.

It was a mouth-watering aroma of spicy sizzling marinade but it was eye-wateringly close, about two centimetres away. Blood dripping from his smashed nose spat and bubbled on the hotplate. Cato could feel his face beginning to burn. Was that new smell of over-cooked meat him?

'That's enough Keith.'

It was Jim Dunstan, sounding quite masterful. Stevenson pushed Cato closer to the hotplate, he could feel something dripping from Stevenson's head on to the back of his own neck. It was a lukewarm greasy concoction of sweat, French mustard and blood from the deep cut just above his tormentor's left ear.

'Keith. Enough.'

A pit bull being called to heel. Stevenson hissed in Cato's ear, 'Keep away from me and my family or next time I'll fucking flame-grill you, you cunt.' He released his grip. 'Now fuck off.'

As a conversation point, the scene took some beating. It was what the Australian chattering classes call 'a real barbecue-stopper'.

Cato Kwong bowed his head and slunk dejectedly out of the side gate, all eyes on him. An embarrassed hush amplified his lonely footsteps on the limestone paving. He held a handkerchief over his shattered nose to try to stem the flow. The blood-soaked cloth also helped hide the wide grin beneath. As his face was being pushed into the hotplate, Cato knew he was so close to the truth he could almost taste it.

It wasn't until he was halfway down Wilkinson Street that Cato remembered. He was meant to catch the evening flight to Perth for Jim Buckley's funeral. He saw the tiny silhouette of the plane against the dying orange of the western sky, banking around to swing north. The horizon tilted and swung, Cato steadied himself against someone's gatepost.

'You look terrible.' It was Tess Maguire, seated on her front porch at the house next door, a gin and tonic on the low table next to her.

'Thanks.'

Cato lifted his head and Tess could see clearly now the damage Stevenson had done. She was down her front path in three quick strides, leading Cato back to a seat on the shaded verandah.

'Don't you ever eat?'

'Sorry?'

Cato, head back and handkerchief to nose, waved the half packet of frozen peas. 'Same ones we used for my thumb.'

Tess smiled grimly and placed a gin and tonic on the table beside him. 'Keith Stevenson I presume?'

'How'd you guess?'

'I can see his driveway from here. Saw you stagger down it.'

'So much for the dignified exit, stage left.'

'I hope you left him in a worse state.'

'Yeah, it might take him a while to get the sauce stains off his shirt.'

'My hero; so what happened?'

Between sips of Gordon's and tonic and dabs at his streaming nose, Cato told her. The forensic report on how Hai Chen really died; the conflicting interviews with Guan

Yu, the other Chinese workers and Travis Grant; the bank statements; the RSPCA; and the four-by-two. Tess tutted mock disapproval when he mentioned the anonymous phone tip-off about the sheep. He wrapped up with Guan Yu coming clean; the confrontation with Stevenson.

At the end of it all Tess sat back on the cheap cane chair and frowned. 'Do you really think Stevenson shot Chen?'

Cato shrugged, not so easy to do with your head right back.

The sun was gone but the breeze had dropped. It was a still and not-too-cold evening with a big round moon hovering in the eastern sky. The muffled sounds of Stevenson's soiree drifted down the hill to the Maguire porch on the humble side of the street. Cato looked at Tess properly for the first time since he'd stumbled down her path. She wore jeans and a loose cotton shirt and her bare feet, crossed at the ankles, rested on the low table in front of her. Her toenails were freshly painted and the little bottle of polish sat beside a bowl of peanuts. She looked good. He glanced down at his own blood-encrusted clothes and smelt the animal grease and marinade from his close encounter with Stevenson's hotplate.

'Hungry?' Tess inquired.

'Not any more.'

Tess returned to her theme. 'We know Keith Stevenson's a thug from way back and it's no surprise that he's a nasty boss. But a cold-blooded murderer?'

'Those Chinese don't have access to guns, cars or boats, which are what was needed here.'

'How do you know?'

'They're totally dependent on Grant and Stevenson for moving them around. Nobody has mentioned guns at Paddy's Field. They agree a fight happened and Guan Yu hit the victim with a stick but the news about the bullet in Chen's head came as a real surprise. Somebody else did it and my money is on Grant or Stevenson or both.'

Tess sipped more of her drink. 'So how do you prove it?'

Cato peered up the hill at the steep floodlit driveway and the fairy lights at Stevenson's Palace. The good ship Kerry nestled on the trailer with a silver Prado flanking it and Stevenson's company ute parked in front. Cato patted his pockets for his mobile and found the number for Duncan Goldflam.

Call finished, Tess eyed Cato over the rim of her glass. 'Don't you need a warrant to turn his place over?'

Cato tipped his head back, placed the melting pack of frozen peas on the bridge of his nose and closed his eyes. 'Assault on a police officer, very serious offence. That whiz-bang barbie of his has my blood all over it.'

Tess put her drink down and crunched an ice cube between her teeth. 'Don't get too comfortable. I've got something to show you.'

Jim Buckley had taken a keen interest in somebody over to his left. He'd looked over that way four times in less than two minutes. Whoever Jim was interested in, he or she was off-screen and outside the frame offered by the pub security camera. Tess found it on disk two about a quarter of the way in: the time code said it was 8.46 on Friday evening. Jim Buckley still had about three or four hours to live. On their way fast-forwarding to this point Tess had also pointed out Riri Yusala and his companions shepherding her daughter Melissa and her friend out of the pub. A look passed between Tess and Cato, no words needed. After the first unsubtle stare, the following glances to Buckley's left were lingering but seemingly casual, discreet. Tess described the looks as being like those of a man trying not to seem like he's staring down your cleavage. At which point Tess had smiled enigmatically and sat back up from the position she'd been in. Cato realised he'd been busted. He wondered if he'd driven through an invisible cloud of libido recently. He put his head back and dabbed at his nose to remind her that he was, after all, out of sorts.

A short while later, three and a half minutes to be exact, Jim

Buckley finished his drink and left the picture. He returned twelve minutes later and made straight for a new position at the bar over to the right of frame.

'He orders his drink and ...' Tess paused the footage, 'there. He nods to someone off-screen, male I reckon.'

'Why male?'

'It's a blokey nod. Reserved, a "how's-the-ute" nod. Happy to strike up a conversation but don't care if you don't. That kind of nod.'

Cato was impressed and a little scared, he knew he didn't stand a chance of hiding anything from intuition like that. They'd moved on from gin to coffee. Tess sipped hers and winked at him like old times.

'There's more.'

She fast-forwarded a minute or two. Jim Buckley was now half in, half out the right bottom edge of the frame and facing the person off-screen. The body movements suggested conversation. Buckley then turned to the bar and ordered another drink, his own Jim Beam and Coke still over half full. A barmaid's hand delivered a middy of beer and Jim passed it off-screen.

'Buckley shouting a round: official, on the record.' Cato could have wisecracked a bit more but he remembered he was talking about a dead man.

Tess fast-forwarded again. 'After a few minutes more the conversation ceases and Buckley retrieves his seat by the rear wall. He doesn't look in that direction again for the rest of the evening.' Tess found the spot she wanted. 'At 11.49, pub almost empty by now, Jim leaves.'

They watched him finish his drink, scrape loose change into the palm of his hand and pocket it. Unsteadily now, after eight bourbon and Cokes, he nods towards the bar and exits left of screen. Across the road from the pub is the path that leads him down to the groyne. A hundred-metre walk in the rain across wet gravel and potholes will bring him to the short wooden fishing jetty which points west across the bay to the national park. There somebody will cave his skull in with a lump of jagged rock the size of a soccer ball. As they watched the last of the patrons leave the pub from right to left across the screen, Cato and Tess saw him at the same time. Tess pressed pause. Slightly blurred by the freezing of the frame, there was still no doubt about the short, wiry man in the beanie: Billy Mather, Herman the Hermit from Starvation Bay.

'Coincidence?' Cato didn't even believe it himself.

Tess sat back and took a long gulp from her cooling coffee. 'The usual line is that there's no such thing. That's the line the Mick Hutchenses of this world take. How much of the case against Justin Woodward is "coincidence"?'

Cato recounted what he'd gleaned from the file. 'Forensics; Buckley's hair on Woodward's jeans; phone calls between Buckley and Woodward; drug traces in the van; and last but not least, he was dobbed in by Riri Yusala.'

'Pretty-Boy, now there's a reliable witness. A drug pusher and probable date rapist facing several years in the clink and deportation at the end.'

'But what about the forensics?' Cato insisted.

Tess nodded, conceding the point, then frowned. 'The forensics, however rubbery, are usually good for getting juries over the line. But if they had that from day one why did they release Woodward in the first place? Surely the phone records and the forensics should have been enough to hold him?'

Cato wasn't familiar enough with the case to answer that question. His head was throbbing and he had an early morning search party to organise.

Tess started clearing glasses and cups away. Cato stood up to help her and wobbled; he'd stood up too quickly, not a good idea when you've recently been head-butted. Tess put out an arm to steady him and their eyes locked. They leaned in to each other; his hot breath on her face, his hand cupping her neck below her ear, fingers stroking her hair.

Tess closed her eyes, pushing her head against his hand like a cat starved of affection. 'Why did you go, Cato? What was so wrong with us?'

Cato still didn't know the answer after all these years. 'I'm a coward. An idiot. I dunno ... sorry.'

She felt the tension in his body. The caresses that seemed so natural just a moment ago now felt distracted and clumsy. The moment was gone.

Tess stepped back from the embrace. 'Sorry, it's been a shitty twelve months. I'm just getting to the other side of it. This isn't a good idea. The last thing I need now is a nostalgic fling with Cato Kwong,' she smiled apologetically, 'however tempting.'

He sighed. 'Story of my life.'

She looked at the familiar self-deprecating pity-me smile. The one that said this situation is not of my making. The one he used when he left her.

'Cato, don't take this the wrong way but you're a gutless, self-obsessed bastard.'

He looked like he'd just been slapped, then hid it with a rueful grin. 'Don't beat around the bush, say what you mean.'

'You ran away from me because you were gutless, you rolled over for Hutchens and landed yourself in trouble, same reason, and you're even hanging on to your shitty job in Stock Squad because you haven't the guts to make a stand on what's right and what's wrong. If you really feel hard done by, then leave and get a proper job. What are you waiting for, somebody to say sorry and admit you were right and they were wrong?'

Cato looked at the floor. Flushed and pissed off.

Tess placed her hand gently on his chest. 'Say something.'

He stared over the top of her head. 'You seem to have worked it all out already.'

She took a step back from him. 'Fucking grow up, Cato. You helped put an innocent man away because you did the wrong thing but what's really eating you is that you got busted when others didn't. Now you're wallowing in this bitter martyrdom crap. It doesn't matter who else got away with it. You did wrong, so take it on the chin and move on instead of infecting everyone around you with your ... poison.'

Cato's head was swirling; was it Stevenson's handiwork or something else? Tess had certainly done her homework: was that what the little car ride with Jim Buckley was all about? How long ago, a week?

Tess's look was gentler now. 'And your marriage is up the spout too, isn't it? Tell me I'm wrong.'

'Are you finished?'

She shook her head. 'You really need to stop running away when stuff gets too hard. Take it from a girl who knows, Cato, if you don't get that poison out of your system it's going to eat you up.'

Step Forward–Walk Away. First Greg Fisher, now Tess Maguire. What was this, Hang-Cato-Out-to-Dry Week?

'Finished now?'

'Yes.' She gave him a kiss on the cheek. 'Think about what I'm saying. Please?'

Cato never took his eyes off that neutral spot on the wall.

33

Friday, October 17th. Dawn.

It was a motley crew: Duncan Goldflam and one of his offsiders were ready to roll wearing blue forensic coveralls and face-masks. They would be assisted by Mark McGowan, decked out in blue paper shoe covers, mask and rubber gloves. Paul Abbott and Mitch Biddulph from Ravensthorpe and a couple of young uniforms drafted in from Esperance would help settle things in the house. It was a motley crew because Cato didn't have a more senior officer's permission for this raid. He'd worry about that later. He stifled a yawn. Instead of sleeping he'd brooded over the home truths Tess had presented to him. He met her eyes; she still didn't seem very sorry. He knew he was asking for even more trouble inviting her along. Although not actually suspended in the strict disciplinary sense she was still meant to be stood aside pending the outcome of the taser inquiry. To hell with it–she was one of the very few people he trusted.

Blue-black, orange-flecked cumulus billowed and jostled in the eastern sky awaiting the sun's grand entrance. A soft breeze blew along Wilkinson Street and an empty can of purple UDL rolled with it. Cato nodded to Tess and she pressed her finger to the bell on Keith Stevenson's front door. A dog barked somewhere inside. It was a deep meaty bark from a hound with more substance than Justin Woodward's lamented Lily. Cato noticed Tess's hand hover over her taser. Two more presses of the bell and through the frosted glass Cato saw a blurred figure descend the stairs and curse the dog back into submission.

'Who the fuck is it?

Keith Stevenson slept in yellow Homer Simpson boxers and a Billabong T-shirt. He looked hungover and Cato noticed with some satisfaction that the top of his ear was wadded with elastoplast.

Stevenson squinted at his callers and shook his head in disgust. 'Fuck's sake.'

Tess did the formalities, announcing that she was arresting him for assaulting a police officer, declaring the premises a crime scene, and waving what looked like it might be a search warrant in his face.

Stevenson never took his eyes off Cato the whole time. 'Weak cunt,' he hissed.

Cato ignored him, instead issuing orders for the search of house, backyard, and shed.

Kerry Stevenson's smoky croak echoed from the top of the stairs. 'Keith, what the fuck's goin' on? Who's at the door?'

'Jackie-fucken-Chan. Get up and make us a coffee will you, love?'

'Fuck off.'

Tess and Paul Abbott led Stevenson into the open-plan lounge room, cuffed him, and pushed him gently but firmly into an armchair. The penny finally dropped at the sound of a truck's reverse beeper.

Stevenson's eyes hardened. 'What's happening out there?'

Cato had his answer ready. 'I believe I brushed against the boat last night when I left. My blood is on it. Helps us build a complete picture of the sequence of events for an assault charge.'

'Bullshit. What do you really want the boat for?'

Cato repeated the line about assault being a serious offence, et cetera.

'Any witnesses to this alleged assault?' Stevenson's eyes twinkled.

'About thirty in your backyard.'

'Any that have come forward?'

'Inquiries are continuing.'

'This is a fucking joke and my lawyer's going to enjoy doing you.'

Cato didn't mention the fact that a second tow truck was on its way to collect the Prado and the SaS ute as well.

There was a commotion on the stairs which led directly from the open-plan family area to the floor above. Cato wandered over to the bottom step to investigate. Kane Stevenson was acting tough for little brother Jai's benefit; he was now facedown at the top of the stairs with the two Esperance uniforms kneeling on his back to snap the cuffs on. He seemed to have picked up his parents' vocabulary and florid language. At the top of the stairs, eleven year old Jai stood wide-eyed in his green Bart Simpson boxers. Cute: father and son, mix and match boxers.

His mother brushed past him in a hooded purple velveteen dressing gown. 'Jai, get some fucken clothes on and get down here.' She glanced down at her older boy, face deep in the shagpile.

'Kane, stop being such a dickhead, love.'

Duncan Goldflam poked his head through the back door and nodded for Cato to join him in the backyard. His forensic helper and Mark McGowan were standing by the shed door with the chainsaw, an orange petrol-driven Huskie, and an evidence sack.

'Don't get too excited yet,' cautioned Goldflam, 'it's not covered in your Chinaman's blood, it's been cleaned recently. But ...' Goldflam allowed himself a grin, 'first impressions are of a not very thorough job.' He nodded back towards the house. 'These blokes are usually either too lazy, cocky, or stupid to cover their tracks properly. They think they're untouchable. That's where they usually come undone.'

Goldflam signalled for his bloke to put the chainsaw into an evidence sack.

Cato was warming to him. Despite the man's obvious tribal loyalties to his boss Hutchens he was still, in the end, a pro who revelled in nailing bad guys. 'Let's hope you're right. Any sign of a firearm?'

Goldflam shook his head. Cato frowned, there should have

been one. In the pub, Travis Green had said something about Keith taking the younger boy, Jai, roo-shooting, something he never did with older brother Kane.

That's when they heard the gunshot from inside the house.

'Put the gun down, Jai,' said Cato.

The Disaffected Youth was armed and dangerous. Nobody knew precisely where he was, just that he was upstairs somewhere with his dad's .22: the one he'd just shot Steve Dempster with. That was the name of the young cop from Esperance, now lying face down at the top of the stairs. A patch of dark blood spread across the back of his blue uniform shirt and dripped through the open staircase on to the jarrah floorboards of the kitchen below. Kane Stevenson, still handcuffed, lay on his stomach. Steve Dempster's partner, Corey something, lay between Kane and the wall, eyes pleading for someone to get him out of the line of fire. The poor bugger had pissed himself, maybe worse, judging by the nasty smell hovering in the air. Everybody else was downstairs behind the kitchen counter.

'Jai, put the gun down.' It was Tess this time, she'd come out from behind the counter and was at the bottom of the steps.

'Get back here,' hissed Cato.

Tess ignored him. She unclipped her gun and lifted her foot to the first stair. Cato couldn't believe he'd brought people into this situation unprepared and unprotected. Admittedly, the nearest supply of body armour was three hours away in Albany but it had never occurred to him that they were walking into anything more dangerous than a possible scuffle with Keith Stevenson.

'Jai, it's me. Tess. Remember?'

There was a snort and a chuckle. 'Course I remember.'

Cato crouch-walked over to Kerry who was sipping serenely from a mug of coffee.

'Is there another way upstairs?' he whispered.

She shook her head and waved her mug vaguely in the direction of the stairs. 'If I were you I'd tell Wonder Woman not to chance it. My Jai's a real grudge-bearer, gets it from his father's side. Scots. Never lets anything go.'

Keith Stevenson glared at her. He held up his handcuffed wrists to Cato. 'Get these off and I'll go up and sort him out.'

Cato shook his head but couldn't think of any better ideas right now.

Stevenson growled. 'I don't want my son getting shot. I'm the only one he's going to listen to. You've already lost one.' He gestured with his chin towards Tess who was now three steps up with seven to go. 'Do you want her to die as well?'

Tess's head was nearly at upper floor level. She was now just a few centimetres from the line of fire. Two more steps and she would be able to touch the limp outstretched hand of Steve Dempster.

'Jai, I can see from here he's still breathing, but we need to get him to a hospital quickly.'

She was acutely aware that the last time she and Jai met he'd ended up with a fifty thousand volt hangover. Jai Stevenson was a boy with a gun in his hand and scores to settle.

'He can die. He shouldn't have jumped on Kane.'

Tess looked up the stairs into Kane Stevenson's eyes. He read her signal.

'Jai, mate, I'm okay. No worries. But we need to get that cop to a doctor quick. Chuck the gun down and let them do it, okay?'

'No.'

'Do it, you stupid little runt.'

'Fucken shut up Kane or I'll shoot you as well.'

Tess climbed another stair. Depending on exactly where Jai was, and whether he was lying down, crouching, or standing, she would be in the firing line on the next step – if she wasn't already. Corey from Esperance had stopped trying to merge with the wall and floor. Tess tried to ignore the smell of his fear. He opened his eyes and realised how close Tess was. If he reached out his hand he could touch the top of her head. Beside him, lying on his stomach, Kane Stevenson's expression was unreadable. Was he going to warn his little brother of Tess's every move or would he help her end this? On the other side of Kane, the blood-soaked body of Steve Dempster seemed to be growing colder and smaller.

'I can see you!' Jai was playing a singsong, peek-a-boo game.

Tess instinctively crouched and flinched. The eleven year old chuckled.

Out in the backyard, Goldflam and his bloke were placing a ladder against the outside wall. Mark McGowan, pistol in hand, waited at the foot of the ladder for the word to go, but they didn't know which room Jai was in. They signalled through the door to Cato to find out. He turned to the boy's mother.

'Which room is he in?'

Kerry shrugged and looked away.

'Your son is in real danger of dying today, Mrs Stevenson.'

'Only if I help you lot and I'm not going to.'

'Let me talk to him.' It was Keith Stevenson, pleading.

This was a side to him that Cato hadn't expected. 'I need to know which room he's in. I have a badly wounded officer needing urgent medical attention. Time is running out.'

'The middle one, but let me talk to him. I can end this.'

Cato mouthed 'middle' to Mark McGowan and turned back to Stevenson.

'We both know why we're here don't we? The real reason.'

Stevenson kept his face neutral. 'The alleged assault.'

'The real reason.' Cato's eyes bored into Stevenson's.

Stevenson shook his head in disgust. 'Jesus you're a piece of work. Turning the screws at a time like this. Bargaining with my boy's life. You're a fucking disgrace.'

'I don't know what you're talking about Mr Stevenson, I'm just trying to bring this situation to an end.' Cato looked over

Stevenson's shoulder at McGowan and gave him the nod to start climbing. McGowan checked his Glock one final time and started the ascent.

'What's all that whispering down there?' Jai's voice, uncertain.

'Jai mate, we need to stop this. There's ...'

Cato placed a warning hand on Keith Stevenson's shoulder and leaned in close to his ear. 'If you warn him you'll restrict our options even further. That puts him in even more danger. Think about that.'

'There's what, Dad? What's the whispering, is something happening?'

Jai's voice sounded more and more childlike, nervous, afraid, the game was no longer such fun.

Keith Stevenson's lower lip trembled. 'There's ...' Cato locked eyes with him. 'There's ... no need for all this, Jai. Let's call it a day, eh?'

'Dad. There's a bloke at the window! He's got a gun.'

With Jai distracted, Tess leaned forward and grabbed Dempster by the back of his collar, dragging him down three steps out of the line of fire.

'Dad.'

'Throw the gun down, son.' Keith Stevenson's eyes brimmed over.

'No.' The boy's voice was rising in panic.

'We need to stop all this, Keith.' Cato looked from Stevenson to Goldflam, who was outside waiting for a signal to pass up to McGowan. He turned his gaze back to Stevenson again.

Stevenson slumped. 'I did the Chink. Stop this. Now.'

Cato gave the signal to Goldflam to hold fire and uncuffed Stevenson. Dad was up the stairs in a few quick strides talking calmly to Jai all the way. Cato followed close behind, gun drawn. The boy put the .22 down as he was told and his father crushed him in a desperate, anguished embrace.

Cato placed a hand on the man's shoulder. 'Keith Stevenson,

I am arresting you for the murder of Hai Chen ...'

Stevenson released his grip on his son and turned to face Cato, his voice low and accusing. 'What you did today was plain wrong. If you had a kid you'd know it was.' Stevenson's finger prodded Cato's chest. 'And God help him if you do.'

Cato couldn't read the expression on Tess Maguire's face. She was busy calling an ambulance.

34

Friday, October 17th. Late morning.

Steve Dempster would live. His shoulder would never feel quite right again. He would never feel safe or as self-confident again. He would probably not come back to the job after treatment and rehab. He'd find something a bit safer and more rewarding, maybe real estate, or the mine. Already Cato knew that Jai Stevenson would probably not face trial or retribution for what he had done. Nobody had actually seen him pull the trigger. Nobody could prove evil intent: it would be put down to accident. He was eleven, for goodness sake. Across the table in the interview room at Ravensthorpe cop shop, Cato could see that Keith Stevenson knew it too.

'Hai Chen,' said Cato.

Stevenson seemed overly calm for someone who had confessed to a murder, even if it was while a gun was pointed at his son's head. Mark McGowan had switched on the recording equipment and done the honours. Now he waited, pen and notepad at the ready.

Stevenson had waived his right to a lawyer. 'I got a call from Chen. Must have been about 11.00, 11.30 that night.'

'Where from? Isn't Paddy's Field out of range?'

'He'd walked over the paddocks to the airstrip. There's coverage there. That's where we arranged to meet.'

'Where were you?'

'I'd been out in the ute, spotlighting with the boy, we were on our way back. Bagged a few rabbits, a fox, and an emu. Kept the emu for the cat. She loves it.'

The mobile records would confirm the call. The emu blood in the back of the ute tray would muddy forensics up a bit.

Cato pressed on. 'So you dropped Jai off and went to the meeting?'

An eye flicker and an overly quick reply. 'Yeah that's right.'

'Or did you take Jai with you?'

'Dropped him.' Firmer this time: Cato didn't pursue it.

'What time did you get to the airstrip?'

'About midnight, maybe later, didn't check.'

'Where was Chen?'

'In the undercover area, in front of the terminal, didn't look too good.'

'How do you mean?'

'Blood all over his head, shivering, mumbling. He's hard to understand at the best of times.'

'What next?'

'I cleaned him up. Gave him a drink of water. Asked him where he wanted to go.'

'And?'

'He started going nuts. Babbling in Chinese. Started hitting me.'

'Why?'

'Ask him. Psycho he was. Mental.'

'Was it because his scam had been busted and he needed your help to get out?'

'What scam was that then?' Stevenson cocked an eyebrow.

'Skimming off his workmates. His brother-in-law.'

'Naughty, naughty, but sorry, no, I didn't know he was doing that.'

'Why did you get Guan Yu to put his hand up for it?'

'Who?'

'Guan Yu, the brother-in-law, the one with the sick kid. He told you he had a fight with Chen that night. Was he your insurance policy if things started going pear-shaped?'

'Pear-shaped?'

'The body washes up and the town is crawling with cops, even if they are interested in something else. It all just goes a bit ... pear-shaped?'

'Look, this is all news to me, do you want to hear my story or what?'

Cato caught Stevenson's drift; it was his word against Guan's that there was an 'arrangement'. He tried a different angle. 'What about Travis Grant?'

'What about him?'

'Didn't he ever ask you what happened to your gangmaster Hai Chen?'

Stevenson looked at a poster on the wall. 'Travis isn't your inquisitive type. Minds his own business. It's served him well so far.'

Cato knew now where this was going. Keith Stevenson had used the last few hours to work out his story. Or maybe he had been waiting for this day all along. An argument, a violent struggle, Chen had grabbed at the .22, it had gone off accidentally. Stevenson had a body on his hands. With his criminal history it wouldn't look good. He had to dispose of it, that's all he would own up to. Not murder, just manslaughter at most and the illegal disposal of the body. It would be almost impossible to prove anything else. With a good lawyer he would be looking at five to seven years with a third off for good behaviour.

Cato sighed. 'So how did you get rid of him?'

'Took him out in the boat, Starvation Bay. Went out a few miles. Cut him up on the deck with the Huskie, chucked him over the side, hosed the deck down.' Stevenson opened his arms, mildly regretful but really all in a day's work.

'Chen's clothes, wallet, phone?' asked Mark McGowan, pen poised.

'Same, everything over the side and into the drink.'

Cato went through the story with him again, dotting i's and crossing t's, checking for inconsistencies. It still looked the same. Around 11.00 that night Chen must have woken dazed and bleeding from his encounter with Guan Yu. His workmates were by now asleep and drunk, believing Chen to be dead, and in no fit state to worry about it until the morning. Chen wanted to meet Stevenson and, after stumbling across darkened paddocks until he was in mobile range, called him to arrange it. Why? Maybe Hai Chen believed that he was finished here, his scams rumbled. Again, why? Nothing so far suggested Guan Yu knew he was getting ripped off any more than the basic fifty bucks a week. The argument they had earlier that night was about Guan's inability to pay his weekly dues, nothing more.

At the airport another argument ensued, this time with Stevenson, and Chen was shot. Cato sat back and folded his arms behind his head.

'Tell me about the argument again, just so we've got it straight.'

'He was nuts. Babbling in Chinese. Started getting aggro.'

'What about?'

'Fuck knows.'

Cato leaned forward again, resting his arms on the table, interlocking his fingers. 'C'mon Keith, you told me you, quote, "did the Chink". You must have had a reason. Babbling in Chinese and getting aggro aren't reasons; you could have laid him out with one punch, a man with your experience.'

Stevenson mirrored Cato's arms-on-the-table pose. 'When I said I did the Chink you were threatening my son's life. I think it's known as duress. However I am here of my own free will volunteering to help clear this matter up.'

'Please go on.'

'He made a grab for the gun. It went off, hit him in the head, end of story. That's what I meant by "did the Chink". I was responsible.'

That was all he was giving. The forensics were inconclusive as to the details of the struggle and, like Keith, were never going to tell Cato the real reason for it. The story was coming to an end with plenty of i's and t's left undotted and uncrossed and Cato couldn't do anything about it. Maybe Stevenson and

Chen were splitting the rip-off proceeds fifty-fifty and Chen was threatening to tell all unless he got what he wanted. Maybe Stevenson or maybe someone else shot Hai Chen. Jai was the only other candidate; he'd certainly shown he could handle a gun. Keith Stevenson then took the body in his ute, picked up the boat from home and went out to sea. And now he was probably taking the rap for his son. He was turning out to be a better dad than Cato had ever shown himself to be.

'Okay, thanks Mr Stevenson, that should be enough to be going on with.'

Mark McGowan formally charged Stevenson with various counts including assault on a police officer, obstruction of justice, and manslaughter. Stevenson sat back in his seat and yawned.

Cato stood to leave. 'Okay Mark, let's bring Jai in, and his mum as a responsible adult of course, and check his version of that night he went out shooting with his dad.'

Keith Stevenson smiled and kept his thoughts to himself.

Jim Buckley's coffin rolled through the dark red velvet curtains to the strains of 'Whiter Shade of Pale'. DI Mick Hutchens had never figured Jim for a Procol Harum fan; then again he'd never figured him for anything except maybe a dickhead. At least he had the grim satisfaction of assuring Buckley's grieving sons that their father's killer was in custody. Justin Woodward's appearance before an Albany magistrate the previous day had been headlines on the evening news. Mick Hutchens was flavour of the minute–even the Commissioner had deigned to zap him a congratulatory email. He sensed rehabilitation and reward in the offing. He wanted out of Bogan Town, he wanted Fremantle Detectives. He wanted luscious Lara Sumich but she was as coy as ever. He wanted to bring Cato Kwong back in from the cold; Kwong was too smart and too tenacious for bullshit like Stock Squad, but he had fucked up yet again. Missing the plane and missing Jim Buckley's funeral. Did he have some kind of self-destruct button he pressed whenever he got too near to the big league?

The mourners were filing out. Cigarette packets and lighters already in hands. Mobiles were being switched back on, messages beeping. Among the crowd he could see Jim Buckley's sister-in-law, Stuart Miller's wife; she'd been pointed out to him before the service began. Poor bugger, she looked dreadful. She'd lost her sister and brother-in-law in fairly quick succession and now had a husband blinded and burnt beyond recognition in the hospital. She was staring at the screen of her mobile phone like she had just seen a ghost.

Hutchens went over, fumbling in his head for some words of condolence. 'Mrs Miller, I'm Detective Inspector Mick Hutchens, I ...'

Her face had turned white and there was a look of fury in her eyes. 'Fucking animal,' she hissed.

'What? I ...'

'Look at this.' She passed him the mobile. It was a text message.

Sorry about ur husband. Feel like have known him years. Lovely man. DA

'I don't understand.'

'It's from Stuart's phone.'

'What?'

'DA. Davey Arthurs has my husband's phone.'

Hutchens tried desperately to catch up. 'Davey who?'

Jenny Miller snatched the phone back out of his hand, tears streaming down her cheeks. 'The man in the caravan, you fucking idiot.'

Kerry Stevenson seemed bored. An early morning armed siege, a wounded cop, blood on her kitchen floor, a son seconds away from being shot and a husband looking at several years in jail. Not a flicker. Cato wondered if there was something missing up top. She had a glossy women's gossip magazine on the table in front of her, a collection of Hollywood yummy mummies on the cover. Next to her in a hooded top and board shorts sat eleven year old Jai with a half-sucked Chup-a-Chup sticking out of his mouth. Back on Cato's side of the table, Mark McGowan looked like he could think of a thousand places he'd rather be.

Kerry declined a lawyer. 'What the fuck we need one of them for?'

Cato couldn't think of a reply. He took them back to the night of Hai Chen's death. He focused his questions on Jai, he figured he'd get a bit more sense out of him.

'What time did you go out shooting with your dad?'

'Eight-thirtyish.'

'Sure?'

'Yeah, the second Simpsons wasn't finished and I wasn't going before that, no way.'

Midweek, school days, bedtimes: obviously a loose concept in the Stevenson household.

'Right. So where did you go?'

'Usual place, out John Forrest Road near Phillips River. Always heaps out there to shoot.' Jai paused. 'Oh yeah, how is the cop? Steve, is that him?'

Cool as a cucumber. Inquiring about the man he'd shot in the back this morning, as if asking after somebody with flu. Great joke.

Cato didn't give him the satisfaction. 'Fine. Thanks for asking. Get anything that night?'

Jai Stevenson looked at Cato like he was a moron. Of course he got something. 'Five rabbits, a fox, and an emu, kept that for Millie.'

'Millie?'

'The cat, she loves it.'

'She doesn't have to fucken clean it, skin it, and chop it up does she?' muttered Kerry. 'Stinks the place out.'

'So do you with your cigarettes.' Jai's eyes darkened.

'Watch your lip.' Kerry Stevenson pointed a nicotine-stained index finger at her son's face.

Jai dabbed at his scar, an involuntary reflex; he was doubly furious when he realised what she'd made him do. Kerry smirked, she'd hit home.

Cato tapped his pen on the table as if in deep thought and also to remind everybody where they were and why. 'What time did you finish?'

Jai shrugged theatrically. 'Dunno, late.'

'Did you come straight home?'

He looked Cato straight in the eye and said, 'Yes.'

They'd been prepared for this since day one.

'You sure?'

'Yeah, dead sure.' A spark of amusement flickered in the boy's dark eyes.

In for a penny, thought Cato. 'I think this is what happened. Your dad got a phone call some time after 11.00. He drove over to the airport. You were with him. You met the Chinese man there. Mr Chen. Right so far?'

Jai looked up at the window, feigned bored.

'There was an argument. It got violent. You had the gun and you decided to help your dad out. You shot the Chinaman didn't you?'

'No.'

The dark eyes held just a hint of bravely held-back tears, the voice soft and so genuine. A performance like that in court would win hands-down on the day. Cato had what he wanted, he had the truth, but he knew he'd never be able to prove it. This doe-eyed eleven year old had shot two men in the last couple of weeks, one of them had died. He was getting a taste for it and he was going to get away with it. Cato shuddered at the thought of what this kid might be capable of in the future.

Kerry Stevenson fidgeted with her cigarette packet. 'You done now?'

35

Friday, October 17th. Midafternoon.

There should have been celebratory drinks or something, a ritual to wind everything up. The case of Flipper the headless torso was solved. It was Keith Stevenson and/or little Jai, with the gun, at the airport. But nobody was in the mood. Senior Constable Steve Dempster had been airlifted to a hospital in Perth with a bullet in his back. His colleague, Corey Withers, was lining up the first of many counselling sessions having soiled himself on the Stevenson staircase. Everybody knew the chances of Jai Stevenson facing any real consequences were remote. Cato surveyed the scenery as it sped past him on the road from Ravensthorpe back to Hopetoun. Some days it was vivid, lush and grand, a timeless tableau bigger than all of us and reassuringly so. Today it looked grey, bleak, and mean.

Black clouds billowed and boiled in the western sky. The wind had whipped up and thick drops of rain spattered the windscreen. It wasn't just the shooting of Dempster and general disillusionment with the likely outcome that had dampened the idea of a celebration. In truth, nobody really cared about Flipper in the first place, nobody except Cato Kwong. Flipper had become Hai Chen who turned out to be a greedy little mongrel ripping off his colleagues and countrymen. Hai Chen, an itinerant Chinaman brought in to fill a labour shortage, an outsider and an interloper. Not very welcome and only barely tolerated.

Cato fitted that bill too. A wandering Chinaman called in to fill Mick Hutchens' labour shortage. An outsider and an interloper, not welcome and only barely tolerated. Certainly Desk Sergeant Bernie Tilbrook had made no secret of his contempt. Mark McGowan for a while had shown some grudging respect for the tenacious oddity that was Cato Kwong. Case closed, McGowan's mind was clearly back on returning to Albany and the next job. Released from his bondage, he seemed to have shaken Cato Kwong out of his system like a dog coming in from the rain.

Cato needed to snap out of this. Cresting the rise that brought him down into Hopetoun, he switched the wipers to full bore to cope with the deluge pounding the windscreen. Through the gloom he could see at the end of the road the foaming steel grey Southern Ocean battering the groyne, walls of spray rearing over the spot where Jim Buckley had been found. Today it looked like the bleakest and loneliest place to die. Cato glanced over at the empty passenger seat where Buckley should have been. Jim's funeral would be over by now. Cato Kwong, obsessive as ever, had not been there to send him off, to show some respect for a colleague: so much for feeling responsible for the man's death.

The recruitment poster said Step Forward ... but just when we need you, you Walk Away.

Greg Fisher and Tess Maguire had him pegged. He pulled up on the gravel of the motel car park and turned off the engine. He sat staring through the windscreen, trying not to think about anything much.

The crime-scene tape was gone. Jim Buckley's room must have been released by Goldflam that morning; one of the forensic loose ends he was finally able to tie up before heading back to Albany. The door was open and a cleaning trolley was parked outside. The last time Cato had stood so near this threshold, Lara Sumich had been coming out. Why was that? Something about hearing a noise and wanting to check the room was secure. At the time he'd taken it at face value, he was off the case and had no cause to give it second thought. Now Mick Hutchens had raised doubts about Lara. Whether or not his doubts or concerns had the purest of motives was another matter. Was it just that he wanted to get inside her knickers or did he know something more about Lara that he was holding back? Knowing Hutchens, you'd have to say it was about fifty-fifty.

Cato popped his head around the door, nobody there. There was a bustle of movement behind him.

'I was just about to start cleaning that room.'

It was Pam, she had a determined set to her fleshy jawline; this was a room left unused for too long while good business went elsewhere. She was over the drug syndicate thing now that most of the police had decamped. She'd probably moved on to new rumours.

Cato smiled a greeting, adding in a wistful sad look for effect. 'Sergeant Buckley was my colleague, my partner. I just wanted to take a last quick look. Old times' sake.'

Pam looked at him like he was a bit mad. 'It's just a room. The other blokes will have taken everything out by now.' She looked at his doleful face a moment too long and relented. 'A couple of minutes, okay?'

Cato scanned the room not sure what he was looking for. It was a mirror image of his own, functional, easy-clean mauve carpet and a queen bed, unmade, with a heavy synthetic multi-coloured floral covering. The kind that have the big fold-over envelopes for the pillows and always feel too heavy and too hot, even in winter, before sliding off in the middle of the night and leaving you shivering. There was nothing in the drawers of the bedside cabinets except the Bible and phone directory. The wardrobe sported only empty wire hangers, spare bedding and pillows. There was nothing here to advance the case. On his way out he glanced over at the waste bin and peered inside; an old *West Australian* newspaper stood to limp attention. Forensics had obviously not deemed it to be of interest. Cato picked it out; he flicked through the pages to the middle section where he knew he'd find the crosswords. Jim Buckley had filled in most of the quickie but the cryptic was untouched. Cato folded the paper and pocketed it. He had just looted a dead man's crossword – how low can you go.

Pam the Cleaner returned with a firm smile of dismissal, Cato reciprocated. He knew he really should head over to Tess Maguire's place and pick up the Buckley file and disks but after an early morning armed siege and a resolution to the Chen case he was, to put it mildly, stuffed. He nudged open the door to his own room, chucked his phone and keys on the bedside table and fell on to the bed. He kicked off his shoes, reached for the crossword and a pen and flicked on the reading light. *Diana's debut is a no-show.* Easy. 'Disappearance'. *Positive result of a snap decision.* Doddle. 'Photograph'. He was asleep halfway through reading the next clue.

Cato woke up and reached out for the flashing phone vibrating on his bedside table.

'It's me. Hutchens. What happened to you?'

'What?'

'The funeral, where were you?'

Cato finally shook himself into the moment. He looked at his watch in the gloom: 3.30. He could see daylight through the crack in the curtains – 3.30 in the afternoon.

'So?' Hutchens was waiting for an answer.

'Sorry. I got ... sidetracked.'

Cato laid it all out: how sense was finally made of Guan Yu's version of events, the fracas at the Stevenson barbecue. Hutchens ummed and sighed and asked for clarifications along the way, particularly the details of the dawn raid and the shooting of Steve Dempster. Cato then summed up the interview with Keith Stevenson and his son. He realised he was running out of steam as he explained the difference between what he believed to be the truth and the likely court outcome based on the available evidence. Then he waited for Hutchens' response. He could almost see his boss shaking his head in despair at the other end of the phone.

'Manslaughter at best, although I wouldn't be surprised if he gets off with self-defence. Fuck's sake, you had the Chinaman offering to be locked up for murder and you turned him down. Trust you to turn a simple open-and-shut confession into a ... a fucking dog's breakfast.'

'The truth isn't always so cut and dried, sir.'

'Tell that to the bean counters in Perth. That raid wasn't sanctioned, an officer was seriously wounded. I could finish you for that.'

There was a pause for it to sink in. Cato didn't bite. Hutchens was right, his fate was out of his hands. Just the way he liked it.

Hutchens grunted. 'So where's Stevenson now?'

'Ravy lockup, heading to Albany tomorrow.'

'Paperwork?'

'Same. Also you'll need to phone through to Bernie Tilbrook to authorise the release of Guan Yu.'

'Yeah? Sure there's nothing we can do him for? Assault, wasting police time, hindering the inquiry, pain-in-the-arse, something like that?'

'Your call, sir.' He tried changing the subject. 'So how did it go?'

'What?'

'The funeral, Jim Buckley.'

'He's gone. But something did come up.' Hutchens explained about Stuart Miller's wife and the text message from her husband's phone. How it wasn't from the hubby as he was out cold in the Burns Unit.

Cato beat him to it. 'Billy Mather?'

'Yes, or Davey Arthurs as she calls him. Any developments on that?'

Cato outlined how far he'd got. Not far really as he'd been a bit busy. But the pub security camera footage and now the text message all pointed towards Billy Mather as a person of definite interest for Jim Buckley's murder.

Cato voiced the obvious. 'So where does that leave Justin Woodward?'

Not to mention Lara Sumich, instrumental in building the case against him. Buckley, blackmail, drugs, it was all beginning to look like fabricated bullshit. It was beginning to look all too familiar.

Mick Hutchens muttered one from his collection of fucks into the phone. Prick, thought Cato, he'd dug himself into a gaping hole by pinning it all on Justin.

'Leave that to me,' said Hutchens. 'Forensically, Woodward's still in the frame. But we need to find Mather.'

Cato had in his mind's eye the image of Lara emerging from Jim Buckley's motel room and from the shadows of the town hall late one night. The smouldering kiss, an age-old ruse to distract him from her real purpose, tampering with and tainting evidence. Buckley's DNA from his motel room possibly finding its way onto Woodward's clothing, drugs appearing in the coffee van, none-too-subtle pressure applied to a star witness. He knew all the tricks, he'd been there and done that. What were her words when she came that morning? *Well and truly fucked.* Cato wasn't the only one. Justin Woodward had been trussed up like a Christmas turkey.

Cato suggested a fine toothcomb over the forensic evidence; it probably wasn't all it seemed to be.

'Meaning?' Hutchens' voice had taken on a cold, sharp edge.

'Meaning one or more of your officers has possibly tampered with it.'

'Do you know what you're suggesting?' hissed Hutchens.

Cato was running out of patience. His time on this job was coming to an end; he had little or nothing to lose. 'Yes. And so do you. Don't come over all hurt and surprised. You've suspected her for a while now, haven't you?'

The silence at the other end of the line spoke volumes.

Hutchens inhaled. 'Keep it to yourself. I'll square things away at this end.'

'I'm not sure I like the sound of that.'

'No more games, Cato, I'll square it. Properly. Just find Mather. Please.'

The line went dead. The last time Cato heard Mick Hutchens say 'please' was when he'd agreed not to dob in his old boss to the internal review. The one that saw Cato cast out to Stock Squad Siberia. He wasn't sure if that was a good omen or bad. Cato checked the digital alarm clock on the bedside table and yawned. Another hour's kip wouldn't harm anyone, if he could get back to sleep. Once again his mind was buzzing and obsessing. He reached for the newspaper. A crossword could be as good as a sleeping pill sometimes. The paper had slipped off with the synthetic doona cover and was lying open on the floor. A large photo caught his eye.

The paper was dated Thursday, October 9th, the day after they'd arrived in Hopetoun. The day before Jim Buckley met his death. The photofit was on page four, part of a story about a cold-case review of a 1981 murder in Adelaide. This man had apparently electrocuted and bludgeoned his wife and kids, then put them in a car and left them in some bushland; his name was Derek Chapman. The photofit picture of how the suspect might look today was, to his eye, a fleshy, bald, jug-eared and big-nosed approximation of Billy Mather. Jim Buckley couldn't have failed to see the story and the picture. Had the Pommie ex-cop, his brother-in-law, tipped him off about it? Is that why Buckley left the pub midway through the evening? Did he come back here to double-check the paper? Then he returned to talk to the man to confirm his suspicions. Obviously he didn't ask him outright. Hey mate, are you that murderer on the run? The CCTV disks would have shown significantly more commotion if he had. So why didn't he act on his suspicions instead of just quietly phoning his brother-in-law? Or did he want Miller to be in on the take? By all accounts Miller was an obsessive man who hadn't been able to let go of a thirty-odd year old case; Cato could identify with that. He recalled now the text message on

Jim's phone midway through the morning he died.

how's it going? stu

Stuart Miller wanting to know the upshot of the previous night's call. So what was it in the conversation that convinced Jim Buckley he had the right man?

Nearly ten to four. Where do you start to look for a possible killer on the loose, late on a Friday afternoon? He grabbed his briefcase and took out Stuart Miller's notebook hoping for inspiration. All he found were puzzles and cryptic notes.

Who is CK!!!

Cato Kwong? Well he was the centre of the known universe after all.

Father, shell-shock, suicide?

Vicki Munro – survivor, DA said he didn't have childhood

DA, mum and brother, still alive? How much did they know?

There were dates, telephone numbers, names but all from a long time ago on the other side of the world. They weren't going to help him find Billy Mather, here and now. One name he recognised from the news article: DSC Tim Delaney, South Australia Homicide, the cold-case cop. Cato flipped open his mobile and keyed the number on Miller's list.

'CK?'

'That's what it says.'

Cato had Tim Delaney's full attention. No, he hadn't been aware of developments in the case as regards Stuart Miller, he was shocked at what had happened to him and intrigued by the possible link to the murder of Jim Buckley. Tragedies aside, he was also a bit pissed off that Miller had held so much back from him and let Cato know he was hoping for a lot more glasnost from here on in. Delaney was in a taxi leaving Adelaide airport when Cato called. The WA trip had been fruitless and he had been called back home empty-handed to regroup. Now, with rain thundering against Cato's motel window and the sound of Adelaide traffic honking in the background at Delaney's end, they were trying to decipher Miller's notes.

'Haven't a clue who CK is. Next?'

'Father, shell-shock, suicide, question mark.'

'Nope.'

'Vicki Munro – survivor, DA said he didn't have a childhood.'

'She's a survivor of one of Chapman's attacks. Lived in Bunbury until she topped herself a couple of years later. Miller must have picked something up from the brother Brian. I'll follow it up. Next?'

The blizzard of names was confusing Cato. The man he knew as Billy Mather was known as Chapman to some and Arthurs to others. Cato scratched notes to keep track. Next clue from the Miller chronicles.

'Mother, brother, still alive, question mark, how much did they know?'

Delaney grunted. 'We did an immigration check. He'd got in to Australia using his little brother's passport. As to whether it was with his permission or not, we don't know. Stuart put us in touch with his Pommie police mates. I'll get them to follow up some of these things and get back to you. As soon as you find this Mather bloke give us a bell, yeah?'

Cato promised he would and they rang off. He looked at the notebook again. CK. Calvin Klein? A missing FU? A girlfriend? A boyfriend? Whatever it all meant these were clues to the man's past and maybe his state of mind, not to his present whereabouts. He needed to start using up some good old-fashioned shoe leather.

36

Friday, October 17th. Late afternoon.

Billy Mather's Ravy motel room had been locked up and sealed off. Cato collected the key from reception and let himself in. It looked like any other country motel room except maybe more jaded and faded. It was hardly lived in; Mather hadn't stuck around. A plastic bag of toiletries and some replacement clothes had been supplied by Ravensthorpe Police. Everything of Mather's had been destroyed in the caravan fire. The bag and clothes lay seemingly untouched on the spare bed. He hadn't bothered to take them with him when he did his runner. Why? He didn't need them. Why? Maybe he already had his own stash? Cato had a flashback to the fire scene: the holdall in the back of the jeep. If he was the man he was shaping up to be, a cold-blooded killer who had struck several times and evaded capture for thirty-odd years, then a bit of forward planning was obviously not beyond him.

That got Cato thinking about the theory of the booby-trapped caravan. An open gas tap, matches on the doorjamb, neat and simple. But why not just disappear quietly like he had done so many times before? Why draw attention to yourself with such a melodramatic flourish? That begged a further question: in order to set a trap he had to have prior knowledge of who was coming and when. Maybe Mather had recognised Miller in town and put two and two together. Maybe he set the booby trap because he knew with the cold-case team and Miller closing in, it was time to do his disappearing act again. And hadn't his previous disappearing acts been signed off with an act of spectacular violence? Maybe if you create a big enough sideshow people get distracted from the main game. It buys time. Cato shuddered at the memory from the newspaper story: the man had killed his wife and kids and left them to rot in the bush. Cato could speculate until the cows came home but it wasn't going to help him find Billy Mather.

He checked the cupboards and drawers. Nothing. The bathroom was bare, the towels unused. He checked the phone for messages and previous numbers called. Zilch. The man really seemed to have vanished without a trace. Outside in the courtyard Cato checked for any security cameras. There was one high on a pole by the gravel entrance from the main road. In the motel reception area there was another camera high in the corner behind the counter. He arranged with the bored-looking young woman in charge to view the footage later. Then he went to check on the welfare of Keith Stevenson.

Stevenson was polishing off an evening meal of sausage roll and chips brought to him from the cafe down the road from the lockup. Cato gestured at the almost empty plate.

'Don't let me interrupt you.'

Stevenson didn't. With a malevolent stare he forked up the last three chips and shoved them into his mouth. He clattered the cutlery down onto the plate and shoved it away from him.

'What do you want?'

'I need your help.'

'Fuck off, I'm busy.'

Cato took the newspaper clipping out of his pocket and spread it on the table between them. 'Do you know him?'

'No. Didn't you hear me?'

'Look at it.'

'Why the fuck should I?'

'Because I want him more than I want you.'

Keith Stevenson looked at the photofit and shrugged. 'Who is he?'

'He's Derek Chapman, Billy Mather, David Arthurs. Take your pick.'

Cato told Stevenson what the man in the photo had done to his wife and kids in Adelaide, and a few years before that to another wife and kid in the UK, and what he was suspected of doing to Jim Buckley.

Stevenson listened impassively and shrugged again. 'Crow-eaters, Poms, and cops, who cares?'

Cato held his temper. 'Not you obviously, but all you do need to care about is the fact that I want him badly enough to help you with your problem.'

'Meaning?'

'I'm prepared to speak on your behalf in court, help mitigate whatever is coming your way.'

'Big deal. The kind of lawyers I can afford, I'm expecting to walk anyway.'

It was worth a try. 'Sorry to waste your precious time, Mr Stevenson.'

'Yeah, no worries.' But still he couldn't contain his curiosity. 'How am I supposed to help anyway?'

Cato couldn't tell if this was a wind-up. 'You're connected, old contacts from your glory days, new ones now that you're a pillar of the community. I want him found. Quickly.'

Stevenson sat for a while staring at the smudge of tomato sauce on his dinner plate.

'Okay, get me a phone.'

Cato frowned, not sure he'd heard right. 'Why?'

'So I can make a phone call, dickhead.'

'I mean why are you helping if I'm not offering anything?'

Stevenson gave him a thin smile. 'Because I can, because I'm not necessarily what you think I am and because then you'll owe me. Now get me the phone.'

'The mother's dead but little brother is still kicking.'

Tim Delaney had heard from Northumbria Police. They'd gone back and asked the questions that should have been asked thirty-five years ago. They'd always known whodunnit but they'd never caught him and, without a trial, had never felt the need to pursue 'whyhedunnit'. Delaney's call came through as Cato was in transit from Ravy to Hopey. He had left Keith Stevenson to his devices and headed back to the prospect of a lonely dinner and an early night. The crappy weather had settled in.

Apparently, according to the little brother Andy, young Davey Arthurs had taken his father's suicide very hard. The old man had been a basket case since he came back from the war. He had a crater in the side of his head the size of a fist, it was a wonder he was alive at all. They'd found an easy job for him in the shipyards but he hadn't even been able to do that properly. The homecoming hero thing didn't last very long. Workmates started taking the piss, playing practical jokes. Eventually he'd quit and topped himself not long after. Davey started acting up and became a handful, fighting, truanting, stealing, smashing stuff up. They were all scared of him. His mother, unable to cope, had him committed to the local mental hospital. The standard treatment in those days was electro-convulsive therapy: shock treatment.

'Only in those days they didn't use anaesthetic or muscle relaxants. Not nice. Apparently one time he jerked so much it broke his arm.' Delaney had clearly done his homework. 'Plenty of clues in there about the MO then,' he observed redundantly.

Cato had to concur, it wasn't rocket science: electrocution and ECT, bludgeoning and the father's fist-sized brain injury, mothers and children as the target group – it was mum who signed him up for it and little brother who got away scot-free.

Delaney was on a roll. 'It also ties in with Vicki Munro's comments about Davey saying he never had a childhood. ECT really fucks with the memory.'

'So the family never thought to mention all this at the time?'

'Nobody asked them, according to little brother. Northumbria Police reckon he's being a bit cute. He probably did know about the passport and big brother's propensity for violence but wasn't about to give the cops a free kick. I can see his point, he's not going to do their jobs for them.'

'Fucking hell.' Cato couldn't think of anything cleverer to say.

'Nicely put,' said Delaney.

'What about CK? Anyone know who she or he was?'

'No, maybe when you find him you can ask him.'

Cato squinted absent-mindedly at a spot on the wall. 'Will do.'

He rang off. So they knew whodunit, maybe even why. All he needed to do now was find the bastard. As was so often the case, Davey Arthurs career as a psycho was rooted in a disturbed childhood, a sprinkling of unlucky genes, and a propensity for mayhem. Cato had a mental image of Jai Stevenson sucking his Chup-a-Chup.

37

Sunday, October 19th. Midmorning.

His bags were packed; Cato Kwong was ready to go. The Sea Rescue hut was locked until either Tess Maguire or Greg Fisher returned to work in the hopefully not-too-distant future. Hopetoun was once again temporarily without a police presence but Sergeant Paul Abbott, Mitch Biddulph and the ever-helpful Bernie Tilbrook were just a phone call and thirty minutes' fast drive away in Ravensthorpe should any emergency crop up.

Cato had paid an early morning call on Tess to say goodbye. She and Melissa were at the kitchen table going through old photographs, laughing, reminiscing, putting some in an album, binning others. He felt unexpectedly envious, and as if he was interrupting something. Tess had protested otherwise but she hadn't argued too strongly when he made his excuses and left. They'd hugged at the doorway, Melissa peering inquisitively down the hall.

Tess looked up into his eyes, expression completely open. 'Have you made any big decisions lately?'

'I'm thinking of chucking the job in,' he said.

'Really?' She didn't look like she believed him.

'Really ... probably. Maybe.'

Tess kissed him lightly on the mouth. 'Well if you fancy being a beach bum, kept man, and occasional sex slave, drop me a line. If I haven't found Mr Right by then I might still be open to offers.'

'I might take you up on that.'

A last little wave and that was it.

Rain hadn't stopped falling since Friday. Hopetoun was eerily quiet, not just because of the wet Sunday morning. It was as if the unsavoury events of the past few weeks had finally taken their toll on the town itself. The boom had revealed its festering ugly side: greed, exploitation, drugs, sleaze, and brutality. As always, prosperity comes at a price. Mostly this face never showed itself to the good citizens of Hopetoun. Just as well. Hopefully this rain would wash the past few weeks away. Maybe all Hopey needed was a nice cup of sweet tea, a cuddle and a good night's sleep. Cato fancied a bit of the same himself.

Keith Stevenson had made a couple of calls and Cato arranged for copies of the photofit to be scanned and emailed to Stevenson's dodgy contacts out in the ether: nothing so far. The Ravensthorpe Motel security footage showed Billy Mather walking out within an hour of being dropped off after the fire. That was it. It looked like the Pommie Pimpernel had evaded capture yet again. Cato had tried to deliver more to DI Hutchens but more didn't exist. Hutchens could sort out his own–what was that pet term of his?–'fucking dog's breakfast' in Albany. Cato was out of here. He slung his holdall and briefcase into the back of the Stock Squad Land Cruiser and climbed in. His mobile went. It was Desk Sergeant Bernie Tilbrook.

'Message for you from Mr Stevenson.'

'Yes?'

'I'm fine thanks. How's your day?'

Cato sighed impatiently. Tilbrook, point made, proceeded.

'BIG 4 Caravan Park, Esperance, under the name of Stuart Miller: Cabin 21.'

Cato thanked him and gunned the engine.

The young woman had just finished strapping her sleeping baby girl into the booster seat, put the shopping bags into the boot and climbed up into the driver's side of the Nissan Patrol. It wouldn't start. She gave a tight low scream of frustration. Her husband had said he would sort this out last week. He hadn't, and now he was away at that bloody mine for another four days. It had rained all weekend and the streets were empty. Out on the bay, the isles of the Recherche Archipelago were either shrouded in low cloud or had disappeared completely. The water was flat and oily black. A few determined anglers fished disconsolately from the jetty. The baby was starting to stir and grumble. Cold rivulets of rain ran down the back of her neck. It was at least a three-kilometre walk into town but they were out of key supplies, like nappies. So be it. The pram had a hood, the baby would be fine.

She was caught up in her own thoughts and hadn't noticed the car pull up just ahead of her, a green jeep. The passenger side window was opened from the inside. An old man with a kind face said something she didn't catch.

'Sorry?'

'I said are you havin' a spot of bother with your car, love?'

The old man's eyes twinkled, he had a singsong kind of voice. He reminded her of her grandfather back in England. In no time at all he had the Nissan's bonnet up and his toolbox out and was jabbering away.

'Pardon?'

'I said you'll catch your death of cold out here in this rain. Hop in the Land Rover and you and the bairn can keep dry, I'll have this fixed soon.'

The baby was now fully awake and beginning to whimper. She hauled her out and folded down the pram, passing it into the back seat of the old jeep.

Cato parked down the street from BIG 4 and walked the last hundred metres. He didn't announce his presence at reception, instead making directly for Cabin 21. Heaven knew how Stevenson's network had found Mather, if indeed they had, but it was a society that lived by different rules and they noticed different things about comings and goings. Maybe that old Land Rover gave him away. The cabin looked unoccupied. The vehicle space was vacant but had a few fresh oil stains. Cato wasn't game to go too close just yet. For all he knew, this place was also booby-trapped. He sneaked up to the back of the cabin and looked through the windows. The curtains were wide open. Nobody home. He went around the front, sniffing. No apparent gas odour. He unclipped his gun. A grey nomad en route to the toilet block saw the gun and halted mid-shuffle, wide-eyed with fright. Cato waved his police ID, mouthing to her to keep quiet. She flapped her hands at him, clutched her cardigan closer into her chest, and disappeared into the toilets.

Cato edged towards the cabin door, glancing in again through a window as he passed: still no sign of life, still no smell of gas. He cut to the chase and reached for the door handle. It was unlocked. He braced himself and yanked it open, wincing involuntarily. There was no explosion and no Billy Mather. Cato holstered his gun and looked around. The bedroom was a curtained-off section of the main cabin, taking up about half of the floor space. The rest was a compact kitchen and dining-living room combined. It was neat as a pin. The fridge was empty except for half a carton of reasonably fresh Hi-Lo milk. The dishes were washed and stacked. The floor swept. The holiday cabin looked the way it might at checkout time.

Cato turned to leave, glancing in the rubbish bin on the way out. It contained the usual: fruit peelings, tea bags, eggshells. Something glittered. Cato looked closer. It was the gold under-stripes of a mobile phone SIM card. He fished it out of the bin, wiped it down, and put it into his own phone. The display, address book, recent call lists, and text messages sent and received all confirmed what he'd already guessed. It was from Stuart Miller's phone. Cato read the text sent to Jenny Miller.

Sorry about ur husband. Feel like have known him years. Lovely man. DA

Cato didn't need any more convincing that Billy Mather and David Arthurs were the same man. Taunting. Cruel. Cocky. Even the cabin booking was in the name of his old nemesis,

Stuart Miller. He seemed to think he was untouchable. After thirty-five years it wasn't surprising.

'I think Mr Miller has checked out. Can I help you?'

It was the park manager, alerted by the grey nomad that a Chinaman with a gun was at large. He seemed strangely calm. Maybe this was an everyday occurrence at BIG 4 Esperance.

'Did you notice what vehicle he was driving?'

The park manager nodded. 'A green Land Rover, 1978, a real classic.'

He had the rego too. How hard would it be to spot something like that in a town the size of Esperance?

'Found it.'

The call came from Esperance cop shop, Cato had enlisted their help to find the Land Rover. The vehicle in question was in a street about three kilometres from the centre of town. Cato took directions and arranged to meet them there.

The street was deserted; the steady drizzle helped keep it that way. There was nobody at the Land Rover except for two Esperance uniforms. The jeep had been abandoned. Cato, still fearing booby-traps, urged caution in their approach. Having never worked in Belfast, Beirut or Baghdad none of them really knew what to look out for as telltale signs of a booby-trapped car. There didn't appear to be any loose wires, packages taped to the underside, funny smells, or ticking noises. Cato opened the passenger door and found something that chilled him a whole lot more. The passenger seat was splattered with a few drops of blood and on the rear seat, more blood and a baby's pram.

38

Sunday, October 19th. Late afternoon.

The weather improved the further inland Cato drove. By the time he reached Lake King, three hours northwest from Esperance, the sun was dropping behind a copse of salmon gums. Pink and grey galahs hopped at the side of the road pecking the ground absent-mindedly. He still had a good four or five hours left of his drive back to Perth. In Esperance the Land Rover had been taped off and Duncan Goldflam and a minion were on their way over to check it out. Billy Mather was long gone. Nobody had seen what vehicle he might have used for his getaway. DI Hutchens probably had the wrong man locked up and Jim Buckley's killer was, it seemed, a diminutive ageing Pom with an uncanny ability to disappear into thin air. And a vicious old bastard at that. Cato was finished. He needed to get back to Stock Squad, if only to type up the resignation letter he'd been composing in his mind during the drive from Esperance. He needed to get back to Perth, to his family – even if it was only shared custody every other weekend. He hadn't worked out yet whether what he was doing was Stepping Forward or yet more Walking Away.

If you blinked you'd miss Lake King. Hopetoun was a thriving metropolis by comparison. There was a tree-lined main street that consisted of a general store, the sports oval and the cemetery. Then it was on to the next milestone on your journey to somewhere else. He and Jim Buckley had passed through it on the way down, what was it – ten days ago? There were only really two or three routes between Perth and Hopetoun or Esperance and two of them went via Lake King. The 'lake' had dried up probably a hundred years or more ago leaving behind a blinding white saltpan. It was one of a chain of dry lakes snaking for hundreds of kilometres through the southern wheatbelt. It made Cato thirsty; good time for a fuel stop. He pulled in at the general store beside a four-wheel drive Nissan Patrol with tinted windows.

It was Sunday quiet. Cato filled up and gave the windscreen a wipe with a squeegee. He triggered a loud electronic beeper as he crossed the threshold into the store. He nearly jumped out of his skin.

'Gets me like that as well and I've been here twenty years.'

The storeowner was perched precariously on a stool beside the checkout.

'I'm Troy.' He gave a little wave.

Cato hadn't seen anyone that big fit on such a small stool before, except maybe David Tahere the man-mountain Maori. This was no man-mountain. This was more like a bouncy castle with a damped down central parting and creepy kiss-curls along the fringe.

Cato smiled like everything was completely normal. 'G'day, Troy. Cold drinks?'

'Back there in the fridge. Best place for them ey?'

Cato found a large bottle of water and supplemented it with a can of something cold, fizzy and sugary, and a Mars Bar, and handed his credit card over. 'See you mate. Drive safely,' wheezed Troy.

'Cheers,' said Cato, waving the Mars Bar at him.

The Nissan Patrol was still there. Maybe it belonged to Troy: there was certainly no one else in the store. Cato opened the driver's door on the Land Cruiser and chucked his purchases on to the passenger seat. He held on to the lemon fizz and cracked the can open. A baby whimpered somewhere near. Was it in the Nissan? Hard to see with tinted windows. Another whimper, but not a baby this time. Someone older. Cato's skin prickled. The abandoned Land Rover in Esperance – a pram, some blood. He cupped his eyes close up to the side window of the Nissan. The engine roared into life and the four-wheel drive reversed at high speed. The passenger wing mirror caught Cato a solid blow in his side before snapping off. The Nissan was on its way leaving Cato doubled up with what felt like a fractured rib.

The road northwest out of town bisected the large saltpan aka Lake King. The Nissan Patrol was about two hundred metres ahead of Cato and even though he had his foot to the floor he didn't seem to be gaining. He'd flicked on the flashing blues and reds but the Nissan wasn't interested. Every time Cato breathed, a sharp pain stabbed through his chest. Who or what was behind the whimpering? Had he imagined it? He didn't know who was in the car ahead. Was it Mather? That whimpering. Had he done it again?

Heading their way about three hundred metres further on, Cato saw the orange flashing lights on a ute and behind it a roadtrain carrying what looked like a Tonka tip truck for the mine. Oversize Load was the warning sign flashing on the pilot ute. The Nissan would have to slow.

Surely.

It did. But Cato didn't. He was gaining. The Nissan was now less than a hundred metres ahead and the extra wide load was still bearing down on them. With less than a truck length to go, the Nissan slowed and veered off the bitumen as the roadtrain thundered by. Now less than fifty metres behind, Cato was still flooring it as the truck-carrier loomed with horns and lights blazing. He waited until the last possible moment before swinging on to the gravel to allow it to pass.

He could feel his back wheels sliding, the rear of the vehicle fishtailing. Instinctively he did the wrong thing and braked, spinning the Land Cruiser to face the way it had come. For a moment it seemed to float a couple of inches off the ground. There was a sickening thump at the back end and an acute awareness that he was going into a roll and he couldn't do anything about it. Cato gripped the wheel tight and braced himself as the horizon flipped. He closed his eyes and waited to die.

'Wake up, wake up, sleepyhead.'

Cato opened his eyes. It was a beautiful sunset. One of those purpley-orangey glowing ones with wispy clouds fanning out across the sky and the bush burned into silhouette. A soft breeze whispered across the salt lake and a waning but still huge yellow moon hovered low on the opposite horizon.

'Now then, son, what's all this about?' Billy Mather crouched above him, concerned and inquisitive.

Cato tried to sit up and felt the stabbing pain in the side of his chest from the broken wing mirror adding to a splitting headache. He was aware of something sticky on the side of his face. Blood? 'What happened?' he croaked.

'You rolled. Me and the roadtrain driver got you out. He's gone to get help along with the lad from the pilot ute. There's a police and ambulance post in Lake King. They'll be back in another twenty minutes or so, I expect.'

A few metres away the Land Cruiser rested on its roof, windows shattered, one wheel slowly spinning and catching the last rays of sunset. The axle must have sheared. The bull-mobile was a write-off. Silver linings. Cato wondered if Mather remembered him from their brief encounter at the smouldering caravan.

'You haven't got me thermos have you, son?'

Question answered.

'No. Sorry.'

'Nee bother. So, how did you find me?'

Cato couldn't bring himself to say blind luck so he kept quiet.

Mather sighed and shook his head like a disappointed parent. 'You and your mate, Beefy, don't know when to stop sticking your nebs in do you? He thought he had me twigged, thought he'd play it cool. I can read you lot like a book. Fucken amateurs.'

Beefy? Buckley, he assumed. Nebs? Cato's head was spinning.

'How did he know it was you?'

Mather snorted. 'Soon as I opened me mouth when he bought a round in the pub, his piggy little eyes lit up. Then I heard him on the phone out on the jetty saying, "Course it's him, how many other bastards talk like you?" It was only later I realised he was talking to my old marra Stuey Miller.'

'But why kill him? You could have just disappeared, you've done it before.'

Mather shook his head dismissively. 'Nah, things were closing in. I needed a diversion. Your body on the beach provided that. Plus there was a rumour around town about drugs. All helped to add to the confusion.'

Cato's guts curdled. His Chinese Whispers campaign had provided a smoke screen for a killer to hide behind. He may as well have handed Mather the rock, pointed him at Jim Buckley and said go for your life.

Then with a jolt Cato remembered the scene at Lake King general store. The whimpering in the Nissan: who was it? Where were they?

Mather was still in full flow. 'Ah well, enough small talk. I've got to be getting on now.' He dragged a holdall closer to him and started rummaging. Muffled metallic sounds.

Cato tried not to think the worst. 'Who have you got in the car?'

Mather smiled and patted his arm. 'No need to worry about them, bonny lad.'

Cato started to rise but Mather pressed him back down with unexpected strength for a man over twenty years his senior.

'Stay down, son.'

Cato felt weak as a kitten. Was he really going to let himself be at the mercy of an old-aged pensioner? He tried wasting more time, more time for help to arrive. 'Why do you do it?'

Mather raised an eyebrow, 'Do what, son?'

'You know what I mean: the women and kids–bashing and electrocuting. Bit over the top doing both?'

Mather smiled playfully. Was there a trace of pride in there too? 'I was just seeing if it worked the first time, me little invention, just curious really. After that it just became a kind of signature. Like on a work of art. Know what I mean like?'

His answer was actually more of a 'how' than a 'why' but the worrying thing was that Cato did know what he meant. Sometimes horror has an internal logic all of its own, like those seemingly nonsensical cryptic clues.

'Bonny lass, lovely bairn.'

'What?' Cato looked up.

Mather was flicking through a wallet. It was Cato's. He showed Cato the photo of Jane and Jake on Rottnest.

'What's their names?' the old man asked with childlike curiosity.

Cato's blood ran cold, he closed his eyes and concentrated, trying to think of a plan. When he opened them again he realised it was all a bit too late for that.

Mather's hand was raised high, he was holding a tyre lever. Cato could see the initials CK tattooed on Mather's forearm but realised he was never going to get the chance to ask him about it. He managed to turn, raise his arm and take the force of the blow on his right elbow. He felt it shatter and almost vomited with the pain. With his good arm he grabbed a handful of salty gravel and flung it feebly into Mather's face, rolling and scrambling desperately to get out of harm's way. Mather brought the lever down on the back of Cato's neck and shoulder. Everything went white and the shock sent his whole system into shutdown. He had to hold on. Cato knew he was just another blow or two from death, he'd read the files on what Mather was capable of and he'd seen the results of his handiwork on Jim Buckley. Three strikes and you're out, right out. He crouched on the balls of his feet and launched himself forward, driving the top of his head into Mather's face. He heard the crunch of breaking bone, Mather gasped and the tyre lever dropped. Cato grabbed it with his good hand and set about finishing the job.

At some point the Lake King cops arrived and eased the tyre lever out of his grip as a dark stain radiated out across the white salt lake.

EPILOGUE

Thursday, 22nd January, 2009. Late afternoon.
Perth, Western Australia.

There was someone in his room. He could hear it. Soft rhythmic breathing and the occasional rustle of fabric. Stuart Miller's skin, already raw and tight beneath the gauze and bandages, tingled with fear. It wasn't a nurse or auxiliary, they usually announced themselves and clattered about regardless. He was the tetchy blind man in number 7 and he knew their strategy was to smother him with their good-natured life-goes-on noises. This morning they'd announced a new bunch of flowers had arrived. They read the card out to him: *Get Well Soon. Tim Delaney & Colleagues. South Australia Police*. The personal touch, very nice. The flowers smelt sweet and cloying.

It wasn't a doctor either. They usually introduced themselves too and got straight down to business asking stupid questions about how he was feeling today and then moving on without really hearing the answer. Like shite again, thanks Doc.

It wasn't Jenny, he knew her smell and her trembling fearful touch of his hand and sometimes he thought he could almost taste the tears he knew were running down her face. So who was it?

'Who's there?'

A soft clearing of the throat and a rustling of movement in the bedside chair accompanied by a sharp intake of breath.

'Sorry. My name is Philip Kwong.'

So it was a doctor, probably a young med student or intern, come to gawp at the English Patient.

'Come to check my blood pressure?'

'Actually, Stuart, it's Detective Senior Constable Philip Kwong. Some people call me Cato.'

The voice had firmed up, gained five years or so, maybe a bit of a chip on his shoulder. That was more like it. Cato?

'Like in The Pink Panther?'

'That's right.'

'I used to love that. He was always ambushing his boss, leaping out from behind the curtains when he least expected it.'

'That sounds about right. By the way Greg Fisher says hello, we shared a ward in Esperance together for a few days.'

Miller nodded, his guess had been right; the visitor was nursing an injury. 'Fisher's a good lad. The only one who listened to me. How's he doing?'

'He'll be fine. No permanent damage.'

Miller heard the last few words trailing off apologetically. He changed the subject and injected some brightness into his voice to reassure the visitor. 'So, have you found Arthurs then?'

'Yes.'

Stuart Miller's pulse quickened, it had been a rhetorical question and he was expecting a no. 'Tell me more.'

'He's dead. I killed him.'

'Bastard.'

'Yeah, I suppose he was.'

'I meant you.'

'What?'

'Ever read *Moby Dick*?'

'The first few chapters.'

'Well I'm Captain Ahab and you've just gone and killed my fucking great white whale.'

So Cato Kwong told Stuart Miller his story, including the bit at the end about the bludgeoned near-dead body of a young woman found in the boot of Davey Arthurs' stolen Nissan. The baby on board was unscathed although a bit dehydrated. The mother would spend the next three months in intensive care and, perhaps mercifully, may remember nothing of her ordeal.

'So it was that same bloke from the caravan, Mather,' said Cato.

'Yes.'

'And he killed Jim.'

And Christine and Stephen Arthurs. And the four members of the Chapman family in Adelaide, jeez he couldn't even recall their names. And Vicki and Shelly Munro. At least Brian Munro now had his wish; Arthurs was dead. Miller sighed and shifted his weight in the bed.

'Can I get you anything? Water or something?'

Miller shook his head. 'No, ta. So that bloke you had in the frame for Jim. What happens to him?'

'The case is being quietly dismantled as we speak.'

'That would please that little bull terrier boss of yours no end.'

A derisive snort. 'He'll survive, he always does.'

Miller paused. 'I don't suppose Arthurs ever told you why?'

'Not really, he bragged about his gizmo. Called it his signature on a work of art. But we did pass on your family history notes to Northumbria Police and they found some stuff out.'

Cato told him all about Davey being committed to a hospital, the shock treatment the brain-damaged war hero father. It made as much sense as any in trying to pin down the MO.

Miller sat on the thought for a moment and smiled. 'CK. I think I might have cracked it.'

'Who was it?'

'Not who, where. Cherry Knowles was a mental hospital just outside Sunderland. If the ECT was playing havoc with Davey's memory maybe he wanted the tattoo to make sure he'd never forget.' Miller sipped from his cup. 'Looks like Delaney's profiler was right.'

'What?'

'Mad as a cut snake, as you Aussies say.'

They said their goodbyes.

'Thanks for dropping in, son.'

'All part of the service.'

Stuart Miller heard Cato Kwong's footsteps recede down the corridor. He was weary. Closing his eyes he drifted off and dreamed about the 1973 FA Cup Final: a sea of red and white, Ian Porterfield's match-winning volley on the half-hour, Jimmy Montgomery's miraculous point-blank double-save, Bob Stokoe racing across the pitch in his brown trilby and little Bobby Kerr lifting the cup for Sunderland. And for the first time in nearly thirty-five years he didn't wake up in a cold sweat.

It was still light when Cato Kwong walked out of Royal Perth Hospital. He saw his reflection in the sliding door and realised he looked more like an escaped patient than an official visitor. The sky was blue, the sun was still high and the concrete shimmered. Listening to the same flattened vowels and singsong rhythm of Miller's accent, it was easy now to see how Jim Buckley drew his conclusions about Billy Mather being Davey Arthurs. Cato shuddered at the sudden recollection of the spreading red stain on the salt lake and wondered how long it would take for his bad dreams to go away.

He rolled up his copy of the *West*, bought out of his own money and cryptic crossword completed on the train journey from Freo. The headline was about the shock closure of the Ravensthorpe nickel operation due to the global financial crisis: so much for the fifty-year mine. From boomtown to ghost town in the blink of an eye and the counting of a bean. It was far worse than the rumour mill could ever have imagined. A photograph on the front page showed graffiti on the town sign; somebody had sprayed 'NO' in front of 'Hopetoun'. Apparently the first for the chopping block were the foreign guest workers, now surplus to requirements and set for the next flight home. Concern was expressed for those plucky battling locals who had set up shop to service the boomtown and how they would fare now the bottom had dropped out of their market. Cato suspected that the Keith Stevensons and Jimmy Dunstans of this world would always find a way to turn a buck somehow, somewhere.

Cato thought about hailing a taxi for the journey home to Fremantle. Driving was out of the question with a badly broken arm and his neck still in a brace. At least he was able to breathe again without it hurting too much. He opted for a stroll over to the Northbridge food halls for a laksa and then the train home again. Cato switched his mobile back on and it beeped with three waiting messages. The first an SMS photo: Tess and Melissa on Mount Barren with the long white stretch of Four Mile Beach, blue Southern Ocean, shimmering Culham Inlet and a hazy Hopetoun behind them in the far distance. Tess was laughing and Melissa was attempting sultry but couldn't pull it off because of the mischief curling the edges of her mouth. Underneath were the words:

Wish u were here?

Cato sniffed the fumes from the rush-hour cars grinding past on Wellington Street and texted his reply.

Yes

Next a characteristically terse greeting from DI Mick Hutchens.

Call me–worth your while

Cato sighed. He was enjoying his time off, even if it was enforced and painful. It would take another four to six weeks for the broken arm to mend and about the same time for internal affairs to conclude that his killing of Billy Mather was indeed self-defence. He needn't make any rash decisions about quitting or returning to Stock Squad until then. But he was intrigued by the 'worth your while' bit and Hutchens no doubt knew he would be. He dialled the number, it rang once.

'Cato mate, how's the arm?'

'Good thanks. You rang?'

'Heard the whisper?'

'I've given up rumour-mongering for Lent. But go on, humour me.'

'Stock Squad is for the chop. You're all dead meat.'

Puns like that and Jim Buckley in his grave less than three months.

Cato shook his head in disgust. 'Go on.'

'Budget cuts across the board plus an epidemic of kiddie-fiddlers up north and volume crime in the electorates. The likes of you chewing straw and talking about the weather in Mukinbudin is a luxury we can no longer afford, mate.'

'Thanks. Is there a point to this?'

'Tetchy, tetchy. Not so relaxed back in the big city are we? Look, got an offer for you, mate. The game is afoot, change is in the air, and I'm in charge of it. You'll be needing a job.'

Hutchens outlined his plan. Help downplay Mather's candidacy for the Buckley killing and keep quiet about his early reservations about Justin Woodward. In short, help cover Hutchens' arse yet again. In return, Bob's your uncle, a job in Hutchens' new squad. As plans go it was desperate and stupid.

'Could be the making of you, mate.'

Or the undoing, thought Cato. Step Forward. 'No, I'm not going to help brush Billy Mather under the carpet. He was the one that killed Jim Buckley, not Woodward.'

'But the little prick will sue the arse off us! I'll be back up shit creek again. Fuck's sake,' whined Hutchens.

'You'll think of something.'

The silence at the other end of the phone was deafening. It was broken by a petulant sigh. 'So, is that a yes or a no?'

'What was the question again?'

'Can I depend on you to keep your mouth shut at least until I take care of the Woodward fiasco?'

'No.' said Cato. It felt good.

'Fuck's sake, come and work for me anyway. It's that or the scrap heap and no cunt else'll have you.'

Cato scratched his chin with a spare finger. 'When do I start?'

The final message was another text, this time from Jane, his very soon-to-be ex-wife.

Can we talk?

Good question. He didn't know the answer to that one. He did know that he wanted Jake to be happier somehow so he texted back

Sure

then pocketed his mobile and started walking. He had plenty to ponder so he unravelled his iPod and scrolled down to some walking-and-pondering music: a Schubert impromptu. Cato's arm throbbed in protest at the memory of the movements it took to play this particular piece. He wondered if he would ever play the piano again.

ACKNOWLEDGEMENTS

Prime Cut was shortlisted in the 2010 Crime Writers' Association Debut Dagger Award as a manuscript titled *Chinese Whispers.*

I would like to thank the following. Jamie Steele – who makes the best coffee in Hopetoun and is a man of impeccable character. Georgia Richter and Wendy Jenkins for keeping me on the straight, narrow, grammatical, and correctly punctuated. In particular Georgia for those suggestions that helped me out of a few deep dark holes. Early readers Ron Elliott, Peter Pritchard, Tess McGinty (my mother-in-law) who said 'it was very nice dear but maybe a few less F words', and my brother Brian who put me straight on a few matters of Sunderland football history and local language and customs which I'd forgotten in my long years of exile. Many who remain nameless who shared their insights into small-town life, the universe and everything.

There are some divergences from the real Hopetoun in the text: the boomtown colour-code of orange and yellow fluoros is a figment of my imagination; there is no breakfast restaurant overlooking Murder HQ; and the prisoner lock-up arrangements are pure artistic licence.

All characters appearing in this work are fictitious. Any resemblance to real persons, living or dead, is purely coincidental.

First published in Australia by Fremantle Press in 2011
First published in Great Britain in 2014 by
Michael O'Mara Books Limited
9 Lion Yard
Tremadoc Road
London SW4 7NQ

A CIP catalogue record for this book is available from the British Library.

Papers used by Michael O'Mara Books Limited are natural, recyclable products made from wood grown in sustainable forests. The manufacturing processes conform to the environmental regulations of the country of origin.

ISBN: 978-1-78243-284-5 paperback
ISBN: 978-1-78243-262-3 ebook

www.mombooks.com

Cover design by Ally Crimp
Cover photograph by Erik Wollo/Shutterstock

Printed and bound by CPI Group (UK) Ltd, Croydon, CR0 4YY